I0761489

FIVE
FUNERALS

Choose Your Own Perilous Path

FIVE FUNERALS

by Jeff Somers

RUADÁN BOOKS

Boston, MA

Five Funerals: Choose Your Own Perilous Path

Paperback ISBN: 978-1-968143-04-6
Library of Congress Control Number: 2025946772

Edited by Anna Koon
Illustrations by Ruth Ann Sellars, Barnacles and Moss
Cover & Interior Design/Formatting by Leah Donell

First Edition

ruadanbooks.com

For Danette, who is my partner in every sense of the word, who I love more than normal words can express so we have made our own: I love you infinite iogis!

TABLE OF CONTENTS

FIVE FUNERALS

FOREWORD

The Staple and the Hypertext: About Jeff Somers

I've known Jeff Somers for nearly twenty-five years. We met only once, twenty-two years ago. I'm not describing some far-flung Internet friendship either. At the time, I lived in Jersey City, New Jersey, and he lived ten minutes away in Hoboken. We just never got around to it, until I held a reading for the first anthology I edited, *The Urban Bizarre*, at a café/performance space called The Lucky Cat,[1] in Brooklyn. We chatted for several minutes, held the event along with a couple of other writers,[2] and then he went home and didn't hang out after. Then I moved across the country to California. Then back East. Then back again. Over the same course of decades, Jeff moved from Hoboken to Jersey City, which is typical of natives of the Garden[3] State.

---

1 The Lucky Cat was co-founded by the writer Joi Brozek, another online acquaintance who I mostly knew online despite living twenty minutes away. The place is long-gone, and in fact I had to go to Livejournal to refresh my memory of whether the place was in Brooklyn or the Lower East Side of Manhattan. There are now a million places called Lucky Cat (with or without the article), including a number owned by Gordon Ramsay.

2 I recall they were the zinesters Frank Marcopolos and Ann Sterzinger, who both rather rapidly jerked toward the right-wing. Ann is a talented writer; Frank never quite made it. Ann, Jeff, and I were all published in Frank's zine *The Whirligig*, alongside Khaled Hosseini—yes, before *The Kite Runner*, Hosseini was involved in both the zine and small-press horror scenes.

Why didn't we ever meet again? The answer was we were too busy trying to be writers, specifically writers with one foot in the underground and one foot in genre fiction. That, you should know, is an excellent way to pull your groin.[4] I was doing a lot of work with Soft Skull Press, a tiny "punk publishing"[5] outfit run out of a janitor's basement on Ludlow Street on the Lower East Side. We were very radical, and hip enough to get some occasional help from rock stars. For example, Soft Skull had published, in print, a book of online diaries from musicians touring with Lollapalooza back when the Web was young.

And Jeff? He was *The Inner Swine*. That was his zine, saddle-stitched and photocopied, homemade and hilarious. Unlike many zinesters of the 1990s era, Jeff *wasn't* a radical, but that just meant he wasn't tediously earnest.[6] I loved the *Swine*[7]—imagine if *McSweeney's* was as funny as it wanted to be, and cheap! He was also working on fiction and publishing it here and there, in zines, and online, and in small horror journals. Soon enough, so was I.[8] The two of us also spent a lot of time online

3 They grow concrete 'round there!

4 All my footnotes in the this foreword are tributes to Jeff's tendency to use them, but this one in particular is to tell you that the sentence to which this note is attached is very much a Jeff joke, circa 2003.

5 The *Village Voice* called us that once. We called ourselves that a million times. Anyway, Soft Skull went bankrupt and is now only a logo on a spine owned by an heiress to the diabolical Koch fortune.

6 It also meant that he didn't lurch to the right, like so much of the underground of that era. Some people have fringe politics (hello!); others have fringe *personalities* and adopt whatever politics seem to get them validation from the rest of the fringe.

jousting with a crowd of weirdo[9] zinesters calling themselves the Underground Literary Alliance, which was embarrassing for everyone involved, but least of all for Jeff, who published his first novel, *Lifers*, with Creative Arts[10] in 2001, and somehow it got reviewed in *The New York Times*.

---

7 I could never get it together to produce a zine of my own, but I did contribute to a couple here and there. Even now, decades later, when I'm editing the Billions vs Billionaires series of anti-Elon Musk zines (*It's Okay, Just Set Me on Fire*, and *Bread and Jam for Big Balls* so far), I had to beg a friend to do all the layout.

8 In fact, I'd made a little promise to myself that if I was unable to publish any fiction by the end of the year 2000, I would (ugh!) start my own zine, and maybe even (double-ugh!) apply to the Clarion Writers' Workshop for help. Thank God my first short story was published in *Talebones*, another venue that hinted at zine while being a solidly genre publication, accepted my story "Your Life, Fifteen Minutes from Now" and paid me eighteen whole dollars, in the futuristic year 2000.

9 The Alliance included: an Indian-American Holocaust denier with a Jewish girlfriend; a guy who challenged me to a boxing match when I objected to him sexually harassing Ann Sterzinger who was twenty years his junior; a pretty nice guy from Philly who was in the wrong place; another nice guy who collected stamps and drank too much; and a couple of off-the-grid types who thought the real problem with publishing was the existence of ISBNs and barcodes (and Social Security numbers). They were offline and would only communicate by writing entire zines about their daily lives and mailing them to you.

10 A small press in Berkeley that collapsed just two years later. It published artsy-fartsy stuff, noir reissues, non-fiction of interest to the (insert group here) and all sorts of other titles. The foolish owner got involved in "co-publishing"—a vanity scam in which the author pays for printing and the otherwise-legitimate publisher pretends to like the book—then went bankrupt, because you can't perform a labor of love *without* love. I happen to be typing this footnote just over mile away from where the Creative Arts office was—the same distance I lived from Jeff back in Jersey. The world is extremely tiny.

Was it a capsule review? Yes. Mixed? Yes. Did it make Jeff a superstar? No. But did it change everything? In a way, yes. Finally, someone in our dumb little hothouse had escaped, if even just for one week. Anything seemed possible.

Jeff got involved with another small press, and then when one of its leading lights, Lilith Saintcrow,[11] was called up to the Big Leagues, she took Jeff with her, and suddenly my friend, whom I'd met once and published once, was himself Big Time. His Avery Cates series of cyberpunk novels were among the best[12] and funniest[13] this century. You might even say the vision behind the series was radical![14]

Have I mentioned that he was still publishing *The Inner Swine* through all this? Only when he shifted into urban fantasy with the Ustari Cycle of books about modern[15]-day blood mages did the zine finally die. I published him, too, in my anthology of Japanese-inflected crime/SFF for VIZ Media, *Hanzai*[16] Japan.

---

11 Tiny world: I met her when she was in the small press and I was working for Night Shade Books at a regional bookfair. I asked if Lillith Saintcrow was her real name. She showed me her driver's license. Then a year later she had become extremely famous. Not as famous as Khaled Hosseini though!

12 Best science fiction novels, that is. Not just best cyberpunk novels, of which there were only a few, or post-cyberpunk or post-post cyberpunk novels, of which there were many.

13 Admittedly a smaller subset. Nothing is less funny than science fiction, especially when written with an eye toward being humorous.

14 "Don't fuck with the System Pigs!" and all that.

15 Mentally insert the prefix "post" before modern. As someone who went to graduate school in the 1990s, I just cannot bear to do it myself.

Even after eight novels and assorted short stories in his genre settings,[17] Jeff kept one foot in the DIY underground. He self-published a pair of novels, though unlike most self-published novels, the problem wasn't with the books, but with the publishing industry. Jeff is hilarious. You're not allowed to be funny in more than one genre at a time, and you're certainly not allowed to experiment with form. A writer in the twenty-first century can be:

1. a prolific genre hack
2. a clever chronicler of middle-class anxieties and vices[18]
3. a formalist who enjoys engaging in typographical trickery and unusual narrative structures

Jeff dares to be all three. He dares to believe that one should write without rules, as he describes in his familiar-sounding writing handbook, *Writing Without Rules: How to Write & Sell a Novel Without Guidelines, Experts, or (Occasionally)*[19] *Pants*, which I highly recommend.[20] Thus, he turned to the small press[21] two very funny novels: the polytropic[22] *Chum* and

---

16 "Hanzai" means crime, but it also has a connotation of corruption and political criminal activity—you know, like in the United States as you read these words.

17 Don't call them "universes;" it makes you sound like an idiot. "But Nick! Everyone calls their science fiction or fantasy setting a 'universe!'" Yes. *Everyone* sounds like an idiot.

18 For Jeff, booze is his muse. I mean, the feature in his books, not that he's a lush. Jeff is never a cliché.

19 Or in my case, never. We all have our vices and our muses. Writing without clothing is mine. Yes, including while writing this footnote.

the unjustly neglected *The Ruiner*.[23]

And now, *Five Funerals*. Not self-published, thanks to the excellent taste[24] and Scrooge McDuckean money bin[25] of R. B. Wood of Ruadán Books. This is how publishing used to work. Someone with money, or taste, or both, got it together and put out a book, and if the book was off-trend or hard to market or a curiosity, or a subtle work of genius, or a giggly wtf novel of hypertext-on-paper, it would come out, and the author would earn a few pennies instead of having to split them with Jeff Bezos after uploading a file onto Amazon.

I will not engage in what people call "spoilers"[26] but I'll say one thing. You haven't read a book quite like this one, but you've wanted to. You've wanted Julio Cortázar's *Hopscotch* to

---

20 The cover features lots of fun clip art, including an image of a giant ape clutching a flailing person. My son, then just five years old when I brought home my copy, was very upset that I wouldn't read to him from my new "King Kong book."

21 *The Ruiner* was published by Damnation Books, a *haw-rawr* (you know, horror but not good) micropress that made the foolish era of trying to publish a print magazine, *Realms of Fantasy*, in the twenty-first century, despite two companies with actual money failing to turn a profit and selling the periodical. *Chum* was published by the very good Tyrus Books, which also shuffled across three owners before being shuttered only six months after being finally acquired by Simon & Schuster. So Damnation was too small to promote one of Jeff's books, and Tyrus too big to promote the other.

22 "Many turns," the way Homer describes Odysseus. Read a book!

23 Even I didn't read this one. But I will. The "Read a book!" in the prior footnote was really a message to myself.

be more fun, and *House of Leaves* to be less precious, and *Infinite Jest* to be shorter, and Choose Your Own Adventure books to be as good as you remember, Agatha Christie to be less redolent of mothballs and colostomy bags, and your DVD set of your favorite prestige show to be hypercognitively bingable—that is, to watch your favorite episode from every season at once. Well guess what, Jeff Somers, Jersey's own pantless wonder, spent twenty-five years working to create what you wanted, and now you're soaking in it.

Jeff, may one day we meet again!

—Nick Mamatas
Berkeley, California
September 2025

---

24 He acquired and published my anthology 120 *Murders: Dark Fiction Inspired by the Alternative Era*. Hell, he published this foreword!

25 This footnote is just to recommend *The Complete Life and Times of Scrooge McDuck*, by Don Rosa, which is one of the best works of historical fiction, much less one about a cartoon duck, of the twenty-first century. Like Jeff's work—and this foreword—it is rich in extra/sub/super/hypertextual goodness.

26 I am immune to spoilers. When I was young, my mother took me and my sister to go see *The Empire Strikes Back*, but first we decided to get lunch at the Pizza Hut across the street, where my cousin Ioanna worked. She had seen the movie the night before and promised us that we would love it. "You won't believe it," she said, "as it turns out Darth Vader is *Luke Skywalker's father*!" Yeah, yeah, I know what you're thinking, but here is the real punchline: I loved the movie! Knowing the twist had not an iota of impact on my enjoyment of the film. So I'd love to spoil *Five Funerals* for you, but *Riiiiccchhaaaard*, that guy can't stand spoilers!

INTRODUCTION
by Jeff Somers

When you ask an author how long it took them to write a novel, there are usually several equally truthful answers. I started working on *Five Funerals* in May of 2018, so it took me six years or so to complete a manuscript that wasn't totally embarrassing. But I'd been *thinking* about the book for at least three or four years before that. It was one of those ideas I'd pull out of my pocket, admire, and put aside until I had the time and energy to pursue it.[1]

But really, I started working on this book in the early 1980s, watching TV with my parents. *Mystery!* airs on PBS, a spin-off of *Masterpiece Theater* that offers up detective stories and thrillers and the like,[2] and in my childhood we'd gather as a family to watch. I don't remember a single episode. What I *do* remember is the opening credits, composed of animated Edward Gorey drawings.

Gorey's surreal, creepy ink drawings have fascinated generations, and they sank into my tiny brain and set up shop. When I grew a bit older, I began searching for his work, and eventually came across *The Gashlycrumb Tinies*, which quickly became my favorite Gorey work. A parody of alphabet readers, *Tinies* is rightfully famous for its morbid humor, rendering the deaths

---

1 Of course, a lot of my time is invested in napping and eating snacks, so I guess I could have written this book in 2015, is what I'm saying.

2 In case the words "*Masterpiece Theater*" imply that I was some sort of genius child, I should note that I once had to receive medical attention as a child after eating crayons.

of 26 children in ways that range from the relatively mundane ("A is for Amy who fell down the stairs") to the decidedly less so ("X is for Xerxes devoured by mice").[3]

I purchased a poster of *Tinies* when I was in college, and had it framed a few years later. It's hung over my desk for decades now. I stare at it for an unhealthy amount of time.[4] I started to imagine I know these children: these lonely, apparently abandoned children with access to chemicals and liquor, these doomed children who wander into bar fights and onto train tracks, who dress like Dickensian urchins, who lack even the most basic skills of self-preservation. As someone who roamed the streets of Jersey City as a largely unsupervised child with a decided lack of self-preservation skills and who had most likely come near death many times without even realizing it,[5] this spoke to me.

This novel is inspired by Gorey's work and is a kind of homage to it. It's not a literal interpretation of *The Gashlycrumb Tinies*, but it jumps off the bleak nihilism and hilarity of it, both of which are perfect. Like all art, the novel took on a life of its own, became its own thing—and as a necessary result, less brilliant. I could never hope to match Gorey's genius, so I didn't even try. But if you like *Five Funerals* even a little bit, you will absolutely love Edward Gorey's amazing work.

---

3 See I'LL BE JUDGE, I'LL BE JURY: AN ACCOUNT OF THE DEATH OF XERXES BARTOKOMOUS IN JANUARY, 2004, page 473.

4 Basically, what I'm saying is, between napping, snacks, and staring at this poster, I just don't have time to do much else.

5 Endearingly, this sentence still describes me quite accurately today.

How to Read This Novel

I knew from the very beginning that the story in *Five Funerals* would begin near the end, after most of the kids—most having grown into adults—had died. I wanted to explore the curious chaos of time's passing; something happened years ago, but when you first learn about it, it happens all over again—to you. Your old high school friend dies in a bizarre accident years after you lost touch, and when you hear the news it happens all over again—to you. The way time telescopes, contracts and expands, the way our lives become unmanageably filled with old connections and shames and regrets in a frenzy of connections, I wanted to try to capture that.

The best way to read this story is to start with Chapter One and read until you hit a redirect—a footnote pointing toward one of the stories at the end of the book. Sometimes these will be the story of a character's death. Sometimes it will be something else. Sometimes you'll hit another footnote, and it will point you to another story. Eventually you make your way back to where you started and proceed until you hit another footnote.

But you can read this book in other ways. Straight through from the beginning? Sure, you can do that. Randomly? Yes, that also works, as long as you can keep the dates straight. You could read all the stories at the end before you read the main arc of the story, so you enter into it with omniscient knowledge of everyone's fate. In some cases, you can do a deep dive into a single character, reading just the chapters that center on them.

However you choose to approach the story, thanks for reading it. If you're a fan of Edward Gorey, I hope it in some way lives up to his standard. Now, if you'll excuse me, it's time for my nap.

—Jeff Somers

CONTENT WARNING

Please be advised that this book deals with potentially disturbing topics such as bullying, teen death, suicide, addiction, body shaming, assault, and spousal abuse.

Zillah

Chapter 1: Another Bullshit Night in Bergen City

An Account of the Death of Zillah Scott on October 15, 2015

The sound of bottles floating in the pool. That guitar lick, the note soaring up. *So-ah-ah-uhn*, Eddie Vedder sang, *havai gotta little storee fer you.*

She'd decided that Cliffside was a lot of people's last stop. It wasn't a bad neighborhood, not really; it was close to New York, offered several ways into the city, and bustled respectfully enough. The buildings were worn and wind scarred, the apartments cheap and unrenovated, the tiny groceries on every other corner all smelled like onions. People sat on their front stoops and watched you go about your business, apparently without any business of their own. Kids drove around at night playing loud music that rose and fell outside her window like ocean waves.[1]

The apartment wasn't bad, either. It was five rooms in a line, with floors painted brown and kitchen cabinets that were permanently sticky from decades of other people's cooking, but the water pressure was fine and there was a lot of light,[2] and she'd discovered that she could climb out onto the fire escape

1 She imagined their cars shaking so violently they simply fell apart in the middle of the road. The mental image brought her peace.

in the back and ascend to the roof, where there was something close to open air.

But everything was worn smooth and handled, handed-down and rubbed. None of it was new; all of it was off-center and settled. When she signed the lease and moved her stuff into the place, she knew she was leaning into a decline she'd begun some time before. She'd been in the city, hustling, and now she was outside the city—still hustling, but she'd lost her grip and slid down a few rungs. Instead of climbing back up with trembling limbs and sweat stinging her eyes she'd decided to say fuck it and find cheaper rent.[3]

The bodega on the corner was called Pedro's on the faded, weathered sign, but was currently owned by a bearded man of indeterminate ethnicity who seemed to believe he was part of the resistance in some sort of blasted dystopia. When she entered and plucked two plastic bottles of gin from the back shelves, he watched her approach as if preparing to chase her when she ran. As he rang her up, he insisted in musical, accented English that he could get anything she wished: all she had to do was ask and he would track it down for her like he was running a blockade or crossing the front line to bring nylons and cans of sardines back to the trapped city dwellers instead of clicking a mouse or making a phone call.

---

2 She knew, instinctively, that when there was nothing else to feel good about in an apartment, people started talking about the light as if they were plants.

3 The first sign that she may have miscalculated was the fact the rent, while cheaper, was not that much cheaper.

Her neighbors were mostly older folks.[4] The woman downstairs spoke English with an imperious energy that was disconcerting, like she was physically producing words from within herself, spitting them up as physical objects. She had a son who was obviously a challenge, an overgrown body and underdeveloped mind, and she wore the exhausted, deep-eyed look of someone who would die so deeply in sleep debt her body would immediately turn to dust.

The superintendent was a tall, gangly man named Spencer who spent his days acting as if he was single-handedly holding the building together via the magic ritual of polishing everything with a greasy rag. He was nice to her, though she began avoiding him on her second day when he helped her carry some boxes up to her apartment and then stayed for forty minutes telling her the Complete and Total History of the Building According to Spencer, composed of lengthy recitations of names in a biblical rhythm that meant nothing to her.

Up above on the top floor was a shy, quiet Japanese man who was a particular friend of Spencer's. She found his silent, ninja-like movements around the building disconcerting; she always expected to find him lurking in a corner, filming her.[5] He appeared to speak no English. She wondered what in the world he and Spencer did, two old men with no shared language. All

4 The second sign she might have miscalculated was when she realized that they weren't that much older, because she was no longer exactly young.

her theories were unsavory.

Down below somewhere was the middle-aged white man who favored the sort of shapeless, too-large shirts and trousers exclusive to middle-aged white men, giving them the appearance of having shrunk slightly since getting dressed the day before. He was polite and disinterested in the halls, and looked like a drinker to her jaundiced eye, though she never smelled any liquor on him. His last name, according to the mailbox he opened promptly at noon every day as if expecting it to not be empty, was Marks.

The demon who lived above her was also a middle-aged white man, because Cliffside was the sort of neighborhood where the dregs of prior immigrant waves were still clinging to the bottom of everything like barnacles. The first night, when she collapsed in drunken exhaustion onto her mattress, one bottle of gin empty, she enjoyed five minutes of being too head-spinningly tired to sleep before ludicrous jazz music began thumping down from above—and not the sort of tinkly, coffeeshop, jazz-for-people-who-hate-jazz jazz, but the Buddy Rich-on-Speed kind that was all syncopated drums and sweaty, spitty trumpet. The man also wore shoes while walking on his old wood floors, which as far as she was concerned made him a complete, irredeemable monster.

She'd marched wearily upstairs. She was no rookie; this was the seventh apartment she'd rented in her life—if only

---

5 Zillah could not decide if she was being racist or not because she could not, in all honesty, recall whether ninjas were Japanese or Chinese, or perhaps Korean.

the second without roommates—and she'd had her share of assholes who imagined they lived in some cocoon of privilege. She banged on the door for five minutes and got no response, so she marched back downstairs and dug through boxes. She found many wondrous treasures, several of which she had no memory of packing. At one point she lifted her old high school yearbook from a box and held it for a few bars of music; it felt warm and alive in her hand. Then she put it down, found some paper, and wrote her upstairs neighbor what she hoped was and intended to be the nastiest note he'd ever received in his life.

"Comes from money, Mr. Hammond," Spencer said the next day, working his rag over a random doorknob. He glanced at her. "You're Number Three, right?"

"Zillah," she replied, nodding, making a private bet as to how long it would be before he started calling her *Zill*, a nickname she despised but which followed her like bad luck. It was eleven o'clock in the morning and she was in the process of forcing herself to wait until the afternoon before dismissing her pounding headache and sour stomach with a cocktail. "Money, and he lives *here*?" she asked.

Spencer scoffed. "He ain't *got* money. He comes *from* money, same way I come from Newark."

She accepted this and contemplated a new theory that life was just an immense sorting algorithm, and she had been sorted down to Cliffside Heights, Bergen City, New Jersey.

In the warm afternoon, all the heat below her rising into her apartment, she dozed in a sweat and dreamed of voices raised in alarm, bottles clicking in the pool, that guitar riff soaring and twisting and already old-fashioned when she'd gotten to it.

The war escalated the next evening when the music and the stomping was repeated. She'd been dreaming about Quentin, a recurring dream she'd been having for four years which began with their first kiss—her first ever kiss—timid and weird in a movie theater dark and sticky. He tasted like Southern Comfort and the warm jelly burn in her stomach from the liquor spreading through her. Then the scene shifted and they were underwater, a thick viscous darkness that was cold and clingy and slimy, the surface up above like a sheet of plate glass. And when she turned to Quentin—sweet, odd little Quent—he was dead, swollen and pale, his skin flaking and peeling just as she imagined it had when they pulled him from the pit.

She woke up suffocating as if the air had been sucked from the room. The sound of drums dripped from above, the pulse of a dying, terrified man.

She once again dragged herself up to pound on his door. Then she went down into the basement, where the breaker boxes were lined up on a piece of plywood directly across from the single coin-op washer and dryer. She located #5 and with savage glee she slapped all the breakers over to OFF.

When she got back to her apartment, the quiet was bliss.

She worried for a moment about retaliation, then poured herself the last of the second bottle and fell asleep. She didn't see Quentin again.

The quiet held for a few days. She imagined that Hammond was trying to puzzle out what had happened, was perhaps superstitiously keeping his volume low in case it was ghosts, or aliens, or Acts of God. But then she was startled out of a nap by the thunderous roll of snare and clarinet, and she was staggering down the stairs and through the basement door, only to discover the man had locked his breaker box with a padlock. She retrieved the old ball peen hammer that constituted exactly one-third of her toolbox (the other two-thirds being a rusted flathead screwdriver that served a multitude of purposes and a tape measure that had never actually been used), returned to the basement, and a few seconds later the blessed quiet had returned.

She bought two more bottles of gin from Pedro's for fifteen dollars. The price should have concerned her, made her suspect that Not Pedro was distilling his own in the basement from whatever rotting vegetables were left in the dirty bins at the front of the store—but she thought it more prudent to concentrate on the budgetary angle. She'd crunched some numbers and realized that in order to survive the winter with her rent paid she was either going to have to find a much better job or live on approximately five dollars a day, total. This was theoretically possible, but it required that her liquor budget be Pedro-sized.

Back in her surprisingly warm apartment, she set the bottles on the old wooden table that had been left behind along with three chairs, her only pieces of actual furniture aside from an expensive bed frame purchased in better days, its solid wood now deeply scratched. She studied them with red eyes and runny nose. She'd discovered gin twenty years before, at the Outing Party. She could remember George Heffernan, his shirt collar popped, sunglasses on at night, serving her cocktails he called GSTs—for *gin sans tonic*—which were just gin with lemon wedges. They were horrible and terrible and disgusting and she'd consumed about seven, never felt drunk, and had no hangover the next day despite all the horror and awfulness. She'd been chasing the experiment ever since.

Years and years later, George had gotten extremely drunk and died at a party.[6] She could still see him at Bishop Carlbus Prep, seashell necklace and Vans, sunglasses propped on his head.

In her youth, during college and her early days in New York as a broke young professional as opposed to a broke middle-aged professional, gin as a drink of choice, as a signature move, felt baller. The proles could have their lite beers, their whiskey sours, their low-class flights of shots. She ordered gin with a twist and smiled at the reactions she imagined. It made her feel unique and interesting.

Her tolerance became part of the legend. She was the cool young girl who drank neat liquor and kept up with the boys.

---

6 See COAT CHECK: AN ACCOUNT OF GEORGE HEFFERNAN'S DEATH, page 217.

Hangovers were part of the game, comparing your misery, sneaking off at lunch to a bar to get some medicine. Being lightly hammered in the afternoon after being sick in the morning felt naughty, wild. Days went by in bleary, blurry jump cuts. The most recent of which saw her snapping awake in HR, being informed that she was being let go, she would get no severance, she would be escorted from the building as soon as she'd gathered her things.

She'd waited for the elevator, but when several coworkers emerged, she'd turned and taken her box of possessions to the stairs. As she turned around each landing, she thought for a split second she could see Amy at the bottom, her head twisted around. She thought she could hear music: that guitar riff like a piece of barbed wire, Eddie Vedder's voice sinking like gas into the notes.

Just as she was beginning to suspect that the smell of onions pervading her apartment would not actually fade away over time—that perhaps it was part of the molecular structure of the place and not just the lingering impression of the previous occupant, which in turn led her to worry over the possibility that she herself was beginning to smell like onions without realizing it, that the smell was getting into her skin, her clothes, her very DNA—the strange Japanese man upstairs died.

She'd begun the day with resolve. Head pounding, stomach churning, she'd decided *this* was the day she planted her feet, caught a branch as it hurtled towards her, and hung on. *This* was the moment when she began the climb back. She might never make the summit she'd once thought within reach, but any altitude gained would be better than the wind in her ears as she plummeted.

She was working at the kitchen table when she noticed the commotion—steps up and down the stairs, doors opening, sirens. She closed her laptop carefully, the left hinge held together with duct tape, and listened at her front door for a moment, trying to ascertain whether she should grab her things and light out the back, shimmying down the fire escape and fleeing into the weeds and junky yards of Bergen City to start a new life as an urchin.

When she crept upstairs, she found paramedics standing in the hallway, filling out paperwork along with Spencer and Marks. They didn't notice her, and Spencer's obvious posture of grief made her retreat without inserting herself, feeling for the first time that perhaps her neighbors were human beings instead of demonic, distorted homunculi placed there solely to torture or amuse her.

This led to her contemplating the fact that if the Japanese man was a real human being, then his death was a warning: she'd been sorted into Bergen City, into Cliffside, into this apartment building, and if it was her final destination and not simply a step on her way to the bottom, then she had to seriously consider the possibility that she was going to die there.

After all, she was practically the last one alive.

She poured herself a stiff drink and didn't bother chopping

up any lemons. Later, so drunk typing a single word into a search engine took two minutes, she found the song and played it on repeat until she passed out.

She made her living as a transcriptionist. It was all freelance, all over the Internet. She downloaded videos and audio files, she listened to them, she typed up the words. It was the sort of job any monkey could do, and she felt ridiculous doing it. She had a degree in Communications. She'd gotten good grades. She'd worked for advertising agencies; she'd had people report to her.

But that was the thing about the city. It spun you around, and if you didn't hang on you lost your grip and started hitting things on the way down.

The fact that it wasn't complicated work didn't mean it was easy. It was, actually, quite difficult. The audio was usually muddy and very difficult to parse. She slowed it down and looped it, sometimes sitting for long moments with her eyes closed, listening to the same incomprehensible blast of audio over and over again, a second's worth of speech that had turned into a blob of noise because of a passing bus, a cough, or an accent.

The hourly pay was terrible, so she cheated industriously. She created three distinct freelance identities and took on more jobs than were technically possible, then did Internet searches to see if the audio had already been transcribed, which sometimes happened with videos that had already lived online for a while. She then extracted the audio and uploaded it to a free machine transcription site, which spat back garbled, terrible text files, but this at least gave her something to work with. Then she aggressively guessed and sometimes made up entire sentences from whole cloth. As she sank lower the proportion of bullshit in her transcriptions grew, but no one ever called her out on it.

The sorting had begun, she realized, eight years ago. She'd still been at her first job out of school, comfortably writing copy as part of a small team. Then she'd been downsized. She'd dutifully refreshed her resumé and set up interviews and was pleasantly surprised to find she was relatively popular among hiring managers, all of whom saw great things for her.

One, a brusque middle-aged woman who leaned back in her chair with Zillah's resume held aloft as if seeking invisible ink messages on the thick, creamy paper, told her that she would, of course, have to take on a manager's role at her age and her level of experience. She remembered vividly the air of received wisdom with which this was communicated, the matter-of-factness of the statement impressing her. Two weeks later she started a new job that came with four people reporting to her. She'd arrived on her first day in a new suit, carrying a new briefcase. She felt grown-up. She felt like she was in a music video or a commercial, cast as Bright Young Thing. This made her think of Desmond Brady, who'd once asked her to dance with him at a school social and who she'd seen from time to time on television in small acting roles, and once in a fast-food commercial eating hamburgers like his life depended on it.

Just a month later, she knew she'd made a terrible mistake.

Some people, she thought, were born for management. They somehow effortlessly compelled others to do their jobs while dealing with paperwork, their own work, and the many headaches of managing human resources. Zillah found it confusing and dispiriting. Two of her direct reports thought they should have been promoted and treated her every decision as the mistake of a rank amateur. Deadlines slipped, details were missed, and within six months she'd found herself having regular check-ins with her own boss, who greeted her every statement with a pinched expression of doubt.

Panicked, she fled. And then fled again. Slowly, her options constricted, and she began to wonder if she'd always been secretly incompetent, if her sheen of professional success had always been an illusion. When she was fired from her last job, the firing that had finally pushed her out of New York and sent her drifting downward to a five-room railroad apartment in Cliffside Heights, Bergen City, New Jersey, she'd felt something akin to relief instead of despair.

She became obsessed with the social media of old friends, colleagues, relatives, and complete strangers, all of whom had better careers. Her old high school friends—the ones who hadn't died yet—especially seemed to be charmed; short weirdo Leo Barone looked like a millionaire, working in finance.[7] Kate Huxtable was an executive at a top insurance company,[8] her Instagram a parade of amazing hair styles and new frocks.[9] George Heffernan's career had been mysterious, but he'd left behind a pretty little thing for a wife and a nice condo in the city.

The ones who hadn't made it this far, she knew their stories by heart. Una fell into an old, forgotten drainpipe, landed on her head, and was dead by the time they pulled her out. Ernest had gained a thousand pounds, inhaled a peach pit and died, his face turning purple.

She knew, on one level, that she'd been one of the Poor Kids at Bishop Carlbus Prep. A scholarship kid. Out of twenty-six kids in the Senior Class, there had been three of them on scholarships; the rest were rich, ranging from merely wealthy to Illuminati-scale rich. So, it wasn't a fair comparison. Fanny Heck, who'd spent her life dashing around the world doing charity work of some kind before getting sick and dying in Africa, hadn't *had* to work.

But she knew better. Whatever advantages the other kids

---

7 TWEET FROM @LeoLovesLoot3314: "Does anyone know how to crack a Bitcoin cold wallet password? Asking for a friend."

8 Kate Huxtable's LinkedIn Bio: "Driven marketing professional with sharp instincts and red-soled shoes. Creative, obsessed with success, and intolerant of subpar chocolate, fools, and wasted time. Experienced working with international brands and for Fortune 500 companies, running multi-million-dollar campaigns as well as astroturfed subliminals targeting market slices identified through data deep dives and finely-honed psychic abilities."

9 Visible in every photo: a yellow backpack.

had, they were *killing it*. They were being promoted, being taken seriously, moving upwards. At least they had been before they all died. If she was never going to have the access they had, she could have at least paralleled their success on a different, lower track. Instead, she'd boofed on the fifty-yard line.

Even though it was painful and horrifying, she couldn't stop herself from following along, living vicariously through doom scrolling. Every promotion, every new house, every baby. And it made her sick—and when she noticed how many of the BCP crowd were dead, she felt better. Then, worse.

She thought she detected the pattern, finally. She began searching for the obituaries. At night she heard the bottles, and the guitar riff, and saw Amy Keaton's face staring up at her.

Sometimes, late at night when she was being especially creative with her assignments, interpreting muddy monologues as epic speeches about man's duty to a universe of random chance and increasing entropy, she contemplated the likely possibility that Cliffside Heights and the yellow brick building were not her final resting place in the existential sorting machine: they were simply a plateau where she would idle away a few months or years before being tipped down to the next level.

The freelance would dry up. She would get sick and have no insurance. She would miss two, three, four months' rent, and be evicted.

Or the freelance would hold steady, allowing her to hang on

by her fingernails until she was the weird old lady in #3, and one day she would be found dead in her bathtub, a neighbor drawn by the smell, the eerie silence, and no one would have the energy or impetus to figure out if it had been suicide or simple despair. She contemplated the other ways her classmates had expired: Hector Ricardo, beaten to death by a mob. James Forman took lye in an apparent accident. Yorick Evans was hit over the head when his house collapsed. Desmond Brady, Prue Nelson, and Basil Jefferson. Thrown from a snowmobile, trampled in a brawl, killed by bears during a bizarre incident at a party. Quentin sunk into a mire, Olive killed herself. Susan Petrie, who crashed her car when she had a seizure on the freeway. Bluth and Huang, drowned and natural causes despite a clean bill of health. Clara Addams and Xerc Bartokomous, art and *mice*. Fanny Heck, extreme anemia.

She thought drinking herself to death at least sounded purposeful.

She sipped gin and tapped her fingers to the beat of Mr. Hammond's music, pounding down from above, pushing her under.

At the age of thirteen—as her parents went through what turned out to be a long and bitter divorce that might not even be entirely over, as far as she knew, twenty-five years and both their deaths later—Zillah began experiencing Exploding Head Syndrome.

It didn't happen every night. Sometimes three or four times a week, sometimes once a month, but for years she was semi-regularly awakened at night by an incredibly loud, terrifying bang that sounded like her house collapsing around her. But then she would sit up in bed, soaked with sweat, trembling, listening to the suffocating hiss of the fan, the drip of the bathroom faucet, and, later on in the infinite process of the divorce, possibly her father's thunderous snoring.

She never told her parents, who had demonstrated a disturbingly itchy trigger finger when it came to her mental health. She diagnosed herself in the library. There was no cure. There was not even an official disease.

It reached crisis levels in her Junior Year of high school. She lost so much sleep huge black bags formed under her eyes and her grades fell. The explosions that sent her, rigid and damp, hurtling from sleep, sounded like an atomic bomb going off in the next room, and the sudden, perfect silence that followed was just as horrifying. Going back to sleep was impossible, so she found herself roaming her room with headphones, exhausted and bored.

She had her first drink at Prudence Nelson's[10] house, red wine stolen from her parents' cellar, where there were so many bottles they'd never notice one or three missing. They'd gotten silly and sloppy, and then she'd dozed off on Prue's couch. She woke up with a headache and a sketchy stomach, but she realized she'd slept for almost three hours without hearing a thing.

10 See MEDICATIONS IN AN EMERGENCY: AN ACCOUNT OF THE DEATH OF PRUE NELSON, page 233.

Zillah flipped blearily through the yearbook and thought incredulously that this had been her high-water mark. Senior Year at Bishop Carlbus Prep—until the After the Outing Party and Amy Keaton's death—had been the literal best year of her life. This was so utterly basic and cliche she was offended. But it was undeniable. With her nights peaceful, with her parents in a momentary holding pattern that she recalled as Truce Mark One, with her class at BCP winnowed down to twenty-six kids with whom she had a passing familiarity if not an intimate relationship,[11] things were calm. She was able to think. Catch her breath.

She stared down at Amy Keaton's photo. Her face, round and squinting distrustfully at the camera, reminded her what a total bitch Amy had been. Loud. Bullying. Always angry, always disappointed. Always *easily* disappointed.

The head explosions started again after the Outing Party. Except, instead of explosions, she started waking up to the sound of Amy Keaton screaming in her ear.

She threw up a lot, but it wasn't so bad. When she'd been younger, she'd had a morbid fear of puking, and she'd put a lot of effort into avoiding the experience. But now she did it fre-

11 Her brief love affair with Quentin Cunningham—which had consisted of six dates of varying levels of awkwardness and approximately two hours of fumbling in darkened spaces—had ended when Zillah became the last person to notice how Quentin's attention was almost entirely absorbed by Rhoda Anderson.

quently, and didn't mind—it was a relief, a pleasure. She began to feel poorly, but all it took was a quick trip to the bathroom and she was ready to have another drink and get back to work.

She took a creative spin on her transcription services, crafting sentences and even whole paragraphs from an artistic understanding of the subject matter and the speaking style without the benefit of actually listening closely to the recordings. Superstitiously, she continued to play the recordings as she wrote. She just didn't pay any attention to them.

Surprisingly, no one complained. She kept snagging assignments, and being able to make up most of the text made it go much faster.

When she came across someone's obituary, she opened the yearbook and put a thick red X over their photo, along with a date. It made her feel better for a moment. Then it made her want another drink. And another drink made her remember the bottles floating in the pool. The braying laughter coming from the living room in that huge, cold house. The throbbing music. And the sudden silence and then the crowd of bodies, overheated, pushing for a view.

And Amy. Staring up at them, as if in on the joke, but unamused.

The war with Hammond turned into a cold war that ruined her sleep. He spent some money on a real lock, and no matter how she pounded away at it, squinting in the gloom of the basement as it dodged and ducked away from her, gin singing in her veins, it held. Every time she managed to drink herself into a fitful slumber, a spray of snare and bass, trumpet blast and clarinet call would yank her back. It was worse than the explosions, in a way.

She would drag herself from the bed and get up on top of a chair to hammer at the ceiling. She shouted. The mystery of why no one else complained, why everyone else seemed able to ignore not just Hammond's boozy jazz concerts but also her own screaming into the abyss that *was* Hammond's boozy jazz concerts was inscrutable. She wondered if she was dead, if she'd slipped off the edge one evening, rolled out of bed insensibly drunk and cracked her head on the edge of the frame and bled out—and this was her gasping Owl Creek Bridge moment.

She rejected the idea for one simple reason: not enough ghosts.

She thought of Prudence, who'd been dead two years before she heard about it. She imagined her, crushed under the weight of bodies, merciless steel-toed boots and stiletto heels her final sensations. There was, she knew, no dignity in death. Everyone died badly. But Prue had died worse than some.

Twenty people under the age of 45: two decades of deaths. Twenty pictures in her yearbook with a thick red X over their faces. And then her own photo, beaming back at the camera, the photo taken weeks before the Outing Party, when everything had been wonderful. She wore her hair up, her mother's cat necklace, a simple black dress. She looked young and fresh. She had great teeth. She'd always been oddly proud of her teeth, which had erupted inside her mouth perfectly without any dentist's intervention.

The page before the Senior Photos was a spread devoted to the Senior Outing. She remembered how exciting the Outing sounded to her when the older kids described it, all the Seniors and Juniors talking like past Senior Outings had been transformative, spectacular—possibly illegal. Lives had been changed, virginities lost, fortunes made on past Senior Outings. Among her tiny, insular class, shrinking over the course of four years from forty-three kids[12] to twenty-six, the Outing had taken on an occult aspect. Rumors involved international trips, elaborate character-building alternate reality games, survival challenges—the only thing everyone was certain about was the awesomeness of the Outing.

But the Outing was just a retreat. They were piled onto a bus, driven to a campground, and for two days they got a lot of bullshit group therapy. There was only one phone on the grounds; they were encouraged to roam around, and at night they were gathered around a campfire to engage in various weird chants and confessions. And on the morning of the third day as they hastily packed their shit back onto the bus, they were solemnly warned to never reveal what they'd experienced, in order to preserve the surprise for the next class.

Then, as was unofficially traditional, there was an After-the-Outing Party. Amy Keaton hosted, because her parents were away, taking with them her little brother Alton.

Zillah remembered the bottles floating in the pool. She remembered Amy raging, pissed off that no one was paying attention to her party rules.

She remembered the guitar riff blasting from the stereo: the perfect song, the *ideal* song for the moment.

So-ah-ah-uhn, havai gotta little storee fer you

---

12 Over time the graduating class had erased the also-rans from their memory so thoroughly many died believing in their hearts that there had always only been twenty-six of them, forever and ever, world without end. Zillah did remember one of the also-rans very clearly, however: a boy named Michael who had been home-schooled by incredibly strict parents until high school. Then there had been a divorce and a battle royale and his mother had thrust him into BCP.

Michael, she remembered, was not ready for this new adventure. On the first day of their freshman year, he had expressed ignorance and puzzlement over a wide variety of common things, including music videos, *Sesame Street*, evolution, and cola.

This could have led to a misery of abuse and heckling, but instead something more subtle and sinister was inspired by Michael's ignorance: a committee devoted to corrupting Micheal was established and quickly swelled impressively in membership.

The protocol was simple: all members of the Secret Sinners Committee were tasked with tempting Michael. At all times, in any way possible. Every day at school became a gauntlet of forbidden pleasures and dangerous knowledge, ranging from his first exposure to candy bars for lunch to Prue Nelson flashing her bra at him for a count of five Mississippis in an empty third-floor classroom.

Michael was one of the first casualties of their class, going home for holiday break and never returning. Zillah sometimes felt pangs of guilt when she thought of him and followed the news for stories about religious types going on killing sprees and cults involved in mass suicides. As she sat in her hot, ugly kitchen in Bergen City, she began to wonder if she'd been looking for suicide cults in the wrong place.

Zillah remembered that the Keaton Party was earmarked for legendary status from the beginning.[13] Mainly due to the conspiracy to ruin it that sprung up organically, fueled by everyone's general dislike of Amy Keaton herself and resentment towards the way she'd simply claimed the party as her own. She could remember the palpable sense of excitement. People talked about it as if the world would be forever changed in its aftermath. She could remember walking the halls of the BCP and hearing it spoken of in dewy tones of awe: The Keaton Party, After the Outing. All in Implied Caps, like some sort of historic event.

Amy was red hot for the party to be epic, but Zillah remembered Amy as red hot for everything. For weeks, plans were laid. Liquor, wine, and beer were acquired through various means including older siblings, sketchy neighbors, unmonitored home supplies, and outright theft. People pledged to bring weed, pills stolen from medicine cabinets, and an exotic list of

---

13 The second-most important Senior Outing party dated back forty years or so and was enshrined in the June 5th issue of the Bergen Journal as a report about a raucous party that resulted in Mr. and Mrs. Steven Douglas being arrested on charges of supplying minors with liquor. The legendary status of this party began with lurid tales of the parents working as bartenders for their children and their schoolmates and includes, in the most recent tellings, intimations that Mrs. Douglas—an attractive older woman of some distinction—being quite drunkenly free with several of the kids. The fact that this party made the papers in an era when the papers were the Internet made it a very important piece of BCP folklore no matter how old the story gets. Every incoming Freshman class heard a version of the legend.

other pharma, most of which was known to be fanciful but still ignited visions of a bacchanalia unlike any previous Senior Class had ever managed. Everyone worked under extreme secrecy. A legendary party of this magnitude could be so easily ruined by loose lips, concerned parents, unfortunate misunderstandings.

The audio recordings she downloaded from her transcription clients got muddier and muddier, the words slurring into a wall of noise. Occasionally a word would rise to the surface as she sat there sipping her GSTSL, a new variation of her favorite cocktail now sans tonic *and* lemons, but mainly it was static and noise and she began writing a lengthy epic novel in short bursts of ersatz transcription.

When her login credentials stopped working, she realized it had been some time since she'd been paid for the work.

She busied herself with collecting information about her dead classmates, sitting on the bed with her laptop and the yearbook, bopping along with puffy eyes and labored breathing to the lurching rhythms beating down from above. She imagined she would write a book about them, chronicling their deaths, something moving and revelatory. She knew this would mean discussing and revealing what had happened to Amy, but she realized she was okay with this. It would be necessary, for one thing, and for another it didn't matter. Most of them were dead, and she knew she couldn't last long.

It would be a relief.

Head spinning, breathing feeling like entirely too much trouble, she roamed the apartment glass in hand, breaking into little spins and balletic moves as the beat went on from above. Then she would sail back to the bed and spill gin and push the soggy clippings and notes around and flip through the yearbook.

And then she paused, going quiet, the emptiness filled by a sudden crash of snare and cymbal muted by the ceiling. She realized she'd seen something—something in a dream, or maybe in real life—something long ago but quite recently. A dark figure—a tall, spectral figure in a heavy overcoat and a fancy hat—looming over each of them. She'd seen it: she'd seen *him*, Death, visiting each of them. When Rhoda had burned alive in her house, he'd been there in the mirrors, grinning. When Fanny drank water infested with leeches in Africa and they attached themselves to her throat and bled her to death, he'd been there, a black umbrella shielding his face from the hot sun. When Xerc died alone with just the mice for company, he was visited by this looming figure, she was sure of it.

As she poured the last of the bottle into her glass she felt a warm sense of completion. She'd finally cracked the code. She'd finally understood. She was part of something enormous, and inevitable.

It was Hector who switched the music. This Zillah remembered clearly.

Hector Ricardo and Ernest Bundy arrived early with their

guitars and portable amps and began setting them up in the informal living room with Amy's permission and played the four songs they'd composed with their almost aggressively terrible mathcore band *Polybius*. All well and good, until Hector had decided it was time for an encore. And Amy had lost. her. shit.

Amy Keaton losing her shit wasn't unusual, of course. Amy lost her shit constantly. Amy's default setting was SHIT: LOST. Everyone knew that the After the Outing Party at the Keaton Compound was going to be a prime-time Amy Shit Losing Moment; that had been part of the fun, happily lapping up all of Amy's rules and regulations about the party with the sure knowledge that everyone would ignore her, making her ragey.

Ragey Amy was very popular.

Zillah remembered the escalation. The painter's tape across doorways torn down. The stolen diet chocolate bars passed out to everyone. The invasion of the master bedroom and bath. Throwing bottles into the pool and laughing.

And Amy raging, raging, raging.

Zillah remembered the shouts and screams. She remembered being very, very drunk. She remembered feeling weirdly unsafe. They carried all the televisions out to the patio and began searching the house for extension cords. When they discovered the door to the basement was locked, Basil Jefferson took off his shirt and hurled himself against it until it snapped open, sending Basil crashing into the opposite wall hard enough to crack the plaster.

She remembered kids on the roof overlooking the patio,

dancing. She remembered Amy, red faced and crying, screaming that she was going to cut the fucking power if Hector and Ernie played one more single fucking goddamned power chord, and she remembered the silence as Hector stopped tuning up to shout at her. She remembered Amy standing at the top of the basement stairs to marvel at the cracked plaster, her rage reaching incandescent levels as a red glow began to leak out of the cracks in her skin. She remembered Amy stopping and turning to shout back at Hector.

Zillah remembered Yorick slamming the basement door. The sound of everyone shifting their weight at once, bleary and blurry, amazed.

There was a beat of silence. Two.

And then the stereo, loaded up by a spiteful Hector. That guitar riff, forever seared into her mind, Eddie Vedder singing about someone's daddy.

She woke up in the hall at the foot of the landing, one arm draped on the bottom step leading up to the floor above. She squinted around, working her mouth, wincing as she moved her shoulder and was rewarded with a sharp stab of pain. The sound of drums drooled down from above, a thick cloud of percussion that sank down like smog, smothering her in heavy bass.

She rolled over onto her knees, head pounding. She pulled herself onto her feet with laborious effort, fought back a wave of nausea, and hung onto the banister for support. She rifled back through her memories for clues as to how she'd wound up in the hallway and found nothing going back some time, just empty blankness. Smoothing her clothes and shaking herself, she staggered back towards the open door of her own apartment.

In the bathroom, she didn't have to kneel down and throw her arms around the toilet like an amateur. She'd perfected the art of simply bending over and throwing up, a stream of clear liquid, pinkish when it hit the water. This was followed by cramps, and she remained bent over the toilet for some time, breathing hard and humming as her guts convulsed.

Sweating, she walked unsteadily into the kitchen and found the plastic jug of gin. She swallowed some, then took another swig and rinsed her mouth out. She felt better, and everything clarified.

For a moment she just stood there studying the mess of papers and photos on the kitchen table. Ancient artifacts, mementos of her high school days. Standing in Cliffside in her railroad apartment, she couldn't believe she'd once attended a pricey private school, that she'd once dreamed of being a superstar, a force of capitalist nature ramming Corporate America's wretched things down everyone's collective throat, a master of the universe. That scholarship had once seemed like her ticket to riches and fortune.

She couldn't believe she was probably the last one standing. Picking up her laptop, she stared at obituaries beaming out misery and death. They used high school photos. They always did, she'd noticed, for some reason. Every obituary she'd found for a classmate showed them when they were eighteen—except for Desmond, who'd been sixteen when he graduated—bright and young and shiny.

The truth she'd discovered was obvious: they'd all died at the Outing Party. The rest of it had been a spasm, a twitching remnant of life, brain cells dying and firing their last spluttering energy into the void.

The drums pounded from above. They'd lost their jazzy raggedness and become insistent, regular, compulsory. She picked up a random glass and sipped from it, swaying back and forth.

They were dead. *She* was dead. It was the only explanation.

They danced. For years she'd told herself that she hadn't known what had happened—and it was all just *hilarious* anyway. They were all loaded, and Amy had been such a bitch. The music had dropped as if on cue and it was perfect, so they'd all turned away from the basement door and danced and sang along. And she told herself that she'd expected Amy to come crawling back at any moment, foul-mouthed and red-faced. They were kids. They didn't *die*. Dying was for old people.

Then they panicked. And then, they were told not to worry. The grownups came. Statements were rehearsed. Lawyers were hired. A narrative was shaped. *We have to stick together. All you have to do is nothing.*

But for one moment, she was certain, with aching heads and scratchy eyes, they'd all seen things clearly; they all saw their futures: ruined, in the main.

She realized she was dancing in the hallway. Her apartment door was wide open, light and heat pouring out of it like a portal to the sun. Her head spun, dizzy and light-filled. Hammond's music had gotten to her. It was in her blood, in her ligaments, invisible strings to make her sway and jerk, something dissolved and bonding with gin and red cells to create a new kind of energy.

It was so hot. Sweat dripped off of her. Her heart was pounding. The drums beat.

Snare. Cymbals. Tom. Bass.

She started walking up the stairs. *snare. cymbals. tom. bass.* Each step felt like it was a mile high, and she kept both arms wrapped around the railing as she moved. *snare. cymbals. tom. bass.* She couldn't breathe enough. *havai gotta little storee fer you.* They coached each other. *snare. cymbals. tom. bass.* Her parents didn't speak to her for weeks. *havai gotta little storee fer you.* The police were so gentle, so kind. *snare. cymbals. tom. bass.* She never saw Mr. and Mrs. Keaton again. *havai gotta little storee fer you.* They did everything they had to do, which was nothing. *snare. cymbals. tom. bass.* Statements were written for them, forms were signed. *havai gotta little storee fer you.* It was a tragic accident. *snare. cymbals. tom. bass.* They had done nothing wrong.

The upstairs hallway was undulating, rippling with the sonic impact of each drum hit; walking down it was like riding dry, dusty waves. Hammond's door was open, too, but instead of heat and light it was darkness and cold, a purplish glow leaking out. It felt good, splashing against her hot skin with every beat as she crawled closer.

Most of the surviving members of the graduating class of Bishop Carlbus Prep walked on stage for graduation. They wore black armbands. They kept their faces correct. They didn't look directly at the empty chair draped in a black sash and filled with flowers their parents had arranged for. Amy's death had become something they could only see out of the corner of their eyes.

Hammond's kitchen was exactly like hers but shrouded in darkness and mystery. She squinted around, realizing it was her kitchen. She was floating, unmoored from gravity, passing through walls. The music was no louder; it was still syrupy and thick and pounding. She pulled herself up to the table and lifted a glass. It was the heaviest thing she'd ever picked up and trembled in her hand. She put it to her lips and tipped backwards, falling and falling and falling.

She panicked, suddenly, the absence of gravity sending a thrill of terror through her. She tried to scream for help, but the drums drowned her out. *My name is Zillah!* she tried to shout. Then, more quietly.

My name is Zillah, she whispered. *And I drank too much gin.*

Zillah

Chapter 2: Funeral Weather

An Account of Zillah Scott's Funeral on October 18, 2015

It was, Titus thought, a beautiful day for a funeral. Bright, clear, lots of sun, but breezy, an early autumn chill in the air. The cemetery was verdant and buzzing with life, birds and butterflies and thick-bodied middle-agers in dark suits and sober expressions. He compared himself to the people gathering around a fresh grave a few hundred feet away. Despite the thinness of his soles and the threadbare nature of his one remaining good suit, despite the DIY aspect of his haircut and the new holes in his belt,[1] he was not as fat or unwell-looking as the friends and family of Zillah Scott, recently found dead in a shithole apartment in a shithole town surrounded by empty plastic bottles of gin.

He glanced at his sister. Winnie turned to look back at him from behind enormous dark glasses that gave her narrow, angular face an insect-like appearance. Somehow, she managed to look chic wearing a dress that was fifteen years off-trend.[2] She turned back to look at the funeral assembly.

"Not a bad turnout for Godzilla," she said. "No one will be at *our* funeral."

This was undoubtedly true. The Sandford twins had once

---

1 The Sandford Family's fortunes had been declining rapidly ever since Titus's father, Harry, had suffered what experts call a Total Existence Failure after consuming 65 tablets of Oxycontin and a generous pour of Glenfiddich 15.

2 See WINNIFRED AT THE WEDDING, page 247.

been good-looking and wealthy, and thus popular. Now they lived together in the slowly collapsing house their dead parents had left them,[3] and the weirdness of being middle-aged siblings shuffling around inside a damp, leaky house still furnished as it had been during their childhood was beginning to give off serious Shirley Jackson fumes. People instinctively stayed away.[4]

Snapping twigs made Titus turn. For a moment he experienced a feeling of dissonance. The man approaching, tall and Black and wearing a sumptuous overcoat, his shaved head making him possibly 25 or 65 years old, resembled his old high school classmate Victor, but a stretched and thinned version of him. The Victor Titus remembered from Bishop Carlbus Preparatory School had been vibrantly fleshy, a kid who wore turtlenecks that made him resemble an exotic species of turtle.[5]

This weird alternate version of Victor didn't look at them but walked to a spot next to Winnie and studied the scene before them for a moment.

"Decent turnout for Godzilla," he said quietly. "I heard she wasn't found for three days."

"Apparently she was wandering around her apartment building pickled on gin and raving," Winnie said without turning to look at him. "You look good, Vic."

---

3 See THE ROOF IN THE BANANA ROOM IS LEAKING: A PORTRAIT OF MODERN SANDFORD LIFE, page 255.

4 Having been born wealthy, the twins had four degrees between them and no marketable skills and thus had been unemployed more or less their entire adult lives. This deprived them of the office spouses that would otherwise have filled out their social lives.

5 Victor Drummond's Yearbook Quote: "If you know, you know."

Victor glanced down at his shiny black shoes. Titus thought they were probably Italian and custom-made. For a moment he contemplated the unfairness of life, that the most boring man he had ever known would have money and means wasted on him. Vic was the sort, he thought, to leave waiters encouraging notes in lieu of tips.[6]

"Good to see you, Winnie," Victor said. "You too, Titus."

The Sandfords nodded in unison.[7]

Behind them, from the direction of the parking lot, there was the sound of a late car arriving, then the slamming of a door. None of them turned around as the sound of crunching footsteps crept up behind them.

Titus smelled perfume as someone took up a spot next to him. "Hello, Hux."

Kate, short and broad-shouldered and somehow wearing an elegant black suit angrily, nodded, pushing her Wayfarers up onto her head and adjusting the incongruous yellow backpack on her shoulders. In contrast to the suit, the bag was ancient, tattered, and stained. "Good showing for Godzilla, huh?"

Winnie turned and beamed her big, round, black eyes at Kate for a moment, said nothing and looked back at the funeral as it staggered into motion. Next to her, Victor leaned forward, turning slightly to wave.

---

6 This was not true, but Victor was the sort to engage waiters and bartenders in earnest discussions about achieving their full potential, which was somehow worse.

7 It is undoubtedly true that the whole "creepy twins who definitely have developed their own secret language they use to mock everyone" vibe had cost the Sandfords friends and opportunities.

"Hey, Katie Kat."

Kate nodded. "Hey yourself, V for Vic. Nice coat."

They stood for a moment. More steps crunched behind them. Vic turned and smiled, his teeth white and straight, the result of parents who had been fanatical about dental work.

"Leo Barone," he said, holding out a hand. "I thought you hired people to attend things like this?"

"Aw, fuck, for Godzilla? Had to be in real life," Leo said, shaking the proffered hand. He was a short, dark-haired man in an expensive suit. His body was narrow at the top, widened out in the middle, and then tapered to two surprisingly delicate feet.[8] As they shook, Victor's eyes jumped to the woman next to Leo.

"Ms. Oglvie," he said. "I didn't see you there."

"It's Tanner again," Ida responded. She was the same height as Leo, and rectangular, her whole body presenting as devoid of curves or bumps. Her hair was pulled back in a tight, prudish bun and she wore delicate, metal-rimmed glasses perched on her nose, somehow emphasizing her large, watery eyes. "Peter died last year." She jerked her chin at the crowd. "That's a lot of people for someone who drank themselves to death all alone with, like, no one anywhere near her."

"Good turnout for Godzilla is the headline," Titus said dryly.

Leo looked around, pushing his hands into his pockets. "This

8 Unbeknownst to Leo, there were several videos online of him at various events, receptions, and parties, all titled in a variation of "THIS GUY LOOKS LIKE A FAT LOSER BUT WAIT UNTIL HE HITS THE DANCE FLOOR!!!!"

is it for the Carlbus crew?"

Kate smirked, leaning to look past Titus and Winnie. "Leo, honey," she said, "we're all that's *left*."

The Everly Diner had been there at the approximate creation of the universe, the germ around which the rest of the world was formed, like the pearl in an oyster if that pearl served precisely four meals[9] and bottomless cups of coffee. It was pink and white and there was a perpetual ten-minute wait for a table, and no matter the time of day, an endless din of noise. They were given a table in the back by the restrooms and settled in among a flurry of coats and scraping chairs, immediately picking up the conversation.

"Fanny Heck?" Leo said, already tearing paper napkins into shreds.

"Leeches," Winnie said. When she felt four sets of eyes on her, she leaned forward. "Oh. She used to go on humanitarian trips to places: build houses, dig wells, that stuff," she said, adjusting her enormous sunglasses on the bridge of her nose. "She drank the water—or went swimming, I forget which—in some African shithole and there were, like, leech eggs or leech tadpoles or something in it, and she fucking bled. to. death."

9 Hamburgers, pancakes, grilled cheese, and eggs any style. Legend has it that one time a man strode into the Everly and perused the sticky menu the customers had been ignoring since time immemorial and ordered the Linguini with Clam Sauce. Legend has it the waitresses, immortal and elemental, were still chuckling about it.

When the eyes remained on her she leaned back. "Don't fucking tell me you can't say *shithole* anymore."

Kate glanced at everyone else in turn, then took a deep breath. "Ernie? Don't tell me Ernie's dead."

Titus raised his hand. "Wait, you never saw *Ernie Eats Everything?*" he said, frowning. "His channel? Fuck—he was some minor Internet god for a while, doing these videos where he would eat ... well, everything. And a lot of it."

"Enormously fat," Leo murmured.

"*Enormously* fat," Titus agreed. "He ended up choking, live during a stream, and died with all these idiots' comments streaming past his face."

"Fuck," Ida said. "We'll never hear Polybius again."

Victor jumped. "Oh, fuck, *Polybius*," he groaned.

"Greatest mathcore band I ever heard," Leo said with a grin. "Also: *only* mathcore band I have ever heard."

"Hector?"[10] Ida said. "There was no Polybius without those sweet incoherent guitar licks."

"Died in a bar," Victor said. "Head bashed in."

"This is fucked up," Kate said heatedly. "Rhoda? Neville? Maud?"

Leo held up a hand, a shower of paper napkin shreds raining down on the table. "Dead," he said, extending fingers one at a time. "Dead, and dead."

Ida nodded. "Rhoda died when her mom's house burned down. Maud was on a yacht or something with some rich kids,

---

10 See COCKSUCKER BLUES: AN ACCOUNT OF THE DEATH OF HECTOR RODRIGUEZ, page 261.

and fell overboard, I think." She sighed. "Neville, I don't know."

Titus cleared his throat. "I stayed in touch with him for a bit. He fell into ... a depression." He paused, looking down at his hands. "He moved upstate, bought some old house and was ... renovating it, I think? But he just sort of ... faded away. They found him sitting in a chair, and it was obvious he hadn't moved in a long, long time."

"Died doing what he loved," Kate said, gazing down at the greasy table. "Nothing."

They all stared at each other. Leo almost broke, his face dissolving into the beginnings of laughter before he mastered himself.

In the silence, the waitress crept up like an overweight, elderly cat wearing a control-top girdle. "Can I start y'all off with coffee?"

Orders were placed, then phones came out and names were typed.

"Clara?" Titus said.

"Were there two Ds in Addams?" Victor responded, reading his screen. "I think she died a few years ago, something about an art piece she was working on. I want to say ... starved to death?"

"Jimmy Forman!?" Ida asked. Somehow an element of raucous energy had crept into the conversation, and Ida was enjoying herself.

"Fucking hell, he poisoned himself by accident," Kate said. "Who knew? We really have a fucking shit alumni association, don't we?"

"That's because The Heffer was the only one who would

have been interested in organizing anything like that," Leo said, turning his phone for everyone to see. "And Georgie died last year. Took the brown acid at some party, passed out in the spare bedroom, and smothered under a hundred coats."

Everyone paused. "Poor Heffernan," Winnie said. "Poor Little Heff. He wasn't built for this world."

Suddenly Leo slammed his fist onto the table. "Dammit!" he shouted. "Don't tell me The Baldest is dead!"

Titus glanced at his phone. "Xerc is dead," he announced. "Like, twelve years ago. He used to post stuff about the collapse of civilization. He was a prepper, started renovating a house or something out in the sticks. Wasn't found for weeks. Mice had eaten him."

"I'm sorry, I thought for a moment you said *mice had eaten him*," Victor said. "But that obviously can't be true."

Another silence fell over the group. More names were shouted: Susan, who died in a car wreck; Yorick, hit over the head when his house collapsed; Prue Nelson, trampled in a crowded bar when a fight broke out; Basil, who wandered out of a party in the suburbs and was killed by trespassing bears[11] (Victor, deadpan: "I'm sorry, I thought for a moment you said *killed by trespassing bears*."); Desmond Brady, thrown from a snowmobile; Olive, suicide.

"That one tracks," Kate said. Then she leaned back and crossed her arms under her chest. "So ... we're all that's left? Bishop Carlbus Prep Class of—shit, how does that happen?"

---

11 See EXIT, PURSUED: AN ACCOUNT OF THE DEATH OF BASIL JEFFERSON, page 283.

she demanded. "There's six of us here, that means twenty of our graduating class are dead. We're not even that *old*."

Ida looked around. "Am I the only one who's gonna say it? Why everyone else in our graduating class is dead and we're the last ones?"

"Shut the fuck up," Victor hissed.

"Don't say it," Titus said quietly.

"I will," Kate said, leaning forward, face flushed. "It's because of Amy."

The Stairs

Chapter 3: Scenes from the Class Struggle in Bishop Carlbus Prep

An Account of Amy Keaton's Outing Party on May 27, 1995

Compiled from emails, video artifacts, audio recordings, diary entries, and public comments made by Amy Keaton and the attendees, all of whom are no longer living.

Amy Keaton had been born furious. By the age of seventeen, eight months, and sixteen days this had become her defining trait.

Decades later, underclassmen who had never really known Amy at all remembered her, mainly as an incandescent ball of fury. Amy didn't walk, she rampaged. Amy didn't talk, she fumed. Amy didn't make out with her boyfriend, she assaulted him. Amy juggled six or seven revenge plots at any given moment and was so flushed with rage it was said that her freckles were the last thing many people saw before death.

Amy was not popular, but she was feared and this was almost as good. When she ran for Student Council President, she received twelve votes mainly because many in her small senior class wished to avoid the consequences if she lost. The joke was on them, of course, as twelve votes got Amy the consolation prize of being *vice* president. She stood on stage listening to the results and many kids swore for years afterward that the lights dimmed and Amy began to glow with an unholy, terrifying radiation.[1]

As her last year at Bishop Carlbus Prep crawled towards graduation and a long, hot summer full of endless arguments with her mother, frequent physical altercations with her insufferable little brother, and mute tolerance from her father back at the Keaton Compound, Amy became furiously obsessed with one goal: hosting the Outing Party.

Bishop Carlbus Prep had been founded one hundred and sixty-three years before as an all-boys school. Its transformation into a coeducational facility had been driven more by economic necessity than anything else: they needed more tuition dollars. But age had a way of imbuing even the rattiest old academic institution with a patina of respect, and BCP had evolved into the sort of school the comfortable-but-not-quite rich, the utmost tier of the Upper Middle Class families sent their ambitious-by-proxy kids. It was expensive, had a good record of college admissions, a strong alumni association, and a long list of hallowed traditions—the most important of which, to the students, was The Outing.

The Outing was a trip reserved for the senior, graduating class—no underclassmen allowed. It was an overnight trip to a cabin the school owned, chaperoned by several faculty members best described as the Cool Teachers.[2] Each graduating class was sworn to secrecy regarding the events of the Outing, so

---

1 Next to her, Student Council President Kate Huxtable appeared to flinch away from her star-like heat.

2 Every school has at least one Cool Teacher, marked by longish hair, a casual approach to dressing professionally, and a certain vibe of I-would-totally-smoke-weed-with-you-do-you-still-call-it-weed.

naturally the rumors were intricate and largely fictional. And every year the Seniors threw a huge party after they returned, an unofficial, unchaperoned rager that itself had developed a matrix of legend and mythology.[3] This year the Seniors left for the Outing on Wednesday and returned on Friday. Saturday, six days before graduation, was the date.

---

3 The most important Senior Outing party, however, would forever be the Seaver Shit Party.

Brett Seaver was a Big Man on BCP's campus, and his photo and several trophies still adorn the awards case in the lobby of the main BCP building. He still held a few records for BCP in the track and field category; BCP was too small for team sports. He was, if you dig up his yearbook photo, a good-looking kid, great bone structure. He was popular and off to Stanford. He did not host the Senior Outing Party that year. He did, however, shit his pants during it.

As the story goes, Brett was actually a ball of quivering stress. He'd cheated industriously through BCP, knew basically nothing, and, worse, was aware of being an idiot. His acceptance to Stanford—he hadn't written the essay himself—filled him with so much unease he stopped sleeping.

Telling no one, he affected to be the same laid-back kid who never wore socks. But inside he was a mess, and self-medicated using whatever he could steal from his parents' medicine cabinet. At the Senior Outing Party, he parked himself by the pool with a bottle of Jack Daniels, a pack of cigarettes, and a pair of sunglasses, and proceeded to drink, smoke, or eat anything he was handed. He slipped into a near-total nervous system shutdown, passed out, and shit his pants. A fact discovered some time later when the party had mellowed out and slow jams were tinkling in the night and several virginities were being lost in the upstairs bedrooms, and someone remarked on the smell.

The night that Brett Seaver shit his pants was immediately codified as the greatest party anyone had ever attended. It became a part of BCP jargon. The Masons had "are you a traveling man?" and the BCP had "well, that was great, but it was no Seaver Shit Party, was it?"

The Outing Party therefore came with tons of pressure, but also the potential for glory. Amy Keaton knew pressure: her sphincter had not relaxed in thirteen years. She had yet to know glory, and she was hungry for it.

The Outing itself had been anticlimactic: it was all touchy-feely trust fall bullshit, although the kids had smuggled beer to the cabin and this made the evening eventful, at least. Amy was determined not to suffer the same anticlimax at her party. The last day of the Outing, however, she overheard Prue Nelson and Susan Petrie complaining about her and plotting to host the Outing Party themselves. This made her so furious she vibrated and rose up off the floor.

Incensed at this attempted coup, Amy got to work.

Amy, enraged at the need for an education, did poorly in school and was often criticized by her teachers for a lack of drive, ambition, and organization. She was, in fact, only graduating by the barest of margins, and her seat in the freshman class at a nearby university was contingent on her completing a short list of make-up assignments.

Properly motivated, however, Amy was a juggernaut. Studiously ignoring Prue and Susan, she worked the pink phone in her room and began nailing down RSVPs. Bargains were struck. Threats repeated. Blackmail was used at least twice. Blatant lies concerning the entertainment and the available liquors were invented. She promised at least one handjob to Desmond Brady, uncertain in her heart whether she would follow through with it. But the greatest single concession she made to the other 23 members of the graduating class of Bishop Carlbus Prep, the one decision that had the potential to shift the personal histories of everyone involved, was her agreeing in principle to allow Ernest Bundy and Hector Ricardo to perform at the party as the band *Polybius*.[4]

Amy notably did not let Prue or Susan know whether they were still invited or not. She decided it would be best to let them twist in the wind, uncertain. Let them decide if they would dare show their faces or if they'd opt instead to sit home together, alone, and miserable while Prue recited some of her terrible poetry.[5]

Amy was furious that her family was leaving so slowly. She had assumed they would be gone by the early morning and she would have all day to prepare the Keaton Compound, as it was known among her classmates.[6] Instead they were making what appeared to be negative progress towards embarking, and Amy paced around her room with the blood pounding in her ears.

She was furious with Titus Sandford, who was, for a time, her boyfriend. Titus had stopped taking her calls. He was polite and even friendly in person at school, but whenever she called and left messages he did not respond, or ever acknowledge the contact. She supposed he had broken up with her, but this did not prompt any sort of introspection, just anger. She often laid in bed and plotted his violent death. Now, as her plans for a

4 See THREE CHORDS AND A DRUM MACHINE: THE STORY OF POLYBIUS, page 277.

legendary party seemed to be curdling into a parent-infested, under-attended disaster, she began to re-imagine it as the setting for her revenge on Titus, who had been, she suddenly realized, a terrible boyfriend.[7]

When her parents finally ordered the car and began assembling their bags, Amy crept down to ensure they actually left. Alton[8] was nowhere to be seen, but Amy assumed he was already in the car, waiting to be dropped off at his annoying little friend's house for several days of sugar highs and what-

---

5 Prue Nelson's poetry was regarded as not just terrible, but legendarily terrible. Once a notebook containing several hundred of her poems was discovered unattended during gym class, and James Forman (a kid so unmemorable his nickname was simply "Jimmy") sneaked it into the library and photocopied the whole thing, distributing it to everyone in their class. For the rest of her time at BCP, Prue would arrive at her locker or her seat in classrooms to find one of her poems left there, usually with a rude comment, sometimes with a disgusting erotic doodle, occasionally with a bit of trenchant criticism.

Prue wrote all of her poems as if they were lyrics to rap songs, and they were all set to the same beat.

THE BEAST LIKES IT ROUGH v2 by Prue Nelson

what rough beast
its time come round
is worming its way to me?

like a continental shelf
it gets passed down
from family to family.

like a patient on a table counting coffee spoons
fits of passion
beneath an evening-moon

Nothingburger
Non-event
another day's useless energy spent

ever else eleven-year-old boys did—masturbate, most probably, Amy thought.[9] She supervised the sloppy, disorganized work of her parents, exasperated and wondering when this sort of brain rot set in, summoning a frozen smile as she waved them into the car and down the driveway.

Summoned via imperious phone call, Fanny Heck and Rhoda

---

6 There was the main house, six bedrooms and seven baths, everything too large, too far apart. Changing a light bulb required a work order and construction permits because the sconces were so high up. There was a four-car garage and a mother-in-law unit which was essentially a small cottage, plus a large shed in the backyard. There was a pool and a finished basement with a wet bar, as well.

Later, many blamed what happened on the size of the Keaton Compound, the sprawl of it. How could they possibly know what was happening halfway across the place, with all the music, noise, and mayhem?

Only a handful of students had ever been to the Keaton House. The Keatons didn't approve of kids. They regarded them as barely housebroken chaos agents who had no respect for property or appreciation for the time and effort they'd put into the design and decoration of a home they spent a maximum of seventy-four days in every year. The place was like a museum; there were entire rooms no one was allowed to actually use, and even in the common areas there were chairs or other features that Mrs. Keaton had clearly marked as untouchable.

In fact, the square footage of the Keaton Compound that was off-limits to everyone but highly trained professionals from various fields (including, but not limited to catering, cleaning, security, and interior design) grew at a rate that threatened to engulf nearby homes within a few short years.

That this added some fuel to Amy Keaton's desire to tear the roof off the place and enter into the pantheon of legendary parties was fairly obvious.

7 When asked why they'd broken up, Titus had thought for a moment and then told Victor Drummond that Amy kissed like she was eating your face.

Anderson arrived a few minutes later to assist in the setup. Fanny and Rhoda had long been Amy's lieutenants.[10] They put on a mixtape that Amy had curated called PRE-PARTY, opened a bottle of vodka and a bottle of pineapple juice, and started moving furniture and bringing supplies up from the basement.

Whenever they found themselves alone, Rhoda and Fanny would phone out updates on the party prep, warning everyone of the debacle that was shaping up. First, the girls conducted reconnaissance, discovering four landline phones (in the kitchen, the informal living room, the study, and the master bedroom). They suspected that Amy had a cordless phone in her room but neither was willing to take the risk of being caught in there, so the story remained unverified.

---

8 In the only public statement he ever granted, an obviously inebriated Alton Keaton was interviewed by phone on the *Kids Fucking Dying* podcast and said, "Amy was not a nice sister, to me. We had a prank war, but her pranks were always meaner by one degree than mine, so it escalated. After a while it wasn't pranks, it was just violence. I would smash her stuff; she would burn my comic books. My sister taught me to choose violence, man." After this interview sparked some minor renewed interest in Amy Keaton's death, Alton never spoke in public again, and in fact almost completely vanished from public records. The only evidence of his continued existence were several stays in mental institutions that popped up at irregular intervals.

9 Correctly.

10 Rhoda and Fanny had launched a zine called *Amy's Brain*, adopting elaborate alternate personalities as co-editors, in order to shit talk Amy. Calling herself Amelia Dongle, Fanny Heck reported every secret Amy shared with her. Rhoda created a persona called Miriam de Rasta and wrote elaborate descriptions of Amy's temper tantrums in a clipped, journalistic style that the other kids found hilarious.

They employed a simple plan for calling in updates. One would seek out Amy and engage her in a debate concerning some urgent detail of the party—the proper placement of the single bowl of pretzels Amy had prepared, or whether there were sufficient throw pillows on the couch in the informal living room, assuming no one actually entered the informal living room but rather viewed the couch exclusively from the dining room where the prized bowl of pretzels would reside. Then the other would secure the phone, dial and make their report in the breathless tone of a war correspondent huddling in a foxhole.

For her part, Amy became increasingly irate as she began to suspect her two friends of undermining her party by misinterpreting her instructions and ignoring her admonishments to stay out of her parents' room. As the vodka bottle's level sank, the girls' moods soured; Fanny and Rhoda began whispering ideas to take Amy down a notch, a prank that would be legendary in both conception and execution. This idea took off like wildfire once shared to several other guests, and suddenly everyone was in accord: they all wanted Amy Keaton's Outing Party to be epic.

Victor

Chapter 4: The Unfuckable Victor Drummond

An Account of the Death of Victor Drummond on October 19, 2015

I am unfuckable. I cannot be fucked. My whole life people have been trying to fuck me, and no one's done it yet.

I woke up the day after the funeral feeling myself again, the previous few days a minor nervous breakdown someone else had experienced, not me. Sometimes the road gets icy under your wheels, and it is easy to believe that you are a shitty driver, but then you hit better blacktop, and things smooth out and you realize it was just black ice. The last few days had been black ice. It was finding out that literally everyone else was dead. Made one think, and what it made *me* think was that no matter how much black ice I'd been spinning around on, I was better off than those people.

I watch the skinny guy running towards me and I feel sorry for him because he is not Victor Drummond. It's true that things have recently not uniformly gone my way, but life is not a sprint, it is a marathon. It is a graph of tiny peaks and valleys, but the velocity is up.

Skinny Guy is overdressed for the autumnal weather, and I can only imagine the swampy state of his ass. And since he's a middle-aged white guy, he probably never washes that ass. He's shouting for someone to hold the subway doors. I do not move. You can't just hand things to people. You either work for something and earn it or it's up to fickle chance. People who do not do the research to know the subway schedule and arrange to be there on time have put themselves in the hands of chaos and entropy, relying on the brittle physics of circumstance and coincidence for everything, and the end game of that kind of fuckery is Neville sitting in a chair and staring at a wall until he dies.[1]

Zillah's funeral. Twenty-four hours later and I was still processing the horrors—it was shocking to see them all. They were so *less*, and it was because they'd surrendered. Someone says to you, you're *old*. And you believe them. You say to yourself, well, I'm old, so I'll wear these ugly shoes because they're more comfortable. Oh, I'm old, so I'll start napping on Sunday afternoons in a sunbeam like a fucking cat. I'm old, so I'll eat whatever the fuck. I'm old, so I'll stop trying to keep up, stop listening to new music, stop trying to get laid.

Skinny Guy is just a few feet from the doors when the little *ding-dong* sounds and they slide shut. Our eyes are locked on each other as this happens. He looks maybe a few years younger than me—but with more wear and tear: he's wearing a cheap winter coat that looks like a deflated balloon, and he's sweating under it. His shoes are black sneakers that look like they're on the verge of dissolving into a pile of fine, rubbery dust. His skin is thin and pink. He's like a human raspberry.

If he'd managed to catch his train, I could have educated him on the importance of a decent skin care regimen. That is me:

---

1 See SLOW AND STEADY: AN ACCOUNT OF THE DEATH OF NEVILLE HUANG, page 295.

I add value. No matter where I am, who I'm talking to, I add value. I raise the bar.

"Fuck you!" he shouts through the smeared glass, outraged, but I am, as I may have mentioned, unfuckable. Guys like this like to imagine that there is a system, that the universe keeps track. The universe does not keep track. There are no punishments, there is no karma, no throughline. It's all just a game and some of us are better at it than others. I should start a podcast on this shit.

The train sways into motion, and Skinny Guy is swiped right by the universe, and I am left staring at myself. Handsome. A man with a moisturizer plan like a civilized human being instead of an animal who assumes that eczema is God's plan or some shit.

Leo got fat. Like, *really* fat, but he's wearing a thinner man's suit. The suit was nice, I had to admit. Leo looked like a sausage in it, and it's incredible—frankly, amazing—that he thinks we don't notice.

Kate has gotten *broad*—wider, flatter, more florid. Kate thinks she can bluster her way through everything, but you can't bluster your way through high cholesterol and thin artery walls. And that yellow backpack suggests several undiagnosed mental problems. She's going around in $5,000 worth of clothes and carrying a filthy $15 backpack. I watched her always keeping it in view, always keeping it within reach.

Ida is already a little old lady. She dresses like one, wrapped up like a sewing kit, everything neat and tidy, her movements birdlike.

Winnie is almost invisible. She was always a pale, slender girl—lord knows I'd thought a lot about her pale, slender body back in high school—but she's been stretched over the years. Now she's barely there.

And Titus, Titus is all about bare minimum survival. He's like a piece of living jerky.

And everyone else is fucking *dead*, which is a trip. One day you're doing Jager shots with these assholes, the next you're going to their funerals.

This makes me think of Zillah,[2] and that makes me sad. I'm not used to being sad. I spent two decades diligently not thinking about Amy or the rest of them specifically so I *wouldn't* be sad. Sadness is a waste. It's a negative emotion. It's an energy sink that increases the gravity around you, making your limbs heavy, slowing you down so the universe can fuck you. But I am the Unfuckable Victor Drummond.

I am also: middle-aged, unemployed, and fresh from the biggest social occasion of my recent days, a funeral. I stare at myself in the smudged mirror and sway with the train.

The day gets away from me and when I come back to myself, I'm in the train station standing on the old platform, and the old reliable is pulling in. And then I'm on my way to Bishop Carlbus Prep. I haven't been to the old campus since graduation. The old campus kept reaching out begging for money, though, the filthy beggars. They tracked me down to every new address. No matter where I went or what steps I took, magically a copy of

2 See VICTOR DRUMMOND, INNER, *INNER* MONOLOGUE, page 313.

the BCP newsletter would arrive, and then a few days later the familiar maroon envelopes along with a message from some kid who was at BCP on scholarship, telling me how alumni donations had changed his life. I could picture the kids being held in a basement, told they would be returned to their families once they produced a bucket of tears each for letter-staining purposes.

Even when I was raking it in, I sent these envelopes back empty. BCP was a cash-hungry monster. Once your unsuspecting parents enrolled you, you were marked for life as a sucker, a soft touch from a long line of soft touches. The way I saw it, my parents paid the tuition. They bought the books. They bought the play tickets, the fifty-fifty raffle tickets. That fucking place soaked them for every dime they had. We paid our fare, I got the ride; I didn't owe those motherfuckers anything else.

And here I was, on the train back to campus for the first time in twenty years.

I class up the train car. The further you burrow into New Jersey, the closer you get to Bergen City and BCP's downtown campus, the grimier everything gets, even the people. I'm wearing a black double-breasted topcoat that emphasizes my broad shoulders and absolutely slaps next to my skin tone, my shoes are Paolo Scafora, and my shirt cost more than most of the people on the train with me earn in a week. My father knew how to dress, and I remember how people reacted to him when he walked into a room, everything perfect. I go to meetings and people—people who I'm supposed to take seriously—are wearing shapeless jackets over wrinkled shirts, the sort of clothes you don't bother cleaning when you spill coffee on them. You just throw them in the trash. I'm surrounded by idiots, is what I'm saying. Idiots who are confused as to their lack of success when all they have to do is look at what they're wearing.

I barely recognize the campus. In my day, Bishop Carlbus Prep had been a runt school, a block of buildings held together with tape and old gum. My father had attended the place, so me and *mio fratello* attending was a given. My brother barely made it out alive. I was the star. Until Amy. After the Outing Party, Dad looked at me differently.

Now BCP was fat on the largess of the morons who somehow believed their own success was due to attending a mediocre private school; the campus is huge. They've taken over what had once been a public street and erected a gate, which sits open. Inside, it's all new buildings and busy students hustling about. I stand there for a moment trying to map my memories to the place and wondering if me and the rest of the No Luck Club had been *this* tragic.

The kids all look skinny and pimply, desperate, stressed-out, and unhealthy. My own memories—right up until Amy's untimely death, of course—were Vaseline-smeared soda commercials: good-looking teenagers living the American dream, cadging beers, failing classes, masturbating furiously. These kids looked like they'd just gotten blasted at their performance review and would have to tell the spouse there would be no bonus money this year.

You save yourself a lot of time knowing how to spot the sure signs of a loser. BCP was absolutely teeming with them. I considered offering myself up as a teacher, but I didn't think

BCP could afford me, even in my present low state.

The day has gotten breezy, and you can feel winter on the edges of everything. I sit down on a bench paid for by an alumnus named Gloria Fenner. A fucking *bench.* I had a sudden suspicion that the whole campus was covered in tiny brass plaques with tiny names engraved on them. Brass plaques for the power outlets, the floor tiles, maybe even tinier plaques for the other brass plaques.

Kids stare at me as they troop by. I figure I'm a few minutes away from being arrested for perversion of some kind, which would be quite the ending to this particular period of my life.

For the first time in years, I try to remember Amy.

Amy and I developed along different tracks. The first day at There But for the Grace of God Preparatory School, when I was still molting and still kind of an off-brand Victor Drummond, I was awkward and unhappy, she was confident and imperious. I was wearing clothes my mother picked out for me according to BCP's fascist dress code, Amy was rockin' an oversize boy's jacket and had six earrings in each ear.

Over the next few years, I filled out. Wrestled, ran track. Grew a dramatic hi-top fade.

Amy shrank. She cut her hair short, always a mistake, and spent most of her time pissed off, red-faced and shouty. Bit by bit people got tired of it, edged away from her in increments so small she didn't notice. Until she did, and that just pissed her off even more. Amy didn't have friends. She had People Who Had Disappointed Her in Various Ways.

By the time of the Outing Party, I hated Amy. Was looking

forward to being rid of her, to not having to worry about the Amy Situation every damn day. And when she died ... I was happy. For one mean moment, I was fucking *delighted.* I remember staring down at her and this little laugh escaped me, this snicker, involuntary but very, very sincere. Then I looked up at Quentin Cunningham, that smug motherfuck, and the look on his face made me hate *him*, too.

But now I sat there, and I thought, fuck, am I the bad guy here? Were we *all* the bad guy?

Nah. Amy had been trash, and I was Victor Drummond. I was aces. Were mistakes made? Sure. Not by me, but they were made on my watch, maybe, and so I had to take some sliver of responsibility. But I didn't plan that disaster of a party, I didn't antagonize every single person in attendance, and I sure as fuck didn't kill Amy Keaton. If it seemed like the universe was punishing us for it, that was just survivorship bias: just because most of the people at that party were dead didn't mean shit. And if it did, then me being still alive was just as meaningful.

I'd let Godzilla down, it was true. That was on me. But the universe does not keep track. They're dead because they fucked up. I'm alive because I'm Victor Drummond, and I'm unfuckable.

Heading back from campus, I stood on the subway platform again and strategized.

I'd made it my business to be popular. I followed sports I

didn't care about; I was in six fantasy leagues in three sports I didn't give a shit about, on three softball teams, and I spent thirty minutes every day liking and commenting on every single LinkedIn post I came across. I could make a couple of calls and have at least a dozen interviews set up by next week. I had already selected outfits for them.

The train is late. I creep toward the edge of the platform and lean out, and there are the lights.

My father would have told me that I took my eye off the ball. No more wallowing, he would say. Get over yourself. And he would be right. I'd been wallowing in the shallow end with the rest of them, the Poor Mes who believed they were being punished for some crime or other. It was time to shake it off and become Victor Fucking Drummond again.

The train was rumbling in, fast and bright, like my future. Without warning, someone shoved me from behind, two hands, making me stumble forward. I barely caught myself before tumbling onto the tracks.

"Asshole!"

I turn and there is my old friend, Skinny Guy. He looks just as unhealthy as before, and I think that if he hasn't made any progress, if he is still on the same platform, then I *really* haven't been his biggest issue.

I open my mouth to tell him that mouthwash is cheap and plentiful and he ought to look into that, but he surges forward.

"Fuck *you*!"

and shoves me again, surprisingly hard for a guy who looks like he's survived on a diet of Pop Tarts and bile his whole life. I windmill my arms like a cartoon character and then I'm in the air and then I hit the tracks below with bone-crunching force, and I turn my head and, wouldn't you know it, there's the fucking universe, keeping track.

Victor

Chapter 5: Funeral Club: Assemble

An Account of Victor Drummond's Funeral on October 25, 2015

Titus is not often impressed by other human beings, but the guests of the Holiday Inn Express impressed him with their determination to make the most of the complimentary breakfast. There was no overt violence, but there was a certain physicality to gently thrown elbows and aggressive darting moves to claim melon slices, syrup containers, and butter packets. He was also impressed by the number of condiments slyly slipped into pockets for later use. Here, he thought, was Late Stage Capitalism on full display.

Winnie appeared at his side. They finagled the funds for the trip and the hotel via a supply of credit card points Winnie had stumbled across in an old account, enough for train fare and a single room in the World's Thinnest Hotel. Titus detected a thinness to everything in the place. When he ran his hand over the walls, they were so thin he could feel the screws in the studs and sense the respiration of the people next door, the walls bowing and sinking with every breath. When he raised a towel off the rack after a shower, he could see through it plainly. At night, he felt every spring and enthusiastic bedbug under the nano-thin sheets.

"Pushed," Winnie said quietly. "Definitely."

Titus frowned. "Did you see Kate? Ida? Leo?"

Winnie nodded, expressionless. "The bar."

The Sandford twins skirted the feeding frenzy as they made their way through the restaurant area into the hotel's small bar, where Kate, Ida, and Leo sat. Kate wore a heavy coat despite the warmth of the day and the heat of the hotel, the yellow backpack slung over the back of her chair. Ida was apparently in the same lacy black dress she'd worn to Victor's funeral the day before.

Leo was wearing a bright red tracksuit. Titus considered it the most Leo Barone outfit he had ever seen. Anyone else, picking it up from the floor of Leo's bathroom and putting it on, would instantly become Leo Barone.[1]

"Boy howdy, the family Drummond aren't the friendliest bunch," Kate said brightly. "I got so much stinkeye yesterday I needed three showers when I got back to this lovely celebration of lowest bid construction."

"One gets the feeling," Ida said in her precise way as she plucked a possibly imaginary speck of dirt from the bar, "that when Victor spoke of us, he did not speak well."

"He was pushed," Winnie said, sliding onto a stool next to Kate. "I overheard a bunch of Drummondses in the elevator."

"I fuckin' knew it," Leo barked, leaning back and crossing his arms over his chest. "Someone's killing us."

"Someone's *hunting* us," Kate snapped.

"I did some confirming last night," Titus said slowly. "We're all that's left. *Everyone* else is dead."

---

1 Leo's penchant for tracksuits was legendary and stemmed from an influential viewing of *Reservoir Dogs* and identifying with the least interesting character.

"Shit," Kate snapped, leaning forward and hunching over. "That's just shit, Tighty."

"Fuck," Leo said. "Quentin?"

Titus closed his eyes. "Vanished, actually, presumed dead. Last seen back home."[2]

"That's ... that's actually just like Q," Leo said, more quietly. "To just fade into the night like that."

"Maybe he's not dead?" Ida said, looking around with her wide eyes. "*Missing* doesn't mean dead."

Leo leaned over and patted Ida on the arm. "Yes, dear."

Kate grunted in apparent frustration and stood up. She walked briskly around the end of the bar and grabbed a bottle of vodka from the shelf. She placed it on the bar and knelt down, searching for glasses.

"Just because someone pushed Vic, doesn't mean it was first-degree murder," she said, breathing hard as she straightened up with glasses in her hands. "And even if it was, it doesn't mean anyone else was murdered."

"Sure," Leo said, grinning. "Sure, twenty-one out of the twenty-six people we graduated with are dead before the age of 40, but it's just a coincidence." He threw his arms out. "Kate *fucking* Huxtable, everyone!"

"The *logistics*, Leo," Kate said, opening the bottle and splashing vodka into the glasses with what could only be described as *wild abandon*.[3] "Think about the *logistics*. I've been thinking about this since Zillah's. Amy died twenty years ago. At that

---

2 See QUENTIN GOES HOME FOR GOOD, AN ACCOUNT OF THE DEATH OF QUENTIN CUNNINGHAM, page 331.

moment there were twenty-five members of our class alive and ... okay, not *well*, but alive. So, we're talking about an average of—" She paused to calculate. "A little more than one murder a year. And somehow no one notices?" She shook her head. "That's crazy."

Ida shrugged. "We haven't exactly stayed in touch." She raised her hand. "Who else was surprised to find out how many of us were dead?"

Everyone but Kate raised their hands as she served the drinks without asking.

---

3 Kate Huxtable's casual relationship with legality was well-known at Bishop Carlbus Prep, where she masterminded a Latin translation scheme involving three underclassmen who provided overnight translations of homework for a set fee, which she then marked up significantly and sold to her classmates who regarded Latin as not only a dead language but a personal insult.

In college, Kate continued to pursue extralegal income when she discovered that the coin-operated laundry facilities, which required quarters to operate, would also accept 20-gauge wire that had been wrapped around a nickel. She manufactured these slugs in her dorm room and made a significant profit selling them for 15 cents each.

At the various office jobs she held down in the years since graduating college, she engaged in petty larceny on a steady and unrepentant pace, sometimes carrying home computers or other pieces of equipment, and she became a master of inflating her expense reports whenever she had to travel somewhere, going as far as inventing several clients she could take out to very expensive dinners, including the legendary Amelia Dongle, who had grown up to be the EVP of a very successful company.

When an employee named Phil robbed the office where she worked, Kate could have dropped the proverbial dime on his surprisingly idiotic scheme to simply haul all the office equipment out of the place and sell it on the black market, but she didn't. She kept the secret and admired its ballsy nature.

Ida nodded. "We're only getting into this because we all ... noticed Zillah's passing."

Titus studied the glass of vodka in front of him with thinly veiled horror. "Another aspect is the clumping," he said. "Last night I made a spreadsheet."

Leo looked around with performative confusion, but no one looked at him.

"The first death was just a few months after Amy's," Titus said, closing his eyes and folding his hands in his lap, the spreadsheet—fully mobile and complete with working equations—on display in his mind. "Una, fell into a storm drain."

"Not exactly a malice aforethought kind of situation," Kate said, taking a deep pull from her glass.

Titus nodded without opening his eyes. "But if we stipulate these are murders, they seem to have been designed to appear as accidents or coincidences," he said. "As in—what if someone chased Una into that drain? Arranged it?" He paused. "Then Maud drowned—"

"*Presumably*," Leo said. "No body."

"Eaten by sharks," Winnie said quietly, staring at her hands with a small smile on her lips.

"The next three are spaced out three or four years each—Yorick, Xerc, Fanny. Then Jimbo a year after Fanny—swallowed lye, apparently by accident."

"By accident," Kate said.

"Ooh! Ooh! I got this one!" Leo said, raising his hand excitedly.

"The council recognizes Mr. Barone as long as the words

cryptocurrency or *Ayn Rand* do not appear in his statements,"[4] Titus said.

"Fuck you, you Poor. I happen to know that lye looks a lot like sugar. It's not unheard of that people accidentally mix it into their coffees and shit and ... kind of dissolve from the inside out."

Titus nodded. "Correct. After that, a year goes by before Clara withers away—I know, I know, Katie, that *withering* away is a *terrible* way to kill someone. Then it's pretty much

---

4 Leo Barone's greatest moment came in his Senior Year at Bishop Carlbus Prep. A town in the vast, unexplored Midwest of the country that the entire student population at BCP was alarmed and surprised to learn existed had been battered by a series of terrifying tornadoes, and the faculty delivered a series of somber homilies on community and empathy, largely ignored by the students.

The next day, however, Leo asked his homeroom teacher, Mr. Rogey, if he could address the class. Leo proceeded to make an impassioned plea for empathy and announced he was raising funds to send to the poor people of Whereeverinthefuck, Kansas, and that he expected every student at school to give generously to prove that Bishop Carlbus Prep was molding the sort of young citizens who would make the world a better place.

Leo was excused from his regular classes and allowed to wander the school with a donation box. He repeated his speech everywhere—in classrooms, in the cafeteria, at the gym, in the parking lot among the school's small but dedicated population of burnouts. Estimates as to how much money he raised varied from several hundred to nearly a thousand dollars.

Leo never mentioned the disaster, or the money, again.

By the time anyone noticed this or realized that Leo had most likely walked home and kept all the donations for himself, it was too late to do much; Leo claimed he had not kept records and would assume a beatific expression and say something about how good it felt to help others.

one or two a year—until this year, when *four* people bite the dust." He paused, opening his eyes. "Shit, *five*, counting Victor." He leaned back in his stool. "The point is, if we assume there is a murderer hunting us down, these gaps could be meaningful. Why the pauses? Why the clumping?"

"Logistics, again," Kate said, pouring herself more vodka. Titus thought her voice betrayed a slight tremor of doubt, however.

Titus nodded. "Yes. One assumes murder takes a lot of planning. And murders that look so accidental, even more. But it could also mean a lack of access or freedom of action. Prison, travel, something like that." He shrugged. "It's a data point. If you think someone is killing us all, it would be one way of tracking cross-referencing."

"We're really talking about this?" Ida asked in a quavering voice, reaching for her glass.

Titus contemplated the weight of age, how everyone felt it differently. Ida had shriveled under it, which at least demonstrated an ability to evolve and change—withering under life's horrors was a sign of perception and intelligence. But Leo and Kate were still more or less as they had been. As if they'd stopped changing or evolving in any way since they'd been 17—as if the Outing Party had frozen them. Not physically. But in every other way, they were the same.

Winnie was not, as far as he could tell, human, so the normal laws did not apply to her.

"You don't think this is a little hinky?" Leo barked. "You think this is all coincidence? Fuck, Ides, if someone's hunting us down, I'd like to know."

Left unspoken, Titus thought, was the question of *why* someone would be hunting them down. The answer was obvious, but no one wanted to say it.

Winnie suddenly looked around, pushing her fine, long hair out of her face. She looked excited, her face lit with a terrible purple light from within. "You're all missing it."

Everyone turned to look at her. She stared at each of them in turn.

"We're the only ones left from the class," she said. "So that means if someone is killing everyone from Amy's party, it's one of *us*."

The Stairs

Chapter 6: All the Rage

An Account of Amy Keaton's Outing Party on May 27, 1995

Compiled from emails, video artifacts, audio recordings, diary entries, and public comments made by Amy Keaton and the attendees, all of whom are no longer living.

About four hours before the official party kickoff, Amy Keaton was in a state of surly tipsiness and growing increasingly irate. Fanny and Rhoda had been less helpful doing setup than Amy had hoped, spending much of their time mixing fresh cocktails and sitting together in hushed conversation, ignoring her. Hector and Ernest had arrived with their gear and were setting up in the living room, moving furniture without asking her and insisting that several hours of sound check and warm-up were absolutely necessary.[1] The steady blast of poorly-fingered power chords and tinny drum loops from their sampler dug into her brain and strummed her fury. Having Polybius play your party was not exactly the key to legendary status.

Also, she suspected someone was sabotaging her party.

There were small signs. The bags of chips she had specified *several times* were for the *party* had been opened and raided

---

1 Largely because Polybius had only performed in front of an audience once, at the legendary talent show, and neither Hector nor Ernie had actually practiced or even mildly discussed their performance that evening, resulting in a plan that called for infinite tuning up and sound check with the hope that no one would notice. No one did.

with impunity. A six pack of beer she'd placed in the main kitchen's fridge had vanished, and no amount of denial from the four motherfuckers actively mooching off her proved convincing. At one point the power cut out, and a quick descent down the basement's narrow and shaky stairs revealed that someone had punched all the breakers off, fingerprints in the red dust that covered the box and switches.

Again, there were vehement denials. Ernie, at least, assured her of his innocence with what appeared to be honest anger at his careful drum programming being corrupted by the power cycle.

When Clara, having promised to supply outdoor lights nicked from her own backyard, arrived, Amy greeted her floridly. Normally, Amy found Clara to be dull beyond words—a girl whose main reaction to any event was cow-eyed blankness. But on the day of the Outing Party, she greeted Clara with a warmth that alarmed the girl.[2]

"Thank fucking *god*," Amy hissed, gesturing with a glass that appeared to be entirely vodka. "I'm stuck with a nest of vipers here."

Clara, who knew for a fact that this was twice as many words as Amy had spoken to her all year, fell back on monosyllables. "Yeah?"

For a moment, Amy wondered if she'd misjudged Clara, who she punished for being thin and pretty, with wide blue eyes that always seemed alarmed. Amy always imagined a girl

---

2 See WASTE NOT, AN ACCOUNT OF THE DEATH OF CLARA ADDAMS, page 349.

that thin and clear-skinned and with such firm, perfect tits must despise a troll such as herself, with her freckles and her flabby stomach and her unruly, bright red hair.

"First, let's get you a drink," Amy said, taking Clara by the arm.

Clara shook her head. Clara considered herself an artist and spent much of her time carefully examining people for interesting details that could be leveraged into artistic works. This was often misinterpreted as a kind of hyper-attention, the impression that Clara was *very* and *extremely* into what you were saying, thinking, or feeling. "I'm good," she said.

"God," Amy sighed, pulling her deeper into the enormous house. "I love you."

The possibility that Amy did, in fact, love her was unsettling to Clara. If Amy was love, then nothing made sense.

Amy began pouring her heart out to Clara, who had, apparently, been her secret best friend for some time now. The party was a disaster. Her friends were all traitors. Her parents were clueless narcissists. Her little brother was a plague upon her life.

Clara blinked. This was the most vivid expression she had displayed in years, as she had always sought a clear neutrality so as to capture the unbiased truth of her subjects. Anyone who had spent time paying attention to Clara would have been shocked at this uncharacteristic display of concern.

"I spent three *hours* in the *emergency room*," Amy said, cheeks flushed. "And did my parents punish the little shit? Of *course not*." She sighed.

Amy instructed Clara, as her only trustworthy deputy, to

put the outdoor lights up around the patio and the pool. She wanted it to be bright, bright, bright, because the night would be mild and she anticipated people would want to hang out by the pool, especially if it glittered with reflected lights.

Clara worked slowly but deliberately, the same way she approached everything. When she'd slung the varied lights around fence posts and shrubberies, she wandered back into the house. She could hear Amy shouting, somewhere, but found her way to the living room, where Hector and Ernie were happy to pause their rehearsal.

She and Hector had hooked up three weeks before at George Heffernan's party, a subdued affair involving just ten attendees at which she'd been deeply impressed by Hector's emotional thoughts on the power of music. Since then, she hadn't thought of Hector once. Sitting there talking to him, she found it impossible to figure out if things were awkward or not.

She slowly became aware of the possibility that it was, in fact, incredibly awkward. It also dawned on her that she was unaware of this awkwardness due to having burned out the emotion synapses in her brain long ago. The dual realizations wigged her out. She decided to go find Fanny and Rhoda, who were sitting on the floor in the Great Room, being filmed by Desmond Brady, who had brought his father's VHS camera with him with the stated intent of making a documentary about the party.[3] Clara sat down with them and began wrestling with the possibility that Miriam de Rasta and Amelia Dongle were real people and she, Fanny, and Rhoda were not real people.

When Amy discovered the painter's tape she had stretched

across doorways had been removed, she immediately became suspicious of her new best friend, Clara, who had lacked a certain amount of sympathy in her reaction to Amy's Report of Abuses Committed Against Her and then mysteriously disappeared. Someone was trying to destroy her party, and they had to be in the house with her. That made her list of suspects exactly five.

---

3 ***Timestamp 3:51 on the Desmond Brady tape.*** *Fanny Heck and Rhoda Anderson are seated on a couch in the informal living room of the Keaton household.*

FANNY HECK: Go!

RHODA ANDERSON: I'm doing it!

‹girls collapse into laughter›

Timestamp 3:53 on the Desmond Brady tape. *Fanny Heck and Rhoda Anderson are standing against a white wall, location in the Keaton house unknown.*

FANNY HECK: I want the caption to say, "Amelia Dongle."

RHODA ANDERSON: Yeah, I want to be "Miriam de Rasta."

DESMOD BRADY: Why?

FANNY HECK: Jesus, D Baby, it's a bit, all right?

Timestamp 3:56 on the Desmond Brady tape. *Fanny Heck and Rhoda Anderson are standing in the Keaton kitchen. Fanny Heck is holding a spatula like a microphone. Rhoda has a metal colander on her head as a hat.*

DESMOND BRADY: Fine. Go ahead.

AMELIA DONGLE: We're reporting live from The Keaton Compound, where Amy Keaton has now been screaming continuously for three hours. Miss, you're an objective stranger. Can you tell me what's going on?

MIRIAM DE RASTA: ‹leaning in toward the spatula› THANK YOU AMELIA. I can report that the survivors trapped in this party are terrified. We're now officially calling this RAGEATHON.

continued on next page

continued from previous page

AMELIA DONGLE: Interesting.

MIRIAM DE RASTA: Come rage with us! Our host, Ragey McRageface, is producing rage in wholesale quantities. Come git sum!

Timestamp 4:22 on the Desmond Brady tape. *Fanny Heck and Rhoda Anderson are standing in the informal living room with Prue Nelson.*

AMELIA DONGLE: I must say, the Keaton Compound is quite tasteful. What I've seen of it, anyway.

MIRIAM DE RASTA: Many mysterious halls and caverns here are off-limits to the Great Unwashed.

AMELIA DONGLE: Ragey has deployed copious amounts of green painter's tape across doorways. As we all know, this green form of painter's tape has magical properties and can. not. be. crossed.

Camera pans away to show crisscrossed green painter's tape over a doorway, then back to the girls.

FIVE FUNERALS

Ida

Chapter 7: Let It Drift

An Account of the Death of Ida Tanner on November 21, 2015

Ida Tanner lived quietly. It was a skill she'd learned from her father, whose vision had been based on movement, his temper based on how often he noticed his children. Along with her sisters and brother she'd learned how to freeze, independently inventing the lost art of Mime. They'd developed a secret and surprisingly complex sign language. They'd all become champion breath-holders.

She spent so much time holding that breath she began to see spots in her vision on a constant basis.

Ida remembered the hurricane when she'd been eleven. The twins, Astrid and Hazel, racing through the house, excited by the blackout and the candles and the wind and the chaos. Giggling until they burst into the spare room, where their father was inspecting an ominous, damp stain on the ceiling, veins throbbing on his forehead. The twins instinctively went still, but the damage had been done, and they spent the rest of the storm playing a slow-motion game of hide-and-seek, creeping from one spot to another in an effort to avoid further encounters. They eventually found Ida sitting on the floor of the foyer coat closet and silently joined her.

Her little brother, Jeremy, had eagerly sought deputation from their father in storm preparation. Ida knew that volunteering for attention was always a mistake, and when their father discovered that Jeremy used duct tape on the windows the storm seemed to recede and the whole house became encased in some kind of gelatin. She remembered sitting in the closet with her sisters, holding her breath until she felt dizzy, listening to their father rage. And then she remembered the wind howling and the rain hitting the roof like sparks from a fire. She remembered hearing him right outside the closet, breathing hard, straining to listen, and how still she made herself.

She remembered how her siblings had been punished for being noticed. Ida had plenty of opportunities to practice being invisible, happily sacrificing her more active siblings to their father's keen eye and powerful hearing.

By high school people were frequently startled to discover her standing nearby and often turned off the lights as they left rooms where Ida was still sitting.[1] Still, she made friends easily. People found her to be a calming presence. The stillness and silence she cultivated around her made people feel good, and resulted in people thinking fondly of her, often without knowing who, exactly, she was.

All 25 kids in Ida's graduating class at Bishop Carlbus Prep assumed she was their best friend—or, more accurately, that

---

1 In sophomore year at Bishop Carlbus Prep, Fanny Heck posted flyers around the school demanding an investigation into the ghost haunting the campus, a "creepy presence that always seems to hover nearby" that had been sighted "out of the corner of many people's eyes, though the apparition vanishes when confronted directly." Each flyer used a different photo of Ida, usually in the background with a thick circle around her to draw the eye. It did not help that Ida did, indeed, resemble the ghost of a tragic Civil War widow in each photo.

they were *hers*. Ida's silence and lack of reaction made her a blank slate, and familiarity polished it into a mirror. Everyone who spent time with Ida became convinced that no one understood them better.

Ida never intended to be a gold-digger.

For one thing, she was aware of having been born into—as she herself described it in a diary entry dated July 13, 1992—the body of "an ambiguously gendered scarecrow." She was thin and tall, her body devoid of curves, her face without edges. She was a walking confusion and had, by age thirteen, accepted her fate as the girl everyone was startled to discover *was*, in fact, a girl.

For a brief period in her freshman year at Bishop Carlbus Prep she'd attempted to emphasize what she thought of as, with some hesitation, her feminine charms. She felt utterly ridiculous in skirts and crop-tops, her hair piled on her head in complex patterns that pulled everything tight enough to give her a semi-permanent headache from November 1991 to March 1992. To her dismay, no one noticed, and when they did, they didn't seem to realize they were looking at Ida Tanner.

By the time of the Outing Party, Ida had retreated into overalls and a tendency to subtly announce herself with a variety of polite coughs, throat-clearing, and hummed songs so as not to startle anybody.

She was twenty-eight when she met Peter Oglvie, who was fifty-nine at the time. She'd just become an Associate and was part of the team that descended on Oglvie's uptown townhome as he navigated a divorce involving so much money, it was the seventh-largest economy in the world at the time. She marveled at how the team took over, commandeering rooms, ordering in food and supplies, and constantly talking to Oglvie himself. He walked about with the hollow look of a man who'd recently discovered that there was, actually, a limit to what money could buy and that limit was the soon-to-be-former Mrs. Oglvie, who apparently considered punishing him to be worth more than any amount of treasure.

Peter Oglvie had been born into obscene wealth and had used it mainly to insulate himself from the rest of the world. He had, on average, four conversations a year and made eye contact perhaps once annually, usually by accident. Ida, trailing behind the team as they appeared to herd Oglvie through his own house, noted how he flinched away from their loud, aggressive advice, constant questions, and profane descriptions of his wife and her own enormous team of attorneys. Ida sympathized.

Once, she lingered behind after the other attorneys had drifted off in search of a rumored catered lunch, and watched as Peter sagged visibly and leaned forward until his head was pushed against the wall. She stood observing him for several moments. When he turned and saw her, he jumped, stepped back, and leaned forward to squint at her as if seeing her for the first time.

"You're very *quiet*, aren't you?" he said.

Peter began requesting Ida at all meetings, and when he suddenly noticed her hovering nearby, he would grin, delighted to have met someone so unobtrusive as to be nearly invisible. The way Ida slipped from his mind without complaint was powerfully erotic. He envisioned a life of silence and peace, discovering Ida in unexpected places and remembering, in a rush, that she existed. She accompanied him on private plane flights to secretive resorts where she would follow him around, smiling whenever he glanced at her, blinking in shock.

He sometimes left her in restaurants, and once had to turn his plane around when he suddenly realized that he'd forgotten to tell her his plans to leave for Las Vegas in the morning, then left without her while Ida was standing in the hotel spa's reception area, hoping to be noticed.[1] Ida never complained, and these incidents served mainly to convince Peter that he'd found the woman of his dreams: Ida was there when he wished her to be, and when he *didn't* wish her to be she didn't exactly *vanish*, but the effect was very similar.[2]

For her part, Ida found Peter to be kind enough, and his lifestyle was certainly pleasant. He put few demands on her

1 Far too late, Ida realized that her skill at not being noticed had evolved into something primal and beyond her control.

and could be funny when he put his mind to it. She drifted from her work—due to her relationship with one of the firm's biggest clients there was no official firing or resignation; she simply factored less and less into the everyday operations until her employment was theoretical, almost Heisenbergian in its nature. Until someone looked into the matter—and no one would—she both worked for the firm and didn't work for the firm.

One day, Ida woke up in a hotel room in Belize the fourth Mrs. Oglvie.[3] She wasn't clear on how it had happened but had no objections.

Ida never became more visible. The staff routinely forgot her, removing cups and plates she was actively eating from, occasionally dusting her, and frequently reacting to her presence as if a ghost had materialized in the room. They occasionally had to toss together a dinner in a panic when they discovered an extra person in the dining room. She had introduced herself so often to Roger, Peter's security person, she considered creating a printed card that read HELLO ROGER I AM IDA PETER'S WIFE.

---

2 Peter's first wife, Gillian, had been largely silent, but wealthier than him. She imposed her will on the marriage via multiple layers of assistants, lawyers, and relatives. At one point, midway through their marriage, Peter had not spoken directly with his wife in six years, and yet he frequently complained that she was the loudest woman he had ever met.

3 The second Mrs. Oglvie had been Peter's third cousin, named Patrice but known as Piggles via obscure Old Money tradition. She had been the perfect wife in most ways, but had been cursed with a loud, braying laugh that could be heard through walls and made Peter flinch each time.

Life with Peter aged her.

Not physically. In fact, through the magic of money—the magic of a personal dietician, a personal trainer, and a team of doctors who sat around all day waiting for the Oglvies to call about a mysterious pain or a boil that needed lancing—she was soon in the best health of her life, glowing and vivacious.

In other ways, however, she acquired Old Lady Manners. Peter went to bed at nine o'clock every night, sometimes earlier. While he did not demand she do the same—in fact, he often went to bed without even thinking to wish her a good night—she soon found herself following his schedule. Peter liked tea—sweet, weak, and with a dollop of milk—and soon Ida found herself sitting in chairs, wrapped in a shawl, sipping tea and nibbling cookies. They did crosswords in total silence, watched classic black and white movies, and ate dinner at five o'clock most evenings, the strongest spice available being table salt.

Ida felt like she'd fast forwarded several decades, but for the most part she didn't mind.

The Third Mrs. Oglvie having acquired the townhome in the divorce, Ida moved with Peter to a penthouse apartment so high up it was often shrouded in clouds. Peter showed little inclination to leave, and Ida found the process of leaving the apartment tedious, involving interactions with multiple staff members, the world's slowest elevator, and the need to update her digital calendar, the use of which Peter insisted on because he regularly lost track of her and found this irritating. They shared the penthouse for five years and Ida left less and less frequently, pulled into a decaying orbit around Peter that drew her closer and closer.

Peter died on his private jet en route to New York. His staff, having developed a Death Protocol decades before, leaped into action and made all arrangements. These arrangements did not include informing the Fourth Mrs. Oglvie of the event until several days had passed. The staff braced for Ida to assert herself as the controlling interest in Peter's fortune and properties, but she said nothing, changed nothing, and made no demands. Without Peter's gravity, she floated.

She soon faded from the staff's memory. They continued to perform their duties, paying invoices, ordering supplies, cleaning and maintaining, Peter's existence transformed into an automated museum of his preferences with Ida at its center. The staff, used to operating silently and invisibly around Peter, continued to do so. Weeks went by with the only evidence that Ida was not alone in the penthouse being the constant supply of fresh linens and groceries and the complete absence of dust.

On the day of the storm, she woke up to find the staff had all left, locking the place up behind them. This was not immediately obvious, but Ida thought the space had a peculiar, unique kind of quiet to it and went searching for people. The building itself was almost always largely empty; Peter had purchased the penthouse apartment, as well as the apartments on the floor below, to act as a buffer zone. Most of the other apartments had been purchased by shadowy figures through shell companies and had been unoccupied ever since. Ida had become very attuned to the silence of the building, and as she walked through the rooms she grew apprehensive. She soon realized they'd followed the protocol Peter developed for sudden departures years before: the furniture was covered in sheets, the kitchen and pantry denuded of all foodstuffs, the windows shaded. The penthouse was dark and cold, the thermostat turned down to fifty degrees.

She stepped into the kitchen and somehow knew that she was absolutely alone in the building.

It took an hour, but she managed to make some tea, spelunking in the dry pantry until she discovered an old box of supermarket-brand tea bags. She boiled water in a large metal mixing bowl after navigating the seventeen knobs on the restaurant-quality range. Everything she did echoed, filling the space with the sounds of her scraping, breathing, and shifting over the growing din of rain and thunder.

She sat at the kitchen table and read Victor's obituary on her phone again, half-listening to the television as it dimly described the storm—lancing rain, dangerous flooding, the usual horrors. New York didn't get huge storms often, but when it did it was usually disastrous. The worst storm she ever survived, in fact, had also come in November, one of those "once in a century" storms that seemed to reliably occur every five years or so. Why she hadn't headed to one of Peter's other homes to avoid the storm, she wasn't sure.

She squinted and held the screen up close to her face—either it was getting dimmer, or her eyes were failing. The apartment was enormous and felt like a space station ever since Peter's death. It was spotless and extremely white, everything done up in colors named Whitesmoke, Snow, Ghostwhite, Linen, Chalk, Cream, Powder, Salt, Alabaster, and Frost. Just looking around made her shiver, and she pulled her shawl tighter around herself, resolving to figure out the thermostat, which required a login and a wireless keyboard to operate, neither of which was at her disposal.

She considered the fact that no one asked about Peter at Zillah or Victor's funerals. She was used to people forgetting things about her life shortly after she'd told them.

When Ida moved into the penthouse with Peter, after a six month honeymoon spent traveling more or less incessantly, she'd found a single box containing her possessions left on the kitchen counter. Peter had sent one of his people to her tiny apartment in the Village, locks and legalities no matter, and collected everything. A single box. She stared at it for a moment, contemplating the fact that she was married to a man who owned entire city blocks and she barely had enough stuff to fill a box.

Opening it, she'd come across the old yearbook, *The Bishop*, and paged through it. Now, with the rain hitting the floor-to-ceiling windows in the sitting room like a spray of machine gun fire and the wind shaking the glass, she recalled the single-box moment and thought about all of her dead classmates. Alcoholism, set on fire, suicide via awl—none of them had been good deaths. There was no such thing, really. She thought of Peter—no good death there. According to staff gossip she'd overheard simply by standing very still, his body had been snarled in a rictus of pain, his face a mask of terror. Someone somewhere undoubtedly described his death as "natural," perhaps even "peaceful." But death was always a violent transaction, she knew.

Looking at her own photo,[4] she didn't recognize herself. Stern and melancholy, a stupid string of obviously fake pearls around her neck. There was no quote under her name, no activities. She took the yearbook into the bathroom and stared at herself in the mirror, making sure she was still there. She realized with some amount of alarm that without Peter she was truly alone in the world.[5]

The lights flickered and went off. Somewhere far off there was a hollow *boom*.

In the darkness the apartment seemed to grow, to expand with additional rooms and hallways that hadn't been there

---

4 With the sole exception of her senior portrait, Ida appeared in the background of photographs in *The Bishop*. She could be seen in photos of clubs she didn't remember joining, standing just to the left of clusters of underclassmen she didn't remember ever speaking to, accidentally caught behind crowds of kids hamming for the camera, and, once, standing framed in a window far behind the spot where the six members of the Chess Club posed.

5 Ida routinely forgot the existence of her own siblings, who had come to occupy mythical status in her memories, as if they'd been imaginary friends instead of blood relations.

before. It was all unfamiliar, everything draped in ghostly sheets, and unsafe, the fury of the storm kept at bay by a few fragile panes of glass. Every time she had to traverse the sitting room she imagined the enormous windows bursting inward, a torrent of wind and rain smashing into the place, into *her*.

She tried calling Roger, but could only reach his voicemail.

She decided she needed to take definitive action. She was 1,400 feet in the air, her phone was at 23% charge, and she was increasingly certain she was, in fact, invisible. No help was coming, and her meager supplies wouldn't last.

Feeling determined, she searched for her phone charger, which was not in its usual place by the bed, or on the floor, or in one of the bathrooms, or any of the other dozen or so locations she checked. The staff, she assumed, had packed it up accidentally.[6]

Next, she went to her closet, which was actually a series of connected, cave-like rooms. She had never penetrated beyond the first room, which contained most of her apartment clothing. Whenever she and Peter ventured outside, staff packed for them, clothing magically appearing wherever they landed. While she assumed that this clothing was stored in the deeper depths of the closet system, she did not actually know that for a certainty.

Initially, she penetrated the closet without a light in an attempt to save her phone battery. She quickly became disoriented, barked her shins on several sharp corners, and was almost

6 She did not consider the possibility that the staff had packed her things around her as she slept, then neglected to wake her.

strangled by a dense cloud of silk scarves. Gasping, she fumbled for her phone and dropped it on the floor, where it vanished into some sort of wormhole. She spent a few sweaty minutes on her hands and knees, swishing her hands around in an effort to locate it, but it had been claimed by some elemental force.

A tipsy feeling swept through her—maybe she was a ghost, had always been a ghost, and she was only now experiencing the inverse of what everyone else did: her lack of presence. Worried that the dark elemental force of the closet might next claim her, she began grabbing clothes blindly, trying to feel for a good coat, some watertight boots, and a voluminous bag.

When she emerged from the closet the faint light from outside was bounced and amplified by the bedroom's moon-like whiteness. She discovered that she'd secured a pair of thigh-high leather boots with skyscraper heels whose provenance was a mystery, one of her old nightgowns that she'd taken for a large bag, and an enormous puffer coat that one of Peter's adult sons had left behind.

She briefly considered diving back into the muffled hell of her closet, but something about the cottony silence of it made that impossible while the loud roaring of the storm outside the bedroom windows alarmed her in completely different ways. So she pulled on the boots and the jacket and fashioned the nightgown into an ersatz bag by tying off four corners, and set about seeking provisions.

After an exhaustive search, the only provisions she acquired were a tin of mints, found by sheer luck in the pocket of the puffer coat.

Unexpectedly buoyed by this discovery, Ida zipped up the coat, wiggled her toes in the too-large boots, and strode purposefully to the front door of the apartment, which was heavy and required all her strength to open—Roger or other staff normally opened doors for her—stepping out into the dim hallway, lit by yellow emergency lights. When the door *snicked* shut behind her with a distinct vacuum-like sound of finality, she realized she had no way of getting back *into* the apartment until the power came back on and she could use the passcode. Unless the concierge office was staffed down below, which seemed unlikely.

In the hall, the wind and rain were less noticeable. She stood for a moment, uncertain. She looked down at herself and frowned. She had scored 172 on the LSAT. She'd passed the bar on her first try. When she'd met Peter she'd been firmly on the partner track. A lifetime of silent observation made her sharp: she had once been a keen collector of details, she thought, grasping patterns and systems faster than most.

Now she stood in a ridiculous outfit, and she realized that she'd never accessed the stairs. She'd only ever followed others into the elevator. She had no idea how to contact any of Peter's staff, who had now been *her* staff for almost a year. It suddenly seemed possible that being as still as she had for so long had shrunk her brain, parts of it shutting down for want of use.

Listening to the muffled scream of the storm, she thought she might be in a bit of trouble.

She crept toward the imposing metal door marked EMERGENCY EXIT which had never, as far as she knew, been opened. Her heels made it difficult to walk. She found herself sweating in the oversized jacket.

Taped to the door was an official-looking memo dated several days before announcing a general evacuation, and making it very clear that the building staff would be elsewhere before, during, and for at least a day after the storm. It asked politely that all routine maintenance calls and requests be held until the existential threat had passed. Ida studied the memo for a moment, blinking. Then she looked at her boots again, amazed.

The stairwell was lit in the same moldy yellow light. The stairs were wide but shallow, and as she stepped onto the first one the sound echoed against the walls. She clung to the railing, her boots threatening to betray her, sweat streaming into her face as she descended. When she'd gone down two floors she realized she could feel the building swaying in the wind, a palpable vibration. Imagining the whole thing pancaking on top of her and squeezing her out of existence, she clung to the railing for a full minute, eyes tightly shut.

She remembered a similar feeling at the Outing Party, the first time she'd seen Amy's body. She'd screamed, though no one reacted. Then she'd closed her eyes, and for a while she couldn't bring herself to open them again. But it had passed. Hours later, she'd found comfort in helping everyone organize their thoughts as they waited, what they would say about the incident. The experience had actually inspired her to become a lawyer.

She opened her eyes and forced herself to move. One slow step down, then another. She picked up speed, and soon felt like the building was pushing her downwards, faster and faster, until she was more or less falling without ever actually hitting the floor. When the first floor doors loomed up from the twilit gloom she crashed into them, feeling nothing thanks to the padding of the puffer coat. She bounced back gently, teetering in the loose boots, then re-launched herself with careful aim, bursting into the lobby at a stumbling run.

Staggering to a halt, she stood for a moment, staring. The lobby was enclosed in plate glass, and outside was water. At least four feet of it, sloshing up against the building, roiled by ceaseless, powerful winds. She could just make out the whipping power lines and swaying streetlights outside. She watched as a yellow taxi cab floated past, headlights still on.

She shuffled forward, eyes squinting as she tried to peer into the gloom. There was a strange, low groaning noise, almost subaudible. As she approached the front lobby doors, she watched the taxi slowly turn toward the building like the *Titanic*, a graceless swerve that put the weakening headlights right on her like an anemic spotlight. As she watched, transfixed, a surge of water pushed the car in her direction. It rode the sudden wave, rising up and then smashing down into the doors, which shattered on impact.

A second later, Ida was swept off her feet by the flood. Knocked over, she found herself bobbing gently on the surface, her puffer coat acting as a kind of momentary, inflated raft. She moved her arms and legs ineffectually as the water swirled her around, disorienting her. She was sucked out into the street, spinning, thrashed by contradictory currents.

She could feel water seeping into the lining, and she began to sink. She stopped struggling. She stared up at the black sky for a moment, dark shapes of buildings speeding past.

She didn't cry out. It had been so long since Ida Tanner had drawn attention to herself. She'd simply forgotten how.

Ida

Chapter 8: Going Viral

An Account of Ida Tanner's Funeral on November 24, 2015

Titus approved of the attitude shift. They sat in the small chapel on black folding chairs and said nothing. There was no sarcasm, no flippancy. They all looked haunted.[1] Leo was extra puffy, his jowls overflowing his bright white shirt. Kate looked hungover, rough, her chic clothes a mess, like she'd dressed in the dark. Winnie, never a talker, had a pinched expression that conveyed deep concern. And Titus himself was very proud of his sad, silent demeanor.[2]

At the front of the almost empty chapel there was an enormous photo of Ida. It was the photo of her from *The Bishop*, taken senior year. Titus wondered why they chose that particular photo, a person Ida hadn't been in decades wearing some truly dreadful pearls and a haircut he found inexplicable.[3,4] He wondered about the low attendance and again contemplated his own death—which was apparently approaching much more quickly and in a much more organized manner than he'd expected. He used to imagine that his death would be spectacular and messy—most likely involving a murder-suicide situation

---

1 This brought everyone in line with Titus, who had always looked haunted and who had once been excused from wedding party photos because of the gaunt sepulchral aura he brought to all photographs.

2 Titus was a collector of expressions. He rarely had an instinctive understanding of how to arrange his face in social situations, so he had long practiced mimicry.

with Winnie—so this was surprising.

He'd also imagined Ida—so careful, so timid, like a piece of china wrapped in tissue paper and covered in choking dust—would outlive them all. He'd imagined her, elderly and frail, tenderly dropping roses on the cheap plywood box containing his viscera and several unidentified bones. Instead, she'd apparently drowned during the hurricane, which was low on Titus's list of good ways to die. Or *possible* ways to die.

Outside there was still the lingering dampness of the disaster—pools of brackish water, evidence of property damage, soggy piles of sandbags. He'd never associated Ida, the driest woman on earth, with water.

Kate, sitting next to him with the yellow backpack slung over the back of her chair, nudged him with one elbow. Titus didn't understand Kate's wardrobe. Everything she wore was expensive, designer labels. Everything she wore was *wrong*, somehow, in ways that his brain found slippery and unsettling.[5]

---

3 A last-minute decision involving some sort of unholy cross between a pixie cut and bangs-based experiment, Ida knew the moment the photographer excused her that she had made a terrible mistake. Her inability to do anything about this had been her number one source of anxiety for approximately seven weeks, at which time her involvement in Amy Keaton's Outing Party took the title and held it for the next twenty years.

4 Susan Petrie, horrified, referred to Ida's haircut as The Thing.

5 In this instance, an oversized camel hair coat, a loud silk scarf with a pattern of purple orchids, a blood red blouse, brown pants, and black boots. Each individual item was fine on its own but put together they vibrated on an ancient frequency most human brains interpreted as *danger*.

Kate raised her eyebrows and jerked her head to her right. Then she stood up, hefted the backpack, and stepped into the aisle. She took two steps towards the exit, paused, and turned to violently gesture at the rest of them to follow her.

The funeral home was like every other one Titus had ever been in. It was tastefully decorated in pastels and grays, the carpets were thick and absorbing, and the furniture's aesthetic was Senile Grandma 1987. There were plenty of spaces for quiet conversation, general weepery, and joking in poor taste. They found an unused sitting area and crowded onto the couch and the stiff, ornate chairs while Kate stood, producing her phone.

"Y'all don't remember," she said, breathing fast, "but Desmond recorded, like, *hours* of the party."

Titus raised an eyebrow. He didn't remember that at all. High school predated the era when he worried about consequences. At the age of 17 he would have done anything on camera with a defiant attitude and a radiant smile. More than two decades later, he was far too jealous of his frayed dignity.[6] There was no such thing as privacy anymore.

"I don't need to see my younger self," Leo complained. "I was fat, and I thought frosted hair was cool."

Titus thought this was the most honest Leo had ever been.

"Fuck you," Kate said in a reasonable tone. "You think *anyone* wants footage of their stoned 17-year-old self existing?"

---

6 As a collector of expressions, Titus knew that when walking around in public he was probably being recorded at all times—doorbells, strangers with phones, municipal surveillance—and thus he had cultivated a facial expression he called Beige.

"Des[7] was only 16," Winnie murmured. Titus thought that she, alone among them, was unconcerned. Winnie had been born 40 years old and would never change until one day she simply vanished.

"Des was supposed to erase it, destroy it," Kate said. "That was the agreement. But he didn't, and eventually he gave it to me."

"Wait a second," Leo said, nose quivering. "Is there ... does the video show..."

"Fuck, *no*," Kate snarled. "Fucking hell, no it doesn't show the fucking *moment*, you freak. It's like a random hour of us standing around like assholes." She tapped on her phone and a video filled the screen. "I digitized it. This is timestamp 5 minutes 43 seconds. I've got a five second loop set up."

She tapped the screen, and everyone leaned forward.

Titus experienced a strange moment of horror. He hadn't thought about Amy's house since that night. He had deleted it from his memories. Seeing it again—all that wood, the floors scratched from moving the furniture, Hector and Ernie's gear and guitars—it was disorienting.

The video was grainy, the lighting dim. The scene was shot from a high angle and captured more or less the entire room. It showed a bunch of skinny kids. Music played, a thumping beat. Everyone had a red plastic cup in their hands. Everyone swayed and shifted. In one corner, Olive Partridge, a tall girl with a permanent slump, threw her head back and barked a

---

7 See AND SCENE: AN ACCOUNT OF THE DEATH OF DESMOND BRADY, page 361.

laugh so loudly the phone shook in Kate's hand. In the center of the room, George held court, entertaining a loose group of classmates—Titus thought he could still hear George's horse-like braying in his head. Towards the bottom of the screen, Quentin and Rhoda were leaning into each other, mouths near ears, having a typically secret conversation.

Then the clip started over.

Titus looked for himself. He stood alone, which matched most of his memories of parties, during and after high school. He was overly familiar with the perceived brutality of parties, the alpha predator nature of people who did well at them. In the loop, he looked around the room incredulously, as if he couldn't believe that kids who spent almost all of their time together every single day would choose to spend *even more* time together.

The clip started over.

"Kate," Leo said slowly, rubbing his nose. "You know I have nothing but the highest respect for you. You know that of all the people I haven't spoken to in literally decades, you are my favorite. So, take this the right way: What the fuck are we looking at?"

Kate sighed, a quick, sharp inhalation-exhalation cycle. "Look, every single one of us is there on the screen. All 26 of us. This is probably an hour or two before. And we're all there, right?"

They all leaned in again. "No," Leo said. "No, Ida's not there."

Kate closed her eyes for a moment and clenched her fist.

"Yes, she is. She's behind the couch, holding a can of soda or something."

Leo scanned the scene again. After a moment, he realized that what he'd taken to be a plant or possibly an odd shadow was Ida Tanner.

Titus let his eyes roam around the screen. It did look like everyone was in the shot—even Amy, all the way in the back, enthusiastically berating Fanny Heck in front of an X of painter's tape across a doorway, her body language an exclamation mark.

"Wow, maybe," Winnie said quietly. "Even Una.[8] I forgot she was even at this party."

"I forgot *Una*," Leo said.

"We're all accounted for," Kate said. "So, who's *that*?"

She jabbed a finger at the screen. Titus stared at the indicated spot, which showed a sliver of the hallway off the living room, and a few feet of the stairs leading up to the second floor. It was pixelated and blurry.

They all leaned forward, faces scrunched.

"Who's *what*?" Leo asked.

Kate jabbed her finger again, more violently. "*That*."

They all stared again. After a moment, everyone turned to look back at Kate expectantly.

"Kate," Titus said slowly, "maybe this goes better if you tell us what that is."

"That's a *hand*," Kate said triumphantly.

---

8 See MANHUNT HA TERMINADO: AN ACCOUNT OF THE DEATH OF UNA TAYLOR, page 373.

Everyone's head swiveled back to the screen. Everyone stared for a moment.

Titus frowned. "*Is* it, though? This video appears to have been filmed in a previous century."

"Hand," Kate repeated emphatically. "Look, I wasn't sold on the logistics. But I started thinking about the *odds*. And then I saw the hand."

Titus tilted his head. "*Is it*, though? That blob of ancient pixels could be anything. Block of cheese? Yes. Someone's shoes? Possibly. Our youthful hopes and dreams, calcified into physical form? Why not."

"*Hand*!" Kate hissed.

"Yeah," Leo said. "Shit. Who the fuck *is* that?"

They got deadly quiet. Even Winnie, Titus thought—even his sister was suddenly concerned, which was very difficult to achieve, as Winifred Sandford sailed through life floating on a mist of unconcern and unearned confidence. They all spent a good minute counting heads and then re-counting.

"Fuck me," Leo said quietly, leaning back against the couch. "There was someone else at the party."

Titus looked around, considering the wisdom of once again pointing out the video quality involved. Not to mention the dim lighting, Desmond's shaky-cam approach to direction, and the general air of desperation to explain what was happening to them. But before he could, Kate pulled the phone back and slid it into her pocket. Then she nodded, looking around.

"There was someone else at the party."

The Stairs

Chapter 9: Definitely Not Baked Beans

An Account of Amy Keaton's Outing Party on May 27, 1995

Compiled from emails, video artifacts, audio recordings, diary entries, and public comments made by Amy Keaton and the attendees, all of whom are no longer living.

The party was a disaster.

There was Jello in the guest toilet. There were muddy footprints on the white carpet in the off-limits sitting room, though the green tape crisscrossed over the entryway hadn't been disturbed. Someone had unplugged the refrigerator. The carpet in the hallway was soaking wet and water bubbled up every time someone stepped on it. There were maraschino cherries in odd, unexpected places.[1] Someone had gone onto the second-floor deck and opened the umbrella, which had caught the wind and now resided in a tree a few hundred feet away. There was a head-shaped hole in the wall just outside the upstairs bathroom. All the televisions in the house had been set to Spanish without subtitles. A complex fort had been constructed from books and leather seat cushions in the library, which also had been invaded despite the presence of green tape across the doorway. Someone had placed an entire package of frozen burritos in the microwave and set the timer to thirty minutes, causing an explosion of black beans and cheese. People were on the roof. There were three different sound sys-

1 To be fair, finding maraschino cherries *anywhere* is generally unexpected.

tems playing wildly different music and Polybius kept trying to win the Loudness Wars.

Worse, no one would own up to the sabotage. Everyone was acting like she was crazy, giving her blank stares and attitude when she demanded answers.

"I got here early," Jimmy Forman[2] said, his mouth wet, his close-cropped hair shining in the light. "That fucking toilet was already bright orange *hours* ago, Ames."

In the dining room, Olive, Una, Susan, Xerxes, and George were playing a game of Truth or Dare that was slowly blurring into a game of Strip Dare that already saw George, pale and fleshy and shockingly hairy, down to his tighty-whities.[3]

"You are losing on *purpose*, you pervert," Fanny wailed from the couch, where she sat with Desmond and Rhoda. "You just want me to see your *nethers*."

"Perv!" Rhoda shouted.

"This behavior is inappropriate," Fanny added. "I'm gonna

---

2 See I AM INEVITABLE: AN ACCOUNT OF THE DEATH OF JAMES FORMAN, page 387.

3 ***Timestamp 1:47:32 on the Desmond Brady tape.*** *Prudence Nelson stands next to a potted plant in the upstairs hallway. A loud buzz of voices and music makes her voice difficult to hear. She holds a small notebook up and reads from it.*

PRUE NELSON: I call this one "In the Air Tonight."

all that stands
between me and doom
is a thin layer
of Fruit of the Loom

Prue purses her lips and closes the notebook.

PRUE NELSON: That was terrible. I apologize.

report you and get you investigated, asshole. Your career in politics is *over*."

George stood up unsteadily and gyrated, hands laced behind his neck.

"I am traumatized by that," Fanny said as Amy stormed furiously past them. "I may have to sue."

Initially, Amy received vaguely reassuring responses to her attempts to discipline her guests—there were apologies, promises, and even some half-hearted efforts at cleaning. But a few hours in, everyone was lubricated and her furious demands for better behavior were met with sneers and jeers.

When she came upon Maud, Neville, and Yorick throwing empty bottles into the pool and demanded they stop, Maud turned and threw a bottle at her feet, the explosion of glass driving her back into the house. When she asked Ernest[4] and Hector to fucking *stop* playing their magnum opus, the sixteen-minute-long *Order of Sex Change Operations* and its apparently random key changes, Hector wordlessly turned up the volume on his amp. When she found Olive and Winnie lying on her parents' bed in the dark, she turned the lights on in a manner that could best be described as *furiously* and ordered them out. They just burst into laughter, hugging each other tightly as they howled.

When she burst into the guest bathroom on the first floor and found Leo and Basil standing in two inches of water while Quentin worked a plunger in the toilet, all three froze for a moment.

---

4 See STOP. DON'T. COME BACK.: AN ACCOUNT OF THE DEATH OF ERNEST BUNDY, page 397.

"It was like this when we got here," Leo said.

"It was *not*!" Amy hissed, her voice cracking.

"Something's wrong with your toilet, then," he said.

"There is *not*!" She craned her neck. "What's *in* there, anyway?"

"Definitely not baked beans."

When she walked into the dining room, which had been explicitly marked as forbidden, she found Yorick, somehow larger than he'd been just a few moments earlier, hanging from the chandelier, spinning slowly around while fifteen of her classmates clapped and cheered. As she stood there, dumbfounded, a sharp cracking sound presaged the chandelier tearing free from its moorings, perhaps the most predictable event in human history.

Yorick fell to the floor, still clutching the chandelier, and the crowd exhaled a unified *ooooh*.

For a moment, he lay very still. Silence descended, the sound of Polybius in the background. Someone gasped. Then Yorick sat up, pushing the chandelier off to the side and raising his arms up.

Everyone cheered.

At this point, Amy was almost totally consumed by rage.[5] She turned and stormed over to the basement door, tearing

---

5 ***Timestamp 2:31:12 on the Desmond Brady tape.*** *Fanny Heck stands in the kitchen. Behind her, the refrigerator is open and appears to have been filled with wet toilet paper.*

FANNY HECK: At this point, Amy has ceased to be a human being and became a creature known forever more as Rage Ginger, Destroyer of Good Times.

it open and racing down the narrow, steep stairs that shook with every step. She was trailed by a burst of laughter from her guests, but this mutated into a groan of dismay when the power was suddenly cut.

"Fuck you, motherfuckers," Amy hissed as she ascended the stairs. "Come into *my* house and act like a bunch of damn barbarians."

As she mounted the stairs again, however, she heard music from above, and a cheer rippled through the air. Boom boxes had been deployed, cassettes and CDs produced. Amy, covered in a light coating of blood-red dust, stood for a moment in the basement doorway, so angry she couldn't move or breathe.[6] She vibrated. She had *invited* these people. These people were supposed to be her *friends*. Friends didn't act like your house was a playground they could shit in.

Worst of all, Amy was belatedly realizing that her Outing Party would, in fact, be legendary, but for none of the reasons she *wanted* it to be legendary. It would be remembered forever as the party when Amy Keaton went berserk, as the party that started the definitive decline of civilization, as the inflection point when everything went bad.

She stared at her classmates as they laughed and joked. And then she started to scream.[7,8]

---

6 *Timestamp 2:33:24 on the Desmond Brady tape. Fanny Heck stands in the darkened kitchen.*

FANNY HECK: Future historians will report that a recently erected statue of Amy Keaton provided enough heat and light for the party to not only survive in these harsh conditions, but to thrive.

continued on next page

continued from previous page

---

7 ***Timestamp 2:34:14 on the Desmond Brady tape.*** *Prudence Nelson and Victor Drummond stand in the informal living room holding red plastic cups. Victor has his arm around Prue's shoulders.*

VICTOR DRUMMOND: This girl writes the best fucking poems!

PRUDENCE NELSON: Shut up!

VICTOR DRUMMOND: Do one! Right now, make one up!

PRUDENCE NELSON: Shut up!

Prudence looks down at the floor, then back at the camera.

PRUDENCE NELSON: This Is a Party, Not a Democracy:

This is not a
party
this is a
democracy
and I am staging a coup

Victor begins performing an off-rhythm beatbox.

PRUDENCE NELSON:

this is not a
fun time
this is
serious business
and you will respect
my authority

Off-camera, cheers and applause.

8 ***Timestamp 2:36:41 on the Desmond Brady tape.*** *Fanny Heck and Rhoda Anderson stand in the darkened kitchen. Rhoda is holding a can of beer and a cigarette. The camera is very close and the light is very dim. The girls' faces loom out of the darkness, indistinct and pixelated.*

FANNY HECK: The bit again, D Baby.

DESMOND BRADY: Uh, sure. The bit.

Fanny and Rhoda look at each other and nod, then look back at the camera.

AMELIA DONGLE: ‹*stage whispering loudly*› We are back here at RAGEATHON, bringing you the latest. As you can hear in the background, Rage Ginger, Destroyer of Good Times has gone thermonuclear. We fear for our lives.

MIRIAM DE RASTA: Allow me to translate for those who do not speak Rage.

AMELIA DONGLE: Sing it, sister!

Rhoda mimes listening intently, one hand to her ear as if she was wearing an earpiece.

MIRIAM DE RASTA: I have invited you to a party but now that you are partying, I am enraged by your partying!

MIRIAM DE RASTA: I provided you with everything you might need to enjoy yourselves! My goodness, people, there were three pretzels allocated for each attendee! What more do you want?

MIRIAM DE RASTA: It is now occurring to me that some of you may have attended this social function ironically!

MIRIAM DE RASTA: This is unacceptable!

AMELIA DONGLE: Fuck, you are hilarious! (indistinct) I can't feel my face.

MIRIAM DE RASTA: The punishments will begin presently and will continue until you assholes start to enjoy my fucking party!

Fanny Heck leans over and grabs Rhoda by the shoulders.

AMELIA DONGLE: Not that you aren't always hilarious! I don't need to be high to think you're hilarious, sweetie!

MIRIAM DE RASTA: ‹*shouting and laughing simultaneously*› But do not enjoy it in any way but the way I have outlined in my current five-year plan!

MIRIAM DE RASTA: Or the punishments will continue!

Leo

Chapter 10:
The Little Chimp Cashes Out

An Account of the Death of Leo Barone on December 1, 2015

The divide between the Smarts and the Stupids was especially obvious at airports, Leo thought. It wasn't just money, though the Stupids tended to not have any and thus wasted so much of their lives standing in lines and lugging around heavy suitcases instead of paying convenience fees to make those problems disappear. It was more than that. The Stupids just plodded along and never saw the *angles*. Every moment in life was an IQ test, and so, so many people failed.

Leo had long ago mapped out all the convenience fees in life. The upgrades, the extras, the services you could pay for that gave you back some time or energy. Because everything was time. The moment he paid Maud Bluth[1] to do his geometry homework sophomore year at Bishop Carlbus Prep he'd realized this fundamental truth: Maud sold him an hour of her life. He used that hour to play video games. Today he paid people to clean his house so he could use those hours to play golf. Or he paid people to buy his groceries so he could use those hours to play with his kids.

Stupids sold their time. Smarts bought it.

The things behind the counter at the food kiosk were Stu-

---

1 See THE WORST TRIP I'VE EVER BEEN ON: AN ACCOUNT OF THE DEATH OF MAUD BLUTH, page 411.

pids. Not just because they were selling their time for minimum wage and spending their lives turning into mushrooms at the airport, the place scientifically proven to be the most depressing location in the modern world, but because they literally presented as stupid, as slow, as finding his food order too complicated to comprehend.

"Chicken salad," he said with deliberate slowness that would have been insulting to anyone with more than one brain cell. "Except in a wrap, and no onions. It's not fucking complicated."

One of the Stupids blinked slowly. He was tall and pale and all Leo could see was his vacant eyes over the mandatory face mask, and glimpses of red hair leaking out from under the mandatory cap. The Stupids always had to wear shit like that. Leo was wearing a pair of shoes that probably would have cost this asshole more than he made in a year.

He got the sense the Stupids didn't like him. When one of them wordlessly handed the wrap to him, Leo stepped over to the self-checkout and scanned a pack of gum he'd grabbed, slipping the wrap into his coat pocket. Let the asshole explain to his boss why he was ten bucks short on the till, Leo thought. Maybe there's a lesson in there for him.

He ate the wrap as he walked back to his gate, almost choking on a rock-hard piece of gristle that got lodged in his throat. He leaned against a wall for a moment, trying to gag it up, then managed to swallow it, grunting as he felt the lump working its way down. Scowling, he pulled the receipt from his pocket. He made a note of the customer service number and store number, and decided it was time that the silent, staring Stupids of the world learned about consequences.

Then he thumbed through apps and checked his position. His scowl deepened. The numbers were going in the wrong direction.

Leo woke up on the plane and stared around for a moment, uncertain of his whereabouts. It was dark, and there was a low, intense hum. He was tucked into his first-class seat with blankets and a pillow, neither cold nor warm. He felt sweaty, though, and had heartburn like a motherfucker. He grimaced as he arranged himself, using the buttons on his armrest to adjust the seat. *Those fucking Stupids at the airport*, he thought. He should have known better than to trust idiots whose best efforts in life had brought them to an airport convenience kiosk. The downside to buying people's time was that you couldn't always guarantee their time was *worth* buying.

For a moment, he sat there and enjoyed First Class. He didn't mind flying the way other people did. He viewed it as a break, a forced time out when all he had to do was sleep, eat complimentary snacks, and drink complimentary cocktails. His time was valuable, so normally he insisted on always using it very consciously, purposefully. Every hour had to have a purpose: playing with his kids so they wouldn't kick him into a care facility when he was old? Worth the investment. But in the air he was absolved.

He called for the flight attendant and bought some of her

time to get a refill on his bourbon. He admired her lithe, graceful form and imagined that her father had probably called her *princess* or *Legs*, or *sweetheart*. His own father had affectionately called him the Little Chimp, owing to how hairy he'd been, even as a child. Yet the princess here was serving drinks in an uncomfortable-looking uniform, and the Little Chimp was poised to make a shit-ton of money any day now—fuck you money, life-changing money.

If the numbers went in the right direction.[2]

When the plane landed, Leo didn't move immediately, letting the rest of the assholes fight to be the first off. One of the benefits of buying time was that you got to be wasteful when it suited you.

Instead he turned his phone on and checked the position.

---

2 Leo's life was defined by the apocalyptic financial philosophies he'd followed during each period of it. As a man in his twenties he believed in property, believing that controlling arable land would ultimately guarantee wealth if the world suddenly and violently regressed to a feudal state. In his thirties he'd become a Goldbug, hoarding wealth in tangible, solid forms that might retain value in the event of global collapse. With the advent of cryptocurrency he'd evolved into a libertarian, believing that all forms of regulation—both governmental and internal—were ultimately anti-profit and thus to be avoided. Most recently, he'd been asked at a party what would happen to his crypto if the power grid failed in an apocalypse, and Leo decided he needed to make hay while he could and amass so much wealth he could build some sort of self-sustaining bunker in New Zealand.

The numbers jumped at him, making his heart pound and his guts gurgle. The burning sensation became sharper, a line of agony running from the back of his throat into his belly. He grimaced. The fucking numbers weren't budging, and they should have, by now.

When he stood up, flinching at the acidic wave of pain that washed through him, sweat popped out on his forehead.

At home, shaking the snow off his shoes, he knelt down with a wince so his girls could jump onto him, but then he found he couldn't stand up. It felt like his stomach muscles were ripping open. He hid it behind an extended hug, then sent them scampering back to his wife. Teresa studied him thoughtfully, but she hadn't spoken a complete sentence to him in months, and did not break the streak there.

To escape her gaze, he went into the kitchen. It was the first time he'd ever been in the room. There were several areas of the house—the kitchen, the garage, the laundry room—that he'd never stepped inside. These places were black holes that devoured time, and he paid steep convenience fees in the form of salaries and benefits for a cook, a housekeeper, and a driver in order to never feel compelled to see what they looked like. He was momentarily surprised to discover that Teresa had apparently chosen to do the kitchen in avocado green, with black fixtures and a veiny white countertop. It was hideous, and standing in the midst of it with sweat running down his face he felt his gorge rising at the sight of it.

He retreated to his study and poured himself a gin and tonic. It soothed him, as did the study, which he'd decorated in rich, dark woods and books bought wholesale from a prop company that dropshipped them to his address. Sitting behind his big oak desk, he held the glass against his forehead and the pain retreated, leaving him merely uncomfortable. When he felt up to it, he fired up his monitor and checked the numbers again. They still hadn't shifted. He stared at them, moving the mouse a little to ensure that his computer hadn't frozen, that this wasn't some sort of cosmic prank. The numbers hadn't changed. He was days off schedule and suddenly the possibility that he wouldn't be able to cover the play was looming.

Sweating again, he scoured the accounts, looking for ready money. There wasn't any. Liquid money was a waste. He invested every dime he had.

That night, Leo woke up in his plush Colorado King soaked in sweat, a cramp of raw agony in his belly. He felt like he'd swallowed a wad of steel wool. He peeled the blankets off and managed to get to his feet, swaying slightly as a wave of dizziness swept through him. When his head cleared, he staggered into the enormous marble bathroom, dropped to his knees, and vomited into the low-profile toilet. The LED lights around the bottom of the bowl lit up, bathing him in electric blue light.

He flashed on a memory: Yorick,[3] the only person ever *born* with an enlarged heart, somehow yelling *fuuuuck meeeee* as he vomited in Amy Keaton's parents' master bath.

When he climbed shakily to his feet and glanced down, he realized that he'd thrown up a quantity of blood. He stepped over to the mirror and saw his lips and chin covered in a chunky, gruel-like sheen of gore. He did, however, feel marginally better.

He cleaned up as quietly as he could. Swallowing acid, he staggered down the stairs to his study and sat for several hours staring at the numbers, which remained resolutely precisely where he didn't want them to be. His stomach lurched, and he belched, the coppery taste of blood filling his mouth. He began researching mortgage rates, even though he knew he would never be able to close a new loan in time to cover his losses.

He walked back to bed. When he slid under the blankets, he felt something slick and cold. He stood up and flicked his phone's flashlight on, discovering a deep red blood stain on the sheets.

"It's a thumbtack," the doctor said. With his accent, Leo thought it sounded more like *dumtick*. He had forgotten the doctor's name, and mentally dubbed him Omar. Omar was deep brown and smelled like antiseptic and cigarettes.

Doctors occupied a liminal space in Leo's worldview. They were clearly Smarts, but they often pursued Stupid careers,

3 See THE VOID IS EVER EAGER: AN ACCOUNT OF THE DEATH OF YORICK EVANS, page 425.

working long hours for shit pay. The ones who specialized and made millions doing plastic surgeries? Smart. The one standing here in hour ten of his shift, his lunch, an energy drink and a candy bar? Stupid.

Leo had warned Teresa to never bring him to the local hospital. It was just a fifteen-minute drive, but it was owned by some Midwestern corporation and staffed by people who'd gotten their medical degrees from places that hadn't yet signed off on germ theory. He'd made her promise that in an emergency she would call Dr. Wallace at Columbia and rent a helicopter to get him there. But she'd panicked, finding him on the bedroom floor, blood leaking out of his ass, and here he was.

"The fuck it is," he said. They'd filled him with painkillers and he was feeling much better, though he was still shaking and sweating. "How the fuck is it a fucking thumbtack?"

The doctor turned and pointed at the X-ray pinned to the lightbox, where an object distinctly recognizable as a thumbtack could be seen in the midst of Leo's guts. "That is how," the doctor said.

Leo resisted the urge to strangle him. A few days ago, he might have, because he routinely congratulated himself on having so much money that he would probably be able to get away with murder. It would be inconvenient and ungodly expensive, but a team of lawyers, some careful bribes, a top-notch team of investigators—chump change. Now suddenly he was stretched thin and at the mercy of the bottom feeders.

"How the *fuck* do I have a thumbtack slicing me open from the inside out?"

The doctor frowned. "My best guess would be that you swallowed it."

For a moment, a vision of an airport chicken salad wrap flashed before him, a Stupid—male or female, he couldn't recall. Had there been one swallow as he'd wolfed it down, racing towards his gate, that hadn't gone down right? Maybe. He thought, *fuck, maybe.*

"We operate," the doctor said, nodding to himself. "Only way. We operate *immediately*."

"The fuck you will," Leo growled, sliding his bare ass off the examination table. "Here? You fucking *kidding* me?"

On the ride home, Teresa insisted on reading out loud the definition of *sepsis*, conveying her absolute horror that he would leave the hospital. He concentrated on not showing how much pain he was in and surreptitiously checking his numbers, which remained stubbornly catastrophic.

"Lee," Teresa said, "you have to go to the hospital. *Now*. We'll call Dr. Wallace on the way."

He shook his head, staring at the numbers. He did the math: the time spent unconscious, the time spent in recovery, weak and confused. The numbers spinning around unmonitored the whole time. He knew people who thought the world stopped when they left the room, that everyone around them was just a puppet or an actor there to populate their existence, but Leo knew better: everything moved when you weren't looking.

"I'm okay," he said, trying to stop his teeth from chattering.

"Lee—"

"*Dammit Terry, I said I was okay!*"

Silence, then. Leo knew his wife well enough to know she now no longer cared if he lived or died, and wouldn't for several hours. That was all he needed. After that he would either go to the hospital, or the numbers would be beyond repair and it would no longer matter.

He was so sweaty he'd soaked through his pajamas and the upholstery of his desk chair. He kept hearing a guitar riff, echo-y and distant, *da-dum-da-da-DA-dum*. His heart pounded so fast in his chest he thought it might burst out and go running around the room like a toddler. The pain in his guts had crossed over from *intense* to *beyond comprehension*, which was a relief. He knew in some abstract way that he was being split in two like an atom, but it didn't bother him.

The numbers had slid in the wrong direction, and he could feel a cold, corrosive radiation coming off of them from the screen, burning his skin and singeing his eyebrows. Everything was being burned. He was leveraged to the hilt and when the market's burning red eye turned to look at him, everything he was and everything he had would burst into hot, white flame.

Then he was on the kitchen floor, an extravagant porcelain tile from Italy. He didn't know how he got there, but he appreciated how cold it was. He lay there and shivered and heard the guitar riff repeating in the distance: *da-dum-da-da-DA-dum*.

He went in and out. Finally, he snapped to attention, staring at a pair of red tennis shoes, the sort a teenage girl would have worn in the 1990s. The cuffs of the jeans were frayed, white threads dangling over the slender ankles. He couldn't seem to twist his body around to look up at her, and he was painfully glad about that.

The shoes turned and walked slowly away. Leo crawled after them, leaving a snail trail of blood behind. *Da-dum-da-da-DA-dum*.

"I'm sorry," Leo croaked. He knew it wouldn't save him. He thought perhaps saying it while knowing it wouldn't help him would count for something, some modicum of mercy.

He followed the shoes to the basement door. He had never been in the basement. He paid a lot of convenience fees to ensure he never had to. As he pulled himself along, lubricated by his own blood and viscera, he wondered if the house actually had a basement. He couldn't recall.

"I'm sorry," he croaked again as the shoes paused and the basement door opened. Or had he opened it? There were no shoes. He was slumped against the wall across from the door, melting into a pool of sweat and blood.

Was there a basement? Suddenly he had to know. His shivering was so powerful his teeth clattered together loudly and he had trouble getting traction on the slick floor. He contemplated the time he was wasting, crawling on the floor when there was triage to be done on his positions, emergency cords to pull on his accounts. But he couldn't stop. Something was looming over him, about to slam down and crush him, and all he could do was mindlessly flee. He wasn't a Smart, he realized. He'd been a Stupid his whole life, banking hours he would never actually have.

He crawled. And then there were the stairs, and the darkness below.

Da-dum-da-da-DA-dum.

FIVE FUNERALS

Leo

Chapter 11: Drinking Outside the Box

An Account of Leo Barone's Funeral on December 5, 2015

"Jesus fucking Christ, this room is horrendous," Kate said, pushing her messy hair out of her face. "For the love of dog, no one check his browser history. This room was 100% a masturbatorium, and there's a very decent chance he jerked it to something we will never unsee."

Winnie nodded. "It was *Leo*, after all."[1]

The study, Titus agreed, was a horrorshow of late-stage capitalism's greatest cheerleader. It was done up as a replica of J.P. Morgan's office in Manhattan, suffocating wood everywhere, windowless and airless. He'd pulled a dozen books off the shelves and discovered they all had EX LIBRIS BARRY HARRAHAN stamped on the inside cover, and none of the copyrights were in the current century.

Outside the room, the buzz of conversation was a muffled sizzle. Outside the house, the weather had turned cold and snowy. Back at the rotting pile Titus and Winnie still, improbably, lived in, the old pond was already mostly frozen. In a few weeks, they might be able to skate on it, if they felt like risking cracking through the shell and eventually being found, years later, embedded in ice. He hoped if that happened society had the technology to revive them. He imagined he would surge

---

1 Leo's main sexual fetish involved paying people to perform sex acts in front of him and then paying someone else to manually pleasure him while he sat and sipped a nice glass of cognac. The less physical activity he had to perform before being brought to completion, the better.

back to life shouting "WINNIFRED, RUN!"

"So weird, this party after a funeral," Kate said. "You bury someone, then you go to their house and eat finger foods, drink box wine." Dropping her backpack on the floor, she started to sit down behind Leo's desk, then hesitated, hovering for a moment, her lips curled in mild disgust. Then she turned and plucked a book from the shelves, opened it, and laid it face down on the seat before sitting. She reached into her pocket and produced a tissue, which she used to fuss with the items on Leo's desk.

"Parties are the worst," Winnie said quietly. "That party destroyed us all. Every one of us. We never left."

For a moment, no one said anything. Titus stared off into the middle distance, contemplating death. He'd been thinking of death more or less continuously ever since the Outing Party, so this was a matter of simply picking up the threads in his looping contemplations and resuming them. Then he paused and wondered who Barry Harrahan had been. The idea that Leo had simply purchased someone's library at an estate sale to decorate his oppressively woody study was both a terrible one and something that felt distinctly Leo Barone.

"Fuck that," Kate growled, opening drawers and peering into them angrily. "That party didn't do anything. It was whoever else was *at* that party. Our unknown 26th guest. *That's* who destroyed us all, Wins."

Titus blinked as if waking up. "*Twenty-seventh*," he said.

Kate shook her head. "Amy wasn't a guest. Amy was the *host*." She jerked, realizing she'd let her arms fall onto the chair's armrests. She leaned forward slightly, bringing her arms in close to her lap.

Titus blinked again. "All right ... first of all, the unknown 27th *person* is a blurry shadow on an ancient VHS tape filmed by an idiot in a dark room," he said. "Second, someone has engineered the deaths of twenty-two people over the course of two and a half decades?" he asked, shaking his head. "Unlikely, Kate. You said it yourself: the logistics. There is no avenger punishing us. The universe isn't that tidy. It's chaos and entropy."

Kate shrugged. "I see a hand. I see someone lurking. Maybe you're right, but if not, I'd still like to know who it was. Because if someone was there that we had no idea about, they witnessed ... everything. And never said a word."

Titus and Winnie exchanged a glance. An entire conversation concerning Kate's competence ensued in a few seconds. Then Winnie's face lit up with the dark radiation Titus had grown to fear, and he knew a social experiment was about to be launched.

"All right," Winnie said in her low, languid voice, turning to Kate. "Drinks in my room tonight. Bring your laptop. Let's do some work, compare some notes. Let's try to ID this fucker."

Titus rolled his eyes but knew that when his sister decided to have a little fun with someone there was no stopping her.

Kate leaned back in Leo's chair, letting her head fall back. After a moment she leaped up and shook herself. "Ah, fuck, I touched it. I touched Leo's masturbation throne."

For a moment, she stood with her eyes closed, breathing deeply. Then her eyes snapped open. "Gross. All right," she said. "Does that mean we have to go back out there? Leo's daughters give me the creeps."

"His wife hates us," Winnie said. "I wonder why?"

"And this house!" Kate said, laughing. "There are rooms literally wrapped in plastic that no human being has ever stepped into."

Titus shrugged. "We stood there at the grave; we were seen and counted here. I think we can leave."

Kate stood up. "All right—until later, then." She paused, eyes narrowing. "But I'm stealing a box of wine on the way out."

Kate stepped into the hotel room carrying two boxes of stolen wine and immediately knew two things: one, the hotel was not expensive, and two, Winnie and Titus were obviously sharing one room. Their clothes were everywhere, and both lounged on the floor in their bare feet. Kate had never understood their sibling relationship—even back in school they had enjoyed a strange, silent link.[2]

She withheld comment on both of these observations, plowing into the room without hesitation and planting the boxes on the makeshift bar the Sandfords had arranged in front of the television. She turned and dropped the yellow backpack on the floor.

"The shittiest Cabernet in the universe," Kate announced. "I'm not kidding. You know how they say rich people are the

2 The most recent BCP odds offered concerning Sandford twincest dated back to their Senior Year and were approaching 100%.

cheapest people in the world? Leo proves it. This shit is ... not expensive."

Titus tried to comprehend Kate's outfit. There were plush-looking purple sweatpants. Green-tinged cowboy boots. A beautiful white cashmere sweater, an off-white scarf, and a voluminous red cloth coat that she flung off like a monarch making an entrance. Once again everything looked pricey, and nothing looked right, and his eyes kept slipping off her as if she didn't quite belong in this dimension of reality. Her clothes also made him very aware of the holes in his own socks, which had been purchased back in better days.

They gathered plastic cups and held them under the spigot of one of the boxes. Kate thought it tasted like the stuff they used to swill back in high school; bland, sweet wine no one ever missed or tried to preserve from theft. Then she turned and extracted her laptop from her bag, along with an HDMI cable. "I've been working all afternoon on this," she said breathlessly as she bent and contorted to plug the cable into the room's aged television set. "The logline is: you're not taking this seriously enough."

"Kate," Titus said, an element of genuine hurt in his voice. "Look where we are. Look where we're *staying*. Look what we're *drinking*. We could not be taking this *more* seriously."

"No, you're not," Kate said, sitting on the floor and flipping open her laptop. The screen filled with her desktop, her wallpaper a photo of a child that Titus and Winnie simultaneously chose not to inquire about. "We're the only ones left; everyone else is *dead*, and you don't seem worried at all."

"I am very worried about the foot," Titus declared, deadpan.

Kate's eyes flashed. "It's a *hand*."

"I am very worried about the indistinct body part," Titus corrected. "Although I say it might also be a lamp. Or just a splash of light. Or a raccoon that crept in from the back yard, seeking the single bag of pretzels Amy provided."

Kate's face tightened. "*Titus*."

Winnie shrugged. "Kate, sweetie, this is like when scientists tell us an asteroid is headed our way, maybe, in five years. There's just not much to be done."

"*Fuuuuuck* that," Kate breathed, double-clicking on a file. A moment later Titus's face melted into a disbelieving smile.

"Wait," he said, sitting forward and spilling wine on himself. "Wait. Are you seriously going to show us a PowerPoint Presentation?"

"Shut up," Kate said. On the screen, a title card read THE SURVIVAL PROJECT. The subtitle read NOT TODAY, MOTHERFUCKERS. Gulping wine with one hand, she moved the cursor with the other. "This is how I organize my thoughts all day at work. It's just easier for me." She grimaced and looked over at the twins seated on the bed. "*Please* take this seriously, guys. We're all that's left."

Winnie and Titus glanced at each other and conducted a silent conversation via nostril flare, eyebrow movement, and invisible twin telepathy. Then Winnie and Titus nodded and looked at Kate. "We're sorry," Titus said. "Please do your perfectly normal presentation about how someone has been secretly hunting us for two decades."

Kate closed her eyes and visibly took a deep, calming breath. Then she tapped the trackpad, and the presentation filled the screen. "Exhibit One: The Hand."

Titus felt Winnie tense next to him and knew she was suppressing a peal of laughter. "I still say it was a foot," he said.

It was the frame from Desmond's video again. All of them crammed into the living room, the stairs off to the side. Titus studied the blurry faces and figures of everyone in the shot again. He picked out Leo, wearing his red tracksuit, a kid who'd valued comfort over everything else. He'd turned into a man who encased himself in wood paneling and wore shoes that undoubtedly pinched his toes. And now Leo was dead. Titus wondered if Teresa had buried him in the tracksuit.

"That's a *hand*." Kate said intently. "Here, I enhanced it," she added, tapping.

Titus blinked. "That is a *spectacular* red circle, Kate," he said. "It does indeed draw the eye. The problem is that blob of low-res, 1990s photons could be a hand, sure, but also a kitten, a plastic bag caught on the warm air currents of the Keaton home, a sleep paralysis demon stalking its prey, or a shadow."

Kate made a *tsking* noise. Before she could say anything more, Winnie leaned forward.

"Foot," she said, her tone very soft and very serious. "I see it now. Definitely a foot."

"*Hand*, goddammit!" Kate growled.

"No," Winnie said decisively, shaking her head. "It's a foot." Then she looked at Kate and smiled. "But it's definitely *something*. Don't listen to my idiot brother."

"*Right?*" Kate said excitedly. "Now, look at this photo I found. There were a bunch of old Polaroids taken at the party; we were passing it around. You remember? I wound up with a bunch of them. Look at *this*."

Titus put a politely bland expression on his face and looked. "This one has everyone in it, too," Kate said. "Except me, because I took the pic. I counted twice. Even Amy." She touched the top part of the screen with one finger. "Look up here."

The shot had been taken out on the patio. He remembered Kate taking charge, browbeating them to assemble, crouching on the other side of the pool to take the photo. The pool, filled with bottles, was lit from below, an eerie blue glow that refracted into multicolored sparkles that danced on the walls of the house. Everyone was gathered together in a pose, smiling, hands up, red-faced and sweaty. Except Amy, who stood off to the side, smeared mascara making her resemble a raccoon, arms crossed. Near the center, Yorick had lifted Fanny Heck[3] up by her waist, and Titus thought her contorted body and expression could either be delight or horror.

He followed Kate's pointing finger. On the second floor behind them, in a window lit by a soft orange glow, there was an outline of something.

"Shit," Winnie said flatly. "That's not ominous at all. If this turns out to be a ghost, I'm going to be so *irritated*."

"That's a *person*," Kate said. "That's Number 27."

"Or," Titus said slowly. "A lamp."

---

3 See TO SERVE MAN: AN ACCOUNT OF THE DEATH OF FANNY HECK, page 439.

"It's not a *lamp*," Kate said emphatically. "Someone was at that party, hiding from us. And I think whoever it was has been killing us off, one by one. And they're almost finished."

"The lamp is almost finished?"

Winnie nodded, sipping wine. "I believe you."

Without warning, Kate turned and leaned her body over, reaching out to grab one of Winnie's hands. "*Thank you*, Winnifred," she said.

Winnie shot Titus a look of naked alarm.

"C'mon," Kate said, releasing Winnie and turning back to the screen. She tapped her finger and pictures began flashing past. "Think about it. Think about all the damage—the house was *so* fucked up. And Amy was so fucking mad at us, but … I don't remember doing most of that stuff. Do you? Did *we* do all that? *Could* we have done all of it? I dunno. It was chaos, right—someone could have been doing stuff in the background, and we all thought one of us was doing it. And remember how the dust around Amy was all messed up? Was someone down there? Down in the basement while we were upstairs?"

"Absolutely," Winnie said, nodding gravely. "None of us would have been down there."

"*Exactly*," Kate said. "We were asshole kids, sure, but if you or me or even your brother went down there, we would have raised the alarm, called for help. Not walked around her dead body and gone back upstairs." She tapped the trackpad. "Now, here I've reconstructed—"

"Kate," Titus said, draining his cup and reaching for the wine box. "*Kate*."

Kate turned around. "*Titus?*"she snapped.

"Kate, let's say you're right and a lamp has been hunting us down. The lamp has spent two decades keeping tabs on twenty-five people. Plotting murders. Murders that were so carefully constructed that not *one* has pinged law enforcement or triggered an investigation. Murders that read as bizarre accidents instead of, well, murders. This lamp is brilliant. This is Doctor Moriarty in lamp form; this lamp is a Bond Villain."

Kate's face was tight and unamused. "Titus—"

He held up a hand. "Kate. People try to plot one murder, and they mess it up. Serial killers, okay, but everyone knows there was a *murder*, even if they don't know who did it. Kate, Katie, Kats—there is no lamp."

"But—"

"We're just unlucky. The universe is a sparking, infinite, convoluted ball of chaos, and infinity sometimes produces stuff that *looks* like a pattern but isn't. It's just interesting noise. Sometimes bad things just happen to bad people. All we've ever been is interesting noise."

Kate closed the laptop with a *click*. The tv screen went blank. "Fine. You want to stick your head in the sand, fine. The math doesn't *math*, Titus. The odds. The actuarials. We're being hunted."

Titus nodded. "By a lamp, yes; we've established this."

Kate's face reddened. She stood up and yanked the cable from the television, then bent to retrieve the laptop. "You wait for someone to come for you, if you want," she said, grabbing her coat and hefting the yellow backpack. "I'm not going to do that. I'm Kate Fucking Huxtable and I'm not going to sit on my ass and wait to be murdered."

"Kate—I know you've spent the last two decades prepping for disaster. I know you've been waiting for someone to try to kill you since the party, carrying that bag around like it's a magic totem against zombies or plagues or fascists—"

She turned on Titus, and he realized she was legitimately furious. "You two are the only people I could hope to talk to about this. No one else is there, no one else is *left*. I don't *talk* about Amy. I don't talk about the Outing Party. No one would understand. But as usual, I'm on my own. So good luck. Good luck beating the absolutely brutal odds. Me, I'm going to start preparing. No one's taking me down without a fight."

She stormed through the small room, tore open the door, and slammed it behind her. Titus and Winnie sat for a moment, staring.

"At least she left the wine," Winnie said.

Titus visibly brightened. "There is that."

The Stairs

Chapter 12: The Opposite of a Party

An Account of Amy Keaton's Outing Party on May 27, 1995

Compiled from emails, video artifacts, audio recordings, diary entries, and public comments made by Amy Keaton and the attendees, all of whom are no longer living.

After Amy's scream ended in a raspy, gurgling fade there was, by all accounts, a moment of complete, eerie silence. Amy, red-faced and tear-streaked, stood for a moment sniffling and blinking in apparent confusion at her own emotional outburst. The first person she saw when her vision cleared was Rhoda Anderson.[1]

In silence, she launched herself into a lumbering run, throwing herself violently onto the other girl. The crowd scattered as the two girls slammed to the floor, Amy raining down punches, spittle flying.

"Fucking *bitch*!" She screeched. "Fucking *liar*!"

For a few seconds the other kids just stared in combined shock and joy. Then Hector and Xerc Bartokomous stepped forward simultaneously, grabbing Amy's arms and lifting her up as Rhoda scrabbled backwards on her palms, eyes wide, face flushed. Amy twisted free of Xerc and turned on Hector.

"Listen, Amy, settle the fuck down," Hector chuckled.

Amy responded by slapping him hard across the face.

---

1 See MIRIAM DE RASTA'S LAST STAND: AN ACCOUNT OF THE DEATH OF RHODA ANDERSON, page 449.

"*Motherfucker!*" she snarled. "I will not be *brutalized!*"[2]

Hector stared at her for a moment, then stepped forward and slapped her across the face in retaliation. The blow sent Amy spinning away, blood spraying from her mouth. The crowd parted and let her stagger across the floor and crash into the entertainment center. The television fell on top of her, the screen cracking.

A thick silence filled the air. As Amy climbed unsteadily to her feet, bleeding from a split lower lip, they could hear every joint pop and grunt.

Then they started to laugh.

"I will not be BRUTALIZED!" Kate Huxtable shouted in a comical falsetto, and the whole place descended into hysteria. Kids staggered around, gasping for breath, clasping onto each other in dark mirth.

Amy spun around, spitting bloody bubbles as she shouted. "Fuck *ALL* of you! Get out! Get the *fuck* out of my house!"

"No un's gon anywhere," Olive Partridge[3] said, blood dribbling down her chin, her face sporting a bright red hand-shaped mark, her eyes wet from tears. She spoke with a distinct lisp produced by the displacement of her braces, knocked out of place by a marauding and clearly deeply inebriated Maud Bluth. "You *inbited* us, you cwazy whore."

---

2 ***Timestamp 2:38:05 on the Desmond Brady tape.*** *Fanny Heck mouths 'oh my god at the camera, then leans in close and whispers that she's going to have T-shirts made that read "I WILL NOT BE BRUTALIZED" as graduation gifts.*

3 See AWL TOGETHER NOW, AN ACCOUNT OF THE DEATH OF OLIVE PARTRIDGE, page 461.

"Get out!"

Olive leaned forward, pigtails swinging. "Shlut upf!"

"I'm *calling* the *fucking* police!" Amy shouted, storming towards the hallway. Just in front of the open basement door, she turned again, her face shining with blood and sweat. "You all fucking *suck*," she seethed. "All I asked was that you respect the house, obey a couple of stupid *rules*. And now I'm gonna be—I'm gonna—"

"Jesus," Fanny said with a snicker, "are you *crying*?"

They howled, taking a step forward, crowding her. Ernie and Hector began a comical pantomime of crying, their faces stretched into clownlike masks of grief as they twisted their hands by their eyes.

Amy stamped her foot, an action that only exacerbated the rolling waves of laughter aimed in her direction. When she opened her mouth to shout something else, Leo Barone stepped forward, trailed by a wild-eyed, freely sweating Yorick Evans,[4] who repeatedly flashed out his fists like a boxer getting loose.

"Amy, come on, calm down," Leo said in a quiet tone of menace that had the immediate effect of quieting the whole room down. In his tracksuit, Leo kept chopping one hand in

---

4 In the school's recently released yearbook, The Bishop, Yorick was listed as MOST SWEATIEST. This was not an actual category students had voted on, but rather a decision made by the Yearbook Editor-in-Chief, Olive Partridge, who had peppered the Yearbook with many jokes at her classmates' expense, including selecting a photo of a clown doll identified as Desmond Brady and consistently replacing Fanny Heck's first name with "Butt." None of the adult advisors working with the Yearbook staff noticed. Or, possibly, cared.

the air as he spoke, rocking back and forth as if suppressing the urge to run straight at her. "For fuck's sake, you want us to go, we're going." He raised his arms into the air and turned to look around the room. "My house, one hour!"[5]

Wild cheering broke out. For a moment, Amy just stared around, bug-eyed with fury. Then she smiled. The smile, curiously, had the same effect of bringing the room to uneasy silence as her classmates noticed it.

"You can all go fuck yourselves. I'm calling the cops and telling them there's a wild-ass party doing property damage at the Barone place. Which is a fucking *dump*, by the way, you fat fuck."

"That's fuckin' *it*!" Yorick roared, stepping forward, arms hanging at his sides, eyes savage. He stalked steadily towards Amy, who began stepping backwards, face suddenly pale with fear. "No one likes you, Amy," Yorick slurred. "Everyone *hates* you. This party was a *travesty*. This party was the *opposite* of a party. All you've done since we got here was yell at us. All you've done for *four damn years* is yell at us!"

Amy continued to back away. Behind him, the crowd advanced in step with Yorick, faces split into grins, fueled by alcohol, substances, and sugar.

"So you know what?" Yorick yelled.

---

5 *Timestamp 2:41:45 on the Desmond Brady tape. Fanny Heck tends to Rhoda Anderson's superficial wounds.*

FANNY HECK: I never thought I would say this, but as God is my witness right now, I would totally fuck Leo Barone.

RHODA ANDERSON: Honestly? Same.

"WHAT?!" the crowd roared back

"We're not going to Leo's shitty house!"

"YEAH!"

"We're staying *right here*!"

Amy backed onto the landing of the basement stairs and stopped, visibly shaking. For a moment she and Yorick faced each other, everyone else fidgeting and shifting behind him.

Then Amy firmed up, opening her mouth to speak.

Yorick suddenly lurched forward and slammed the door shut in her face. A second later, Hector pressed play on the nearest boom box and it burst into life, blasting a triumphant guitar riff that soared upwards and upwards

So-ah-ah-uhn, havai gotta little storee fer you.

And with a guttural cheer, everyone began to dance.

Xerxes Bartokomous[6] had never once experienced a hangover, a blessing he assumed was part of his compensation for being born as hairless as a pink cue ball. His morning-afters were not precisely *pleasant*, but he had never puked after a crazy night, never had to cradle his head in *just* the right way to keep it from splitting open and spilling his brains out onto the floor, never had to slam down electrolytes in desperate, breathless gulps.

In fact, he always woke up at 6 a.m. more or less on the dot, clear-eyed and rested. Sleep was his superpower. With a name

6 See I'LL BE JUDGE, I'LL BE JURY, AN ACCOUNT OF THE DEATH OF XERXES BARTOKOMOUS, page 473.

like Xerxes Bartokomous, having a calm, even-keeled demeanor had been crucial to his survival. Nothing bothered him, nothing got him worked up: the worst, most cutting insults elicited a secretive smile that implied superhuman, godlike tolerance. It intimidated and defused.

Xerc sat up on Amy's enormous couch. The thing was an aircraft carrier, and there'd been a drunken debate on how, exactly, the Keatons had maneuvered it into the space. It seemed far too large for the doors or windows, and an energetic investigation had revealed no obvious way of dismantling it. The final conclusion had been that the Keatons had purchased and installed the couch and then built the compound around it.

For a moment, he just sat. Everyone was asleep, everything was quiet and muffled. He reveled in the dim light struggling through the shades, the gentle respiration of the house, swelling and shrinking as two dozen people breathed in sync. He stood up, hugging himself against the house's early morning chill, and walked barefoot through the place, enjoying the peace and quiet.[7] He liked seeing where everyone had wound up, who they'd slept with, who was alone, who had their head jammed in a bucket.[8]

Xerc thought about Olive. He had come to the realization that he might not be a good person. At least for a moment, while everyone was asleep, he was in no danger of making anyone's life worse just by their association with him.

---

7 Kate Huxtable once remarked that Xerc's willingness to walk barefoot through a house the morning after a sticky, semi-violent party that had involved more than one instance of vomit was an example of true bravery.

After a circuit of the house, he realized he hadn't found Amy. Her performance the night before had been hilarious—enraging Amy had long been a hobby of most of her classmates, but this party had been the greatest performance of her life.

He'd wandered the house twice more before remembering the basement, the last place he recalled seeing Amy—or at least he remembered her standing just inside the basement door before someone dropped-kicked it shut in her face to thunderous cheers. He padded to it and pulled it open, thinking that it was totally like Amy to spend the night sulking in the basement, just to prove a point. She was the sort of kid who had probably run away from home by hiding in a closet, increasingly alarmed when no one seemed to notice that she was gone.

The stairs creaked and shimmied as he stepped down. When he was halfway down, he stopped.

"Everybody," he said in a soft, strangled voice. Then he took one involuntary step, falling back to sit down hard on a tread. "EVERYBODY!" he shouted, as loud as he could. "EVERY FUCKING BODY!"

His throat shredded. When there was no immediate response, he started crab-walking backwards up the stairs on shaking arms. "JESUS FUCKING CHRIST EVERYBODY!"

---

8 Most of the Bishop Carlbus Class of 1995 had not suffered under any kind of curfew since grammar school through a series of bilateral treaties that maintained a fictional network of chaperoned sleepovers. For example, Susan Petrie's parents believed she was staying over at Olive Partridge's house, whereas Olive's parents had been convincingly informed that their daughter was staying the night at Fanny Heck's. While there had been several panics caused by casual phone calls, to date the ruse still held. Victor Drummond had declared the scheme Too Dumb To Fail.

Kate

Chapter 13: Best Day Ever

An Account of the Death of Kate Huxtable on December 12, 2015

TO: Malcolm and Julia Huxtable
FROM: Philip K. Marks, Marks Investigations
RE: Report on Death of Kate Huxtable

Dear Mr. & Mrs. Huxtable,

Attached please find copies of pertinent documents pertaining to your daughter's death on December 12th of this year. As I noted in our initial interview, I am not a police officer and I made no promises of changing the apparent facts of the case; you hired me to provide context and understanding around the circumstances of your daughter's death, and I believe I have done so. I am sorry to say that the executive summary of my findings does not disagree with the official police conclusion: she was killed by a man named Harvey Delacroix, a courier who was apparently acting in self-defense. Kate's motive for the assault appears to *also* have been self-defense. Both parties believed they were about to be killed.

Due to the sheer amount of documentary evidence your daughter maintained, I have been able to create what I believe to be a very clear picture of the events leading to her death. I have included copies of several documents I believe are key, along with a final summary of my conclusions.

I am very sorry for your loss. No one should lose a loved

one in such a violent and shocking manner. I understand your desire to find an explanation and hope my work here has provided some modicum of that. I am, of course, available for any questions you might have or to provide any further context you might need.

Sincerely,
Philip K. Marks,
Marks Investigations, LLC

›''''''''''''''''''''''

EXHIBIT ONE: This is a photocopy of a poem found in Kate's handbag in her office. The paper was very creased and torn; it seems likely she had been carrying it around with her for some time.

TO KATE ON THE OCCASION OF HER 19th BIRTHDAY
by Prue Nelson

Oh captain, my captain
of Team WeDidNothingWrong
you pretend not to know us
you won't return my calls
but everything comes back around
(no matter what you try to do)
all we had to do was nothing
and nothing was all we had to do

›''''''''''''''''''''''

EXHIBIT TWO: I include this student evaluation here because it offers insight into your daughter's personality that I believe played a part in her death.

KATE HUXTABLE

Student Evaluation

Econ 405, Professor Mallory

COMMENTS: Kate is a highly capable and competent student. In fact, "competent" does not properly describe her; the term "hyper-competent" might be more accurate. Despite being a sophomore, Kate is over-prepared for each class and consistently exhibits a clear and comprehensive understanding of the topics covered. Combined with excellent communication skills and a sincere desire to learn, Kate has acquitted herself well in the seminar despite her relative youth.

On a personal note: Kate, as discussed, I have attached an application to be my Teaching Assistant next year. This is unusual for a third-year student, but your knowledge of the topic and work ethic are far beyond anyone else in class, much less at your age. With my support I am confident we can overcome any resistance in the department, but an early submission of the application will go some way towards demonstrating your enthusiasm for and dedication to the role.

‹attached to page via yellow Post-it note›

On an even more personal note, Kate: I have noticed the backpack you appear to carry everywhere with you. In fact, we all have, and it has been a topic of (overheard) discussion among your classmates. Having glimpsed its contents from time to time over the course of the year, I have to ask if you are unhoused. There is no shame if you are. I know you officially have a housing assignment (I checked), but you would not be the first student driven to sleeping in cars or libraries due to roommate issues or financial problems. Carrying so many tools and staples in your bag may give you a sense of security, but it isn't a healthy or safe way to live, if that's what's going on. Please do feel free to contact me if I can be of any assistance in any way.

›''''''''''''''''''''''

EXHIBIT THREE: This is a photocopy of the four-page spread in The Bishop, the class yearbook from Kate's graduation year at Bishop Carlbus Prep. You will note that thick red marker has been used to draw an "X" through all of the photos except Kate's, Titus Sandford's, and Winnie Sandford's (I am not sure if the fact that Susan Petrie's[1] photo had three Xs through it is significant). I have done some follow-up research and confirmed that all the other members of the graduating class are dead, many under mysterious circumstances. Several also had copies of The Bishop with similar markings.

›''''''''''''''''''''''

EXHIBITS FOUR THROUGH SEVEN: The following licenses and certifications were found at your daughter's apartment and are included here for context:

- License to carry a concealed firearm issued by the state of New York.
- Certification as a Hapkido Black Belt, 2nd Dan
- Completion certificate, 16-hour self-defense course

---

1 See SEIZE AND DESIST, AN ACCOUNT OF THE DEATH OF SUSAN PETRIE, page 487.

- Letter of achievement, Mario Supremo's Survival Skills Adventure Weekend

>''''''''''''''''''''''

EXHIBIT EIGHT: Attached are photographs of the contents of the yellow backpack Kate had in her possession on the evening of December 12th. According to several co-workers and other witnesses, Kate carried this bag with her at all times and had been doing so for most of her life.

The photographs depict (in no specific order):

- Two magazines containing 9mm Speer Gold Dot 115 grain hollow-point ammunition.
- An inexpensive phone, charged.
- Three SIM cards.
- A charged TASER Pulse 2.
- A keychain-size canister of pepper spray.
- $1,000 in cash, about half of which was sewn into the lining of the bag.
- Two bottles of filtered water.
- A package containing a dozen 2,400-calorie ration bars.
- One Fallkniven S1 Forest Knife.
- A hardcase mini first aid kit including a suture kit.
- A thumb drive containing a PowerPoint Presentation. I have broken this out as a separate exhibit.

>''''''''''''''''''''''

EXHIBIT NINE: Hard copy of a PowerPoint Presentation apparently created by Kate Huxtable, entitled THE SURVIVAL PROJECT. It is composed of just five slides:

1. Title slide.
2. Image. Appears to be a frame from a video depicting a high school party.
3. Images. Appears to be scans of poorly framed photographs taken at the same party. Comparison with *The Bishop* appears to confirm these are Kate's classmates at Bishop Carlbus Preparatory School. The slide has an animation that flips through about two dozen of these photos.
4. Text. This is a listing of twenty-three names with a cause of death and a date. All the information conforms to what we have been able to determine concerning the fate of Kate's classmates. The only names omitted are her own and the Sandfords'.
5. Slide title: EVIDENCE. The text is a bullet list of words and phrases:
   - Hand
   - Shadow (window)
   - Dates
   - Order of deaths?
   - Titus' attitude: Sabotage? Accomplice? Winnie?
   - Faked deaths?
   - Lack of pattern **is** the pattern.

The presentation contains no notes. It was last edited shortly before her arrival at the office on the evening of her death. We do not know what Kate would have spoken over each slide. Analysis suggests that Kate believed she was being targeted, and that her classmates had been as well. A review of the various police reports and available obituaries suggests a statistically anomalous but not impossible series of accidents.

›‹‹‹‹‹‹‹‹‹‹‹‹‹‹‹‹‹‹‹‹‹‹

EXHIBIT TEN: The following is an email Kate sent 27 minutes before her death. Titus and Winnifred Sandford died five days later in an apparently unrelated accident.

TO: Titus Sandford; Winnifred Sandford

FROM: Kate Huxtable, Vice President, Client Services, Wilson Group

RE: The Lamp

Hey kids,

I'm sorry I made my dramatic exit the other night. But you should know that the Lamp is fuckin-A real. If it isn't someone else who was at the party, then it has to be one of us. And I know it isn't me, right? So, you'll understand that I've decided your hostility toward the Survival Project has to be interpreted as disingenuous, and you are both my number-one suspects for Lamphood going forward. Don't take it personally. If I find—or you provide—exonerating evidence, I'm happy to restore all your old benefits and privileges as a Friend of Kate. Until then, if I see you anywhere near me there will be violence.

Don't call me, Lamps.

Kate

I confess that the references to "lamps" (see Exhibit Eleven as well) are confusing. Neither I nor the investigating officers are aware of a clear explanation. If I learn more I will be in touch.

›''''''''''''''''''''''''

EXHIBIT ELEVEN: The following is a summary report based on a meticulous review of footage from thirteen security cameras in the Wilson Group offices the night of December 12th. The number of cameras and their positioning provided a fairly comprehensive view of the deceased's activities during the hour of 8–9 p.m. EST, eventually leading to her demise.

What follows is a summary of Kate's last 27 minutes, along with occasional commentary in order to surface what I believe to be important details. Note that I engaged Eric Mullins, a lip-reading expert who has appeared as an expert witness in more than a dozen court cases. Mr. Mullins holds a certification from the National Science Teaching Association (NSTA). Mr. Mullins has provided insight into statements made on the security video, which does not have an audio channel.

8:23PM: Kate Huxtable enters the lobby of her office building, which is decorated for the holidays. Rugs have been rolled out to absorb the melting ice and snow and stop the floors from being slippery. She is seen waving at the two security guards on duty. The shift chief was a man named Sam Devine, a long-term employee of the building. Sam told police detectives that from his perspective nothing unusual occurred up to that point in the evening. I confess to having doubts concerning Mr. Devine's reliability on this score. Ms. Huxtable enters Elevator 4 and the doors close.

8:24PM: Ms. Huxtable emerges on the 40th floor. She steps off the elevator. She is seen walking forward but suddenly pauses. She turns her head to the right. Approaches the fire safety ax case adjacent to the elevator and appears to notice that the fire safety ax has been removed from its case mounted on the wall.

Note: Security footage going back several weeks verifies the ax had been missing for some time, and an email complaining about its absence to the 40th floor's assigned Fire Warden, Andrea Browning-Smith, is dated eighteen weeks prior to your daughter's incident. A subsequent investigation found that the ax had been removed by an administrative assistant named Vera Caneli for the purpose of assisting her attempts to open a can of condensed milk for her afternoon tea. Having come upon Ms. Caneli in the act of swinging the ax, her supervisor, Kevin McReynolds, relieved her of the ax and stored it in his office for safekeeping. Ms. Huxtable apparently did not notice the missing implement until that moment.

Ms. Huxtable says something, dropping her bag on the floor. Mr. Mullins suggests she appears to say *Not like this, Lamp.*

Ms. Huxtable kneels down and extracts a small-caliber handgun from her bag. It appears to be a SIG Sauer P365, the gun that was found at the scene by police. She pushes the gun into the waistband of her pants, then stands and extracts the fire extinguisher from the case set in the wall. It is notable that there is almost no hesitation here. Ms. Huxtable either expected this attack or *an* attack. She picks up the backpack and begins walking to her office, shedding layers as she goes: her coat, scarf, shoes, and handbag were found on the hallway floor where she dropped them.

8:25PM: Harvey Delacroix, a courier working for Best Day Ever Gift Services, arrives in the lobby. He is dressed in a black leather jacket and is carrying an arrangement of balloons and a box of long-stemmed roses. The recipient of the balloons and roses was intended to be Susan Lambe, an employee of Certa Systems on the 41st floor, but the delivery address had been misprinted as the 40th floor. Delacroix and Devine have an exchange; Devine says they joked about Delacroix's resemblance to The Terminator, a fictional killing robot in films. Delacroix enters Elevator 6.

8:26PM: Barefoot, Ms. Huxtable arrives at her office. She steps inside and closes the door. Visual was restricted to a camera some fifteen feet away that catches just a narrow slice of the glass wall of Ms. Huxtable's office, so her movements are not explicitly understood. Based on later events it is likely she was standing on her desk triggering the fire alarm sprinkler system with a plastic lighter.

8:27PM: Elevator 6 arrives and Harvey Delacroix steps onto the 40th floor. He is seen checking his phone and referencing the package in his hands. He looks around for a moment, then looks down at his phone again. He appears to be responding to a text or possibly conducting a search. I was not given access to his phone records.

The sprinkler system is activated in the sector around Ms. Huxtable's office. Devine confirms that an audible alarm sounded, and an automatic call went out to the fire department. Devine does not immediately investigate the alarm, claiming that a physical ailment he describes as "lumbago" made physical interventions challenging. I have not been able to confirm later details with Mr. Devine, as his former employer cannot put me in touch with him.

8:28PM: Delacroix appears confused, and is seen walking toward Ms. Huxtable's office, which is dark. He pauses, apparently unwilling to get wet. Something then attracts his attention, and he glances at the sprinklers and then begins to open the door to her office. One of the balloons in his hand appears to come into contact with the sharp edge of the sprinkler and visibly pops as he opens the door.

A plume of dense white fog envelops him, and he staggers backwards. Ms. Huxtable has triggered the fire extinguisher directly in Mr. Delacroix's face. Remarkably, while he does release the balloons, he does not drop the box of roses, which I speculate Ms. Huxtable took for a weapon, such as a shotgun, possibly due to the aforementioned link to The Terminator.

There is no sound in the surveillance video but based on Delacroix's behavior at this point and the six bullets recovered from the hallway wall, it is apparent that Ms. Huxtable then fired her gun at him and missed six times. Delacroix then flees and is shown entering a gender-neutral restroom about fifty feet away from Ms. Huxtable's office, apparently in a state of great agitation.

8:29PM: Ms. Huxtable exits her office, carrying her gun and her cell phone. At this point, the fire alarm had put the elevators into emergency mode, and they had all descended to the lobby and would not respond to calls. It is likely Ms. Huxtable knew this to be the case, based on the clear evidence that she researched and planned for this scenario.

8:29PM: Ms. Huxtable enters the employee break room. Again, she moves deliberately, suggesting this was a scenario she had wargamed. She overturns two tables and then opens the refrigerator, removing plastic squirt bottles of mayonnaise and ketchup. She proceeds to coat the floor just inside the entrance with both condiments. Then she is seen crouching down behind the tables while extracting a fresh magazine from her bag. She reloads her gun. Throughout, Ms. Huxtable demonstrates very good trigger discipline.

8:33PM: Delacroix emerges from the restroom, covered in white powder but still carrying the box of roses, which is now visibly damaged. The balloons continue to drift on air currents, and two more pop in quick succession. Mr. Delacroix jumps into the air and begins to run, shouting something. Mr. Mullins reports he is shouting out Susan Lambe's name, but concedes, in light of Ms. Huxtable's emphasis on the word, it is not impossible that Mr. Delacroix is shouting the word lamp.

8:33–8:38PM: Delacroix moves rapidly through the Wilson Group offices. He stops at the elevators and spends some seconds pressing buttons. Apparently realizing they are locked down, he resumes running and shouting. He enters Kevin McReynolds' office, apparently at random, and emerges a moment later without the box of roses but now carrying the missing ax. He retrieves his phone, but it appears to not be functioning, possibly due to the combination of sprinkler water and fire suppressant foam. Ms. Huxtable remains in the break room, crouched behind the tables.

8:39PM: Ms. Huxtable produces her phone and taps at the screen. The police initially thought she was making a call, but there is no record of the call. I believe she used her phone to produce a sound designed to lure the person she assumed to be an attacker to her location. Again, one gets the impression that Ms. Huxtable had wargamed this scenario to a surprisingly granular level.

8:40PM: Delacroix arrives at the break room. Just outside, he pauses, apparently listening in some confusion. Then he shouts something—*I don't even have healthcare!*, according to Mr. Mullins, or (less likely) *Greetings from hell*, ‹expletive›—raises the ax with both hands, and races into the Break Room. Ms. Huxtable shouts something in return—*Who sent you?*

Delacroix immediately slips on the condiment-covered floor and loses his balance, sliding into Ms. Huxtable's table barricade. For a few seconds they appear to struggle, then Ms. Huxtable flees the room, almost losing her own balance on the condiment-coated floor before she gains traction on the carpet outside.

8:41PM: Delacroix, covered in suppressant foam, mayonnaise, and ketchup, struggles out of the Break Room, ax still in hand. A careful review of the footage makes it clear that in her panic Ms. Huxtable has left both her bag and her gun behind. Both were later found there, undisturbed.

8:42PM: At this point, Devine has deactivated the alarm and re-enabled the elevators. He has not and does not stand up during this time. The police and fire departments are en route. I assume that both Ms. Huxtable and Delacroix were aware that the alarm had stopped ringing. Delacroix changes course and immediately heads for the elevators, clearly seeing an opportunity to escape. Ms. Huxtable is at this time heading away from the elevators.

8:43PM: Ms. Huxtable enters the supply closet. There, she constructs a serviceable spear with a mop handle, duct tape, and a pair of long scissors.

8:44PM: As Delacroix approaches the elevators, another balloon pops. Delacroix startles. He walks to the reception desk and crouches down behind it, concealing himself from view.

8:45PM: Ms. Huxtable steps out of the supply closet. She appears disheveled, bleeding from what the coroner later described as a superficial scalp wound. She is still barefoot and hefting an ersatz spear as she is seen prowling through rows of cubicles. At this point, the police are about two minutes away from the building.

8:47PM: Ms. Huxtable approaches the elevator banks carefully, seeming to believe she is in grave danger. She hesitates at the edge of the reception area. She makes a sudden move, running, and Delacroix springs from behind the desk, swinging the ax. On the security footage, his eyes are clearly closed, and he appears to be screaming (either *I'm looking for Lambe!* or *I'm killing for Lamp!* though Mr. Mullins believes the latter to be unlikely). Ms. Huxtable runs in a wide arc around the desk, shouting (*Who sent you? Not today, motherfucker! Do you work for Titus?*) and slaps the elevator call button without slowing down. Delacroix buries the ax in the wall, missing Ms. Huxtable by a wide margin. Delacroix is thrown off balance while attempting to extract the ax, his condiment-smeared hands slipping from the handle and causing him to stumble off to the left and crash into the reception desk.

Ms. Huxtable runs. Delacroix scrambles up, retrieves the ax, and runs in the opposite direction.

8:49PM: Ms. Huxtable runs a looping route through the office. Delacroix runs past a few offices with a distinct limp, but then stops, standing for a moment, visibly breathing hard. Ms. Huxtable suddenly stops and turns, running back the way she'd come.

8:50PM: Delacroix turns and begins running back to the elevators. When Ms. Huxtable arrives back at the reception area, the elevator has arrived and already closed its doors. She is forced to hit the call button again to open them, and rushes into the cab just before Delacroix arrives. Delacroix, unaware that Ms. Huxtable is in the elevator, attempts to enter. Ms. Huxtable stabs with her spear. Delacroix turns to avoid her thrust and swings the ax in a downward arc that cleaves Ms. Huxtable's shoulder. Ms. Huxtable falls backward. Mr. Delacroix, holding tightly onto the ax, is pulled down on top of her. He appears to panic, leaping up and pulling the ax free and swinging it back down. He repeats this three times.

Delacroix's legs go out from under him. He sits on the floor, the elevator doors continuously bumping into him. He is openly weeping. This is how the police find him minutes later. The police report states the officers on the scene had some trouble lifting and handcuffing Delacroix due to his mental paralysis and the lubricating action of the condiments.

Mr. and Mrs. Huxtable, it seems clear to me that your daughter believed someone was responsible for the deaths of her classmates, and that she was their next target. While it is remarkable that almost an entire graduating class is dead long before middle age, her death is clearly the result of a fatal misunderstanding on the part of an addled mind. While the investigation is ongoing, I have little doubt Harvey Delacroix will be cleared of any charges. His physical injuries are another matter, however, as he does not, in fact, have health insurance.

Enclosed please find my invoice. Mrs. Huxtable, I will also ask that you cease phoning me at home after midnight.

FIVE FUNERALS

Titus

Winnie

Chapter 14: Gaslit

An Account of Kate Huxtable's Funeral on December 17, 2015

It was, Titus thought, an obvious day for a funeral. Gray, snow falling, frigid—a day that felt like the world had simply given up and rolled over. December, and one of the coldest he could remember. There was such a lack of energy he and Winnie didn't even get out of the car. They parked at the muddy edge of the cemetery and stared at the thin group of people standing under a motley collection of umbrellas while listening to music at such low volume it was almost subliminal, the heater on full blast and barely making a dent in the chill.

"I thought Kate would be more popular," Winnie murmured.

Titus frowned. "Did you?"

She shrugged. "She was loud. And bossy. That usually seems to work. Also, she had money."

Titus nodded, conceding these were good points.

The ceremony concluded and the crowd slowly dissolved, people heading back to their cars in twos and threes, hurrying now that the moment of solemnity was over. Titus started the car and slowly backed out of the parking lot. The twins had already silently and wordlessly agreed to skip the gathering at Kate's mother's house. There was no longer any point; they were the last survivors of the graduating class of Bishop Carlbus Prep and the last survivors of the Alumni Detectives Club. Any strategy meetings could be conducted on their own, anywhere they liked.

No strategy meeting was held, however. They kicked off their snow boots and walked across the sagging, ancient floors to the dilapidated living room and wished for cocktails. The bar remained barren, the whole house so hungry for resources that anything brought into the place vanished into its bottomless void. They each sat on the half-collapsed old leather couch. Titus unknowingly occupied the same seat his father had often perched on, deep glass of Scotch in one hand, newspaper spread out on his lap. The siblings slumped down, chins on their chests. In their black funeral attire, they looked like defeated job applicants who had just been informed that it was raining, and the subways had stopped running.

"I suppose Kate was right, after all," Winnie said, sounding quietly amazed.

They proceeded to have a silent conversation entirely via facial expressions and different levels of sighs. The conversation centered on not wishing to just sit around waiting to discover how this malevolent force or supervillainesque mystery person planned to kill them, but, if death was inevitable—as seemed likely—and also incredibly unpleasant—which *also* seemed likely—then it was better to take control of the narrative by deciding how, exactly, they *wished* to die. They had grown weary of trying to figure out ways to avoid their fate. Without speaking the words out loud, the Sandford Twins silently agreed that they possibly deserved their punishment, and had no energy left for avoiding it in any case.

"We could shoot each other," Winnie said. "Dad's old hunting gear is still downstairs."

Titus was horrified. "Absolutely not."

"Poison? Mother probably left some lying around, knowing her."

"Probably expired. Not sure I want to risk eating half-strength poison. Drugs can cramp, after all."

"Good point." Winnie considered for a moment, idly dangling one shoe from her bare foot. "We slit our wrists."

"Only one tub," Titus pointed out. "And a good chance it falls through the floor if we actually fill it with water. And razors pain you."

Winnie bit her lip. As much as she didn't want to die in some horrible way, she also didn't want to leave her death to any sort of chance. "Nooses?"

Titus grimaced. "Too easy to miss breaking the neck. Then you're hanging there forever, choking but not dead." He glanced around. "Besides, this old place? Show me a rafter that won't snap like a dry twig."

They sat for a while, contemplating. Then Titus looked over at his sister. "Gas?" he said.

Winnie chewed her lip. Then she nodded. "Gas. Quiet, peaceful. You just drift off."

Titus nodded. He liked the idea because it didn't require much in the way of equipment. "All right," he said. "But first, cocktails."

They drove through swirling snow to the store and bought supplies with the fumes of the emergency cash. Back at the sagging, sinking house, they mixed drinks and then worked to seal up the place.

Still in their funereal clothes, they caulked cracks and closed windows and doors, stuffed rags under openings, shut vents. Things moved slowly; each room inspired stories and memories from the Sanford family history: isn't this where Mother hit Father so hard his glasses flew across the room? Why, here is the dent in the drywall where they were briefly embedded. Isn't this the spot where Bruno dropped a bird he had caught out in the yard and Mother screamed and called him a dirty beast? The next morning Bruno was nowhere to be found, and Mother refused to ever explain what happened to him. Why, you can still make out the faint blood stain soaked into the wood.

In the Banana Room, the cheerful Banana Men were soggy and peeling, and Winnie had the momentary sense that an entire universe, hidden and silent behind the walls, was collapsing around them. For a split second she was eleven again, lying on her tiny bed and imagining the Banana Kingdom into vivid life, and she thought she could hear them crying out for her, their goddess and creator, to come save them.

When the old pile was as airtight as it was ever going to get, they recharged their glasses and went into the kitchen, brown and yellow and covered in a near-permanent, micro-thin layer of grease. They opened the big old oven and Titus crawled inside and blew out the pilot light. Then they cranked the gas up as high as it would go, then went back to the living room.

They made themselves comfortable on the couch, each lying on opposite ends, their feet touching.

Winnie set her gin and tonic on the floor. Titus balanced his Scotch and soda on his stomach.

They talked about the family lore as if they were children's detective stories. The Mystery of the Missing Marmalade. The Night of The Lost Iguana. The Case of the Stolen Legos. As they talked, the stories grew somehow more hilarious, their laughter shaking the fragile walls of the old place. The house grew younger around them, the walls firming up, the floors stiffening, the wallpaper unpeeling and the divots and scrapes fading away. Warm sunlight filled the rooms and Winnie thought they were going to be the ones to win, the ones who got to choose their ending. The ones to escape their punishment.

She turned to look at Titus. Her brother was lying there with his eyes closed, one hand loosely wrapped around his glass. He looked peaceful for the first time in a long time.

Winnie was light-headed but she felt clear, even as the golden light in the rejuvenated house increased to painful levels, everything melting into a nostalgic haze. She rested her eyes. When she opened them, an army of Banana Men were marching through the room in parade. She waved at them, their benevolent queen, and at first, she thought they were waving back, but then she realized they were shaking their fists at her, their tiny faces stretched into scowls of displeasure and anger.

She closed her eyes. If the Banana Men had turned against her, all was truly lost.

When she opened her eyes again, Amy was standing there,

looking down at her. In the intense sunlight Amy looked beautiful: the perpetual scowl was gone, the unnatural kink in her neck had been fixed, and she looked down at Winnie with something resembling gentleness, something that almost appeared like forgiveness. On her shoulder was a blood-encrusted ax.

Adrenaline slammed into her, and Winnie screamed.

Head spinning, she tried to launch herself off the couch but slammed limply into the solid, heavy coffee table. Pain lancing through her leg, she tumbled to the floor in a chaos of limbs, rolled away, and crawled as fast as she could. The air near the floor was fresher, and as she moved, she felt the cloudy death that had been settling into her brain thinning, breaking apart. Behind her there was a noise, a gurgling, gelatinous sound that might have been her brother trying to speak or might have been a spectral Amy Keaton transforming into an avenging angel, dark wings beating, eyes flashing with unnatural light. Winnie was determined not to find out, her fuzzy brain kicking into a haphazard overdrive. She staggered to her feet and began running, suddenly aware of the stuffy smell of rotten eggs, the way breathing just made her want to breathe more.

The gurgling noise followed her into the foyer, and some supernatural instinct deeply buried in the otherwise disappointing Sandford genome sent her diving to the floor, certain something was about to slam into her. She flipped over onto her back to face her enemy, but there was nothing there. Her eyes stabbed at the darkened doorway leading to the hall closet—whatever it was, it was hiding in there, plotting its next move. She scrambled back to her feet and tore open the front door.

Barefoot, she ran out into the frozen landscape, ice slicing at her soles as she ran.

The cold air made her cough, spasming painfully as she ran, gasping air. The cold smacked into her. Within a few seconds, her feet were numb. Behind her, too close, she thought she heard the crunch of shoes in the ice and snow, and heavy breathing, each breath punctuated by a mean little grunt.

The air lanced her lungs; she had ice crystals in her eyelashes. Shivering uncontrollably, she pushed herself to keep running without thinking about *where* she was running to. The Sandford house was located miles away from town, miles away from neighbors, a paean to privacy. There was only one place to go. A plan, dim and faded, bloomed in Winnie's head. She made for the lake, for the dock. The ice, she knew from childhood, was thin. If she could keep her pursuer just behind her, and at the last minute stop and dive to the side, whatever Amy Keaton or other Eldritch horror chasing her wouldn't be able to stop themselves and would go sailing into the air, then crash through the ice to the frigid water below.

She closed her eyes for a moment, trying to find reserve strength. She ran as hard as she'd ever run in her life, thinking how unfair it was that she hadn't lived long enough to see an even longer list of other people die first.

The dock, rotten and icy, zoomed towards her. When she leaped onto it her feet almost skidded out from under her, but she windmilled her arms and kept moving, racing towards the edge, preparing to throw herself to the left at the last possible moment.

In the living room, Titus, his face dark and his breathing rapid, didn't react when the glass slipped from his chest and crashed to the floor.

The thermostat in the front hall had been set to 75. With the front door left open, cold air infiltrated the foyer, and after a few seconds' delay there was a blue flicker inside the old thermostat. Down in the gas-filled basement, the furnace clicked contentedly, called into action. A moment later it roared into violent life, blue flames jumping, and a moment later both Titus and the Sandford house explosively ceased to exist.

The blast slammed into Winnie just as she reached the edge of the dock. It lifted her up, pushing her several feet through the air before dropping her. She crashed down through the ice and plunged into the black water, everything vanishing in a blink.

For a moment, she sank, the jagged rip in the ice above her shining brightly, drifting upwards. The water was so cold she felt nothing for a moment, her body struggling to process what was happening, the sensory overload. As she stared, pinpricks of light appeared in the ice sheet as things crashed down from the sky, a Milky Way forming right above her.

She convulsed, her body trying to force her lungs into action. She suddenly felt like she was on fire, the water boiling hot. She kicked, struggling to reverse her momentum, to get back to the surface, but nothing seemed to work correctly. Her legs refused to move, her arms were weak. Her vision began to fade, and the last thing she saw, or imagined, was a face peering down at her.

For a moment she imagined she could hear the sound of bottles floating in the pool, and then

So-ah-ah-uhn, she said, havai gotta little storee fer you

The Stairs

Chapter 15: All You Have to Do Is Nothing

An Account of Amy Keaton's Outing Party on May 28, 1995

Compiled from emails, video artifacts, audio recordings, diary entries, and public comments made by Amy Keaton and the attendees, all of whom are no longer living.

Titus had often experienced the feeling that the world was some sort of complex entertainment put on just for him, that everyone in his life—his teachers, his parents, his friends—with the possible (and probationary) exception of his sister, Winnie—was a figment of his imagination or an entity that vanished the moment he looked away. The main defect he could perceive in this worldview was the generally low quality of the entertainment; if he was the focal point of the universe or a supremely powerful being, he imagined the whole thing should be far more interesting.

Waking up sprawled on the guest bathroom floor, Titus discovered a copy of the yearbook, *The Bishop*, and had spent a profitable hour writing in his own Most Likely To captions under each beaming photo of his classmates. When Xerxes began screaming, the distant sound didn't inspire Titus to action. The evening before, after all, had been *filled* with screaming.[1] The bathroom was warm and stuffy, but the floor was cool and soothing, so Titus elected to just stay there for a while.

Clara Addams was the first one down in response to Xerc's

shouts, and her subsequent screams were piercing enough to startle Titus and everyone else out of their hungover torpor. As everyone crawled over a frozen, staring Xerc the basement filled with more screams and shouts of alarm. Someone laughed—a mean, harsh sound that was swallowed immediately but reverberated, stabbing into everyone.

Titus' sense of being an audience to some grand prank intensified as he squeezed past Xerc and stepped down onto the gritty basement floor. Amy[2] lay at the bottom, on her belly, her head twisted around cruelly so that she stared back at them with dusty eyes, her face locked in its perpetual sneer. Titus thought that Amy looked, impossibly, even angrier in death than she had in life, a girl who would speed off to the afterlife on the fumes of supernovareal anger. The red dust that coated the floor had been disturbed around her. Titus thought this implied she'd been alive for some time, struggling to overcome her injuries, but he chose not to say this out loud on the off chance that his classmates were real people.

At first, Titus wasn't sure what the sound was. It reminded

---

1 In the history of Outing Parties, the Keaton Death Party took on special status. If the Seaver Shit Party had become an ironic shorthand for an epic experience of any kind, and the Douglas Family Booze Fest a code for a gathering that stretched social norms, the Keaton Death Party attained platinum status as the Most Legendary Outing Party Ever Thrown, but Not in a Good Way. For years afterwards, kids at Bishop Carlbus Prep would say things like *Tell Marianne she's not going to do seventeen shots of tequila for her birthday, we don't need a goddamn Keaton Death Party situation on our hands.*

2 "Most Likely to Experience Court-Ordered Therapy" in Titus' altered yearbook.

him of trips to the old beach house, lying in the scratchy, stiff bed that was terrible in the way all beds in all vacation homes were terrible no matter how rich you were, listening to the ocean through several walls and interior spaces. He was startled to discover it was weeping, that several of his classmates were openly crying. Astonished, Titus glanced at his sister,[3] seeking reassurance that he was, indeed, awake.

He looked around. Olive, her face puffy and off-center, had coaxed Xerc off the stairs and they clung to each other so tightly they looked like a single, misshapen person. Quentin and Rhoda held hands, knuckles white. Hugs were being administered. Olive Partridge and Susan Petrie had buried their heads in each other's shoulders and stood near the stairs, quivering. Clara Addams clung to Una Taylor. Ernest Bundy and Hector Rodriguez had their arms on each other's shoulders, eyes wide and wet.

Titus himself stood with Winnie, Kate Huxtable, Victor Drummond, and Leo Barone. He was startled when he turned and found Ida Tanner[4] standing just behind them, gaping.

"I—I can't *believe* this," Maud said, sniffling. "Like, I *can't fucking*—she was just *here*, she was—"

Everyone began talking in tones that Titus recognized as solemn and tearful. He heard words—*kind* and *angel* and

---

3 Their anti-twincest PR training was so strong they did not hold hands or, usually, look at each other directly. Careful observation of the Sandford Twins gave the impression of two espionage agents practicing spycraft, their conversations always held while they looked in different directions, often while they were engaged in different activities.

4 "Most Likely to Be Mistaken for a Server."

sweet—that as far as he knew had never been spoken in connection to Amy Keaton ever before in the history of the planet. He felt a new heat source bloom into being and turned to look at Kate. He had never considered Kate to be anything more than basically attractive, but she was glowing with a sudden Eldritch beauty.

"Why are you *crying*!?"

Kate stepped closer to Amy and turned to look at her classmates. "Why the *fuck* are you assholes *crying*? You all *hated* her!"

Rhoda sniffled prodigiously. "C'mon, Katie ... she's, like, *dead*."

"Couple of hours ago she was slapping you in the face, Rho," Kate shot back.

"Jesus," Yorick moaned. "Jesus, I am so *fucked*."

Everyone turned to look at Yorick. In Titus' opinion, this was the most perceptive thing Yorick had ever said. Yorick was, indeed, fucked. An image flashed through Titus' mind: a flushed, menacing Yorick screaming at Amy as she trembled in the doorway, then his aggressive rush, a thousand pounds of sweat hurtling like a cannonball and slamming the basement door. And, apparently, knocking Amy down the stairs in the process.

Yes, Titus thought. He made a mental note to amend Yorick's title in the altered yearbook to read Most Likely to Die in Prison.

"You all hated Amy," Kate went on fiercely, turning and making several of her classmates flinch. "*We* all hated her. So don't fucking *cry*. Des has most of you *on video* talking about how much you hated her."

"Oh, shit," Susan said. "Jesus, Dezzy, erase that tape, right? Like, right now."

Desmond[5] was staring at Amy. After a moment he shook himself and looked around as if not sure who had spoken to him. "What? Oh. Yeah, sure."[6]

"What do we do?" Ernest Bundy said, voice trembling. "Bury her?"

At least four people looked down and toed the dusty floor as if considering the suggestion. Kate rolled her eyes.

"We should call, you know, 911," Jimmy Forman said, and a hush fell over the room.

"*Shit, yeah*," George said amidst a rumble of agreement, and took a step toward the stairs.

"*Don't call 911!*"

Everyone turned to look at Leo Barone. Titus thought that under the present circumstances and in the grimy light of the basement he looked slightly less ridiculous in his tracksuit than

---

5 "Most Likely to *Be* a Server."

6 He did not. He removed the write protection tab and labeled it BORING SHIT. He carried it with him through every move and eventually forgot that it existed, and when he stumbled across it again in 2001, he assumed it was an old acting "reel" he had created in school and was therefore loath to get rid of it. In 2005 he watched it out of curiosity and suffered a panic attack. For two years he kept it in a desk drawer and suffered fits where he found the temptation to invite people over and show it to them almost irresistible. In 2007, He contacted Kate Huxtable via MySpace, expecting her to insist he destroy it. Instead, she asked him to ship it to her.

he had the night before, but admitted to himself that it could be an optical illusion.

"Leo, what the *fuck?*" Zillah hissed.

"You call 911, they come, what happens?" He pointed at Yorick. "What happens to all of us? We left her down here for what like—six hours?"

"That's, like, *depraved indifference*, man," Winnie murmured. Titus suppressed a smile.

Leo was standing next to Kate now. "We gotta *think*, man. We gotta think about what happened here. We have to stick together."

He turned around. "Vic—call your father. He's still tight with Chief Wiggum,[7] right?"

Victor blinked, then nodded. "Yeah—sure. They hang out all the time."

Leo snapped his fingers. "Call your dad. We do this the right way. Through channels."

Victor nodded. "All right."

As Victor moved toward the stairs, Neville asked in a quavering voice "What do we do now?"

Kate put her hands up in the air as if asking for calm. "Nothing. All we have to do now is *nothing*."

7 Earl Wilkins had been Bergen City Chief of Police for 17 years. The kids had been calling him Chief Wiggum since 1989.

Titus regarded Calvin Drummond as the Platonic ideal of a parent. He arrived in his BMW, resplendent in a pair of salmon trousers and brown leather loafers, and a green Izod Lacoste polo shirt, and managed to convey the impression that your instinctively terrified reaction to this ensemble was a failure of imagination on your part and certainly not his problem. His watch was the size of a small baby. He had a slight paunch, but that somehow only accentuated his V-shaped torso and muscular forearms. Titus did not normally notice the forearms of other men, but Mr. Drummonds' demanded attention.

Where Mr. Sandford had jowls and a permanently haunted expression that confirmed Titus' suspicions about life after the age of 25 or so, Mr. Drummond had the tightest fade haircut ever conferred on a man and a facial expression that implied impatience and disappointment with lesser beings, i.e. everyone he met on a daily basis. He exhibited none of the intrusively fake interest in children that some parents manifested nor the aggressively distrustful meanness popular among other adults. To Mr. Drummond children were part of the furniture of his life, which is how Titus thought it should be.

Mr. Drummond arrived fifteen minutes after his son's call, grimaced in Victor's direction, and immediately went to the basement. He walked halfway down the stairs, scanned the room, then looked at the assembled living graduates of Bishop Carlbus Prep and shook his head.

"Fuckin' idiots," he said. "Get the fuck upstairs, idiots. Everyone stay out of the god-damn basement."

Titus liked the way Mr. Drummond split *goddamn* into two

crisp words, unlike his own father, who tended to slur all words together into a mush.

After that, Mr. Drummond set up what Titus thought of as a Crisis Control Center in the Keaton kitchen, making phone calls in rapid succession. He called the Chief, Mayor Cucci, and Principal Murray and spoke to each at length in low tones, pacing around the kitchen, smoking cigarettes.

With adult supervision on site, the graduating class of Bishop Carlbus Prep sat together in the informal living room alternately studying the damage they'd wrought and privately gauging how fucked they were on a sliding scale that started off at thirteen or fourteen and extended well into the hundreds. Yorick[8] was almost comatose, comforted by Susan, Una, and Zillah as he sprawled on the enormous couch, staring at the ceiling where someone had somehow contrived to adhere several dozen jelly candies in a spiral design.

When Mr. Drummond walked into the room, cigarette dangling from his lip, everyone sat up straighter.

"All right, idiots," he said. "You stay right the fuck there until the police and paramedics show up." He stared at them for a moment, then sighed and rubbed his eyes. "It's gonna be fine. I called some of your parents and they're calling the rest. This was a tragic accident. Nice girl, that Aileen. Nice girl. Tragic."

Everyone started nodding. Titus could see the seed being implanted in their soft, runny brains: Tragedy. Nice Girl. Whoever the fuck Aileen was, it sure was sad that a completely unpreventable accident had snuffed her beautiful flame out too soon.

8 "Most Likely to be The Only Yorick in Any Room."

"Victor," Mr. Drummond said.

Victor didn't look up. He stood up in one unfolding motion and walked over to his father, who then led him back toward the kitchen trailing blue smoke. Titus trailed behind. At home, Titus had made a game of eavesdropping on his parents as they conducted an unending and vitriolic argument about money that had started before he'd been born and seemed destined to continue until the bombs dropped and melted everyone and made money, at long last, superfluous. He employed all his usual tricks: standing close to walls, being perfectly still for long periods of time, holding his breath any time he thought someone might be looking in his general direction.

"Listen, Vic," Mr. Drummond said quietly when they were seated at the kitchen table, cigarette burning on a plate between them. "I called Carl Wems, too, and he's gonna be here. He's gonna talk to you first, and then he'll be here when the cops talk to you. Okay?"

Victor was staring at the cigarette. He nodded.

"Good." Mr. Drummond leaned back and sighed. He studied his son for a few seconds. "It's all gonna be fine, Vic. Y'all idiots didn't do anything *wrong* wrong, okay? We're gonna get this mess sorted. All you gotta do is let me and Mr. Wems handle everything, okay? All you gotta do is *nothing*."

Titus drifted. In the informal living room, Leo and Ida were coaching everyone, speaking in whispers.

"Just say what you saw," Ida said to Clara and Ernest. "You didn't *see* her fall."

"None of us did," Leo said to Xerc and George Heffernan. "All we have to do is stick together."

Titus had never noticed the hypnotic cadence of Ida's quiet, monotonous voice and unblinking gaze, but he observed his classmates nodding along, grateful for the guidance. Leo, on the other hand, was in his element, strutting about and persuading people to do the things he wanted.

"We couldn't know," Ida was telling Jimmy and Maud. "Amy sulked. She was a sulker. You know this—she always got pissed off and went off to hide. We couldn't have known what happened."

"You just gotta be honest," Leo was saying to Yorick and Olive, whose face had swollen up in ways that Titus personally found comical. "We just need to stick together and be honest: no one knew. We were partying, the vibe was happy, no one thought twice about Amy. Maybe it makes us bad people. But it doesn't make us *culpable*."

Titus thought Leo chewed the word like he'd just learned it in Owens' English class the week before.

He wondered where his sister had gotten to and knew the answer immediately. Winnifred, he was certain, had attempted to consume him in the womb, and retained a certain bleakness about her. Or perhaps, he admitted, that was just his own fear of being eaten projected onto her. In either case, he made his way surreptitiously to the basement and wasn't surprised in the least to find Winnie kneeling next to Amy.

"A few minutes," he said softly, kneeling across from her. "Before the cops and the ambulance. Best guess."

Winnie nodded. "I think this is the most I've ever enjoyed Amy's company."

"It's the longest she's been quiet since I met her."

A ghostly smile spread over Winnie's face. In the distance, sirens bloomed. "Are we in trouble?"

He shook his head. "Nothing's going to happen."

Titus was afraid, for a moment, that she might reach out and touch the dead girl. But she shook her head.

"Something always happens."

George

Chapter 16: Coat Check

An Account of George Heffernan's Death in March 2014

by Reginald Reloux

My phone leaped into life, playing *Ding Dong! The Witch is Dead*. I studied the screen for a moment, weighing my options. I'd learned through bitter experience that it paid to think before speaking with Regina. Then I picked it up and swiped right.

"Reg," I said, pronouncing it *reeg*.

"Reg," my sister said, pronouncing it *reg*. "I need an assist."

I nodded, sipping coffee. The sun was streaming through the big window over the sink, and it promised to be a beautiful day. I refused to let Regina ruin it. "I'm not helping you clean up."

"It's not that," she snapped. There was a beat of silence. "George is dead."

I paused with the coffee cup halfway to my mouth. This was news. This was interesting. After all this time my sister's presence in my life was about to finally pay off. "How'd you do it?"

There was an indignant squawk. "Reggie, I didn't."

I nodded. "Good. Keep practicing that delivery. Because you have often made what many reasonable people might interpret as threats. Against your husband's life."

"All in good fun."

"It is reliably hilarious."

"Also, no one could possibly have taken me seriously."

"A corpse changes hearts and minds."

"Reg," she said, her voice taking on an unfamiliar note of pleading. "Please."

I'd seen my kid sister Regina in many low states. She had a taste for substances and prior to marrying George Heffernan, the Most Boring Person in the Universe, a taste for sad, broken boys who mistook her symmetrical facial features as proof she was capable of normal human emotions. But when she opened the door, I was taken aback.

"Girl," I said, holding up a tall coffee, "wash your face."

She touched her cheek with one hand. Party Regina had betrayed Morning Regina by skipping her bedtime toilette, and now my kid sister resembled a particularly sad clown-whore hybrid. Her makeup had smeared, leaving glitter everywhere and purplish eyeshadow like a bruise. Her hair had metastasized into a puffy cloud of stiff brunette snarls. She was still wearing her little black party dress, but the rubber underwear underneath it had twisted and bunched up in Unattractive Ways.

"Shut up, Reggie," she groused, accepting the coffee and stepping aside. "He's in the SCB."

This in a tone that implied calling your furiously estranged brother instead of the police upon discovering the swelling corpse of your beloved husband was normal and acceptable behavior. I might have been summoned to dispatch a particularly hairy spider for all the urgency Regina was displaying.

The SCB or So-Called Bedroom was right there when you

walked in, and was officially the third bedroom of the condo, the basis for an extra twenty thousand dollars and many dozens of breathless words in the listing. Many couples, including George and Regina Heffernan, known idiots, had been seduced by phrases like *third bedroom or potential home office and generous floor plan* only to discover that the third bedroom had very likely been a closet in a former life. Through some feat of black magic, a tiny window and an even tinier Caligari-esque wardrobe had been fitted into place, leaving enough room for a bed and your thoughts.

Since George and Regina had no use for a home office, they'd painted the walls a soft gray and bought the most minimalist bed frame they could find in a bid to make the tiny space seem larger. It left a narrow channel that required you to walk sideways to get into the room, and as a result no one ever did.

George was stretched out on the bed, legs and arms spread and covered with his own coat. It was a scruffy peacoat he'd bought at a thrift shop and was inexplicably proud of.

"Did you cover him up?" I asked, shocked that Regina would be uncomfortable with a dead body, since I'd always assumed there were a great many of them in her past.

She shook her head, and a soft rain of glitter fell around her. "No. I found him like this."

I sacrificed my dignity and shimmied my way into the room, hugging the wall and splaying my feet. I looked down at his face, which was red and puffy. His eyes were bloodshot and looked up at the ceiling, his mouth hung open, dried spittle tracing down to the blanket from its corners. His staring eyes made him seem extremely alert and present, which was to say very un-George-like. In life George had been a lump of a person, a depressing man convinced he was cursed and seeing plenty of evidence supporting the presumption. I'd always assumed this lumpiness, mistaken for darkness, had been the key attractant for my sister. Regina was always on the hunt for pain and suffering, her perfect little nose twitching like a rodent's when she sensed misery.

"Yes," I said. "He is dead."

Regina frowned as if this was an unexpected result. "I didn't do anything to him. I thought he'd left."

I nodded. "I heard the fight was epic."

"You hadn't arrived yet. He was being a jerk."

"The version I heard was that you screamed at each other for ten, fifteen minutes, following each other around the place," I noted. "You said he'd better be careful because you knew a dozen ways to poison someone, and he called you a witch."

"That proves nothing."

"People recorded it, Reg. It's on the Internet by now."

She hugged herself. "I didn't kill him. I should have, but I didn't."

I nodded again. My sister was, I knew, perfectly capable of murder and many other things. "So why am I here?"

She sighed. "I need a drink."

I picked my way out of the so-called bedroom and followed her into the main living area, which was a desolation of crusted-over party detritus. I paused in the entryway to survey the damage, which was composed of tipped-over, sticky plastic cups, beer bottles, plates of half-eaten pizza, one smashed vase in the form of a billion razor-sharp shards of glass, and all of Regina's vinyl records snapped in half and strewn about the floor.

The place had a fermented smell to it. Under the crust of party, you could tell the place hadn't been cleaned in a long time. When I'd arrived the night before my impression had been of dirt rearranged as a demonstration of the distinction between *clean* and *neat*. That and the lingering acidic scent of post-fight tension.

"What will you have?" she called out from the kitchen, where she liberally poured vodka into one of the red plastic cups.

I glanced at my phone. Nine in the morning. Close enough. "Scotch."

She brought me a plastic cup filled almost to the brim, and I looked at it in amused bafflement. Then I remembered that Regina Reloux—like our long-dead and unlamented mother—had a long reputation for exacting revenge on people via potions and potables and sniffed at it suspiciously.

Regina sat down at the big dining room table next to the big windows and took a slug of her drink. I sat down in the opposite chair.

"I have ... concerns about optics," she said.

Despairing that my day would regain its orderly shape, I swallowed whiskey. "I'm not going to hide a body for you, Reg."

She shook her head, but in a way that conveyed that was a discussion best saved for later. "I didn't do anything. George and I got into a fight. You know that. He stormed off. You know that, too."

I nodded, though stormed was much too active a verb for George Heffernan, a man made from regret and pocket lint.

"He left, and I didn't see him again. No one did, I don't think. Then I woke up and found him in there, dead as a doornail."

I nodded. "And called me, instead of the police," I noted. "Because optics." I thought for a moment. "Heart attack? Stroke?"

She pursed her lips. "I'm not normally that lucky," she said, then sighed. "Maybe. He just had a physical you could frame, though."

"Ah."

She nodded, pushing her hands through her stiff hair and somehow making it look even more insane. "I may have given him a dose last month. He may have told people I tried to kill him."

On the one hand, I knew that if Regina Reloux wanted to poison you, you would be poisoned, so I believed she'd intended to punish, not kill. On the other hand ... optics.

"So obviously this doesn't look good," she said, leaning back and hugging herself. Regina had never lost her girlishness. It was as if the last twenty years hadn't happened, and she was still the angriest teenage girl in the world. "I need to be proactive." She looked at me. "To do that, I need to know how the fuck George ended up dead in the SCB. So I can craft my narrative."

I sipped whiskey, feeling the nice blurry warmth forming in my belly, soon to spread everywhere and make me think I was smarter and more handsome than I actually was, which was already pretty smart and handsome. If I kept going, I would eventually be the smartest and most handsome man in the world, and that was usually when the trouble began.

Regina's sociopathic honesty was bracing. "You want me to play detective, so you can brief your defense team," I said.

She nodded. "I think we have a few hours. I can plausibly tell people I didn't think to look in the SCB until later today, then immediately called the police and reported George. I need to get my shit in order by then."

I leaned back in the chair and studied my little sister, a demon in human form. She'd lured the bumbly George Heffernan with her anime eyes and preternatural ability to lie convincingly about anything, and the moment he'd asked her to dinner his doom was sealed. But George had always believed himself to be cursed, due to some mysterious high school incident he carried with him like a wound. He'd always been a guy who saw his own death stalking towards him, a little closer every day. That had to have been part of his attraction to my sister, who was the sort of person who appeared in mirrors when you spoke her name three times. It stood to reason that if you considered doom to be your fate and met Regina, everything would click.

I weighed the positives of playing detective—fun and having a powerful witch like my sister owing me a favor—against the positives of doing nothing—being free from Regina for ten to twenty years as she languished in jail without access to the proper ingredients for her terrible spells. And though I'd never cared much for my brother-in-law, this was by far the most interesting thing he'd ever done.

"All right," I said. "Challenge accepted."

While my sister lay on the couch with a pack of frozen peas on her head, dreaming dark things and twitching like a stray dog, I walked through the place reconstructing events.

Past a certain age, parties become a burden. As children, they bloomed naturally, pulling people and supplies in with a fundamental gravity. All you needed to do at age nineteen was speak the word party and you set mysterious gears into motion: a few hours later someone was handing you a can of beer while you shouted *what?* at them, the room slowly filling up with exhaled smoke.

At a certain age, you only showed up because you feared the consequences of being on Regina's bad side.

I'd arrived late, by which time everyone at the party had the hollow look of hostages, but that was par for the course past the age of thirty. At our age parties were populated by people who spent their time checking the time on their phones and doing calculations in their heads: babysitter rates, equations concerning the number of glasses of wine and finger foods consumed and the length of the next day's recovery. All the number crunching left people standing around staring off into space.

I'd arrived determined to gladhand my way through the room, chug a glass or two of mediocre Chardonnay, then excuse myself to the bathroom and slip out, possibly through the window if the exits were blocked. I tossed my coat as I walked in and found the room buzzing about Regina and George. Then I worked the room, throwing winks and nods around to let people know I'd seen them and cared that they were still alive, if you called this living, which I did not.

I was already familiar with the Regina-George dynamic, so I knew how things had progressed even if I hadn't actually witnessed them. Act I, the introduction, involved George emerging from the shower with an enormous towel wrapped around his barrel-shaped body, cinched way too high so it looked like some sort of muumuu. The sight of George's fleshy, pale body inspired a primitive hunting instinct in Regina, who couldn't help but see everyone as prey, and some pointed remarks had no doubt been made.

Act II, I deduced via careful listening, involved a bowl of pot brownies Regina had put out to fuel the party, a desperate attempt to get people stoned enough to enjoy themselves. Regina had become convinced George had eaten all of them in a deliberate act of sabotage, because now all she had to offer was cheap wine, hard liquor, and the entertainment value of George Heffernan galumphing his way through the place like a deranged elephantine ballerina.

George, now clothed in an oversized shirt he refused to tuck in for fear that people might notice he'd gained fifty or sixty pounds since his heyday, his thinning hair slicked back and pulled into a short, stubby tail, would have vehemently denied the accusation while also appearing to hover an inch off the floor because he was so aggressively high.

Act III apparently involved Regina gathering all of her witchy powers, purple electricity swirling around her, and launching into a Statement of Intent in terms of her husband, George. This began with a litany of George's flaws and disappointments—legion—and ended with a repetition of the brownies accusation and the clear resolve to murder George in his sleep.

From there I'd been told George stormed off and had not been seen again. When I'd finally arrived, several people approached me to suggest I might do a wellness check on George. I took this in stride. People have been pulling me aside about Regina since high school. Regina's problem is that she is the walking manifestation of Resting Bitch Face, and any cop or jury member would take one look at her and decide to punish her for a wide variety of crimes they simply assume she had committed.

Regina and George had always been a mystery to me. I had entertained the possibility that my sister was secretly a vampire and George's fleshy body represented an infinite source of sustenance for her spider-like existence, because otherwise George seemed an odd choice to be Mr. Regina Reloux. He wasn't rich, an early and easily disproved theory, he sweated freely and favored Hawaiian-style shirts. He was also convinced of his own damnation for some reason—I always lose interest when people tell me things. It's a real problem.

That their entire marriage had been one long and endless fight was obvious. So, no one was terribly surprised at the histrionics. By the time I'd shown up Regina was already serving the bean dip, the momentary horrors of George gone from her mind. I'd expected George to return, as he usually did, droopy and apologetic. I remembered Regina leading a group of ladies into the kitchen for a tour of her pantry, and seeing my opportunity I downed my drink, turned on my heel, and walked rapidly down the hall. Hearing Regina's voice calling my name, I didn't even pause to grab my coat. I fled the disaster, went home, and spent the evening enthusiastically and much more profitably watching porn.

So, at some point, then, George had silently returned. Or been returned, although I thought he must have come under his own power, because there was no way someone would carry him up from the street and place him gently in the so-called bedroom without attracting attention.

I returned to the SCB and stood in the doorway, looking around. Reverting to form, George had not done anything interesting in the intervening time. I stood there studying his body. The longest interaction I'd ever had with my brother-in-law took place at his Bachelor Party, an event I reluctantly attended, and which had lived down to my expectations aggressively. If you searched for the term "basic bachelor party" you would wind up with the package George's friends—all doughy, overlarge men—selected for him. Hired car? Yes. Steakhouse dinner? Yes. Awkward hour at a low-rent strip club? Yes. Cigars and whiskey enjoyed by men who are not familiar with cigars and whiskey? Yes.

George had grown glum over the course of the evening. His friends were skittish around me, and it slowly became clear that they didn't approve of Regina and George and feared for

George's life but were afraid to broach the subject with me around. And they were right to be, because if Regina grew wrathful and I had to save myself, I would not hesitate to throw each of them at her in a desperate attempt to do so.

This was where an inebriated George told me he knew he would die young, and that he had a fear of being smothered. He told me that almost all of his old friends from school were dead, and in bizarre ways—my mind wandered, but he offered up plenty of gruesome details. George was haunted by guilt and had decided that bad things were coming his way. I didn't ask what, exactly, he'd done to earn this level of guilt because his guilt was the most interesting thing about him. Whatever it was, I knew it would be disappointing, and I didn't want to ruin it.

I pulled his coat off of him, wondering if there was any way to determine if his death was in fact the result of a supernatural retribution. Ectoplasm, perhaps, or some other spiritual residue. He was still wearing the flowy shirt and the too-tight pants, and his bloodshot eyes were still staring up at the ceiling. I pushed my way along the edge of the bed and wormed my way in further. There was a bottle of wine on the floor. I leaned down and picked it up—an unremarkable Merlot, which was the same as saying "a Merlot," almost full.

George had no shoes on.

This fact was disturbing on several levels, the primary one being the state of his toenails, which were thick and yellow and terrifying. With some effort I crouched down and lifted the coverlet, peering into the inky blackness under the bed, but I found nothing but dust bunnies and the creepy sense that Regina never actually cleaned her home.

With difficulty, I maneuvered my way around the bed to the other side of the room and discovered George's shoes sitting on the floor. Sweating, I pulled back and stood in the doorway again, contemplating George Heffernan's pear-shaped body. I wondered how they made it work physically in bed, how they bridged the gap of proportions. It must, I decided, involve harnesses and some kind of pulley system.

Frowning, I scanned the room again. There was, obviously, no way Regina could have dragged George to the bed, being a tiny person made of doll parts and perfume. Moving an inert George robbed of his animating fumes would require heavy machinery and an engineering degree.

I examined his shoes.

They were indoor slippers, the soles immaculate. These were shoes that had never been outside of this apartment.

Which implied that last night George had never been outside the apartment.

I stood and went back to the front door. I could hear Regina snoring from the other end of the place, an animalistic grunting drone that inspired fear and loathing in equal measures. I stood in the doorway and saw myself walking into the party, loins girded for boozy discussions about school districts, tax burdens, and television shows that were inky black holes of bourgeois drama. I remembered tossing my coat and turning for the living area.

Frowning, I stared down at my shoes. I'd tossed my coat.

Like a hundred other times arriving at the Palais des Heffernans, the So-Called Bedroom had been used as a convenient coat-check. You walked through the front door, you threw your coat onto the pile, and you proceeded into the inner sanctum to find out if this was the day that Regina Reloux would murder you, as was foretold.

I pictured the dark rectangle of the SCB doorway when I'd arrived. I knew the room was essentially all bed—you couldn't miss. I hadn't been able to see the bed—or anything. And it was suddenly obvious that George had been lying there in the darkness, his own coat over himself like a blanket. That George had galumphed in, head spinning from THC and wine, and laid down, maybe pulling coats on top of himself for warmth, or from a primitive instinct telling him to conceal himself from the Apex Predator he'd married. And the rest of us arrived and tossed our coats on top of him. Dozens of us. Forty, fifty heavy coats.

"He smothered."

Regina said the word with a peculiar relish I chose not to chase down. "A bowl of brownies, a half bottle of wine. He never stormed out of the apartment—he stormed into the SCB and settled in for a nap. Then he smothered under a pile of coats."

I smiled. "We're all murderers. It's a real Christie moment."

She shook her head, staring at George. "No. I never put a coat in here."

I sighed. Regina was meticulous and was already prepared to sacrifice me and every one of her friends in the name of her legal defense. "He died as he lived: pointlessly," I said breezily. "But at least you have your narrative. No one is going to rule this anything but an accidental death."

She nodded. "I guess I have to go pretend I've been sleeping all day."

This, I knew, would not be much of a stretch. Regina was many things, most terrifying, but ambitious had never been one of them. I turned to go.

"Do you think he was?"

I paused, turning back. "Was what?"

"Cursed," she said thoughtfully. "Like he always said."

I studied my sister, her fine profile, the Reloux nose, the caked-on makeup and the bird's nest hair. "Yes," I said.

Prue

Chapter 17: Medications in an Emergency

An Account of the Death of Prue Nelson in January, 2015

It is an inconvenient fact that the moment you decide to finally, truly clean up your life and get organized, everything will fall apart. In her diary entry dated Thursday, January 3rd, Prudence Nelson wrote:

> *Days Sober, 3. People slept with this year, 0. No more boys and their sticky ways, no more girls and their drama for days. Apparently, one cannot live on pills and liquor for twenty years and emerge on the other end with glossy model-style hair and bright eyes. My teeth are loose, and I look like I am wearing someone else's skin as a suit.*

Having resolved, the morning of the New Year, to sober up, get her shit together, and finally clean her apartment for the first time in six years, Prue got as far as transferring the debris from the kitchen table to the sink before succumbing to exhaustion and sitting down to wish for coffee, the grounds in her cupboard taunting her. She was reminded, as she often was, of some lines she jotted down several years before:

slightly hungover with eyes painted shut
hollowed and raw nothing matters so much
as the moments just wasted, the times just had
yet another care wasted, another unfinished night

As she sat at her crusty kitchen table wishing for coffee, she slowly came to realize that this poem was terrible.

Prue reflected that one main reason people seeking sobriety were so often unsuccessful was the way all the tawdry failure of their lives became obvious once they weren't using psychoactive substances to improve things. All your willful misconceptions and personal deceptions were stripped away.

She distracted herself by cleaning. Prudence had few applicable skills when it came to cleaning, and the accumulated cruft of her filthy apartment—a combination of spilled wine, cigarette ash, various powders, vomit, and blood—had grown to an impenetrable shell. Moving anything revealed an increasingly advanced and complex civilization of ants, the discovery of which initially sent her running into the bathroom to stand in the tub, where she imagined she would be safe, and then sent her back to the kitchen table where she wrote out some lines in her chaotic, loopy script:

If I sat here any longer,
as my house fills up with ants,
they will cover up my shoes
and crawl inside my pants
explore the jungle of my hair,
see what's going on out there
pass the word from front to rear
"We're tunneling in through the ears!"
sounds of chittering growing stronger
as my head fills up with ants

I decipher their language from verbal clues
all I can hear are communist rants
build a city inside my head
my thoughts become the ants instead
I try to resist them when I'm able
as they lace my veins with pipe and cable
If I sat here any longer,
the freaks not giving me a glance
I become a frame of insects, fused
wriggling
I open my mouth and scream ants

After a moment, she moved the pen to the top of the page and wrote: THORAX AFTERNOON.

The thrill of writing something new energized her, and she returned to her cleaning, ignoring the jittery, feverish sense of unease that had settled under her skin. Sweating, she surveyed the horrors of her apartment and decided the best thing to do was just start somewhere, do one thing. So, she began washing the dishes, inhibited slightly by a lack of dish soap or anything resembling a sponge.

But as she worked, her bones fused into one monolithic itch that couldn't be scratched without a lighter and a piece of foil, an intrusive thought began to plague her. After a few moments, she turned off the water and walked back to the table, worrying the bloody cuticle on her right thumb as she stared down at the poem.

It was also not very good, she thought.

This was worrying.

The project of cleaning her apartment was abandoned and replaced with a thorough and increasingly distressing review of the dozens of notebooks she had crammed into various corners of the space. If the dawning horror that every single word she had ever written was objectively awful was an unhappy experience, it did have the benefit of distracting her from the drug cravings.

Poem after poem was revealed to be distressingly simplistic, sloppy in its structure and phrasing, and self-indulgent in its imagery and subject matter. It was enough to send her searching for a crumpled pack of cigarettes and begin chain-smoking the bitter, stale coffin nails despite her All-Encompassing Commitment to a Substance-Free Life of just a few days before. One needed something to steady one's nerves, she thought, when faced with an existential black hole such as this.

The despair over the quality of her work started to give way to another worry.

She found that she barely remembered writing most of it. For example, she found a neat sheet of high-quality stationery on which she had carefully printed the following:

COMMUTING

EVERYONE IS SHOUTING
and pelting him with garbage
AS THE BUS IS ROUTING
spewing out raw sewage
EVERYONE IS DOUBTING

that we'll make it to the garage
and he can't hear us complain because

everyone is shouting.

The circumstances that had inspired this bit of doggerel were stubbornly missing from her memories. Several other poems appeared to describe various emotionally shattering experiences she could not reliably recall. It was as if there had been a second, separate Prudence Nelson, a Night Prudence who wrote while Day Prudence was passed out.

Suddenly, she recalled *Omnes Sumus Reus.*

Thousands of unrhymed couplets. Composed over the course of three years during which she'd been fueled by cocaine, coffee, and Robitussin, it was, essentially, a confession. As memories, long buried by opioid haze and sleep debt, slowly rose to the forefront of her mind, Prue realized that she had detailed every single awful thing that had happened at the Outing Party. Every single awful thing she had done.

There was, she recalled, a photograph. A Polaroid. Of her. Standing over Amy. Smiling.

She couldn't recall why she'd crouched down and posed over her so Desmond could take a picture. But it seemed unlikely that anyone would understand anyway, whatever the reason had been. And she had clipped the photo to the manuscript. Her thought process around this decision was now mysterious to her.

Sobriety, she thought, was just one unpleasant thing after another. Headaches, diarrhea, aches and pains as her body lurched back into stuttering motion. Sudden realizations that cherished epic adventures had actually been horrifying humiliations. And sudden realizations that you had admitted to terrible things, in writing, and that years of living life to the fullest had left you with thin artery walls and an almost certainly shortened lifespan. When she died, someone would find the poem, the photo. and the world would know what she'd done.

The next day, Prudence woke up at Noon and wrote in her diary:

> *Days Sober, 4. People slept with this year, 0. Apparently sudden sobriety leads directly to paying off your sleep debt, as I have been unconscious for most of the new year. Sam called from Narrowbacks four times while I was sleeping. He's down three people and desperately needs a bartender, but I know if I go back there, I'll fall back into bad habits. Narrowbacks is the local mall of drug dealers in this town. Half the clientele pays for drinks with little plastic bags.*

She had forgotten, again, to purchase coffee filters. Or any groceries at all, which led to her making coffee using toilet paper for filters and ice cream for creamer, which worked out much better than she expected. Then she set her mind to the problem of Omnes Sumus Reus, a title she now bitterly regretted as the pretentious act of a young woman very much in love with Oscar Wilde and her own elegantly wasted tragedy, not to mention the fact that in those lines she admitted to something she was certain would qualify as Depraved Indifference and implicated many of her former classmates in worse crimes.

The problem was, she could not recall where the manuscript had gotten to.

This should not have been a challenge, since she had not traveled far from the place of her birth and had lived in precisely four locations, all within walking distance of each other, and held exactly one job that was almost but not quite perfectly centered between those places. But, of course, she no longer had easy access to her two previous apartments, both of which she had fled under cover of night to escape oppressive back rents owed, and her parents had sold her childhood home some years before and moved to Florida, leaving Prudence a terse note that informed her that they no longer recognized their daughter before listing their new address in handwriting that somehow conveyed reluctance.

She knew she had hidden the manuscript, paranoid and convinced that people were coming to steal it and publish it under their own names to rob her of her legacy. But she had no idea when or where she'd actually hidden the book away.

This was not uncommon. An old boyfriend, known to her intimates as Thoroughly Despised Robert, once quipped that you could take possession of everything Prudence Nelson owned simply by following her around. The moment things left her hands, they left her mind, and half her life had been spent in a stupor tracking down wallets, phones, and beloved shoes left behind at apartments, clubs, and county jails.

Somewhere, pulsing with dark energy, was a confession, waiting to be found.

Days Sober, 6. People slept with this year, 0. One of the great things about living in shithole apartments is how easy they are to break into. When you lose your keys as often as I do, you quickly evolve tricks for getting back into your own apartment and thank goodness those tricks still work. The bad news is, I can confirm that the stupid poem is not anywhere in my old rentals, unless I have hidden it so fucking well no power in the universe could ever find it, which is just as well. There's nothing for it: I'll have to search the house.

Prudence had not been back to her childhood home since shortly after her graduation from high school. She stood across the street from the tidy ranch-style house shivering and nauseous. She remembered having a perfectly fine childhood; her parents had never been particularly interested in her or her sisters, but they had dutifully fed and watered them all, and occasionally even offered a sort of dry, grim affection that felt contractually obligated. Her life as a pre-teen and teenager had therefore been spent mainly in her room, getting high in various ways, but this had, she reflected as her loose teeth chattered in her mouth, been generally enjoyable.

The drugs, naturally, helped.

As with her old apartments, Prue knew of several ways to

enter the house without keys, having spent a great deal of time out past her curfew with Susan Petrie and Jimmy Forman and Desmond Brady, arriving home unsteady and giggly and thus unsuitable for interrogations or sobriety tests. Unfortunately, upon arriving at her old house she discovered that the new owners at some point had built an addition, removing one of the sticky windows she'd relied on for after-hours entry. This led to a series of poor decisions: the decision to use a rock to smash a basement window, which resulted in a slashed hand; the decision to enter the house despite this setback, which resulted in leaving a series of bloody handprints on the exterior and interior basement walls; the decision to attempt to break in the basement door when she discovered it locked, which resulted in what felt like a broken shoulder and a startling sharp pain lancing directly into her brain; the decision (somewhat involuntary) to give in to shock and pass out slumped on the basement stairs.

The sound of the new owners returning woke her, and she was forced to scramble out through the broken window, enduring even more cuts and scrapes as she did so. Limping away in the night, Prudence contemplated the fact that sobriety had so far not turned out much better than indulgence. Her whole body itched, she was still nauseous, and now she was covered in as many serious wounds as ever.

So, she headed for Narrowbacks.

Narrowbacks had transformed Irishness into kitsch, with the flag, shamrocks, and vintage Guinness advertisements everywhere, like a theme restaurant whose theme was holy fuck, Ireland! The owners and patrons had long ago ceased being the working-class Irish of generations past, but the crusty old look and feel suited everyone.

The crowd was rough most nights, but when Prue stepped inside the cramped space, it was worse than usual. The place was packed, and a sense of violence hung in the air. Prudence, however, was undeterred: she had remembered, in a fit of surprising clarity, that she had hidden Omnes Sumus Reus in the women's bathroom of the bar. Her reasoning, she recalled, involved the fact that she spent more time at the bar than anywhere else. She often stayed after her shifts to keep drinking and doing bumps in the bathroom, and sometimes then went straight on to her next shift, so high she had to keep touching things to ensure they were real.

The bouncer, a surprisingly normal-sized man named Ribs, thrust out a sleeved arm to stop her, then startled.

"Hey girl!" he shouted, leaning in. "You workin' tonight? These fucking bikers are trash!"

She ignored the question. "Trouble?" she shouted over the noise.

Ribs shook his head. "Not yet! But *soon*!"

She nodded and moved past him, swimming through the bodies and cuts, the dirty jeans and key chains, all of them drinking whiskey with bottled beer chasers. She got some stares. She wasn't sure if it was her fading sex appeal—a 38-year-old woman who hadn't eaten a vegetable or consumed a glass of water in decades—or the slick of blood running down her arm, the tears and rips in her clothes. They let her through, though. With a nod at Benny behind the bar, she made her way to the women's bathroom. Miraculously—due to the dick-heavy presence of the bikers—there was no line, and a moment later she was inside the depressing closet the bar called its women's room.

When Narrowbacks had been founded, it was legal to exclude women from drinking establishments, and so the place had. They'd clung to this prohibition long after the rest of the community grew tired of it and had to be sued to force their hand. Ordered by a judge to have facilities for women, they grudgingly took a small space that had been plumbed for a slop sink and transformed it into a toilet closet, with an airplane-size sink. Many women, heads spinning from whiskey shots and the cologne fumes that clouded the bar's air, had stepped into the space and immediately questioned their life choices.

Prue dropped the lid on the toilet and climbed up onto it. Bracing herself against the wall with her blood-slick hand, the wounds burning and aching, she reached up behind the old-school water tank that fed the ancient toilet. After a moment's search she found the plastic pouch containing her greatest work of terrible poetry, *Omnes Sumus Reus.*

It was thinner than she recalled.

Extricating the pouch, her blood-lubricated hand slid free from the wall, and she tumbled backwards, slamming her head against the bathroom door and landing painfully on her ass, almost folded in half. When she climbed to her feet, she swayed unsteadily, her head filling with a buzzing noise, sparkles floating in her eyes.

Outside the bathroom, the noise suddenly swelled.

She stumbled out into chaos. Clutching the slick plastic pouch, she blinked in what seemed like blinding light and was immediately hit with a wall of humanity as the dense crowd struggled to simultaneously contain and flee a fistfight that had broken out between a group of patrons. Prue found herself swept along with the bodies, dragged under by the current, shoved and pushed in confusing ways.

The pouch was torn from her hands, and as she scrabbled after the greatest, most terrible poem she'd ever written, someone stepped on her wrist, shattering bones and twisting ligaments. She screamed, then she was kicked in the stomach, all the air leaving her lungs. She tried to crawl, gasping, desperate to find the manuscript, to somehow destroy it before the end, before she lost her window to keep her secrets. She felt light in a bad way, her bones bird-like. Dimly, she wondered when she'd last drank a glass of milk or been in full sunlight.

The shouting swelled, and there was something distant and booming that reminded Prue of a gunshot, which weren't as uncommon at Narrowbacks as the employees would have liked. The crowd above her surged away from the front doors, and she felt their suffocating weight pushing down on her relentlessly. A boot heel came down on her hand and pain exploded, shooting up her arm as she tried to curl into a ball to cradle her bent fingers. A flash of light made her turn, and there was the plastic folder of paper, intact. She reached out for it with her good hand, but as her fingers closed on the slick surface a boot stomped, the crack of broken fingers loud enough for her to hear over the thunder of a stampede. She screamed, every nerve on fire.

The packet was kicked away, papers escaping to cling to legs and stick to boot heels. Prue lay on her stomach, hands beneath her, too breathless to cry. She lifted her head, seeking a tunnel through the forest of kicking legs, and saw it: the photo. The little square of white lay on the floor just a few feet away, and hope surged inside her. Despite the throbbing agony of her hands, she thought this was luck: the photo was the worst of it. After all, if trends continued, no one would ever actually read the poem anyway.

She couldn't crawl. She undulated, raising her ass into the air and pushing herself forward, arms tucked under her torso. She used her elbows for stabilization, suffering several kicks to her sides. Someone fell on top of her, the weight crushing the breath out of her before they rolled off. But then she was on it, the photo was right there. She leaned down to take it between her teeth, feeling the faint ghost of that old rush, a flicker of that wonderful, awful golden flame licking at her nerves as her brain coughed and sputtered and wheezed out a trickle of triumphant endorphins.

As she turned her head, trying to get her tongue under the photo, movement made her pause. A boot, larger than seemed possible, hurtled down toward her face, old-school hobnails like tiny spikes. She closed her eyes. She thought perhaps that she deserved this.

Winnie

Chapter 18: Winnifred at The Wedding

The last time Winifred had worn this particular dress was at the wedding of an old college friend named Mary. Winnie and Mary had met in their third year when Mary was brought in as a last-minute replacement for an off-campus apartment shared between six girls, and Winnie had become obsessed with her due to the sense of slow-motion disaster that followed Mary around like a chemtrail.

A superficial examination of Winnie's life at the time would make one think she was a relatively happy and well-adjusted girl. But Winnie had always had trouble relating to other people, who, in her opinion, were typically boring and stupid. Her weakness was ridiculousness. All of the friends she accrued in her years at school were trainwrecks of different sorts, and Winnie greatly enjoyed sitting back like a spider and watching them go off the rails. She liked the idea of cohabitation because it gave her the chance to observe their disastrous decisions from a front row seat while snacking on popcorn and sipping chilled white wine.

Her roommates had been carefully curated from the broken, the deluded, and the dysfunctional. Jessica Froth was so wired on stimulants she slept one hour a day, and ate, at most, a spoonful of cereal before declaring herself "hefty" and going out for a long run. Winnie was carefully noting her fade, and continually revised estimates on when, exactly, she would completely vanish. She hoped she would be in the room when Jess simply disappeared with soft POP!

Tori had come to college unofficially engaged to her high school boyfriend, Tariq. For two years Tori refused most social occasions and worked hard to never be alone with another boy, for fear that Tariq would find out and dump her, because Tariq proved to be incredibly jealous. He never actually visited Tor, however; he simply monitored her moves through regular phone contact and would pounce on any perceived betrayal, resulting in Tor being compressed into a quivering ball of tears and regret for weeks at a time.

When Tariq efficiently ended their relationship via voice message, announcing that he was months deep in a new relationship and couldn't handle Tori's drama any longer, she dropped into a sort of sustained nervous breakdown marked by frequent crying jags and lazy stalking. Any time Winnie was feeling down, she knew she could go find Tor and breathe in her jittery despair.

Grace was a quiet, skinny girl, with big eyes and the longest hair Winnie had ever seen. Grace was a Secret Drinker who pretended, for obscure reasons, that she was actually a teetotaler, but was reliably wasted by noon every day. Grace was never seen without a water bottle filled with vodka, which she sipped on continuously throughout the day. Every evening at sundown, she became a raging slut, like some sort of sex and booze werewolf. Winnie found her daily descent into madness very entertaining.

Deidre was the Saddest Girl. Just sad, sad, sad. Everyone was mean to her; everything made her cry. Being her roommate required the ability and willingness to provide comfort at a moment's notice, because any sense Deidre got that *you* were being mean to her, right there in the *moment*, would result in even higher levels of weeping and clothes-tearing. Winnie didn't enjoy making Deidre cry, but she *did* enjoy those moments when Deidre decided to be brave and venture out into the world with a fresh outfit and carefully-arranged hair, only to be inevitably crushed by the casual cruelty of a world that didn't seem to like her very much. The meltdowns were delightful.

When Allison, who spent her life in a state of thick, perpetual stupidity and confusion and thus hovered on the edges of failing out of college at all times, generating so much anxious energy the lights flickered when she entered a room, finally *did* fail out, skulking home in a cloud of shame so thick it choked all life as she passed, birds dropping from the trees and animals rolling over in the streets as she walked, Winnie took charge of the search for a new roommate to replace her portion of the rent. Winnie engineered an invitation to Mary Harrows, a tall, blonde girl who was, Winnie thought, the loudest girl she'd ever known. Mary was a shouter—she shouted at waiters, she shouted at slow walkers on the street, she shouted at professors, sanitation workers, bartenders, randos at the laundromat she suspected coveted her dryers, and her boyfriend, the high-volume, fiber-rich Samuel.

Mary especially seemed to enjoy shouting at Sammy, to the point where screaming was their main form of communication. The year living with Mary was a loud one, with earth-shaking fights erupting at all times. Sammy could give as good as he got, volume-wise. They shouted at each other when they fought, when they fucked, and whenever they had some spare time to burn. Sam was a dense, short guy who was in a fraternity. The fraternity took up an inordinate amount of his time and attention, in Winnie's opinion, and these activities also meant Sam was constantly standing Mary up, and Mary, who had symmetrical features and, in Winnie's opinion, good tits, wasn't used to being stood up. And thus, the Circle of Shouting never ended.

The main thing Winnie remembered about Sam was his bowel movements, which were so epic they routinely clogged the toilet. He would always simply leave the toilet in a state of horrifying malfunction, and this usually stirred the rest of the house to shout at Sam—even Deidre, tears streaming down her face as she screamed.

Winnie had fond memories.

After college, she stayed in touch with Mary for some time. She found Mary's obstinate and undeserved confidence fascinating, and after burning through a few more boys Mary stumbled on pure gold, in Winnie's opinion, with the tall and strangely damp David. Winnie didn't like David because he was handsome (his face was beak-like) or smart (he often paused for uncomfortable silences when faced with simple questions) or interesting (unless you found frequent drunkenness and a tendency to work his belief that Arnold Palmer was overrated into every conversation no matter the topic interesting). No, Winnie thought David was a winner because he and Mary enraged each other so effectively. The hate-fuck vibe of the happy couple kept Winnie coming back like a tick to bury her head in their crapulence.

She bought the dress the day Mary invited her to the wedding, the invite suspiciously late and last-minute, suggesting her inclusion was designed to fill a sudden gap. The invite also included a lengthy list of irritating instructions, all printed in a cutesy font designed to look like handwriting and using tiny hearts for dots. One of the clear instructions was to avoid wearing certain colors, and to ABSOLUTELY DEFINITELY UNDER NO CIRCUMSTANCES wear black. Winnie chose not to be insulted or to speculate too much on how few friends Mary might have at the age of twenty-six after a lifetime of screaming herself hoarse. Then she bought a black dress and went for the entertainment value.

Initially, it was well worth the effort. Ducking into the bathroom in order to text her brother some mean-spirited impressions from the privacy of a stall, Winnie almost immediately found herself a fly on the wall when Mary and her idiot bridesmaids—tall, loud girls almost as irritating and obnoxious as their leader—burst into the room and began, of course, shouting.

The shouting centered on the motherfuckery of David Bickerman but had sufficient girth and spread to include several of the groomsmen, all of whom were found to be deficient in many ways. Mary's chief complaints about David—greater than his low tolerance for alcohol that produced a braying, unhinged kind of laugh that reminded her of a donkey—was his obsession with golf. She had almost broken off the engagement when he suggested New Jersey as a honeymoon destination, and had almost broken David when she discovered this was because of his lifelong dream of playing at the Pine Valley Golf Club.

"Did you see that bitch in black?" one of the bridesmaids said suddenly. "The damn *audacity*."

Winnie froze.

"I did NOT," Mary hissed. "What is WRONG with people? A simple INSTRUCTION!"

Plans to identify the Black Dress Whore were discussed. One of the bridesmaids suggested the BDW might be one of David's former whores. This was considered, and Mary grew increasingly loud. Winnie began considering the very real possibility that she might never leave the bathroom stall and bitterly regretted her decision to rubberneck this disastrous wedding.

Eventually, the wedding party exited in a flurry of slurred expletives, and Winnie managed to slip out of the venue without being seen. A year and change later, Mary Harrows died under mysterious circumstances—rumor had it David was found by the police and EMTs watching golf in the living room, apparently unconcerned—and Winnie wore the black dress to Mary's funeral. It became her official funeral dress, and as the Sandford family fortunes declined (and the Sandford family condensed) she only wore it when she had a chance to see a dead body.

FIVE FUNERALS

Titus

Winnie

Chapter 19: The Roof in the Banana Room Is Leaking

A portrait of modern Sandford life.

Winnie walked in from the hallway and sat down next to Titus on the bed. They were both facing the balcony, the sound of the rain a hissing, comforting white noise.

"The roof in the Banana Room is leaking," she said languidly, accepting the flask in one tiny hand. "Pretty badly."

Titus nodded in resignation, and you could tell he was doing numbers in his head. Titus had always been good with numbers, and he knew that the house was falling apart, dissolving around their ears. It was all the Sandfords—a family whittled down to two middle-aged, childless siblings—had left. It was a grand place, a large three-story house with classic lines, six bedrooms, and four bathrooms. Not quite a mansion, it was a testament to a long-vanished economic boom.

Titus's expression as he accepted the flask back from his sister was not encouraging. It spoke of immense sums required, of armies of workers, trains of delivery trucks hauling materials the fourteen acres from the road. And there was no money—there was, the twins knew, *negative* money, which is in itself a privilege few get to enjoy. Most people are on the street eating shoe leather before they get to enjoy the sensation of negative money.

To his credit, Titus was somewhat aware of this. Winnie, who had always been considered pretty (if a bit remote and unassailable, the sort of coolness in a woman that makes men irrationally angry), not so much.

After a moment they both rose at the same time, an example of their secret connection. The twins had always done this, suddenly moving in concert as if they'd spent the previous few hours practicing. But it was a completely spontaneous and natural effect, like watching a ballet, or a horror movie.

They got to work. The Banana Room was on the third floor of the house, the yellow wallpaper with the smiling banana men dancing on it peeling off the walls, and all of Winnie's childhood furniture remained, untouched. As a girl, Winnie had created a complex portal fantasy based on the smiling, dancing Banana Men, completely unaware of the connotations of yellow wallpaper and women in various states of mental health. She had never shared this world with her brother or anyone else, and she still occasionally sat in the Banana Room after a few glasses of wine or a few edibles and returned there, always finding it desolate and abandoned, the few cult-like remaining Banana Men waiting for her glorious return, certain of a prophecy promising that she would repair the broken earth and warm the permanent winter.

They carried the furniture down to the Great Room, which was crowded with other salvage from the home's damper regions. When the Banana Room had been cleared, Titus ceremoniously placed a fresh red plastic bucket from the local hardware store on the floor under the worst of the water drips, turned, and closed the door behind him.

Titus's room was across the hall and had been decorated in red wallpaper depicting different heirloom tomatoes performing some sort of conga. Titus always thought of his room as the Redrum and had been refusing to sleep in it for most of his life. His childhood had been a quiet war between him and his mother. She would put elaborate work into settling him into his bed and calming him down with light threats about what would happen should he be found anywhere else in the morning, and then in the morning he would be found sleeping in surprising places: the laundry room, the Great Room, in the spacious pantry off the kitchen. Once during a particularly brutal summer he was found sleeping on the dock leading to the small, shallow lake—a pond, really—on the property. In happier times he remembered his father taking them in a rowboat on the pond. Every winter, the lake froze more or less solid, and he and Winnie were able to skate on it. The dock itself had been a rotting shell when he'd been a kid, and its continued existence was both puzzling and inspiring.

He went into the Redrum now and stood for a moment with his hands thrust into his favorite pair of brown corduroy pants, wondering why the house didn't choose to destroy this room instead of the Banana Room, which at least had a whimsical charm.

The Sandfords had been in steep decline ever since the patriarch, their father, had been forcibly retired from his cushy executive job in response to a litany of misbehaviors beginning with a tendency to touch the young female interns and ending with a reckless use of his corporate credit card. What initially seemed like an early—if involuntary—retirement turned out to be the cork in the volcano of shit Mr. Sandford senior had been sitting on. There were debts—debts so large they seemed impossible. Some of the debts were to well-known online dating platforms and pornography sites, as well as a healthy dose of escort services. Divorce and general collapse followed quickly, Mr. Sandford fled and was found dead in a motel six states away, and by the time the dust had settled the only thing left was the house.

Titus often thought that the word "decline" did not really convey the rapidity and completeness of the family's fall.

He and Winnie found each other in the kitchen, where more yellow clashed with brown and Formica. They sat down at the wobbly table.

"Maybe we'll get lucky," Winnie said with a smile, "and the whole place will collapse on us."

"Let's have a real drink."

Winnie shook her head. "All gone. Bar's dry. It's a calamity."

FIVE FUNERALS

Hector

Chapter 20: Cocksucker Blues

An Account of the Death of Hector Rodriguez in September, 2010

From the zine WITH THUNDEROUS APPLAUSE
by Tim the Angry Clown

HULLO, FRIEND! Once again back is the incredible, the rhyme animal, me. Tim, that is: your old, cranky pal crawling through the shithole bars of The Narrows section of our dear Bergen City and reporting back to you the lousy music, watery beer, and horrifying state of the bathrooms. Which all just get lousier, waterier, and more horrifying every year. Or maybe I'm just an old fart.

Faithful readers, you know that I spend far too much time in Hasty's Tavern. It's the sort of low-rent bar that proliferates in the Narrows area of Bergen City like lice. Say what you will about that shithole, but other shitholes come and go, going quietly into that night, while Hasty's persists. Why do I come back to a place that offers an experience so uniformly and consistently mediocre? Because for decades this bar has featured the world's smallest stage. It's *ridiculously* small! You feel constrained and claustrophobic just looking at it, and yet they have crammed some entire bands up there.

At the risk of being once again accused of *rambling*, something your old pal Timmy hears far too often, I have to mention the record for mostest band on Hasty's tiny stage. You hopefully recall Galactinous, that sad attempt to fuse New Orleans parade jazz brass with speed metal rhythms? You don't. Color me shocked. Galactinous was a band better known for their bright red costumes—satiny jumpsuits, a delight for the senses—than their music. I think they only played once at Hasty's—you'd be amazed (or not) at how many bands began and ended on that stage, a musical crucible few survive. But if you do survive it, your reward is ... still probably failing, because playing at Hasty's can only hurt you professionally, emotionally, and even physically, as Galactinous proved that night. The band was eight fairly brutish souls, three toting brass and one using a stand-up bass. The singer kept falling off the stage, and we all cheered like loons every. single. time. By the end of the set, he was a little loopy, which was, trust me, my beautiful trash ('cuz who else is reading this?) for the best. I pray he does not remember the details.

Did I ramble? Friendos, I rambled, and I am sorry. But you only paid a buck for this zine (unless you're one of the many who traded for it or paid me in promises and lies), so shut up.

The tiny nature of the stage breeds *drama*! *Drama* with a capital "D," drama that is usually the only reason to show up at Hasty's: to see if anyone falls off the stage. You know how your fave angry clown loves drama. Something about the tight space, the way all the cords and amps and monitors become a maze of tripping hazards, the hostility of the crowd—because everyone who shows up at Hasty's for a disappointing five dollar concert is *angry*, my friends, including, of course, me.

The worst is the regulars, who can be cruel. And the worst of the regulars—as anyone who has ever been in Hasty's knows—is Kieran Hoss, aka Special K, a florid middle-aged man sporting a mullet. Special K is something of a thug, a big guy who favors a wallet on a chain linked to his belt loop, the sort who looms over you, his surprisingly small eyes steady and malevolent. After a few restorative beers after his day spent ... doing some sort of noble labor, I'm sure, he is ready to relieve some stress by abusing anyone who approaches the microscopic stage with some very *dark* energy. And since the stage is so microscopic, there is no escape. Once Special K gets you in his sights, it is an evening of suffering. And I am *there* for it. He's one of those people, children, that you pray vociferously gets hit by a truck but also makes you excited because you know he's going to be just absolute trash all night.

That stage has seen bloodshed and despair. As regular readers know, I witnessed several epic moments in Hasty's. Aside from Galactinous proving why Mr. Hasting's makes everyone sign a release before mounting it, I saw The Levon Sobieski Domination *violently* break up over the course of a 26-minute set one winter evening (see Issue 34). I witnessed Slippery Bits spend an entire set madly attempting to tune their instruments, resulting in a brown fog of noise I actually kind of enjoyed? (See issue 76). And I was there when Vulvatine played the same song thirteen times in protest against the two beer limit on comped drinks for the entire band (see issue 57). I have seen some shit, people.

But nothing compares to the night Hector Rodriguez died.

If you've been to Hasty's you know Hector—he's been a fixture for a decade, a specter from a prior age playing old-fashioned music, old-school blues scales and turnarounds, pentatonic solos and copped Zeppelin riffs that were in turn copped Muddy Waters riffs. You might know him better as Freebird, the name bestowed upon him by a fleshily inebriated Special K one evening when he hit a flat note. *Better practice that one some more, Freebird!* Special K hooted, eliciting a laugh from the sparse crowd, and a nickname was birthed.

If I had to come up with a word to describe Hector, it would be *dogged*. Hector has *that look*. You know it. Or I hope you don't: that look, that bland, blank look of despair, my little doggies. He always had that look—that expression implying that Hector suspected he was being followed everywhere, or that he could see a shadowy figure at the edge of the light, enveloped in shadow. Or that a mystery bird perched over his door is croaking *nevermore* incessantly no matter how many shoes are thrown at it. Life, in other words, was flowing past Hector like an existential tsunami and he hadn't seen a log to cling to in a long, *long* time.

But three nights a week for, what, twelve years? Hector showed up at Hasty's, old Epiphone Les Paul in hand, and proceeded to play moderately acceptable blues licks for a few hours, in exchange for two bottles of beer and whatever tips were thrown his way. Which were usually zero, though some nights a few pity bucks made their way into the bucket. Most of the crowd at Hasty's regarded Hector with a sad kind of affection, the way you unconsciously anthropomorphize an old T-shirt, imbuing it with dumb sentience and mourning it when it finally goes to the great laundromat in the sky.

If you found yourself drawn to the midweek drink specials at Hasty's, which came with a thrill not dissimilar to gambling, since you never knew if you were going to emerge into the daylight mildly poisoned or infected with some sort of Andromeda Strain sourced from the bathrooms, then you know Hector's set: Friendos, it never changed. He would arrive, faded old merch in a faded old green backpack. He'd set up, tune up, then launch into twelve songs. The same twelve songs. Songs that had, apparently, been handed down to Hector (or, who knows, his distant, dead ancestors) on stone tablets. And Hector would pick his way through these songs with a stress frown on his face, as if he'd only recently learned them and received mild electric shocks every time he dragged.

That night, the night of Hector Rodriguez's death, was unusual in a lot of ways. Dear reader, you have to believe me when I say my antennae for weirdness was up the moment I *walked in*. You know that electric sensation when a storm is coming? Or when you're eating a burrito from Ayala Brothers and halfway through you realize that special flavor is probably botulism? That *thrill of disaster* is what I'm talking about, the same feeling I—and, since you're reading this, probably *you*, beautiful trash—wake up with every day.

First of all, there were *fucking people in Hasty's*. A *crowd*. I don't think the fire department has bothered to issue an occupancy certification for this swamp in decades, but it's not big, and that night it was filled up. An investigation revealed that a bachelorette party had mixed up Hasty's with a more upscale joint around the corner called Hinky's Roughhouse, where male bartenders danced on the bar. The ladies marched in, every one of them wearing a sash that identified their role in the psycho-drama. Nothing as pedestrian as MAID OF HONOR or THE BRIDE, though. Oh, *fine*, there was a BRIDE TO BE, yes. But after that things got weird. One girl, whose voice pierced the night like a dropping bomb and who I later ID'd as the Maid of Honor, wore a sash that read BAD INFLUENCE. Another's said HOT MESS. Another's was MISS BEHAVING.

They all had tiny plastic dicks on necklaces. The suburbs had arrived! Your pal, Timso, was petrified: the girls were aggressive. Even I, the angriest little clown, was intimidated by them. There was a scent of apocalypse. You might think that these young ladies would have high-tailed out of Hasty's upon realizing their mistake, but you would be so, so wrong!

First, Bad Influence ordered shots, tequila, with the full suburban fanfare—salt, limes, the hand lick—and the girls performed it as if they'd been choreographing it for weeks. They probably had, as these women were what Tim likes to call *saucy*, my friendlies. Coughing and giggling, the women then marched over to the jukebox. Finding it booked for the next several songs, Miss Behaving took it upon herself to get down on the floor, flashing everyone her purple thong, and unplugged the machine, plunging us into a silence that threatened to see the whole place contemplating the life choices that had led them to Hasty's that evening—I thought I heard someone weeping—and then plugged it back in. And all this so the gals could play *Friends in*

Low Places and perform an unwanted karaoke sing-a-long as if the rest of us were an audience who had paid to see them. This culminated in a sloppy can-can where the girls slid their arms around each other and kicked their legs as they sang along.

A girl whose sash identified her as Miss Demeanor sent a chunky shoe sailing behind the bar, where it smashed three glasses. The girls all *woooed* enthusiastically, then raced to the bar for another round of shots. Pulses were pounding. There was something feral in the air, I'm telling you, kiddos.

Meanwhile, during the most dramatic and complicated evening in the history of Hasty's, over at his usual table Special K was dealing with some sort of shitkicker family reunion. He'd brought a dozen or so of his mulleted relations, all pre-gamed within an inch of their blocked-artery lives and ready to throw down. They took an instant dislike to our heroic Bachelorettes, and as Miss Demeanor and Miss Behaving made a clumsy attempt to climb up onto the bar to continue their line-kicking dance (Miss Behaving once again giving us all more of her purple thong than was appreciated in the attempt) the Hoss Clan hooted out derision and a few cruel nicknames.

The two groups were like gangs from *West Side Story*, circling each other, unhappy to have learned of each other's existence. More shots were ordered. Jukebox wars erupted—at one point someone paid real money to play *Achy Breaky Heart* six times in a row (the way the Bachelorettes cheered and immediately broke into an abomination I *think* was meant to be some variation of The Forbidden Dance, my money's on them as suspects), which led to a retaliatory run of *Ace of Spades* by

Motörhead. I, a man whose neighbors routinely play samba music until the wee hours of the morning and still sleep like a baby—I firmly believe, Friendos, that if you can't sleep through music played loud enough to drown out the police sirens you have no business living in a city; get thee to the burbs!—nearly fled the scene due to the increasingly fragile nature of the micro-civilization inside Hasty's that evening.

The Hoss Clan clearly regarded Hasty's as their territory in the same way the surviving Hapsburgs regard Europe as temporarily on loan from their holdings. The Bachelorettes had been promised drinking and the sort of dancing that regularly revealed Miss Behaving's by-now-well-examined underwear, and there was no force in the universe that would stop them.

Except, as we were all about to find out, Hector Rodriguez.

All of the chaotic energy clearly got to Hector. Friendos, I've seen a lot of Hector's performances. Say what you will about Freebird's robotic playing and tendency to startle as if seeing ghosts, but the man was steady. He showed up three times a week for more than ten years, set up his battered laptop (which provided tinny, programmed drum beats and backing tracks), played the same set down to the note, drank his two beers while sitting glumly at a rear table with his old CDs and curled stickers for sale, then packed up and walked out of the place, beaten but never defeated. If you don't admire that kind of determination in the face of utter mediocrity, you aren't human.

Hector's arrival on the tiny stage at least cut off the jukebox, which had apparently been programmed by Miss Demeanor to play Hootie and the Fucking Blowfish for the next hour or so, making him a minor hero of sorts to the regulars who weren't part of Kieran's shitkickers. His presence seemed to augur a return to Regular Order within Hasty's, an end to our recent troubles. And for a little while, it worked, because you can't underestimate the vampiric power of Hector's playing to suck all the energy out of a room.

With the first note, the crowd slumped, and the noise level dropped. Special K, an old hand at surviving Hector's sets, tried to rally his troops for a bit, but they just sank into their seats, gulping cocktails, hypnotized by the soothing cruise ship competence of Hector Rodriguez.

Did Hector look a little more hollow, more peaked, than usual? Hindsight says he did, though I can't swear I remarked on it in the moment. I was distracted, my lovelies, by the Bachelorettes, who were huddled over a tray of Margaritas, plotting witchcraft. Margaritas! If you are familiar with Hasty's, Beauties, I can picture your "O" face of shock, the very *idea* that the place could produce such a drink. I'd seen people berated for asking for Margaritas, or Cosmopolitans, or Sex on the Beaches, or Pina Coladas—laughed right out of the place! It made me quiver in my Dickies, friends, because these were clearly women possessed of a power beyond my comprehension.

But thinking back, I think Hector looked like a man who hadn't had much sleep in recent days. But Hector had never looked like a person who was *thriving*, to be fair. He looked like a man whose financial circumstances forced him to choose between food and prescriptions on a regular basis.

While I was contemplating the sad state of Freebird, one

of the Bachelorettes apparently crept over to the jukebox and committed an act of terrorism by reactivating it. One minute Hector is picking his way through a reasonably pedestrian pentatonic scale, the next *Alive* by Pearl Jam is blasting at us at a volume once thought theoretically impossible.

Chaos ensued.

Everyone was up, out of their seats, shouting. The Hoss Clan was incensed, the Bachelorettes were celebratory—and, yes, kids, they started the line-kicking dance thing again, hootin' and a-hollerin' up a storm. Everyone was, I believe, relieved that Hector's set had been interrupted, his bland spell holding us captive broken. Fresh violence between our two groups seemed imminent, but I again became distracted. Which is my second flaw, after the rambling.

Up on the stage, Hector had frozen. Gone completely still. He stood there staring just over my head, and his face was a mask of terror. Sheer terror.

I twisted around and peered into the dark. The doors to the bathrooms and the kitchen were behind me, bathed in shadows. And while I will stipulate that the bathrooms at Hasty's are *terrifying* in that they are essentially portals to hell, Hector was no stranger to those horrors. It wasn't that. It was as if he was seeing something—or someone—that wasn't there. Anyone else I might have joked that the drugs were kicking in, but let's face it: the last time Hector Rodriguez could afford drugs was at least a decade in the past.

Management strolled over to the jukebox and pulled the plug out of the wall, staring balefully at the Bachelorettes. They booed and hissed and demanded to know if Bernard had ever been in love (the man has a secret tender side, I am convinced, though I confess I have never seen it). Bernard just leaned back against the wall, cord in hand. Bernard Hastings is seventy-four years old and still has the musculature of a professional wrestler who routinely skips leg day, so no one was going to challenge him. And he was committed to giving Hector two beers for his services. If Bernard Hastings owes you two beers he's going to get his money's worth.

Hector didn't move.

He just kept staring, his eyes locked just over my shoulder. The crowd grew restless. Kieran Hoss raised both hands into the air and shouted *Come on, Freebird, you canta forgot them all!* and the shitkickers went wild with hilarity.

It seemed to shock him out of his stasis. His eyes drifted down to Kieran and the shitkickers, and then he shuddered, or shook himself, and leaned into the microphone.

"I wrote this song back in high school, with my best friend Ernie," he said, tuning his guitar, the sounds sour and discordant. "He died a while back. I didn't even hear about it until recently. This is called *Sexually Transmitted Disappointment*."

Friendos, you could have heard a pin drop. Not because we anticipated something amazing, or because we caught the whiff of pathos and felt a momentary affection for a fellow human being, but because it was pretty obvious disaster was at hand. Hector Rodriguez had been playing the same dozen songs for a decade and had not improved one bit in that time, and now he was going to play an *original composition*? The universe is rarely so kind to me.

He fiddled with his laptop. The Bachelorettes were loudly plotting their next move, which involved, apparently, rushing the stage and putting on some sort of cabaret performance. But Kieran, the gravitas of the moment somehow piercing his simian brain, waited patiently to see what kind of glorious fuckup was about to be bestowed on us.

Hector pressed a button and stood back, fingering his guitar. A second later, sounds filled Hasty's. What kind of sounds? I can't really say. They were sounds I was not, and am not, familiar with. There was a beat, although it staggered and slurred so much it evoked active anxiety, the kind of terrified worry you might feel when an insect crawls into your ear. There was a synth bed, but it was pitched in some eldritch way I can't define, each wash slipping between a vertebra and scraping the nerve. There were, I believe, finger cymbals, but far too many of them implying some sort of arachnid performer, or an entity from some other dimension.

And then Hector began to play his guitar.

I can confidently say, dear reader, that in the ten years or so that I have been ... *enjoying* is the wrong word; consuming? enduring? Hector's performances, I have never actually remembered them. His mediocrity is legendary, and many people have engaged in complex and challenging activities while he performed on Hasty's stage, balancing checkbooks and reading Russian novels, completely unbothered by his art. You only need one percent of your attention to appreciate what Freebird normally lays down.

But that night, from the first note, your brain was painfully engaged, desperately trying to make sense of what it was hearing. A kind of resonance cascade was formed, guitar notes bending between cymbals and rippling synths to create a sound that hooked into the deepest recesses of your brain and *yanked*. It was a painful, sudden experience. Several people leaped to their feet, hands in fists. I cracked a tooth, I was clenching my teeth so tightly.

The Bachelorettes fell silent, the clearest sign of the sound's power. I will not, shall not call it music, dearies. For it was not *music*.

When the song ended—abruptly, with a crescendo of grating chords and something that sounded like a table saw being lubricated with cement—relief swept through me, and the whole crowd sagged back into their seats, sweating. And then Hector approached the microphone, staring at us.

"Am I here?" he asked. "Can you see me?" Then he leaned down to the laptop, and I was seized with terror. "This," he announced as a fresh, jauntily and viscerally *wrong* drum beat emerged from the speakers, "is *Colonoscopies Me*."

What can I say, Friendos? You had to be there. It is impossible to describe the noise. It wasn't cacophony, it wasn't random. That was the worst of it. Listening to it was like hearing a muffled conversation in the next room—you couldn't make out the words, but you couldn't ignore them because you could *almost* make out the words. Your brain got hooked on the sounds Hector was producing, and it strained to make sense of them. It strained so hard you began to sweat and tremble.

Miss Behaving, cat's-eyeglasses, tall hair, and purple thong, suddenly jumped up and began shouting at Hector to stop, stop, *stop*, but Hector ignored her. That broke the seal, though, and a moment later the rest of the Bachelorettes were on their feet, shouting him down. Hector, a man who hadn't inspired more than a round of feeble, polite applause in his entire performing career, took this as encouragement, however, and began bending and hammering strings in a demented frenzy as the backing track hit new heights of discordant anxiety.

The seal broken, it was only a matter of time before Kieran made a move. He lumbered up, his crew rising up around him like time-lapse mushrooms, and began staggering toward the stage as if battling a stiff wind—he leaned forward, head down against the aural onslaught, one hand clutching an unopened bottle of rye whiskey like a club. It was like a classical painting, something in dense swirls of oil, a layer of varnish on top, everyone posed around Jesus or some angel as momentous violence was unleashed upon the world.

I looked at Hector to see if he saw the threat. He didn't. As his hands moved on his instrument with a grace and terrifying skill he'd never once displayed before, his eyes were once again locked on something behind me, just over my head. The expression on his face remains one of the worst things I have ever seen in my life, a mask of dread. Moving slowly against the thick air, I managed to twist around one more time, and again there was nothing there. Just the darkness and the ominous bathroom doors and, I noticed, Bernard Hastings crawling on the floor toward the extension cords that were powering Hector's performance, a hero to the end.

I turned back just in time to see Kieran, his adherents swarming up behind him like soldiers scaling a fortification, raise the bottle and swing it into Hector's head with determined force. Hector swung around, guitar spinning around his body on its strap, and crashed forward into the old laptop.

Silence.

For a moment, a soft chorus of sobs and heavy breathing filled the place. After a few drinks and some sympathy, I might admit to being one of the sobbers.

The Bachelorettes fled, most taking their drinks with them, silently citing some obscure provision of the Geneva Convention as justification as they cawed and hooted into the evening, seeking easier places to drink. Kieran stood on stage, breathing the way people breathe when a heart attack is about five minutes in their future, but his followers began the laborious process of dragging him off the stage and out of the place. He stared at Hector the whole time, eyes locked on his unmoving body as he was slid along the floor, his boot heels carving two deep scars into the soft old floorboards.

And then it was just me, Hector, and Bernard, who was lying on the floor with his head down, contemplating his life decisions. Hector was undoubtedly dead. The bottle hadn't shattered and lay in a spreading pool of blood next to him, but the real clue was the ugly dent in Hector's skull. I did eventually call the police, Friendos, but you will understand, I hope, that I spent a few minutes appreciating the silence.

Ernest

Hector

Chapter 21: Three Chords and a Drum Machine: The Story Of Polybius

Ernest Bundy received his first guitar when he was ten years old. His father, who appeared exhausted by his wife's extended family (who were an ever-present and extremely loud fixture in his home), put much of his energy into triangulating their locations in the home and ensuring he was perpetually on the opposite end of the property. This meant he was frequently absent from Ernie's life despite being just a few dozen feet away. The sort of man who threw money at problems, he came to consider Ernest to be not just *a* problem, but *the* problem of his life, and so he threw a lot of money at him.

The guitar was, therefore, expensive: a Les Paul Standard Heritage Cherry Sunburst that made Ernest break out into a sweat on sight. Holding that heavy guitar in his hands and imagining the legendary shredders who had played one like it on stage in front of thousands of screaming fans, Ernest had his first, but not last, panic attack.

Ernest had never expressed any interest in music except for a tendency, as a child, to mime very dramatic air guitar along with the music his father played. His father found this to be adorable and encouraged his son's performances. Slowly, in Mr. Bundy's mind, this alchemically changed into a kind of musical genius in his son that needed to be tended.

So, Ernest took guitar lessons. Exactly three of them. Then

he began a steady campaign of lies and deceit to make his father believe he was still actively studying his instrument when in fact it began collecting dust in his room. He had, once, successfully played three power chords in succession. He considered this an achievement worth savoring and never learned another chord or scale.

By the age of ten, Ernie was aware on some subconscious level that life had played a trick on him. He was vaguely aware of once being adorable and slowly being less and less so. By the time he entered high school at Bishop Carlbus Prep, he knew that his nose was enormous, his hair a floppy disaster, his acne-pocked skin an embarrassment, and his wiry, skinny frame an open invitation to mockery. When he expressed his concerns to his father, his father had cheerfully reminded him that he played guitar like a hero, and that everyone loved a guy who could shred.

Ernest, however, could not shred. He wasn't even certain that the expensive guitar in his room still worked.

This did not stop Ernest from telling everyone he met in those first few sweat-inducing weeks at BCP that he could, in fact, play guitar. He made a point of it, stressing that he'd been taking lessons for years and that he found most popular music boring because it just wasn't complex enough for him. He liked the reaction this got. By the end of the first week of school, he was known as one of the Guitar Guys, the other being Hector Ricardo.

Hector was, as far as Ernest could tell, effortlessly cool. Tall and skinny, but with muscular, well-defined arms, he had lush, curly brown hair and wore an earring and called everyone *muchacho* or *ni–a* with casual confidence.

When Hector approached Ernest in the cafeteria, suggesting they start a band and melt some faces, Ernest panicked and agreed enthusiastically. That night, he picked up the old Les Paul for the first time in years, strummed it, and promptly broke two strings.

Armed with several shaky power chords and a sense of desperation so thick it was suffocating, Ernie met Hector in the school's music room a few days later to jam and work out an initial approach for the band. Like a chess player who only knew one opening three moves deep, Ernie tried to take the lead in order to keep things within his comfort zone, laying down a chord progression that sounded, to his ear, almost competent.

To Ernie's amazement, Hector reacted with enthusiasm. Programming a simple drum beat on his laptop, he asked Ernie to "develop" that progression and began embellishing it with his own guitar licks. And Ernie realized something incredible: Hector, also, could not play guitar. At all.

The dynamic that developed between them, each pretending to an expertise (or even basic competence) they decidedly lacked, was thrilling. They practiced together for weeks, composing complex creations that resembled music only fleetingly and accidentally. It was Ernie's idea to describe their music as mathcore, which no one understood or had ever heard of, but which superficially matched the lurching time changes, dissonant scales, and stridently off-key riffs that became their signature sound. Hector suggested the name Polybius, taken from an urban legend involving a video game supposedly distributed by the CIA that drove people insane. Ernie loved that.

Polybius made their public debut and cemented their legend at the Bishop Carlbus Prep Talent Show, where they played their 15-minute opus "Entropy: Parts 3 and 5." A small-scale riot broke out among the audience of about a hundred and fifty students and a few dozen faculty members. Things were thrown. Epithets were hurled. And for decades to come the word "Polybius" would trigger any BCP alumni who had been there.

For Ernest, he thought this was the best night of his life and wondered if he would ever exceed it. Sadly, he would not.

FIVE FUNERALS

Basil

Chapter 22: Exit, Pursued

An account of the death of Basil Jefferson in April, 2012

From the web series WEIRD WAYS TO DIE, Skype interviews with Malcolm Granville, Donna Blick, Stacey Murrow, and Dean Murrow conducted by Ken Browning in 2014 and 2015.

‹*Intro music*›

KEN BROWNING: Hey, everybody, and welcome to WEIRD WAYS TO DIE! All my Weirdos in the comments, thank you for your support—don't forget to hit up my tip jar and check out my swag page, too! I'm *super excited* to get this episode out the door, because it is *soooo* weird, I love it! This is the *true* story of Basil Jefferson, who was just this guy in New Jersey who went to a party one night out near the town of Ho-Ho-Kus and got mauled to death by bears. Yes, *bears*! I kid you not, Weirdos. Now, you might think that getting killed by black bears in New Jersey isn't so weird, but trust me, this *ain't* your average bear death!

I contacted some of the people who were *actually at that party*! They were really helpful piecing together what happened. And as usual the real weirdness is under the surface! So, like, I edited these interviews together—with everyone's permission—to make it all flow and easier to understand, right? And just FYI we beeped out a few bad words here and there for our moderator overlords. Now, strap in, get comfy, and let's find out about the *very weird* and *very real* death of Basil Jefferson, eaten by *bears*!

THE GRAN MAL: The thing was no one knew the bear was up in the tree. It had climbed up there earlier in the day. No one knew. There's like a life lesson in there, somewhere.

STACEY MURROW: Don't let Malcolm spin this into a rumination on chaos. That's his way of saying, for insurance purposes, if a guest of his attending a party at his house gets mauled to death by a bear it's force majeure.

DONNA BLICK: Poor Basil. It was two bears.

THE GRAN MAL: It was my birthday. Shockingly, no one seemed to care, so it was up to me to plan my own celebration.

DONNA BLICK: Eh, that's Malcolm for you. He has this faux humility thing where he refuses to tell people it's his birthday. Then he gets pissed when no one knows it's his birthday, and throws this angry, weird party that's, like, fifty percent passive aggression.

DEAN MURROW: There was talk of a boycott, of everyone refusing to show up. But Malcolm throws really great parties.

STACEY MURROW: Basil's idea, the boycott. Sent an email to everyone arguing that Malcolm bought friendship and affection and we should start challenging him.

DEAN MURROW: Did I mention the parties are terrific?

THE GRAN MAL: Everyone always hated me because of the money, man. As if it was a character flaw. But all I ever spent it on was showing them a good time.

STACEY MURROW: Basil's boycott didn't get any traction. Basil was sensitive, and it made him kind of tender, and a tender Basil was a damn bore.

DONNA BLICK: Basil suffered from Great Guy Syndrome. He thought of himself as this great guy, a real gem. And because he was a great guy, his motives must be pure and his intentions always good. If you got hurt because of something Basil did, you weren't allowed to be angry at him—because his intentions were good. And that's all that ever mattered.

THE GRAN MAL: We called him Saint Basil. It was not a compliment.

DONNA BLICK: He was sad, really. That level of Unawareness was sad.

DEAN MURROW: Stacey had to let me know about the soiree, because Little Baby was angry at me.

THE GRAN MAL: Dino can eat a bag of d**ks.

STACEY MURROW: The inheritance ruined Mal before he was fully formed. He always knew it was coming, and it took away his ambition and replaced it with this weird kind of insecure spite. Most people throw parties so they can invite their friends. Malcolm threw parties so he could not invite people. As punishment.

DONNA BLICK: Malcolm is sad too, really, in a different way. You realize at some point that the crazy stuff—the famous performers, the circus acts, the catering done by celebrity chefs—he doesn't enjoy any of it. And he doesn't want you to enjoy it, either. What he wants is for other people to feel left out.

THE GRAN MAL: I missed the day they were handing out psychology degrees to all my friends, apparently.

DEAN MURROW: So: the bear. Malcolm knew, of course.

The rest of us only knew some bear had been spotted in the area, but Malcolm had seen it right there at his house. He just didn't tell anyone.

THE GRAN MAL: I'm supposed to call up 500 people to tell them a bear has climbed a tree? Okay—two bears?

STACEY MURROW: Only Malcolm would propose in all seriousness that warning people about a clear and present danger to their safety is a ridiculous thing to suggest.

THE GRAN MAL: I didn't know bears were dangerous. As god as my witness. I thought bears were slow. And ... bumbly. And then I started thinking that it might be cool if the bears were, like, at the party.

DONNA BLICK: So, we all show up even though we've seen this movie before. Even Basil. What's that saying about the definition of insanity? ...It was a great party, though.

DEAN MURROW: Basil walked in with a real hard-on about his failed rebellion. You know, sometimes people attend parties angrily. That was Basil.

DONNA BLICK: Sometimes talking about this makes me so sad. A man died, and we talk about the really good champagne at Malcolm's party.

STACEY MURROW: The thing is no one liked Basil. He was a stealth jackass. When you first met him, you liked him. Then you realized all the man ever did was complain. He wanted everything done to his liking, his way. And if you didn't let him have it, he sulked.

DONNA BLICK: Basil had a thing about *parties*. He approached every party he was invited to with what felt like deep-seated anger and *despair*.

STACEY MURROW: Which was also, like, *our* problem, somehow. Like if Basil couldn't enjoy parties anymore, neither could anyone else.

DEAN MURROW: We always had to worry whether Basil would ruin things because he didn't get to control everything.

STACEY MURROW: So, this was a classic Basil moment. He thought we should have boycotted the party, and he was angry that no one did. So, he set out to ruin it, as usual.

DEAN MURROW: I think Basil wanted to ruin Malcolm by ruining the party. Except, here's the thing—Malcolm's un-ruinable.

DONNA BLICK: He always likes a spectacle at his parties. Malcolm's a showman at heart. I remember New Year's five years ago, he had it catered, waiters and bartenders in uniform. Which was crazy enough, but then at midnight they all started to sing and dance this choreographed routine. It was years after flash mobs were cool, but it was kind of cool, anyway. It was bananas.

THE GRAN MAL: Look, mistakes were made. But I had a sudden opportunity to craft a legendary ending for a party.

STACEY MURROW: I remember thinking that it was one of the most Malcolm-free parties I'd ever been to. Normally he's everywhere, basking in his role as host. But this time I hardly saw him.

DEAN MURROW: Now we know he was trying to figure out how to lure the bears down from the tree.

THE GRAN MAL: I mean, not to sound obvious and basic,

but if you have two wild bears at a party and no one sees them, do you really have two wild bears at your party? I started trying to lure them down. I thought maybe they'd bumble around a bit. I now realize I was thinking of pandas.

DONNA BLICK: I don't believe Malcolm had any idea what would happen. He's an ass, but he's not a murderer. I mean, technically I guess he is, but it wasn't purposeful.

THE GRAN MAL: Basil killed himself. He suffered from an acute case of being an asshole and succumbed to the symptoms, may his memory be eternal.

DONNA BLICK: Basil was haunted. I remember we went to a concert once, a bunch of us in a single motel room after the show, and Basil kept waking me up because he was having a bad dream. Kept shouting some girl's name, saying he was sorry.

DEAN MURROW: He'd obviously come with the intention of ruining the party, and to be fair I was excited about the idea, initially.

DONNA BLICK: I was upset. The rest of us were enjoying ourselves, but Basil acted like you'd betrayed him because you were eating a canape.

DEAN MURROW: He was there just like the rest of us.

STACEY MURROW: He was sophomoric. He put salt in the booze; he shook up all the cans of beer. He dumped food on the floor. It was all very dramatic and very, very dumb.

DEAN MURROW: We all thought it was a blast—it wasn't our money being flushed down the toilet, after all—until we didn't.

DONNA BLICK: When he went for the urn, Basil lost the

hearts and minds.

THE GRAN MAL: Everyone knew Millie was in that urn.

DONNA BLICK: Everyone loved that dog, but Malcolm *loved* that dog. Stacey used to joke—I think it was a joke—that Millie was the best part of Malcolm, his better half. You've never met a more gentle, loving dog.

DEAN MURROW: I didn't quite get it. I mean Millie was a great dog and I love dogs too. But ... she was a *dog*, man.

THE GRAN MAL: Millie was nineteen when she died, and she'd been part of my life for so long I honestly wasn't sure how to get over it. I had her cremated and kept her in this gorgeous black urn, and I still talked to her. I felt like I could still feel her there, you know?

STACEY MURROW: We all loved that dog. And after she passed, we all talked to her, sometimes.

DONNA BLICK: We all knew not to touch the urn. Malcolm got very upset, and ... it was a dead dog, you know? No one was going to argue the point. No one was going to mess with that.

STACEY MURROW: So, Basil's there trying to start an insurrection and he's getting pissed off that we're all ignoring him, so he's making a speech about how Malcolm's a bad person and no one can take him seriously.

DEAN MURROW: We started laughing at him.

STACEY MURROW: He got pissed.

THE GRAN MAL: I was enjoying the moment. I had come back inside because it was getting cold and the stupid bears wouldn't come down, and here everyone was making fun of that prick. It was a nice moment. And then, to tip the scales back I guess, that piece of crap grabs up Millie.

DEAN MURROW: Not gonna lie. Even I was a little shocked.

STACEY MURROW: Basil finally got us to pay attention. Look, Malcolm's friends—we're not the nicest people. But the moment that son of a bitch weaponized a dead dog's ashes everyone turned against him.

DEAN MURROW: At long last, have you no decency, sir?

DONNA BLICK: We all loved that dog.

THE GRAN MAL: They chased him. It was amazing—the party became a mob. I remember seeing his face. Right before he burst through the french doors into the yard, I saw his face, and I can guarantee you the man knew he'd done messed up.

DONNA BLICK: People started shouting, a couple of folks took a few steps forward, and Basil freaked out and ran.

DEAN MURROW: And then he was eaten by bears.

STACEY MURROW: Assaulted by bears. Mauled.

THE GRAN MAL: Animal Control investigated—the bears had been up there all day. They told me the bears were probably scared—too scared to come down, but they were super hungry, too, which is why they were bumbling around outside the house in the first place. They must have climbed down just after I gave up trying to tempt them. I'd left the food out there I'd been using as a lure. It was just bad timing. We had all run out there, and ... well, it wasn't pretty.

STACEY MURROW: I didn't know bears were that fast. Maybe I'm thinking of pandas.

DEAN MURROW: We all ran out there, and all I saw was two dark shapes jumping on Basil. And Millie went flying—and someone screamed. For the *dog.*

THE GRAN MAL: Look, I was right there. Basil came running with Millie held out in front of him—you know, the stupidest possible way—and he didn't see that he was running *right at* the bears. And one of the bears kind of, I don't know, *casually* reached out and it was like it was *petting* him, you know? Like, it looked like a *gentle caress*, except Basil split open down the side and blood started gushing.

DEAN MURROW: There was a soft gasp of shock from the crowd. Like a communal *oh, crap.*

THE GRAN MAL: Basil's legs went out from under him and he kind of folded, and Millie went flying.

DEAN MURROW: Everyone screamed. Like, *shouts of outrage.* For the dog. The *dead* dog. The dead dog's *ashes.*

STACEY MURROW: Millie was a good girl.

THE GRAN MAL: I swear—I will swear on anything you like—that the bears watched the urn and hesitated. Like, they thought about chasing after it. And then they just looked back at Basil—who was trying to crawl away at about one mile per hour, and like I said these bears turned out to be very un-panda-like and are actually quite fast—and they just sort of grabbed him from both ends, roaring. You know, bears don't have fingers. They have *claws.*

STACEY MURROW: And then Malcolm charged at the bears, screaming like a maniac.

THE GRAN MAL: Millie was on the ground next to Basil.

I was afraid she'd get smashed.

DONNA BLICK: The bears took off.

STACEY MURROW: We called 911. Of course. But by this point ... think of ground beef.

DEAN MURROW: In the morning, after the EMS and the cops and most everyone else had gone, we were all that was left. We're sitting in the kitchen and Malcolm walks in.

STACEY MURROW: He had Millie.

DEAN MURROW: Miraculously undamaged. He just carried it in and put her back in place, and he turns to us and shrugs and says, "F**k that guy."

DONNA BLICK: But he saved Millie! We all jumped up and started dancing. Millie was the best girl, so it was a happy ending, seeing that urn.

STACEY MURROW: We lost it. After all that: F**k that guy.

THE GRAN MAL: F**k that guy, you know?

FIVE FUNERALS

Neville

Chapter 23: Slow and Steady

An Account of the Death of Neville Huang in June, 2013

He bought the house sight unseen, and his first call was to have the pool drained.

Debbie Keller referred to him as The Asian, which made some people uncomfortable. It soon caught on.

People asked if he knew about the murders, about the ghosts. She was delighted to tell them she thought they were a big reason why he bought the place.

Parties were immediately planned.

The party culture in town was competitive and cutthroat. Houses were renovated specifically to add Great Rooms, Butler's Pantries, expansive patios, and conversation pits. At least fifty percent of each home went unused most of the year, scrubbed down and brought to life only when a party was organized, then critiqued and slandered by attendees who felt *their* conversation pits were deeper, *their* Great Rooms greater by some inexpressible matter of inches. The risk that eventually the conversation pits would become so deep that ladders would be required was considered a real possibility.

The real competition, however, involved The Theme: anyone, it was generally felt, could throw a party. The real challenge was throwing a *memorable* party. Something people would talk about for years to come. This could be achieved in one of two ways: you could come up with a theme that inspired buzz, or you could secure guests that would inspire buzz. When the Garveys filled their conversation pit with sand and hosted a lūʻau in the middle of January, the level of buzz was historic although marred by their embarrassment when they discovered neither their Filipino gardener, Mr. Cruz, or their Panamanian cook, Miss Aguilar, knew anything about lūʻaus or the energetic dancing the Garveys recalled from a recent cruise. When the Kinseys managed to secure the attendance of Channel 12's meteorologist Kelley Polio for their Spring Forward Soiree in March, the buzz was durable.

The moment Debbie Keller reported The Asian's arrival, the party planning lurched into smoking, churning motion. Orders were immediately placed for large quantities of paper lanterns.

Everyone called it Harrows House. Montgomery Harrows built it in the 19th century as his sawmill and furniture business took over the town. It was a riot of bedrooms and columns and formal gardens that had gone through several cycles of boom and bust, re-arranged and re-planted.

The Harrows family fell into hard times, and the Harrows twins, Peter and Petra, inherited a rotting, ramshackle house in the 1970s. As they bided their time, refusing to pay taxes, and wandering the wooded acres to post KEEP OUT and PRIVATE PROPERTY signs, they actively antagonized everyone in town. This was mainly accomplished via the tried-and-true technique of running up huge bills and then not paying them, but also involved death threats, issued regularly and with real venom. The Harrows' grew unpopular.

And then the bodies were found.

It was the sheriff, serving a notice of seizure. Finding the house unlocked, the door open, he entered the property to search for a Harrows to serve. He later admitted he wanted to see their faces when he delivered the good news. When he came upon Peter and Petra in the backyard in the act of burying a hitchhiker they'd picked up a few hours earlier, a physical confrontation broke out, but the sheriff, a former high school football star, prevailed.

Thirteen bodies were eventually found on the property. Peter and Petra lacked remorse—they fired their attorney and admitted it all, bragging about their murderous acumen. It was just a few days after their execution when their ghosts were first sighted at Harrows House.

Debbie Keller speculated that Neville was a fake name. It was just too much, the thought that some family of Huangs would name their kid Neville. Though she admitted he certainly *talked* like a Neville.

Everyone wanted to hear the pool story from Ben Marsh, and he was happy to tell it.

Harrows House had a tremendous pool. Olympic-sized and

decorated with an impressive mosaic of tile. Ben Marsh loved the pool. There wasn't much call for pools of that size and caliber, and it was one of the few aspects of the house that had escaped the toll of neglect. He was initially excited to get the call from the new owner.

"He wanted a quote on drainin' it and filling it in," Ben said, shaking his jowly head in wonder at such insanity. "Who fills in a lovely pool like that?"

Neville heard bottles in the water and music in the open air. That was why he wanted to fill it in. He lay awake at night hearing the bottles in the pool and the tinny music, and when he rolled over, he saw her, his ghost, in the mirror formed by the television screen on the wall.

That was her way. She never made a direct appearance. He couldn't see her in just any reflection, only a reflection of a reflection, only twice removed. And then she'd be there, neck crooked, hair gritty from the basement floor.

Neville didn't sleep well. Every time he saw her, he took one more pill, and somehow that meant he would see her *more*.

Initially, The Asian's silence in response to several party invitations was taken as a strategy in the Great Game. When Bob Timmons, summoned to Harrows House to deliver supplies from Sam's Market, reported that a pile of unopened invitations remained on the floor under the mail slot, plans were scrapped, deposits sacrificed, and new strategies workshopped.

Everyone felt that the urbane, worldly Mr. Huang had taught them a valuable lesson. Foolish to think that a wealthy, exotic out-of-towner—no doubt the heir to some sort of massive Oriental fortune—would simply show up to any sort of dull dinner party. He would hang back, cultivating mystery, and wait for something irresistible, sustaining his social life with frequent private jet flights to more glamorous villas and mansions. If someone was going to host *the* party of the season, they would need to find a way to attract someone of Neville Huang's stature, and to do that they would need to offer him something more than canapes and a freshly carpeted conversation pit.

Most of the new strategies involved inventing cocktails named after the newcomer. Most of the names were puns on the word *wang*.

Neville had chosen the house *because* of its ghosts, to test a theory. He knew ghosts were real. He knew they were the lasting imprint of a person, a burned-in outline like those shadows at Hiroshima. He knew they would attach themselves to places and people, move through time and space chipping away at your existence. Rubbing at your eyes. Picking at your scabs.

He knew this because of Amy. The girl he glimpsed in reflections of reflections, neck broken and lonely.

He removed all the mirrors, but it didn't help. All it took was a glance in the wrong direction. A window reflected on his phone—she was always there, he'd come to understand, whether he could see her or not.

Ben Marsh reported that The Asian never seemed to move. When Ben arrived for the day's work, Neville could be found slumped in a patio chair, a glass in his hand.

Ben reported an exciting development: Neville had suddenly taken an interest and had blearily called him over.

"Look," he'd said, holding up his phone. "See anything?"

Ben reported that he'd dutifully looked but only saw his own reflection on the blank screen. Then Neville asked to see his phone, and things got weird.

"He held his phone up and told me to turn around, look at my phone's blank screen. And he asked me if I couldn't see a girl standing behind him."

Here Ben paused, looking troubled.

"And maybe there was something," he would say slowly. "It might have been one of the bushes, maybe, but it could have been *something*."

Ben didn't realize it at the time, but at least three rumors regarding his mental health and drinking habits originated in that moment.

Neville had done his research. He'd spent years trying to get rid of Amy and her perpetually judgmental glare, always popping up to ruin his mood, always ready to remind him of that party. Of that night.

And then he'd hear the bottles in the pool, and the tinny music in the air, and that would be it for sleep. Then he'd start drinking, aiming to pass out, at least get some unconscious time in.

He looked for ghosts. Violent, terrifying ghosts. Ghosts that had demonstrated histories of misanthropic and brutal post-life existences. The Harrows twins were ideal and ticked every box, and he'd brought Amy to them in the hope that they might destroy her.

Neville had been cursed by The Assumption.

It wasn't that Amy lacked reasons to torture him, Neville knew. The irony of it all was that he'd dreaded the party. He'd almost begged off. But Amy had been a tough girl to say no to.

It was the Outing Party, after all. The bash at the end of Senior Year that was legendary, that was imagined to cement your legacy at Bishop Carlbus Prep. As if anyone remembered high school more than a few months after it ended.

There was an elegance to it, though. Every year there was a

Senior Outing, and every year there was an illicit, secret, epic party afterwards.

That year, Amy's parents went on vacation without her, which meant The Keaton Compound—her ridiculously large house and assorted other structures—was available. Amy claimed the Outing Party simply by issuing terse, demanding invitations, as if by royal fiat. Twenty-five invites. Neville recalled there was a brief, doomed rebellion against Amy's hegemony that he hadn't been invited to participate in. He'd spent much of his high school years being assumed. People would make plans and simply *assume* he was joining them, or not joining them, as the case might be. And he always did. He'd learned to sense The Assumption and go along with it. When you were named Neville, he reflected, you didn't have a lot of options.

But in the end, they all showed up.

That was why he almost hadn't gone, despite his terror of that red-haired demon. It was suffocating, that small class. Twenty-five people he spent most of every day with. Every morning, classes, lunch, and activity spent with twenty-five kids he wasn't entirely certain he even liked, twenty-five kids who found it the height of humor to make fun of his name.

And Amy had always been the worst.

High school was when Neville realized the world made no sense, and Amy was a big reason. She was stout and broad-shouldered, her skin pale and her curly red hair thin and short on the sides, rising up into a shock on top that he'd always thought of as very punk rock. She wasn't pretty, or ugly. But she was *loud*.

She was volatile. And so, twenty-five kids who were variously better than her—prettier, smarter, more athletic—kowtowed to her simply because they didn't want to deal with her.

Amy was a terrorist, and they negotiated with her constantly.

So, he considered skipping the party. School was over. He'd be in college in a few months and could begin the busy work of forgetting them all and making new and better friends. Or, at least, different friends.

But then gravity kicked in.

He recalled a party in his sophomore year at Bishop Carlbus Prep. An impromptu gathering, everyone said, explaining how he'd missed it. Assuming he would not come. And he remembered the stories. Years later, kids were still talking about mysterious Noodle Incidents from that party. An entire secret language stemmed from it constructed of inside jokes.

The Outing Party began to develop gravity like that. He pictured a reunion, classmates talking about it, mysterious references to life-changing events, epic moments he would be forever locked out of. He reflected that, as it stood, his main takeaway from high school was a generalized fear of white people, and Amy's party could hardly make that any worse, so there was really only upside.

Social gravity was more powerful than regular gravity. It pulled. And he gave in. And he went. And it did change his life, much to his regret.

He spent hours just sitting in the old library, drinking whiskey and staring. The mirrors were smashed and the pool drained but left uncovered so the rain slowly filled it with dark, ominous water, but he could sense her. For decades he'd felt her, a hot coal of rage focused on him. When he closed his eyes, he saw her twice—before and after.

Before, he'd turned away from Hector and some shrill, ridiculous argument about the music. She was framed in the basement doorway and looking back he thought he might have stopped everything, changed everything, if he'd just said something to her.

Amy certainly seemed to think so.

After, everyone had laughed. Everyone made jokes about Amy. How the party was better off without her mooning about ruining things.

But he'd known better. Even then, head fuzzy, limbs loose, he'd known on some level that something terrible had happened. And yet he'd done nothing. And maybe he should have.

Amy certainly seemed to think so.

He woke up at 2:13 a.m. every morning. There was no mystery about why.

Alejandra Costa did Tarot readings for everyone in town and had her shingle out as the town's sole psychic. She was regarded as an amusing eccentric by the old men warming seats at Bulley's Tavern (when they were not speculating about her fuckability and whether or not she invoked spirits if you really hit the spot correctly), a grifter to be sniffed at by the ladies who comprised the Friends of St. Paul of the Cross. They implored a beleaguered Father Bickam to have her expelled from town as if he retained some microbe of the Church's medieval authority, and as a party trick by everyone else, who kept her housed and watered by hiring her for social gatherings.

She reported immediately when The Asian (as everyone in town had taken to calling him, their horror forgotten) scheduled her to come to Harrows House in order to hold a seance. Half the town immediately assumed this was an audition for a party, and suddenly the genius of Neville Huang came into focus: he had refused their invitations because he'd been planning his own party.

Neville sat and stared, listening to the bottles in the pool, the tinny music in the air.

The party had been a rager. None of them knew how to use substances. Their only goal was more, and more. Faces numb, pupils blown, passed out and shaking. You got older, you figured out how to enjoy things. How to savor, how to pinpoint the best point in the curve and surf there.

But at 17, they knew nothing. They staggered around the Keaton Compound. They vomited into everything. They broke things and spilled every possible liquid on every possible upholstery. They tossed empty bottles into the pool, and when Amy screamed they laughed, and when she raged they ignored her, certain she would come crawling back, spitting and cursing.

All these years later she was still spitting, still cursing.

Alejandra dined out on the story of the seance for weeks. It was a grim affair. The Asian was drunk when she arrived, complaining of irritating noises. All the mirrors had been smashed and the glass left on the floor. And the house of course had an evil aura, which she found to be oppressive.

She did her work. She burned a cleansing herb and cleared her mind to channel the angry spirits of Harrows House—here, her audience found her to be wordy, going into unnecessary detail about what it feels like to be in touch with another plane of existence, and silently urged her to get back to the gossip.

She reported that when she opened herself to the energies, she easily found the hateful, bloody-hearted Harrows twins—but there was a third spirit. A spirit so angry, so loud and staticky the Harrows twins were almost drowned out. As if their malevolent spirits wanted nothing to do with the newcomer.

Everyone would lean forward, fascinated. Even the Friends of St. Paul of the Cross, faces permanently puckered, paused their whisper campaigning to lean over casually, curious as to the precise nature of the Devil in their midst, unsurprised that he had taken the form of an immigrant.

Alejandra asked the Asian what he wanted to know. He pulled himself free of his alcoholic depression and told her he wanted to start a fight.

The idea came to him after reading a book on the paranormal explaining the nature of spirits, how they existed on a different plane, how they were inaccessible and intangible to physical presences. The book suggested, not entirely seriously, that to touch a ghost you would just need to become a ghost.

And Neville thought—or, perhaps, somehow *employ* a ghost.

At this point in the story, each time she tells it, Alejandra hesitates, shakes herself, and starts to lie.

She spins a story filled with flash and dread. She speaks of sudden noises, shifting objects, a titanic unseen struggle, and her audience enjoys themselves. And, she hopes to make mental notes to hire her in the future, and soon.

She does not tell them of the bleak emptiness she felt, sitting there in the ruined house with this odd, silent man, whiskey fumes wafting off him so thickly she feared open flames and felt woozy. She did not tell them that he wept, that he begged her to help, that for the first and only time in her life she almost regretted taking someone's money. She did not tell them that her real name was Doris, and that for a moment, basking in the invisible radiation of Neville Huang's despair, she'd felt very much *like* a doughty, lower-middle class Doris, instead of a mysterious, vaguely international Alejandra.

She remembered The Asian's expression as she fled. It had been terrifying in its blankness.

Neville didn't leave the house after the seance.

He set up in the large living room in Harrows House, sitting on a camp chair and drinking a steady supply of White Russians, the cocktail he'd been drinking the night of the Outing party.

He hadn't had a White Russian in decades. The thought of one made him ill. But now he discovered a taste for them, a thirst. He sat in the chair and drank. He pissed himself and drank. He did sloppy calculations regarding the caloric content of White Russians and how long one could survive on them before diabetes or cirrhosis got you.

If he could not eliminate Amy, he didn't see much point in doing anything.

Reports reached the town. Everyone who delivered supplies

to Harrows House found Neville seated in the living room, staring. The door was invariably open; the air was invariably rancid. Bob Timmons said he'd called out to The Asian several times, trying to strike up conversation in the way Bob was known to do, but Neville just shrugged or grunted monosyllables.

Bob's audience privately wondered how many of Neville Huang's possessions they would find if they turned Bob upside-down and shook him.

The excitement passed. The novelty faded. Folks in town forgot about The Asian and his haunted house. Life resumed its prior shape. Supplies of Saki were moved to the rear of liquor cabinets.

When they found him, he was sitting in the living room. The chair and his clothes were crusted in bodily fluids. It was clear that he hadn't moved in days before his death. He'd sat there, unmoving, staring out the window.

Stanley Morris was one of the EMTs who came for the body, and when The Asian was discussed, he said everyone had got it wrong. This, after a few drinks, convinced him it was a good idea to tell the story.

Because Stan saw that the light and the glare on that window made it reflect, like a poorly made mirror. And when he'd caught the reflection of the television screen in it, he'd almost screamed, because for a moment he'd seen—clear as day—the Harrows

Twins, gaunt and grinning.

The part he left out was that when he moved toward the television, he realized it had been a rose bush peeking in through the windows. Market testing had found this part of the story did not play as well as the first, and it was quickly edited out.

One aspect of the story that remained: In The Asian's pocket they found a scrap of paper. It read, MY NAME IS NEVILLE HUANG, AND I DON'T CARE ANY MORE.

FIVE FUNERALS

Victor

Chapter 24: Victor Drummond, Inner, Inner Monologue

October 16, 2015

As I am being escorted off the plane, my mind splits between how I am going to get to Jersey and coming up with a devastating series of comebacks for the shitkickers as they applaud. In years past the last part wouldn't have been much of a challenge. I used to be clever. I used to routinely savage people, effortlessly. Time had smoothed my sharp edges, though—time and Scotch and cigarettes and late nights staring at a screen. I'd let myself be ruined, and now I am a feeble King Lear type sweating through my cardigan as I navigate my way down the narrow aisle, people holding their phones up to capture my ignominy for their cackling cud-chewing neighbors.

"Fuck everyone," I mutter. "Fuck you all."

I was no longer clever. Whatever mild advantage I'd had over the lowing assholes of the world had evaporated, and here I was middle-aged and impotent. Not literally. Existentially. Though, maybe literally too, who the fuck knew.

When I reach the front of the plane, I know I have to do something. I couldn't leave hunched over my carry-on, sweating freely like some shlub. I couldn't let that be the permanent social media record of this event. But in the end, all I can manage is a stiff bow and a smirk I hope conveys disdain. The applause swells, but it is unsatisfying. They think they've beaten me.

The police take me into the guts of the airport, down one of those fluorescent hallways that ends in a metal door with a keypad. They lock me in a windowless room after relieving me of my license and my ticket. I sit with a headache forming behind my eyes until a blank-faced woman enters the room, an official-looking badge clipped to the lapel of her sad little jacket. She has sad short hair pulled back in a sad ponytail and looks like a woman who has several sad cats she dresses up in costumes for major holidays, and probably for the minor ones too, that make them even sadder, contemplating cat suicide. I see a lot of tiny sombreros in her future.

"The airline would like me to inform you that you have been placed on their permanent Do Not Fly list," she says, sliding my license across the table.

"The airline," I say, tongue thickening, "can go fuck itself."

She stares at me. Whether professionally bound to be unamused or congenitally incapable of humor, I am not sure. She stands up. "There will be no charges, but you'll have to make alternative travel arrangements." She pauses with her hand on the door. "If you plan to rent a car, I'd suggest sobering up a little first."

"I drive better when I'm drunk."

She hesitates. I get the feeling she doesn't like me. Then she opens the door and stands to one side. "You can go."

"How many days will you need the vehicle?"

"Honestly, it's a suicide mission, so I wouldn't hold your breath."

The short, disturbingly hairy man behind the counter doesn't look up from his frantic typing, but he frowns. "Excuse me?"

I sigh. "I don't know. How long does it take to drive to New Jersey?"

His typing changes tone and rhythm for a moment. "About six hours," he says.

I do math, moving the mental abacus with more effort than is seemly. "Three days, then," I say.

He nods, his typing resuming its monotonous, crashing rhythm. "Supplemental insurance? GPS for an extra fee? Pre-pay for gas?"

Everything is exhausting. I used to have energy. I used to be able to stay up all night and operate at a high level of energy for days at a time. Now I need six naps a day and frequent snacks like a toddler, and I am getting fat, and my heartbeat has become erratic. I doggedly answer his questions, this little martinet with the bushy mustache and the thick pelt on his head: the kind of hair you have to cut twice a day, or it consumes you. The Werewolf, I decide to name him, and regret not having anyone to tell the story to.

Because we live in low times, I have to find the car on my own, lugging my carry-on, dragging my roller with the broken wheel and my coat. In *Sunset Boulevard* Billy Wilder suggested you could tell how things were going for a man by looking at his shoes. In the modern day it is his rolling luggage. The broken wheel announces to the world that Victor Drummond has lost a step. He's slipped so far down he can't even afford to replace his luggage. Cashed out too early, the old hands would say, stroking their silky beards. Others with more courage have done much better. And he used to be so smug, so certain of his own superior genius.

The car is another sign. It's a box on wheels, white and scuffed. The interior smells disagreeable, but it is impossible to identify the source or nature of the scent. When I turn the key in the ignition the radio leaps to life, incredibly loud, playing a screeching, shuddering nightmare of a song. When I lash out to turn it off, the knob breaks off and falls onto the floor.

I stare at the radio bleary-eyed and tired. It dawns on me that I might be having a bad day.

Pennsylvania is absolutely enormous, and completely unpopulated as far as I can tell. It's a prank. No one lives in Pennsylvania. It might even be an entirely fake state. You can drive for hours and you're still in Pennsylvania and you haven't seen a person or a building in all that time. A man could die in Pennsylvania, and no one would know for decades. A team of researchers arrives and stumbles onto a set of bleached bones next to a derelict rental car. They take samples, they write reports. You become famous as Pennsie Man, the moron who tried to drive through the Forbidden Zone previously known as Pennsylvania without purchasing supplies and weapons.

While driving through territory so flat and featureless it saps at your sanity like a fnord in plain sight, the white box starts to shake and shudder. I press on grimly, willing the car to keep moving even as the headlights slowly fade. Then the dashboard lights, and I am driving in complete and total darkness. I am afraid that if I take my foot off the gas the car will die, so I double-pedal, white knuckled. It doesn't work. The car coughs and splutters and coasts to a stop.

I sit and stare through the windshield into darkness. I've never experienced anything like it before, this total absence of light. This is how people in the past believed the world to be flat, believed that if you traveled too far you would fall off the edge. This was how men on whaling ships went mad, ate each other. The darkness. The sense of tininess, of isolation.

The tow truck driver arrives three hours and sixteen minutes later and is covered in tattoos I suspect, but cannot be certain, represent variously horrifying belief systems and political adherences. He's a big guy, with a big beard, and he smiles constantly. Even when he's leaning into the engine of the boxy rental he's grinning, like something otherworldly is tickling his brain. When he concludes there is no starting the car, he hooks it up, grinning, and then, grinning, he invites me to ride along in the front with him, which requires him to move a pile of garbage off of the seat for me.

As we drive, I study his ink and try to suss out the key detail that will allow me to identify the precise militia he is part of, probably holding a rank like Grand Teton or Supreme Taco.

I suddenly feel blacker, which is something I had previously thought impossible.

I brace myself for the awkward conversation, but The Supreme Taco says nothing, and then I am insulted. Who is he to sit there grinning and not evince polite interest in me, a sophisticate lost in the wilds? I have a story to tell, beginning with a girl I haven't spoken to in twenty years and ending with me being escorted off a plane, but The Supreme Taco is not interested. He drives us to a town with irritating efficiency and drops me off in front of a La Quinta with the grimy business card of ALVIN'S BODY WORKS in my hand and all my luggage piled at my feet.

Inside, a girl who can't be older than twelve watches me warily as I drag my entire shambolic life to the front desk. It's warm and quiet in the lobby, which is filled with ugly chairs no one ever sits in. So much of the modern world is composed of spaces no one uses. The legendary amenities of condominiums, endless tracts of roof decks and indoor pools and party rooms that no one ever uses for fear of being trapped with other people in excruciating social proximity. Hotel lobbies always look so romantic in movies. In reality they're empty, static.

Or maybe that's just the La Quinta lobbies. I am living the La Quinta lifestyle now. The rented beater, Supreme Taco, La Quinta lifestyle.

"Let me see what's available," the girl, whose name tag reads TARA, says in a tone so devoid of emotion my eyelashes freeze. I turn and look around. I've never seen a more obviously empty hotel in my life, and I, an international man of taste and grooming, have been in many hotels.

"I have a room with a queen-sized bed on the third floor," she says in a monotone of impressive steadiness. I have heard that science keeps physical examples of measurements under lock and key as a reference—a block of metal that is exactly one kilogram, for example. Those eggheads could record Tara reading something she finds uninteresting—a violent threat to her life, for example—and keep that recording as an example of True Monotone.

"Thank you," I say, pulling my wallet from my pocket. I extract my abused credit card and put it on the counter.

"There's a $75 pet fee," she says. I cock my head.

"I don't have a pet?"

She looks up at me, suddenly interested. Her nostrils flare. She is, I realize, smelling the air. Smelling *me*. "Oh," she says, glancing back down at the keyboard. "I thought you did." She begins typing. Her typing is a slow wave, inevitable and unrelenting.

Cheap hotel rooms are like slipping out of time into an in-between place, falling into a liminal space like the event horizon of a black hole. The decor is reliably a decade out of date and the technology is pulled from an even more distant past—tiny televisions with thirteen channels, corded phones, drip coffee makers. I take a shower, put on the scratchy white robe, and pour four bottles of various whiskies into a plastic cup. I sit at the tiny, impractical desk and read the email again:

Dear Vic, this is me, I am breaking the glass

and sip whiskey and contemplate my progress, which is disappointing. According to plan I should be in Newark by now, hailing a cab and explaining to the driver that there are no tolls so he shouldn't charge me for tolls because there are no tolls. To be fair, according to plan I should be twenty pounds lighter, much wealthier, and much less likely to die suddenly of an infarction while dragging broken rolling luggage through bizarre unreal twilight kingdoms like the great state of Pennsylvania.

breaking the glass

The bedspread is scratchy, and the room is too hot, and before I'm three sips in, I fall asleep. I dream about bottles in the pool, and *she said have gotta little storee fer you*, and Polybius.

I startle awake, sweaty and dry-mouthed. I go downstairs for some free breakfast and emerge from the elevator in my robe to find I've crossed over into an alternate reality where a bustling community of ambitious businesspeople have invaded the La Quinta and are consuming all of the waffles. I stand there naked under my bathrobe, paralyzed. They're everywhere. The lobby is crammed full of men and women in drab business suits, cups of complimentary coffee in hand. The buffet is a conga line of them. There is buzz. There is energy. There is waffle batter literally everywhere.

After a moment, I cinch my robe's belt a little tighter and join the end of the line at the buffet.

Everyone pretends this is perfectly normal, and who knows, maybe at the La Quintas of the world it is. The woman in front of me, whose little bun of hair is gathered so tightly it is slowly contracting into a diamond, turns briefly to say some pleasantries and pauses, thinks better of it, and turns to look straight ahead.

Following locusts is no way to live. I manage to scrape together some mismatched English muffins and a cup of coffee, the floor sticky with spilled jelly, the plates all gone. I cradle my muffin in a napkin and make my way gingerly back to the elevator, the robe's belt working its way loose and threatening to make me famous. As I cross the lobby my eyes meet the sunken gaze of TARA and I am startled by a depth of exhaustion heretofore unknown to man. I feel shame. I'd spent my night sleeping, and TARA had been psyching herself up for the worst hour of her life.

I escape into the elevator. I consider making the La Quinta my home.

In the room, I check my accounts, as required by the higher law that has governed my life for the last ten years. They are slightly less every time I look at them, as required by the higher law that governs higher laws, which will grind me into dust and spread the impoverished dust onto the sidewalk one sunny day. But it is not this day.

I briefly consider contacting the body shop and finding out what's happened to the White Box, or calling the rental agency and informing them that their car is languishing in a Pennsylvania town so small it's claim to fame is, apparently, a La Quinta. I reject both options as too much effort and turn my attention to my luggage. There is entirely too much of it. I need to travel light, so everything is unpacked and spread out. I change into my most comfortable pants and a decently new-ish white button-down. Then I add layers, because you can always remove layers. Phone, of course, wallet, no, but cards, yes. I can buy anything I need when I get to Jersey. That's the magic of not being a failure: you can buy things. It's great. More people should try it some time; society would benefit.

I realize in the middle of putting on a sweater in case I need one later—adding a plan to purchase a backpack of some sort—that this is probably how people become soldiers in the Crazy Homeless Army. It starts with wearing everything you own out of convenience, and five years later EMTs are cutting you out of your sausage skin-like garments and demanding to know if you know your own name.

Leaving behind most of my possessions, I walk out of the room, down the hall, and into the elevator. On the first floor the breakfast frenzy is still going on. I walk out through the back door into the parking lot, fish out my phone, and call a cab. I imagine Tara's face when she realizes I'm gone, and I'm pleased by the image.

Bus People are fascinating. I'm one of the few passengers with no luggage. Several people have brought complex lunches which require heat sources and whisking pans by all appearances.

Others have created sumptuous nests in their seats, walls of coats and blankets creating tent-like structures they have filled with screens and music, soft lighting and headphones the size of Jupiter. These are professional bussers. If the bus crashed and slid off a cliff and we were trapped inside for weeks, they would survive on snacks in Tupperware and candy bars while I starved and tore my nails bloody trying to open one of the windows.

Riding the bus is slipping back into a more primitive time. It's the steerage of modern transport. But it's contemplative and private. No one looks at you or cares about you because everyone knows the one vital thing: you're going in the same direction as they are, and you are too poor or too despised by the universe to get there any faster. Best of all, the Void Otherwise Known as the State of Pennsylvania is reduced to a black nothingness that slides past without fuss or drama. Before I know it, I am in Newark, with that greasy nostalgia-filtered light that makes everything look like it's in an old instant photo left in the sun, faded and vanishing, becoming more indistinct with every passing moment.

I've never been to Newark, but I am back in New Jersey, my native land. You can feel it in your fingers; you can feel it in your toes. The Chromium. The asphalt. That subtle sinking sensation. That urge to flee to better places.

Since I am spending money like a man who has prospects, I hire a taxi to take me to Bergen City: the old stomping grounds, the ancestral home, a place I haven't been in fifteen years and have little desire to revisit just in case my brother is still alive and bitter about the fact that when our father died I sent him a

Get Well card with the words GET and WELL scratched out and the word SORRY scratched in. The idea of running *mio fratello* on the streets of Bergen City terrifies me. The idea of discovering *mio fratello* has died at some point in the intervening years terrifies me slightly less, but it's still terror.

The drive in is a slow telescoping of the familiar into the unfamiliar. From afar, the skyline and broad strokes of Bergen City remain largely as I remember them. But as we get closer, the details no longer match up. The old pencil factory is now condominiums, a tattered old sign advertising luxury and affordability. The jughandles I navigated as a kid have vanished, replaced with sleek modern off-ramps. The old Zip Soap sign has been dismantled, a new thin slice of greenspace running parallel to the river in its place.

My driver is disturbingly competent. He drives fast, moving smoothly from lane to lane to pass slower cars. He multitasks, carrying on two separate conversations in a foreign language—one quite heated—and also thumbs data into his phone. His front seat is filled with folders and paper and books about day trading and finance, and in-between a practical course on the effects of momentum, I wonder how he's doing. And then I remember: he's driving me to a shitty apartment building in Bergen City, and figure I know my answer.

But he gets me to 293 Griffith Street in no time at all, dive-bombing to the curb with a sudden wrench of the steering wheel and grunting several times as we pass my credit card back and forth. I climb out onto the sidewalk with shaking legs, and he is accelerating almost before the door slams shut. I watch him tear off and marvel at this level of energy and ambition.

I turn and regard the building. The scientific term for a building of this style and vintage is *shithole*. It has the tell-tale yellow brick and broken security door, the doomed gardens installed on fire escapes by people desperate for any glimpse of life, the pollution stains and cracked front steps. This is a place where things end. This is a Final Destination.

The vestibule is reasonably clean. There are eight buzzers with names next to them. Number six reads SCOTT, and I stare at it for a moment—

this is me, I am breaking the glass

so-ah-ah-uhn, havai gotta little storee fer you

—hands shaking. Then I find the buzzer marked with the letter B, B for basement, basement for supers, basement for folks getting a break on the rent in exchange for all the grungy work even Final Destinations require. I press the button for a calculated ten seconds, designed to be as annoying as possible.

A moment later, the door buzzes open. It's surprisingly heavy, and the interior of the building smells unsurprisingly terrible, as if a billion dinners of boiled cabbage and farts had chemically combined into a wholly new scent. At the other end of the hall, under the stairs, the door to the basement slowly creaks open.

"Who are you?" a voice asks. It's a rough, thin voice, stretched by years and cigarettes and screaming matches.

I take a few steps down the hall towards the doorway and address the black gap between the door and the jamb, imagining someone peering through it, suspicious and fearful. "I'm a friend of Zillah Scott's," I say. "Apartment Six."

The door creaks open slightly more. A man emerges. He's a tall Black guy who'd once been super skinny. Now most of him is super skinny but his belly is enormous, like he's swallowed a watermelon—or two watermelons—in recent days and his body is struggling to digest them. "Oh," he says, "she's not here. She's dead."

I nodded. "I know. Most of us are."

The idea that people live in places like this is depressing, because it holds out the possibility that *I* might someday live in a place like this. Especially since I have not held a job in years and the surprising bucket of money my momentary interest in cryptocurrency had gifted me is growing thinner by the day. Especially since everyone I knew in high school, everyone I knew at the place I like refer to as Bishop Carlbus There But For the Grace of God Preparatory School, is pretty much dead.

My self esteem has been on a low ebb, I think.

It's a five-room railroad, too hot, with painted floors and loud music pounding down from above. The kitchen is a jumble of stale fast food and plastic jugs. Gin, of course. Zillah's drink, her whole life, or at least the portions of it I'd glimpsed.

The whole place smells of it, as if she'd doused herself in gin and set herself on fire. Or been dissolved by it.

On the table, a copy of *The Bishop*. It glows like an object in a video game, blinking softly to let you know it's important, because the designers found that test players weren't smart enough to notice it on their own. I walk over and pick up our old yearbook. It looks brand new, like it had been transported directly from twenty years earlier via a wormhole. Or the slow way, time traveling one minute every minute as Zillah packed and unpacked it over and over again, inexplicably carrying it with her wherever she went.

I open it to the photos in the back, twenty-six smiling kids. Most of them have thick red X's through them. Zillah's hobby was, apparently, tracking the wrack and ruin of our graduating class as we failed downward towards death. I flip through the pages; not *all* of us—Leo Barone, Kate Huxtable, the Sandford twins, and Ida Tanner, haven't been X'd out.

I have.

I stare at myself through the red ink. Who is this asshole, I wonder, with his Cameo *Word Up* hair and the suave turtleneck? Hovering over a quote I thought must have seemed *genius* to 17-year-old Victor. Smiling at the camera as if Amy Keaton wasn't about to ruin everything while we laughed and danced. That Victor Drummond is a stranger, a totally different person. I'd worked hard to get away from him—to get handsome, and confident. And rich. For a moment I'd been there, but then all my disguises started to melt and here I was, collapsing like a pudgy, emotional singularity back into its fundamental shape.

I look up, looking for her, for Zillah. There was a time we talked constantly. There was a time we saw each other regularly. Any time you need me, just break the glass, give me a call. I look around, half expecting to see her, hungover and sarcastic.

I want to ask her what, exactly, is this bullshit, but she's not there and hasn't been for a long time.

The train into New York City is crowded, so I let it go and stand on the platform waiting for the next one. I have nowhere to be and all the time in the world to get there. For a blessed two-minute interval I'm alone with the general smell of the place, which is somewhere between a slice of processed cheese food held in an armpit for a decade and oblivion in odor form. You keep breathing in deeper and deeper in a desperate gambit for oxygen, but this just makes the situation worse.

I start researching clothing stores. I'll need to glam up in case I see anyone at the Funeral Event. Half the battle is looking the part.

I open Zillah's copy of *The Bishop* and flip through it. I land on the Student Council—headline: CHILDREN ARE THE FUTURE—and there she is. Amy Keaton, staring at me with that steady, pissed-off glare she'd perfected by age four. Our vice president, six days before her untimely death and still trying to swallow the bitter pill of having lost that election to Kate.

I keep flipping. Everyone signed it. Even me. There's my loopy kid handwriting, *never hesitate to break the glass, love forever, Vic.* I'd forgotten to write that it might take me three or four weeks to respond. I'd forgotten to warn her I might turn into a terrible person.

I'd forgotten.

FIVE FUNERALS

Quentin

Chapter 25: Quentin Goes Home For Good

An Account of the Death of Quentin Cunningham in April, 2013.

The world is a vampire. Most people know about the fundamental forces of the universe. Gravity, electromagnetism. But they forget about the most powerful force of all: The Suck.

Bergen City is the Suck Capital of the world.

Escape velocity from Bergen City is higher than most neutron stars and black holes. The worst part of it is all those years when you *thought* you'd managed it. When you were outside the heliosphere of the place. The illusion of forward motion. The Suck gets stretched so thin under those conditions you don't really feel it. But it's there. It feeds out some slack for a while, and then, when the moment is right, it jerks you back.

Filthy place. All I remember from growing up there was washing my hands, washing my hands, washing my hands. I never felt clean. I'd vowed to never go back to Bergen City. And I didn't, for a long time. And then Rhoda died. And I still didn't plan to go back. Thoughts and prayers, but I hadn't spoken to her in ... since the party.

But then I was lying in a hotel bed in Siem Reap, staring at the ceiling, and I remembered Pontifuss Maximuss.

And The Suck got me.

I tried to remember when I'd last seen Rhoda. A persistent mental image of her standing at the top of the stairs in her house, wearing the green overalls she liked. Watching me leave and looking not sad but angry. But I couldn't be sure it had actually been the last time.

Everything was different. I came in the back way, the old highway by the refineries. But the road no longer cuts through the Narrows. I got lost. The old Two Guys had been torn down, and a hotel had been built in its place, now showing a little wear and tear itself. A boutique place: efficiencies, a micro-kitchen, and a living room. Hotel room as pathetic apartment. Everything was just slightly smaller than the real thing. Subtle shrinkage that left you questioning your sanity. Was washing a dish *normally* a challenge requiring robust knowledge of geometry and the joint flexibility of a much younger person? Did *most* people pull muscles contorting themselves in a vain attempt to wash every part of their bodies?

And then I thought it was strange to take a shower in the same spot Mom had taken me to shop for school clothes.

And it was a *terrible* shower. My first session: fifteen minutes, decent pressure, lots of foam on the body wash, promising. Then the towel felt greasy. Back in the shower, naturally. Couldn't get the slick feeling off my skin. Thirty minutes, scrubbing, skin raw. Finally gave up, air-dried. But that left the soles of my feet covered in dirt, from the floor. So, I had to wash *them* again. Then a complex procedure: sitting on the toilet, feet in the air. Old T-shirt to dry off my feet. Then the shirt draped on the floor so I could step on it. One leg, another shirt for the other foot. Repeat until I got to the suitcase and clean socks. Madness.

The old green house. The Bender house. It was gone, just an empty lot in its place, as if no one could muster the energy to build anything. Across the street was the driveway Rhoda had deemed sufficiently private to take down the top of her swimsuit. I remembered her nervous, unhappy smile. A twitch.

And I remembered the laugh. I'd been trying to get away from that laugh ever since the Outing Party. That laugh broke my heart.

The fucking cat. Pontifuss Maximuss. A sweet blur of an animal Rhoda had adopted in Junior Year as a starving kitten. It fattened up like it couldn't believe its luck and didn't believe it would last. Rhoda imprinted on that cat. It had the run of the property, roaming about and whoring around with the locals. Two litters of kittens during high school alone. Rho, I recalled, delighted. And three more, I knew, after I'd left. the news traveling through social media once I gave in and joined Facebook.

I like cats. They're self-cleaning. How can you not appreciate a self-cleaning animal?

Listen, she'd said, one night in her room. I remembered soft music playing. Ole' Ponty purring in Rho's lap. *Listen, you're my only friend. If anything happens to me, you gotta promise to take care of Ponty.*

I remember grinning. I remember pointing out that it was a cat, that cats had been engineered by our alien makers to live rough. I may have pointed out Ponty's evident joy in carousing with other cats and turning up pregnant and Unashamed at regular intervals. Evidence that she would be just fine.

No, Rho said. Mom *will kill it if I'm not here. She'd poison it.*

I agreed with this assessment. I thought, at the time, that Mrs. Anderson would poison all of us. Every one of Rhoda's classmates, if she had the chance. Mrs. Anderson despised teenagers. And blamed us for Rhoda's love of bowl haircuts, shapeless overalls, and preference for asexual reproduction.

So, I agreed. I *swore*. I also did the math and figured the cat would be long gone before either of us. So, I swore a blood oath that I'd take care of the fucking cat if Rho predeceased me.

The tiny plastic bottles of liquor in the hotel fridge weren't satisfying. Drinking with Rhoda and Xerc and Kate had been fun—at least before Amy died. The weight of a shared bottle. The heft of it. The ritual of passing it around. The tiny doses in the hotel were medicinal at best.

I sat on the bed for a while, drinking shitty vodka doses.

Trying to decide if I was heavier here in Bergen City. I'd made it as far away as possible—Perth, Australia. Then roamed from there. Trying to maintain at least ten thousand miles between me and Bergen City. But I'd just been in orbit. I was still trapped by the Suck.

Half-drunk and headachy, I wash my hands and face in hand sanitizer. The water here, I realized, is no good. It stinks. It's polluted. Then I put on my coat and go looking for the fucking cat. It wasn't just a promise. It was a fucking oath. It meant something. You meet people in your life and you chemically bond with them. You can go decades without seeing them, they're still there, in your bloodstream. That was Rho. I never saw her again, but she was still in me. And that promise scratched at me. Kept me awake at night until I decided to fly out to honor it.

The fucking cat is twenty fucking years old. Still fit as a fiddle, according to its Instagram page. Fatter, dumber, sluttier. I've read that cats can live to be thirty years old.

Everything felt different. The air thicker, lights dimmer. The Suck made walking more challenging. My legs heavier, steps harder. I remember going to the planetarium as a kid. They had these scales you could step on showing your weight on different planets. If they had one for Bergen City I would weigh in at several tons. The ground would crack under me.

I walked by Mom's house. Stood watching the blue flicker of the television through the window. I pictured her in Dad's old lounge chair. Every time I saw her The Suck had pulled her slightly deeper into the torn upholstery. I hadn't told her I'd be in town. Hadn't told *anyone*. Certainly not anyone from high school, Lord fucking forbid. People had their own special gravity. You got sucked into get-togethers and awkward dinners. Endless conversations about the old days, gnawing on the bones of better times.

I walked up to the Boulevard and thought of Rhoda in grammar school. Suddenly grabbing my arm and parading with me when she learned I'd never kissed anyone on the mouth. She had big energy. At least she had before the Outing Party. Before Amy.

I remembered the silence. The sound of her TV. Her breathing. The plasticky noise of hands on the phone. Hours burned off like gas. The two of us connected over several blocks via the invisible link of the phone. Just existing, not speaking.

A few times in college, my phone rang, and I had voicemails from unfamiliar numbers—just silence and breathing. I knew it was her. I never called back. I left her at the top of the stairs, receding from me.

I had the forethought to purchase cat treats at the Shop Rite. A vigorous shaking of the plastic box produced a startling number of eager cats who wanted to be my new best friend. Before long I was being followed by several cats with shifty dispositions and questionable facial scars. This was surprisingly terrifying. I knew from bitter experience that even fat, fluffy cats like Pontifuss Maximuss possess razor-sharp murder claws. The swaybelly gang stalking me was a genuine threat.

In an effort to throw them off, I walked to the outskirts of town until I stood across the road from Amy's house. It wasn't her family's anymore. It had been sold several times since then. A cursed place where the Suck was stronger, attracting even non-corporeal things like despair and horror. It looked smaller than I recalled. In my hazy, eagerly buried memories it was a compound: the large house, a guest house, a pool, the courts. There were acres of land, and the place had always felt infinite.

Now it was like a collapsing star. The Suck was so strong it was warping time and space, crunching everything down.

The night of the party, I sat with Rhoda drinking cheap tequila from a plastic jug. We mocked everyone, Rhoda cackling. We were partners in misery. We hated everyone and we hated ourselves, but we loved each other.

Until that laugh.

Shivering in my thirties, I realized that moment sitting on the ice-cold patio furniture drinking corrosive liquor had been the end of us. Amy didn't survive the night. Neither had we.

The cats were still prowling, snaking between my legs and making declarations of love. Were there more of them? I couldn't be sure. I felt like I was about to be mugged. I considered whether walking out to this empty area of town had been the right move. If I was a cat plotting murder in exchange for treats, this would be *exactly* where I would want my idiot victim to go.

I turned and walked back. Briskly. After a few blocks, I was amazed to discover that Narrowbacks was still open. The grimy old bar had been notorious when I'd been a kid. A perpetual challenge for each generation: get served at Narrowbacks despite resembling an urchin from a Dickens novel.

I stood for a moment listening to the soft yowlings of the cats and the hum of beery activity in the bar. The place was no doubt filthy. The pavement outside was stained. Puke. Blood. Piss. Just being near it made me feel dirty. And the chances that Pontifuss Maximuss was in Narrowbacks sipping on a boilermaker were slim. But no stone unturned and all that. Because I knew where the fucking cat would be found, eventually, didn't I? The Suck was gently tugging me there. A weak but irresistible force. I was in no hurry to follow.

I remembered her at the top of the stairs. Her mom yelling in the background. Her eyes wide, accusatory. I'd told her I couldn't stay. Not after Amy. Not after the Outing Party. She reminded me that we'd sworn to stick together, no matter what. If one of us left, the other did. If one stayed, we both stayed. That was the deal.

I couldn't explain it to Rho. That I remembered her at the Outing Party. So irritated at Amy, nearly in tears because of something she'd said, some mean thing, because Amy Keaton was the Queen of Mean Things. I remembered sitting out on the patio with her, drinking some of Zillah's gin. That awful gin Godzilla had suddenly discovered. Rho, emotional, talking about college and feeling free and being able to leave all the mean bitches behind.

And I remembered later, everyone irritated with the band.

Amy, red-faced with rage, going down, and I remembered Rho had laughed. Rho had *cackled*, amused. And something between us soured and blackened, right there, in that moment. Rhoda had been my Person. My Constant. But the Rhoda I'd sworn to follow anywhere wouldn't have cackled at what happened to Amy as we all stood there, stunned in the damp basement air the morning after the party. It was a single, sharp bark of a sound, an instinctive reaction.

I could never forgive her that laugh.

The fucking cat, on the other hand, had done nothing wrong.

Narrowbacks was just as I remembered: a time capsule. Dark, woody bar with ancient Little League uniform shirts tacked up on the wall to celebrate ancient championships. It still smelled of cigarettes decades after the last one was smoked. I hesitated in the doorway. I could feel the tiny bits of dirt and germs. Slapping onto me like bugs on a windshield. But behind me was a gang of probably murderous cats. Inside the bar was only slightly less threatening, all the customers in grimy jeans and biker cuts. There were a lot of beards that hadn't been tended to in quite some time. The smell of the place was disturbing on many levels. Including the level where I could have sworn I detected the coppery scent of blood.

Steeling myself, I sat down at the bar. Stared down at my hands. I'd spent so much time as a teenager scheming to get into this place. Now I was here and it kind of sucked. Would have to burn my clothes later. Fill the tub with rubbing alcohol for a soak. Had it sucked back then? Almost certainly. Everything did, once you took a close look at it. But at least I was safe from cats for the moment.

"What can I get you?"

The bartender was a tall, skinny woman. Black T-shirt and black jeans. The shirt had several stains on it. Her hair was a stringy brown mess, her ears poking out from underneath, her skin red and rashy in ways that look uncomfortable. She had the look of someone who'd been surviving on Cheetos, vodka, and good genes for a long time.

"Bourbon, neat." I started to specify, then caught myself: this was the sort of place where any sort of palate marked you as an undesirable.

She didn't turn away to pour my drink. Instead she squinted at me, eyes suddenly intense. "Christ—Quentin? Quentin Cunningham? From Bishop Carlbus?"

Panic. The Suck had me firmly in its grip, pulling me toward that enormous drain that we were all making our way to. I blinked at her. A fight-or-flight response rose up like black electricity, jerking all of my limbs at once. I had one chance to make a run for it. Assuming I wasn't immediately eaten by a horde of cats, I could just run straight for the hotel and be in the rental car in half an hour. Leave Bergen City the second time the same way as the first: sweaty and trembling.

Instead, I collected myself. I put a smile on my face.

"Wow—Prue?"

Prudence Nelson looked to be about seventy-five years old.

It had been a rough seventy-five years. I wondered if I looked this bad to objective observers. It didn't seem possible. I didn't have scabs on my neck. My pupils weren't so blown they were like two black plates in my head.

She stepped back and curtsied, raising imaginary skirts. "At your service." She smiled. "Literally. One bourbon, coming up."

She served up a shot glass filled to the brim, her hands shaking. Then she turned to deal with her other customers, laughing and joking so loudly it was alarming. I studied the shot glass for obvious contamination. Then reasoned that 80 proof liquor would kill anything in there. I sipped. Gave into a sense of anxious waiting. I knew she would come back. If I was going to—

"—since what? Graduation? Has it been that long already?"

I'd lost time. She was back, leaning forward over the bar to give me a glimpse of her cleavage. Deliberate, I thought. Obvious.

I nodded. Graduation had been grim. I remembered the panic attack. I remembered Olive didn't come, and how that seemed like an omen. I remembered feeling like I'd been dipped in cement when they called out Amy Keaton. Everyone turned to stare at the empty seat. I remembered the sense of awkward embarrassment and burned with shame.

Prue hesitated, leaning forward and forcing me to flinch away from her breath. It implied a lack of self-care that was, frankly, shocking. Like she was rotting away from the inside.

"You heard about Rho?"

I nodded. I said nothing.

"Fuck, burned up in your own house," she said, shaking her

head. "I heard her Mom fell asleep with a cigarette. I thought people would come to the funeral."

I understood this to mean she'd expected *me* to come to the funeral. Because me and Rhoda had been so close. It was like we were all dipped in amber, trapped in that moment in time. That moment right before we all knew we were damned.

I didn't say anything.

"You going to the house?" She blinked several times rapidly, then hugged herself, rubbing her arms. "It's actually kind of cool, in a sad, weird way. I mean, the house is *gone*, man—burned to the fucking ground. You can see the outline of everything—the walls and shit. But it's *treacherous*. The whole lot is roped off because it's like a big sinkhole. A *mire*."

She was breathing hard as she spoke. The words hissed out like steam escaping. I imagined I could feel her heart pounding from across the bar.

"The house was built over a cave or something. People have fallen through. Couple of dogs lost. City keeps promising to put up some sort of fence, but her family has everything tied up in court." She slapped the bar, smiling, and I almost bolted for the door. "Hang out! My shift ends in an hour. We'll have a drink." She frowned. "Not here, though."

I watched with mixed fascination and horror as Prue put what scientists would term *the moves* on me. Back in school, Prue had been impossibly cool, beautiful, untouchable. We'd been friends in that very specific way you were friends with one of twenty-six people connected only by their choice of a ridiculously exclusive preparatory school. *This* version of Prue Nelson felt ... less exclusive. She'd been to the bathroom six times in forty minutes. Hadn't stopped talking for more than five seconds at a time. Her hand landed on my knee about three minutes in, and had so far crept to my upper thigh. I noticed the nails were painted black, chipped and peeling.

"Have you been to the campus? Jesus fucked it's fucking *huge*, all that alumni money just *pouring* in. It's *metastasized*."

She'd led me to a bar around the corner. It had no sign, no lights visible from the outside. You had to walk down a flight of steps to open a rusting metal door to get in. An after-hours joint where the bartenders, wait staff, dishwashers, bouncers, and line cooks gathered to decompress. Make dubious social connections. Prue had ordered us both doubles, had already consumed three, and didn't seem even slightly drunk.

"You hear about Hector? This little shithole downtown, he used to play gigs. He was *good*! Head caved in right on stage. Shit's brutal."

The hand crept up. I ran some calculations. At this pace Prue would be giving me a fairly professional hand job in about five minutes. Decisions were going to have to be made. I imagined that Prue was vibrating slightly, blurry from microscopic motion, like a hummingbird.

I looked around. Incredibly, the place seemed even dirtier than Narrowbacks. I started to itch. The small, wobbly table was covered in a sort of pelt. My glass had a greasy thumbprint on one side. I had a vision of the near future that involved a restroom stall that had last been cleaned in the previous century and Prue Nelson's underpants. Also, I assumed, last cleaned in the previous century.

"Okay, I gotta pee," she finally slurred. She stood and swayed over me for a moment. "Don't even think of sneaking in there to try any funny business, mister!" she added, cackling. "Oh, gosh, I'm so glad I ran into you, Quentin!"

This was followed by a knowing look and a wink. When she turned and walked to the restrooms she put some extra mustard in her hips.

I broke into a sweat. Which was either panic or the beginnings of a terminal disease recently acquired from my shot glass. I sat for a moment hearing the clink of bottles in the pool and Eddie Vedder in the air. I wondered what Prue saw in her mind when she thought of the Outing Party and Amy Keaton. Or if she thought of it at all.

I stood up. *Not tonight, venereal disease*, I thought. *Jesus, give me back the wheel.*

I started walking toward the front door. Cats or no cats, if I was going to die it was going to be breathing the chromium-tinged air of Bergen City, not suffocated between Prue Nelson's thighs as she did bumps off the toilet seat.

"Quentin!"

Her voice, outraged, sliced through me. Considering how hopped up on goofballs she was, odds were she now possessed superhuman strength and speed. An Apex Predator startled from a nap.

I ran.

I burst out onto the street and experienced a kind of Panic High, the years falling away as I ran.

"Quentin! What the *fuck*?!"

She was behind me, and a splash of adrenaline got my knees higher.

I steered unconsciously toward the Anderson house. The old neighborhood now seemed unchanged. I slowed down to a staggering walk, breathing hard. Chest hurting. I took each turn instinctively and then I stopped. The empty lot was like a missing tooth. I could picture the old place, a house where I'd spent just about every afternoon and evening for a decade straight. Video games. Movie marathons. Walking up to the yellow caution tape that had taken the place of the walls, smoke in my nose, I knew exactly where the front door would be, the little concrete step that tripped everyone, the big bay window.

I stood at the edge of the sidewalk. I stared at the black space. I pictured where the short hall had been. The stairs leading up to the second floor. The last place I'd seen her, the expression on her face as I left.

My eyes roamed around the soggy mess. There, sitting in the middle of the scorched waste, was the fucking cat.

Pontifuss Maximuss looked a little rough. She was thinner than the pudgy thing posing for photos on her social media accounts. Her fur was matted and snarled. We stared at each other across the ruined marsh of Rho's house. I heard her again: *Listen, you're my only friend.*

I pushed the yellow caution tape down. Stepped over the edge. My foot sank down into the muck. It felt warm. I froze up. Could feel the skin rash. The fungal infections. The shit under my toenails that would require scraping, scraping, scraping. Then I saw Rho at the top of the stairs, staring down at me. Her disappointment almost a physical force.

The fucking cat mewed at me. Sad and bereft. It stared at me as I approached. The soggy, charred ground sucked at my feet. Burning my clothes no longer sufficient. On the third step, I lost my shoe, the warm ground refusing to release it. On the fifth step, I was sweating and shoeless. The fucking cat just sat there, staring at me, on the spot where the stairs used to be.

I imagined Rho at the top. The news story said she was found in the second-floor hallway. No evidence she'd tried to escape. It was like I'd left her standing there and she hadn't moved. That I kept drifting further and further, miles and miles away, and she just waited for the flames to come.

Pontifuss Maximuss mewed. I took another step forward and sank above my ankle. I managed to swing my other leg over and it sank in even deeper. The fucking cat just watched me, blinking slowly. The smell of smoke was making me ill.

I frowned. Was I getting shorter? Or was the ground rising up to greet me? I had the sensation of falling in slow motion. Panic. Being enveloped by *filth*. The toxins and smoke smell becoming my world. Ashy mud pushing into crevices. The ground was the consistency of pudding, simultaneously too liquid to hold me up and too dense for easy movement. I frowned and reached for Pontifuss Maximuss. The fucking cat let out a distinct growl and danced back a few steps.

Gravity got soft and insistent. I sank, faster and faster. The burned earth, muddy with soot, swallowed my legs. My hips. My belly. And then the soil was crowding in and choking me, pushing into my mouth, my nose, my—

I sank into the mire and saw her waiting for me.

Clara

Chapter 26: Waste Not

An Account of the Death of Clara Addams in August, 2010

"Still seeing that girl? The artist?"

"*Performance* artist."

"Sorry—the *so-called* artist, then?"

"No. She died."

Clarkson hesitated. "Shit. I'm sorry."

Flick shrugged. "We were only together a few months."

Clarkson frowned around his pint glass. "You were after her for years, man."

Flick shrugged again, studying the amber liquid in his glass. "I just thought she was hot."

"For years you thought she was hot, is my point."

"So, what if I did?"

"Settle down, son. My point is you knew her for more than a few months. Don't be a sociopath about her dying. How'd she go?"

Flick looked down at his glass again. "Hard to explain."

"I'm bright," Clarkson said, holding his glass up and looking at the bartender expectantly. "I am very good at comprehending the incomprehensible ways of my fellow man, even if I didn't go to a fancy, weirdly tiny private school like your girlfriend. Ex-girlfriend. Dead ex-girlfriend."

Flick sighed and set down his whiskey. "She sort of ... gave up."

"She dumped you."

"No, she fucking didn't. She gave up. Just didn't see the point anymore, I guess."

"The point in dating you."

"The point in any of it. She stopped eating and kind of ... wasted away."

"I *will* need more than that to go on."

Flick visibly hesitated. "It involved an art project."

Clarkson leaned forward, long, curly brown hair sliding to obscure his eyes before he pushed it back, then pulled at the collar of the old, faded denim jacket—a jacket too young for him, Flick thought suddenly. "Look, I know I can be an asshole, say all the wrong things, but ... now you absolutely *must* tell me. Did a heavy bronze phallus fall on her? Did she succumb to lead paint poisoning?"[1]

Flick shifted uncomfortably. He was wearing a pair of green work pants, a blue button-down, and a scraggly old sport coat, an outfit that could be seen repeated again and again in photos of him throughout the years. It had given him the effect of a college adjunct for most of his life. "It was a hunger strike."

"Brutal," Clarkson said. "So ... she offed herself?"

"No, it was a project. She did stuff like this—her art always involved *her*, her body. She carved tattoos in her arms, once, with a knife. Shapes and names, took photos. She called it 'Scabs.' She thought that was gonna get her a lot of attention, but no one cared."

"Brutal."

"This one was a hunger strike. She was going to stop eating, take a photo of herself every day for months, portraits, showing her shrinking, or something. Called it 'Guilt.'"

Clarkson paused with his glass partway to his mouth. "Huh. Guilt, huh?"

Flick squinted. "What?"

Clarkson hesitated in a way he rarely did. "You know she killed someone."

Flick did a series of odd things. He looked around as if worried someone was watching them, covered his glass as if afraid it might hear, and rolled his shoulders as if preparing for a fight.

"She didn't," he said. "It was high school, and she was at a party, and one of her classmates died. It was an accident."

Clarkson shook his head. "No. Look, this goes back a while. You were—where were you, Calgary? Someplace Canadian.

---

1 Clarkson first met Clara in late 2009 when Flick invited him to her performance piece, KEEPSAKES. Held in the back room of a nail salon on Bleecker Street, Clara sat on a large, ornately bedazzled chair behind a card table. She was wearing just a bathrobe. On the table was an arrangement of scissors, razors, hair clippers, toenail clippers, and tweezers. As he entered, he was handed a card that instructed the audience to use the tools to take whatever they wished from Clara—hair, nails, eyelashes, etc.

Clara disrobed. After some initial hesitation, Flick got the performance started by cutting a lock of her hair as Clara stared straight ahead, unmoving. The small crowd, fueled by cheap wine and a lack of oxygen in the small, hot room, was surprisingly enthusiastic, and within thirteen minutes Clara had been shaved and plucked completely bald, her fingers and toes clipped painfully short, some bleeding. Clara, who had rented the room for three hours, panicked and summoned Flick. She spent fifteen minutes trying to convince him to take her place and let himself be shaved. Flick refused, and Clarkson decided he did not care much for Clara Addams.

A couple of days, me and Clara met for a drink. We had a conversation."[2]

"Really."

"It wasn't like that. Come on, nothing like that. And it wasn't like we were close—that was the only time we hung out without you, actually."

"Okay."

"You introduce people, expect them to get along for your sake. It's not like you walk away and we all go limp, existing

---

2 He chose a place where he and Flick usually met up, a steak joint with good cocktails. He remembered Clara walking in wearing enormous sunglasses. He thought they had to have been custom made. The lenses were the size of coasters. She looked like the alien from some low-budget '80s sci-fi movie they ran on the less-reputable cable channels after midnight.

She was wearing a heavy coat that draped her like a tent. It created the illusion that she was gliding along the floor, like the nun in *The Blues Brothers*. People watched her. Phones came out.

When she got to the table, she stared down at the chair like she'd never seen one before. Or like she hadn't taken the logistics of her coat into account. After a moment's blank-faced consideration, she lifted one edge of the coat and enveloped the chair, then lowered herself down, leaning forward and laying one arm over the other.

When the waiter arrived, Clarkson ordered a double bourbon. For strength. He and the server stared at Clara for several long moments. She finally turned her head slightly toward the waiter, the only visible sign that she was looking at him.

"I want the driest Stoli martini you can make. Glance at the vermouth. *Glance* at it. Make it dirty. Muddy. Disgusting. Shake it. Jump up and down, get your *back* into it. For a long time. Longer than you think necessary. Four olives. Save the shaker ice."

The waiter and Clarkson exchanged a glance—a whole conversation wishing each other luck with the rest of their Clara experience.

just for you."

"I said OKAY, okay?"

Clarkson nodded. "Okay. So, we met for a drink, just being friendly. An old high school friend of hers had just died."

"James," Flick confirmed.

"Yeah, James. She called him Jimmy. He died and she was sad, so we met for a drink, and she told me ... she told me there was guilt around this girl, Amy, who died at a party. She didn't make it sound like it was an accident. There were what you might call suspicious circumstances." He leaned back and signaled their waiter with one extended arm. "That was the word she used, man. *Guilt*."

Flick frowned. "Like ... what, she killed her?"

Clarkson hesitated. "Well ... something like that."

Flick gulped at his drink.

"But it wasn't that," Clarkson said hurriedly. "Or not just that. It was—she was being haunted. She was seeing the dead girl—the one that died. Hand to God, that's what she told me."

"Amy," Flick said. "Had an accident or something."

"Yeah."

"Haunted," Flick said, as if tasting the word. "She didn't tell me any of that."

"Maybe she meant to, then ran out of time." Clarkson swallowed. "You know."

Flick shook his head. "Nah. That was her, that was Clara. I'm not even sure I ever liked her, you know? Even now. She was moody and ... blank. That was what got me with her. You couldn't get anything out of her. A smile, a frown, a response—

nothing. I got obsessed. My whole day became all about trying to get a reaction. A smile? A laugh? A touch on the arm? Red fucking letter day. Banner day. Then, a moment later, she was acting like you were made of shit and she got some on her shoe. Maddening woman."

"I saw it. Your eyes followed her. Couldn't stay away."

"I just wanted to get a reaction. I wanted ... I wanted her to acknowledge me."

Clarkson was silent for a moment. "She never paid me much attention. Always thought she didn't like me. I was fuckin' shocked when she suggested we meet. But she was ... haunted. That's a good word for it, really. Said a bunch of her old friends were dead, and she kept seeing this Amy." He shrugged. "She had issues, man."

A ghostly smile touched Flick's lips. "She was an *artist*, man—"

"*Performance* artist. That's, like, *extra* artisty."

"—of *course* she had issues."

Clarkson accepted a fresh beer, the waiter racing off without a word. "You think that's why she ... did it?"

"I told you, she didn't. It was an art project."

"Called *Guilt*."

"An *art project*. Like I said, she was always doing crazy stunts like that, always thought the world would notice and give a shit. She had it all planned out—talked to a doctor about how much water to drink, how to avoid bedsores, how to check her vital signs and what to look for, vitamins and supplements. She didn't *intend* to die."

"Okay," Clarkson said. "Death by misadventure. Death by *art*. A series of unfortunate events. Mistakes were made. What went wrong?"

Flick studied his glass again. "She got competitive."

Clarkson cocked his head. "Around starving to death?"

"Clara originally planned to go three months. Ninety days. Then she heard about another artist, out in San Francisco, who'd gone on a hunger strike for a live installation at a gallery space. One *hundred fifteen* days."

"Oh, shit."

"She was afraid she wouldn't make an impact."

"Performance art is notoriously cutthroat." Clarkson traced the rim of his glass with one finger. "One assumes an arms race of literally starving artists. What was the reaction? To the piece and ... the rest?"

"There wasn't any."

Clarkson cocked his head.

"Mistakes were made."

Clarkson raised one eyebrow a calibrated quarter inch.

"A series of mistakes."

"Choice of career, check. Choice of boyfriend, check. Choice—"

Flick shook his head. "Stop, okay? She *died*, man."

Clarkson opened his mouth, then a sequence of expressions on his face told a story of imposed self-control. Finally, he nodded. "You're right. Sorry. What happened?"

Flick sighed. "It started with the sleep-eating."

Clarkson's eye twitched as if he was struggling to control

his response. "Sleep. Eating."

"The first week, she's eating nothing. Drinking water, swallowing vitamins. But she *gains* weight. She's really upset. She can't figure it out. Then she notices: food in the fridge is missing. She sets up a camera in the kitchen, and watches herself: she's sleepwalking into the kitchen, making herself meals."

"She didn't notice—"

"She was also sleep-dishwashing."

"You should have married her." Clarkson put his hands up. "Retracted, with apologies. One assumes she did the obvious thing and threw away all the food?"

Flick grimaced and sipped his drink. "In this economy? No, she paid one of her neighbors, a guy who does handyman stuff around the building, to strap her to the bed."

"Naturally." Clarkson's face twitched again as he fought off an impolite grin. "That sounds ... messy."

"Bedpan."

"Oh. Naturally."

"That solved the sleep-eating problem, but then she realized she was biting her nails and chewing on her fingers. And she started to worry about whether that counted as *eating*, whether it was contributing calories."

"*Naturally*."

"So, she had mittens taped onto her hands. Like, layers of duct tape."

There was a moment of silence. "And?" Clarkson prompted.

"And ... that's when I got out. I told her she was being reckless, and we didn't have much of a relationship anymore. We did nothing, we never went anywhere, she was just in bed all day. I thought maybe my storming out would wake her up, a little."

"But it didn't."

Flick closed his eyes. "The rest I heard about. I wasn't there. There was an assistant she hired, but they quit a few days after me, apparently. I didn't know."

"Good to get that in the record."

Flick drained his glass and slammed it down on the table between them. "Fuck off. So, no one checked on her. And she couldn't get the straps off, because of the mittens. And she was weak, because she'd gone longer than she was supposed to. And there was no more food in the place anyway. So, she just ... lay there. And died. They say—" Flick hesitated, then plunged ahead. "They say she didn't really try to get free. No signs of struggle."

Clarkson pursed his lips, thinking carefully. "Look, that's not your fault, right? She was trying to do art. But ... that's an *impressive* list of poor decisions."

"Yeah." Flick rolled his glass between his hands. "Hey—how?"

"How what?"

"How did she say Amy appeared to her?"

"I'm not sure. She said ... she said it was like she kept catching a glimpse out of the corner of her eye. Like, she'd swear someone was standing just off her side, and she knew it was Amy, but when she turned to look there was no one there."

"Shit."

"What?"

Flick signaled the bartender. "I've ... I've ... I think I've seen Clara. A few times. Since. Just like that, too—out of the corner of my eye. Then, nothing."

"Fuuuck."

"Yeah."

"But there's no such thing, right? Ghosts?"

"Of course not. She was in my head. Just like this Amy girl was in hers. That's all."

Clarkson toasted him. "Maybe that's how ghosts work, where ghosts live, right? In our heads. We think if we move away from this place, we can get away. But we can't. We carry them with us. Everywhere we go."

"Everywhere we go," Flick echoed softly, staring at something in an unfocused way.

Clarkson drained his glass. "Fuck, that got grim. What are you up to this weekend?"

Flick blinked. "What? Oh—no plans."

"Come 'round and we'll do something."

Flick turned his head suddenly, then looked back at Clarkson. "Maybe. No, probably not. I think... I'm beat. Done in. I'll just stay in and have a rest."

"Suit yourself. Talk soon, then."

"Yeah."

FIVE FUNERALS

Desmond

Chapter 27: And Scene

An Account of the Death of Desmond Brady

by Desmond Brady in February, 2012.

The fuck of it is, my death was the greatest performance of my life, and no one will see it. Well, no one who *matters*.

The other fuck of it is, this was a commercial for a fucking eczema medication.

I didn't want to do it. It was one of those jobs that come along with so many requirements that you kind of mentally reject it right off the bat. You see these pharma commercials—they're fucking nightmares. They need to show you, the proud eczema sufferer, living your life To The Fullest, right? So it's all this random shit, but it's *exhausting* random shit. My particular friend, Randy, did a pharma commercial for some mysterious pill designed to temporarily cure some other kind of body horror last year and he warned me: they offer you peanuts for, like, feature-length shoots. It's just a fucking commercial but you're booked for days and they're *physical*.

So I told Marnie no, at first. No fucking way was I going to be skiing, building a snowman, riding a snowmobile—all while freezing my nuts off. Not for *peanuts*. Not for the insultingly low rate they're offering.

But then Marnie says—slowly, so I'll understand—that my last gig was two years ago. That I'm unpopular with casting directors. That I have no name recognition. That, before I know it, I'll be in my 40s and that's where careers go to die. And I had that moment when you think about your recent career and you realize you're living on fumes and yes, it's true, *no one* knows who the fuck you are and yes, it's true, a pharma commercial for an eczema medication that pays peanuts for like a week's work is the best you're doing these days.

It wasn't that long ago that I was on the right track. Twenty years old and starring in *That Old Time Medicine* on Broadway. Fucking *Broadway*. Not the most money and not the biggest hit of all time, but for six amazing months there I was every night, hoofing it in front of the greatest audience in the world. Half-empty house, but it was still the Great White Way.

I remember thinking that all those fuckers at BCP were fucking *jealous*. Prue and her goddamn poetry. Victor and the way he sneered at everyone. Leo, money-grubbing Leo. Jimmy and his biceps.

And then I'd think of Amy. That's a real dick-softener.

You don't know you're in a decline until you're at the bottom of the funnel. There had been a lot of auditions, after the show closed. I booked a lot of commercials. I liked commercials—easy money, no one in the business looked down on them, useful for your resume and your reel. I landed a couple of sitcoms, flying out to L.A. and up to Vancouver to shoot for a day or two or three. But nothing stuck. Nothing got *sticky*. I didn't have any viral moments.

So I called Marnie back and said I'd take the fucking eczema commercial. And she said, "Great! Here's all the things I told them you were skilled at."

I figured I could fake the archery a little. And I'd always been graceful, so the high wire stuff was probably okay. And the running would be just, you know, *running*, and as long as it wasn't too far I'd be okay there, too. But there was a whole fucking sequence of me riding a snowmobile, and Marnie had assured everyone that I could ride a snowmobile like a champ. Had practically been born riding one.

Well, if you're reading this you know that's exactly how I died. And I swear to you I had a premonition. The reason I'm such a good actor is that I'm slightly psychic. The antennae is switched on just a *bit*. You max that out and you're crazy; you're one of those people shouting in the streets about the coming End of Days. But you have, like, 5 percent of it? You're open. You're a receiver. And you can give that back to people. I've got that, and I knew that if I ever had the right opportunity, a *chance*, to show it to enough people—critical mass, no pun and all—I'd be a huge star.

You might think: he's crazy. He's arrogant. But, man, I *felt* it. Audiences, me, live—I felt that connection. People were in the palm of my hand. If I ever had a sold-out show, enough asses in seats, or just one goddamn influencer worth the name, I could have changed the world. You can't fake that.

You have to keep working. If you stop, if you give up, what then? I didn't go to college. I moved to New York and started going to cattle calls, knocking on agents' doors. If I don't get the fucking eczema commercial, there's literally nothing else. And I've never been on a snowmobile in my fucking *life*. I wasn't like the other kids when I was in school, the Keatons and the Addamses and the Nelsons, kids who learned to ski as babies, kids whose families had posh *chateaus* where they frolicked in the snow all the time. I spent my winter breaks doing workshops and community theater. All I ever did with snow was shovel it when Dad woke me up in his bathrobe with the shovel in one hand. So, I had to at least get familiar with the safe operation of a snowmobile.

"You don't *need* to know," Marnie had said. "No one cares. And it's easy."

"I don't *need* to," I said. "But this is a *craft*. You know I don't believe in half-assing things. Besides, it's a one-day class. I'm up, I get familiar, I'm back the next day and when they say, 'Ride that snowmobile like a man who thought his snowmobiling days were over because of a socially-crippling skin condition,' I will be prepared to nail that vibe."

"For fuck's sake," Marnie growled, her traditional way of ending our conversations.

The White Mountains are in New Hampshire and there are snowmobiles there, so I drove up on my doomed research trip, borrowing my roommate Iggy's car with a vague promise of compensation both monetary and service-oriented. I spent pretty much every dime I had on gas and a night at a motel. The commercial wasn't going to make me rich, but it would cover these expenses and then some, and if it aired a lot—and these pharma commercials air *constantly*—I might make a decent lump from it, so the investment was worth it.

As I drove I contemplated how to inhabit the body of a man who had once suffered terrible eczema but was now free to take off his long-sleeve shirts, hang out with friends, ride his snowmobile without fear of getting into a terrible accident and being airlifted to a hospital where the doctors and nurses will cut off his clothes with sharp medical scissors and then recoil in horror at his ravaged, reddened skin.

The answer, as always, was Amy.

Before Amy died, my acting had been rote and artificial. I guess all high school kids suck at everything. But her death was a gift to me, because it was an all-purpose source of pathos. I need to be sad? I simply recall that moment when we discovered her and I thought my life was truly over—I'd never cried before, not really. And rarely since. But in that moment I burst into real, hot tears—and I can get there any time I want by sliding, mentally, into that moment. I need to show anger? I just rewind a bit—Amy was a bitch. A *spectacular* bitch. I was regularly furious with Amy, so all I have to do is remember the time she told me she could smell my onion breath from the back row of the auditorium when BCP's drama club staged *Guys and Dolls* and boom! I am furious. Love? In our junior year, Amy and I had two weeks of detention together for two totally different infractions, and we had an extended, intense *Breakfast Club* experience. I fell deeply in love. We bonded and shared secrets. When detention ended she pretended it had never happened, but now when I need to remember what it feels like to be in love with someone, Amy is my go-to.

The best thing that ever happened to my acting career was Amy. I can't use anyone else. Amy was the perfect blend of not very close to me, yet known intimately well, and also: Dead.

It's fucking freezing, which is good. I can remember this misery and use it when they film me on a closed set. I'll be able to convey not just a man recently freed from the prison of eczema, but also a man who knows exactly how it feels when your balls are tiny, frozen raisins.

I arrive at the snowmobile rental place a little early, check in for the lessons, and begin hoping that I'm the only student. A group of loud, chattering women arrive, but the class is small, so it's not too bad. The other five students are a group of women on some sort of Hen's Weekend, one of them getting married and the rest to support the bride. I'm a student of human nature—you never know when you'll pick up a tic or habit that you can use to make a character feel more real—so I study them. They're staying at a Bed and Breakfast on a package deal that includes a bunch of excursions, and as I sidle closer they're discussing the hygiene—or lack thereof—of the B&B's hot tub. They're all wearing what look like brand-new black snowsuits and big, Russian-style fur caps.

As I watch, they ignore our gray-haired instructor as he grits his teeth and mutters, and they hold some kind of ceremony, where one produces a faded sash from her pocket that reads BRIDE and trades it with another of the Hens for a sash that reads MISS BEHAVING. Then the other Hens pull sashes from their pockets and they all put them on with a solemnity that kind of alarms me.

Then they hoot and holler and it's clear that they're already tipsy from lunch. The instructor heroically ignores both their lack of sobriety and the sashes—very wise—and struggles to review turning safely, how to brake properly, and the dangers of overturning the ride. As Marnie promised, it's not terribly difficult. But it will provide all the data I need to offer my corporate masters a terrific performance. And you never know who will see a commercial. The actors in the infamous Folgers Incest Commercial are still being interviewed about it to this day. Why no one hires *me* to be in a virally creepy and unintentionally horny commercial, I don't know.

When the class is over, Gray Hair shakes my hand and tells me the Hens have paid for a guided tour, and suggests I join them. I glance at the girls and they're passing a flask around and cackling—I don't use the word lightly, there's just no better way to describe the sound of their collective laughter—so I politely decline and he takes his tourists off on their snowmobiles.

I stand there and watch them ride away, then glance at the snowmobile I'd been training on. I go inside the office, where a fresh-faced kid with the sort of wind-blown hair and red skin of someone born into the snow and wind sits behind the register.

"Need any help?" he says brightly. I hate bright people. Tone it down, I say. There's a loudness that doesn't require noise. You get it a lot when you're doing, like, off-off-off Broadway. People in the audience being loud as hell without making a sound, letting you know how *imperially bored* they are.

"Just browsing," I say.

He nods, and I pretend to shop. I know how to do a bit of business—even if you're just Extra #32, you learn to always be doing something that will catch the eye of a casting director—so I do a convincing routine where I pretend to seriously consider some gloves that are supposed to be worn *under* your main gloves, like an insulation layer.

"Those are the best," the kid says. I look over at him. He's got sandy hair that's long on top and short on the sides, and he's one of those kids whose limbs are too long for his body. Everything will catch up in a few years, but right now he's like a Gumby version of himself.

I ask myself if my eczema sufferer is the sort to wear gloves *under* their gloves. I decide—seriously, this is my job!—that he wouldn't, because of the discomfort factor. Even if the miracle drug I'm plugging has cured your skin disorder and given you a new lease on life—the ability to snowmobile like a Normal Person—old habits die hard. A lifetime of minimizing skin contact would kick in, I decide. When I turn to thank the kid for his attempt to help me, I jump: he's standing right next to me.

"First time?"

I nod carefully. "Yeah."

"You gotta respect it. The machine *and* the cold."

I squint at him. He can't be more than eighteen. I'm offended. You don't get to be a broke, unknown actor over thirty just to be lectured by a kid about snowmobiles. I run my eye up and down his lanky, Gumby-ass frame. This kid had been born into snowmobile royalty. Him and his friends and his family probably snowmobile everywhere. To church. To get coffee. To school. He could walk into my audition and get the role without even trying, without even having a shitty high school production of *Guys and Dolls* on his resume.

"Got it," I said, turning and making for the door. "I've had my fill of cold, anyway. Back to the hotel and a warm bath for me!"

The kid says nothing. He looks like he doesn't believe me.

Outside, I walk directly to my snowmobile. I hop back on and fire it up. I drove all the way here, after all, might as well get more familiar with it. The more used to it I am, the more impressed people will be when I shoot my scenes depicting the power of clear skin. I figure I'll go for a spin around, have some fun, have it back in place with plenty of time to spare. And I have serious reservations about the kid's work ethic, so I don't think I'll have any trouble.

As I'm pulling away, I have one of those Antennae Moments. I turn and see Gumby running after me, waving his arms, shouting. And I hit the gas. I'm stealing a snowmobile for *art*. This is too important for my career, I think—this commercial is all I have, and I'm not going to let this asshole ruin it. *That* thought is depressing as hell, so then I'm also stealing a snowmobile out of spite.

It's fun. Without Gray Hair scowling at me, I can open her up. They really aren't hard to handle, though I take the first turn a bit too fast and almost tip the whole thing over. Exhilarating, really.

I pick a path at random and zoom along. When I slow down

for the next turn, being careful—because I *can*, contrary to popular opinion, be taught—I hear another snowmobile racing up behind me. I slow down to look and almost crash into a tree, because someone is chasing me, and for a split-second—just a moment—it looks just like Amy, twisted neck and all.

Crazy, I know. Amy has been dead for a long time. And Gumby is a much more likely suspect—outraged at my lack of *respect for the machine*. And yet, terror and adrenaline burn through me.

I turn back and gun the engine. The snowmobile leaps forward and I almost fall backwards, and then I'm losing control, off the trail, careening down a sharp incline, avoiding trees completely by accident. It's actually remarkable, the number of trees I fail to smash into.

Then I hit something buried deep in the snow, and everything goes silent. The vibration of the snowmobile vanishes, the noise of the engine cuts, and I am in the air. I land with teeth-chattering impact, several bones shattering, and roll into a tree, where I lay in agony. Or what *should* be agony. I'm not screaming, though, because the wind's been knocked out of me. I realize that despite my injuries I don't feel anything. Maybe I'm in shock. Or it's possible I'm paralyzed. Either way, I lay there shivering but not in excruciating pain. I'm recording it all. When Marnie books me a commercial requiring me to feign agonizing pain after an accident, I'm going to have it *nailed*.

Then I hear steps. Boots crunching in the snow.

My antennae keep feeding me fear and terror, terror and fear, like this person is here to hurt me—to hurt me *more*, which seems scientifically impossible. So, I put everything I have into my performance. I open my eyes and stare sightlessly. I force myself to stop shivering, to lie perfectly still. I am death. I am dead. I put everything I have into it, I remember how Amy looked, the stillness, that very specific stillness that conveys lifelessness. I picture it and I become it. If I'm already dead, there's no reason to do anything else to me, after all.

The footsteps come close, then stop.

There is a long moment of quiet, and I am triumphant. I don't flinch. I don't breathe. I don't move a single muscle. All of my training, my technique comes to bear, and I am the perfect imitation of a dead man.

After a few seconds, I hear the footsteps receding, convinced. I hold my shit together until I am certain they have gone. But when I decide it is safe to move again, I find that I can't. I have become death, truly.

And I think: *And, scene.*

Una

Chapter 28: Manhunt Ha Terminado

An Account of the Death of Una Taylor in November, 1995

by Cassidy DiFrancesca

I went to college looking for adventure. What I got was Una. Which was fine, except I already had an Una, an impossibly beautiful girl swaddled in pastels and unicorn decals that boys swooned over. Her name is Caitlyn, and according to our parents, she is perfect. Mom and Dad were so thrilled with her they immediately had me, clearly hoping for a delayed twin and instead getting ... well, *me.*

Our house is small, so there was no escape from Cate. I love my sister but also hated spending every moment of my life with her, hearing from teachers how smart she was as I followed her through school.

Dorm day. Wore my boots. The big ones. Dyed my hair. I hate my hair. Wore Mom's old dress. Mom's dress hides my legs. Was excited to meet new people. Moving day! Big deal. The endless possibilities. Like 10,000 people attend Rutgers every year. I felt like my chances at being someone interesting were pretty good. I wanted to make an impression. Plus, there would be no Christopher. Well, there might be *christophers* but no gorgeous, Unattainable, cruel Christopher.

But then I get to the dorm, and I walk in, and there's ... Una. She's like a clone of my sister. I am doomed to spend my life with beautiful girls, the summer babes who always smell like suntan lotion.

When I say beautiful, I mean it, too. Objectively. Not on the inside, not "in her way," not her soul or her mind. She was objectively, physically beautiful. Tall, but not intimidatingly or freakishly so. Long legs. Graceful—which, *trust* me, is a big part of it. Round face, big eyes with the long lashes people kill for, small nose. Her light brown hair was naturally slightly wavy and looked better the messier it got. She smiled easily and her laugh was goofy.

My first thought was that it was going to be a long year. One look at her and I thought I could predict every CD she'd brought, every show she watched, every poster she'd put up on her side of the room. I could do this because I'd spent so much time with Cate. I knew the type.

But I didn't. That night, Una cried. In her sleep. She was *asleep* and crying. And I realized that Una wasn't just pretty. She woke up crying most nights and had nightmares. She screened her calls and was always just *sad*.

Sad is good. It's a tonic for girls. Sadness just *emphasized* Una's hotness, because nothing makes a woman more attractive in this world than depression, which sinks the cheekbones and cinches the waist. Una was a doll. Standing next to Una, I wanted to die. Life is *unfair*.

Obsessed? Maybe. This had happened before. Kimberly in seventh grade. So pretty, I just liked looking at her. It was worse with Una. She looked good in anything. Overalls? Amazing. Little black dress? Fuckable. Jeans and a T-shirt? Everyone wants to know where she bought them.

Me? Clothes always looked secondhand on me. My hair? A malevolent sentience made it impossible to comb.

Una's sadness was like a heavy gas. It filled the room and smothered her. It was disturbing and briefly made me question my worldview. Because if Una Taylor could be sad with her rich family and her perfectly shaped long legs and that hair—if a girl like Una could be that sad, what hope was there for the rest of us?

You do the whole Found Family thing freshman year.

We were on the Engineering campus, but we were both liberal arts. We had to take a bus to get to College Avenue. We were isolated. The other girls in our suite all knew each other. From high school. Were on a sorority fast track. We never saw them. Our social opportunities were limited.

There was Doug. Tall, quiet. He'd been a fat, pimply kid until quite recently, you could tell, and still behaved like a fat, pimply kid. He had no idea what he was doing with his life. Some people get energized by that kind of purposeless drifting. Doug was the other kind: he was terrified.

His eyes followed Una. I'd seen this with Cate. Doug was so obviously in lust with her from the moment he saw her it was kind of amusing in a pitiful way. Because there were only a few certainties in life: the Sun would eventually swell up and destroy us all. The government would get its tax money. And Una Taylor was never going to fuck Doug Gailey.

Ben was heavyset. A sweaty boy. *Sweaty* was his natural state. He would eventually grow into a man who carried a small towel with him everywhere he went, draped over his shoulder, to mop away his constant sweat. He would lose jobs and opportunities because of The Sweat (possibly more because of the Towel). He was sweet, though, with a ready smile and kinky hair that you could sweep up with your hand, making it stand up like a fez. We did it to him all the time. I was jealous. He had *interesting* hair. I just had *bad* hair.

We became a quartet in that weird way you bond with randos in a dormitory, people who for one semester are the most important people in your life and then you never see again. I heard things here and there about Doug and Ben after Freshman year as they grew ever more distant like comets sailing off into the darkness, giving the stories the appropriate amount of my attention, which is to say: not much.

The boys all chased Una.

Your average eighteen-year-old boy has the emotional intelligence of a five-year-old boy. What they lack there they more than make up for with cunning and predatory instinct. You don't survive high school with two x chromosomes without learning at least some of the tricks. The boys on the third floor of Hershisher Hall demonstrated a wide range of tactics when it came to Una Taylor. I'd seen it with Cate. Boys are all the same, but they don't believe it.

Doug tried to demonstrate his worth by being protective. Knowing what *he* wanted to do to Una at the first opportunity, he regarded all other men as dangerous sociopaths. Doug's mating dance was being a buzzkill. He was constantly ensuring that Una was safe. Under *his* care and feeding, of course. Doug's form of sexual assault was much slower and less violent than everyone else's. Chances of success: zero.

Ben fell in love every few minutes. Deeply, passionately, torturedly. He pursued the objects of his desire by doing absolutely nothing and taking great pains to appear sexless and harmless in their presence. As if waiting for the world to slowly kill off all the alpha males until he was the only option left. Chances of success: very, very low, but not zero, because sometimes a girl just becomes *exhausted*.

I don't think Una noticed. Maybe she was too sad to care. I assumed she was worn out from being chased by boys her entire life, and that was true enough, but it wasn't why she was so sad and tired. That had something to do with a girl named Amy, a name she sometimes yelled out when she managed to sleep.

Una didn't sleep much. I would wake up at any random moment at night and she'd be awake. Sitting on her bed, in the dark. In the study rooms, reading. She told me that she felt herself disappearing. Every day less and less of her.

When she did sleep, it was in odd places. Places she'd been trying to stay awake. Upright, propped against a wall. Slumped on the fire stairs two floors down. If you shook her awake, she'd startle and look at you like you were some kind of monster. Sometimes she shouted that name: Amy.

I'd never slept alone in a room in my life. I kept waking up when she was gone. Horny boys are psychic. Ben and Doug started staying up. Entertaining Una. We began organizing night excursions. The Engineering campus was empty and seemed vast. We started just walking around in the middle of the night. Sometimes we played touch football in the quad; sometimes we held races. Una was up for anything that didn't involve sleeping, or being alone with her thoughts, or parties. You couldn't pay Una to go to a party.

We dredged up all the old schoolyard faves. We chalked hopscotch boards. Played Mother May I under the moonlight. We played games we'd never heard of, each of us importing something from our alien childhoods.

And Doug said, "Hey, we should play Manhunt."

We crashed out of the dorm. Invaded the golf course next to campus. At night, the course was a magical space of shadows and moonlight. There were wide open greens—turned gray in the dark—and wooded enclaves.

Manhunt was Hide and Seek for sophisticates. For people

who are no longer babies. The rules of the game were simple.

First, someone had to be It. This was done via acclamation, and Ben was too slow and got the duty. He accepted the honor with what appeared to be visceral dread.

Second, we scattered and hid while Ben counted to 100, eyes shut. We went laughing into the darkness.

That's it. Those are the rules.

I climbed a tree and sat for a while.

I watched Una run, long legs extended, hair flying, fucking majestic. I watched Doug follow at a walk, determined to fight off anyone who might try to get on top of her before he managed to implement his 27-year seduction plan.

For a little while I enjoyed the quiet. The peaceful breeze. Then I worried that everyone else had given up. Gone back to the dorm and left me. That was what Cate would have done. So, I climbed down and went looking for them.

I found Una sitting by the pond.

She crossed one ankle over the other, feeling the smooth skin of her shaved legs.

"I hate shaving my legs," she said quietly. "But boys just get so weird if you don't. Like they get *angry* if they touch you and it isn't what they expected."

She let me do the exhausting math. I knew that she'd had three boyfriends in high school and fooled around with three others. Six out of thirteen boys in her class in four years. The girl needed a *rest*.

The mood shifted. The thrill of the night and the open space of the course had worn off, and I was tired and cold. I didn't want to be out in the darkness. I went looking for the boys, leaving Una by the pond thinking sad girl thoughts. I couldn't find them. When I got back to the pond, Una was gone.

I was tempted to just go back to the dorm. Leave everyone to their fate. But you couldn't hate Una. Because of the sadness. And the prettiness. And she was kind of sweet, in her way. So, I went looking for her. To make sure she hadn't suffered a terrible fate. Like being lured into an unmarked van. Or a quiet, emotional conversation with Doug while he refused to meet her gaze and stole glances at her cleavage, and, oddly, her ankles.

Boys think we don't notice.

I found her just standing near a copse of trees on the edge of the course. A 1970s album cover in the flesh. Jeans, concert T-shirt, hair teased by the wind. She was, of course, crying. Silent, delicate tears. Even I was reluctant to disturb her, the way you're reluctant to disturb a fawn sleeping on your lawn or a kitten curled up in your lap.

Doug and Ben arrived on the scene almost simultaneously, preceded by their heavy breathing. They were closer to Una, and didn't see me. They both froze. Staring at her. Una was approaching such a combination of sorrow and physical beauty that sex cults could be established around a single discarded pair of her panties. I wondered how, exactly, the boys would make this moment of private pain all about their uncomfortable priapism. Before anyone could humiliate themselves, however, there was a rustling noise. After all that silence, adrenaline flooded me. We all froze in place, listening.

A small, dark shape emerged from the trees. It moved erratically, hunched over. In the silence, I could hear the thing making snuffling, grunting noises, and for a second, I thought that I had never seen anything like it. What looked like a long, sinuous tail dragged on the ground behind it as it prowled.

I stared. My heart pounded. I was suddenly five years old again, and I thought this was how I was going to die: devoured by a monster. Or some sort of golf course ghost. While Una wept silently and Ben and Doug tried futilely to hide their erections. This seemed appropriate for my ridiculous life.

A moment later, the creature stopped and looked at Una. Then it growled, a low, rumbling noise. The trees rustled again, and a taller, humanoid figure emerged.

"Don't worry, miss, his barks' much worse than—"

It was a dog. On a leash.

The dog reared back and launched itself at Una, growling. She spun and ran. She'd told me she once flirted with track and field in high school. A flirtation ruined by her *other* brief flirtation, with Mr. Reynolds, the track coach. But Una hadn't broken a sweat while conscious since my arrival. Sleep sweats didn't count as exercise, I didn't think.

A moment later, Ben and Doug bolted after her. Shouting her name. *Una! OOOOOOOOnnnnnnAAAAAAAA!*

Against the purple-black, star-filled sky Una was like a gazelle. Or a cheetah. Or whatever. Gliding along the grass with surprising, surefooted speed, pursued by an angry—or playful?—dog and three males. Doug looked like he was falling and missing the ground. The wind had pushed Ben's hair up into fez position, further reducing his already limited aerodynamics. And a wildly gesticulating man of middle years I later learned was named Richard McMurdo. He owned a house just off the golf course and liked to encourage his dog to shit on the course as often as possible due to an apparent beef with the owners that went back years.

As I was contemplating the strange beauty of this moment, Una suddenly vanished.

I would say *unexpectedly* vanished, but Una was a girl who was going to vanish someday. The only question was the precise details. I did not have *vanish into thin air after an evening of wine coolers and Manhunt* on my Bingo card, I'll admit.

One second, she was there, sprinting, the next, she was gone. The boys all staggered to a halt, no doubt wondering if they'd had a witch among them all this time. They collapsed onto the grass, gasping. Mr. McMurdo finally grabbed hold of his dog's leash and started back toward his house, grumbling.

I started running, some primitive instinct cutting through everything else. When I reached Ben and Doug I stopped, heart pounding.

I looked at the boys. And realized they were going to sit there. Do nothing. *Boys.*

I started walking. The golf course at night was an alien landscape. The moonlight pushed through a thin haze and made everything blurry, unfamiliar. The boys followed. Eager now that someone else was in the lead.

It was eerie. There was no sound, just my breathing and the boys' much louder breathing. Nothing moved. I opened my mouth to shout her name, but Doug gestured sharply, eyes wide, and I nodded. I felt it. The shadows, the silence, and I swallowed the shout. After the momentary chaos of the chase, I was suddenly unnerved and crept forward slowly. The grass unfolded gray and ominous, unbroken until I came close to the edge of a large hole.

It was a storm drain, its grating missing. I had a sudden vision of Una, running like a unicorn, loping along all grace and skinny, tapered legs, and then the ground vanishes beneath her and she's falling. I crept to the edge of the drain and peered down, but I couldn't see anything. I listened for a moment but didn't hear anything. The darkness and the silence were terrifying.

"What—what do we do?" Ben asked.

I turned and looked at them. Then I started running.

Manhunt was over.

I called the police from the dorm, out of breath and shaking. When they pulled her out, they said she'd landed on her head, basically. That she might have lingered for a while.

I didn't see much of Ben and Doug after that. Whenever we ran into each other they seemed eager to get away, like they were ashamed, or embarrassed.

I never got a new roommate that year. When I returned to school the next semester, her side of the room had been cleaned out and left bare, not a sign of her left. She'd finally disappeared, just like she said she would.

The nightmares started a few days later. Each one was the same. Una, broken and folded-over at the bottom of the storm drain. Asking me to come, asking me to help. Next to her, another presence. Someone I'd never seen before. Someone I found difficult to look at directly in the dream. And just like Una, I'd wake up screaming a name, soaked in sweat. Even when I started actively avoiding sleep, it crept up on me at the most unexpected moments. I'd startle awake, screaming that same name.

And then I always stare around in confusion and think, *Who the fuck is Amy?*

FIVE FUNERALS

James

Chapter 29: I Am Inevitable

An Account of The Death of James Forman in June, 2008

by Andrew Forman

You don't come to despise someone immediately. It happens in increments. You might *dislike* someone right after meeting them, but you don't hate them. That takes time—the meat in your youth and all that.

I didn't love Jimmy when we first met. I *liked* Jimmy, though. Everyone did. Jimmy was That Guy. He had a lopsided, disarming smile, he took everything well, he wasn't difficult, he wasn't an obvious creep. He had opinions, and his feelings could be hurt—the thing that a lot of guys don't understand is that being Overly Nice is a red flag. Never arguing, always agreeing—that shit is creepy as fuck. But Jimmy straddled it well—he was *easy* without being creepy. He was the sort of guy who knocked over your drink in a bar and apologized and bought you a new one and five minutes later your roommates are inviting him to your birthday party the next week and it all seems very natural. He was the sort of guy who just started showing up to birthday parties and after-work cocktails and then you suddenly realize you've been fucking him for six weeks. He was the sort of guy who you started sleeping with because he's easy to sleep with and never fusses or acts possessive and then suddenly you're at City Hall and you're 31 and you're marrying him because it's suddenly, disorientingly legal and you have no idea why aside from the fact that you can for the first time in history.

You feel like the last ten years of your life happened to someone else.

Then, shockingly, things *accelerate*. The time goes *faster*. Boom! You're 32 and you don't remember the last year at all. Boom! You're 34 and you're arguing with Your Person about getting a third dog. Boom! You're 35 and you sit at the dinner table watching Jimmy chew and a burning hot coal of doubt creeps into your brain and starts melting down to your throat.

The problem was simple: Jimmy was *easy*. As Oscar said, the very essence of romance is uncertainty. And Jimmy was a sure thing.

Jimmy didn't care where we went to dinner. He didn't care where we went on vacation. He was happy to watch whatever I wanted to watch. I bought him clothes. He wore them. I demanded his phone password. He gave it to me. At first, this was why I loved Jimmy. He was a man who never got upset, who didn't play games, who was genuinely happy pretty much all the time. People wanted to be around Jimmy.

The only darkness in Jimmy was at night, when he was asleep. He would have these terrible nightmares. I would awaken to him thrashing about, begging someone to forgive him, to leave him be, to understand. I'd wake him, and he'd surge up, sweating, and swear he couldn't remember a thing about it.

And I was disappointed.

Because no one tells you that when you meet someone as happy and perfect as Jimmy, it gets boring. It gets irritating. You start to feel put-on, you start to think he's just not telling you about all the bad stuff, because there *has* to be bad stuff. Which means he's lying to you. Gaslighting you.

And then you win the lottery.

I'd been contemplating Jimmy for months when it happened. I'd sit there and study him, suddenly feeling like he wasn't human, like he was some sort of automaton—an Agreeable Version 2.0, something you bought when you wanted zero pushback on every desire and decision. When you look at someone like that it's revelatory. Jimmy's hairline was solid, but the top of his head was thin and almost bald. He had blackheads all over his nose. He had an odor. It wasn't necessarily unpleasant, but once you notice something like that you can't unnotice it. You start to despise it.

But what I really came to despise about Jimmy was that easiness. Jimmy was so easy it was infuriating. Because you start to think that if the man has no opinion on anything, does he have an opinion on *you*? Jimmy just took everything as it came. Did I just *come* to him?

I began being angry at him all the time.

I started the Coffee Experiment. I brewed the coffee in the morning because Jimmy made shit coffee—he was, unsurprisingly, the sort who thought a coffee pod was the epitome of human development. The first time he served me pod coffee when I slept over at his old place, I waited until he was turned away and dumped it into the sink and almost broke up with him right there. But I was young and stupid. I thought: *I'll change him. I'll educate him.*

I failed. Jimmy drank any coffee I gave him. As an experiment, I started serving him really terrible coffee. Coffee that would get you arrested in any civilized relationship, coffee that should have had him dialing divorce lawyers. I used day-old grounds. I used store brand artificial sweeteners. I used oat milk, almond milk, and powdered milk. I burned it. I added lemon juice. I made coffee out of acorns using recipes I downloaded from the Internet.

He never flinched. He never complained. Finally, one day I asked him how in the *fuck* he was drinking these objectively terrible mugs of shit I'd been serving him, and he just shrugged.

"It just doesn't matter that much," he said. "It's not worth getting worked up about."

I almost killed him on the spot.

At work, Vera insisted we chip in on a collective lottery ticket every day. She was very lawyerly about it—there was a signed contract, and photocopies of the tickets distributed to everyone. A dollar a day, and Vera, four and a half feet tall with her glasses perpetually hanging around her neck and never worn, bustled about the office like she ruled the place, distributing non-binding legal documents designed to control our future financial decisions. God, I loved Vera. She was incredible. She was a perfect organism: a fat, short, nearsighted woman who strutted about like Queen Cleopatra. You have to respect the Veras of the world.

I dutifully paid my dollar every day, collected my documentation without a word, and forgot all about it. Then one night while I was watching TV and ignoring the fact that Jimmy had fallen asleep twice during our show, my phone lit up like nuclear war had been announced. We had hit. Our ticket had hit the big jackpot, split 7 ways.

I remember the jolt of electricity through my body as the realization hit. I remember immediately wondering if it meant I could quit my job and never see Vera strut around again. And I remember turning to look at Jimmy and not waking him up.

The state wanted the whole bunch of us to do interviews and show our faces, but I learned from the internet that I could remain anonymous if I wanted to. Four of us opted out of the media attention. Vera was in heaven. She showed up for every presser, every interview, wearing a truly suffocating amount of makeup and a diamond pendant her mother had given her decades before. Two of my co-workers were there, too, preening for the cameras and sharing how they were going to spend every last dime of their winnings as quickly as possible, like people racing to jump off a cliff on a premise that the ride down was going to be the most exciting six seconds of their lives.

Keeping it all from Jimmy was surprisingly easy. James Forman was a creature of constant forward motion. He only saw what you placed in front of him and was typically content to let you select what that would be. He never expressed an opinion about when to watch television or what to watch on it, he simply paid attention when you turned it on and watched with a blank, dutiful expression until it was over. I'd come to hate watching TV with him, because he simply ... existed during any program.

Jimmy did a lot of simply existing. I would watch him when we went out. He was still popular; everyone loved him. But they loved him because Jimmy wasn't a real person. He was the *idea* of a person. A sketch on the back of a napkin. A "gestures vaguely."

Over the years, I'd come to realize that Jimmy lost something when he was a kid. Something had happened. When you see pictures of him in high school, or videos, there's a spark there. An energy. It's gone. It was gone by the time I met him, but he was so good at pretending to be a normal human being it took me a long time to realize it.

I hired a lawyer and financial advisor.

"You live in a community property state," Megan, my attorney, said, leaning back and steepling her long fingers under her chin. "You get that, right?"

I loved Megan. She had a law degree from a school I'd decided not to research, and she looked at me with such blatant predatory joy I knew I could trust her, because of the money. She wanted to insert her proboscis and suck me dry like I was some backwater lottery goon, hundred-dollar bills falling out of my pockets every time I stood up. She wanted every dime she could suck out, so I was confident she would be protective of my fortune to ensure no one *else* stole it out from under her twitching nose.

Her words stuck in my head. I thought about suddenly becoming rich and then ennobling my husband, who was a soulless husk with dead eyes and a flat affect, who had scraped something off of himself—a soul, apparently—back in high school.

I realized with something resembling a panic attack that I'd been thinking about divorcing Jimmy without being conscious of it, and now, if I divorced him, I'd essentially be giving him millions of dollars.

I started making soap.

Jimmy, of course, didn't understand my sudden obsession with making my own soap, but Jimmy also asked zero questions about it and exhibited zero curiosity about it, which was on brand.

I didn't put too much effort into it. Just enough to actually produce some bars of soap, suffering several chemical burns in the process. I sent Jim to work with some to hand out, and gave a few away to friends. I made soap in the kitchen, storing everything in the cupboards. And one day, I started making Jimmy coffee again. And one day, I put a pile of pure lye into his coffee. And one day, Jimmy was gone.

It sounds ridiculous. Of course it does. That's why it *worked*.

There was an investigation. I had a few dicey moments when I worried. One of the detectives had decided to dislike me, her questions getting more and more pointed. But in the end, it was ruled an accident: Jimmy had reached for the wrong jar. People told stories about Jimmy's famous lack of taste and discernment and one of his old college buddies inadvertently helped the project along by telling a story about a time Jimmy ate expired frozen pizzas for *days*, suffering tremendous gastrointestinal distress, and yet kept *eating them* like the soulless golem he was. Thus, establishing James Forman as a man whose taste buds were so stupid he was destined to eat something deadly eventually.

If I was a supreme asshole for storing my chemicals next to the fucking coffee creamer, no one saw fit to charge me with murder.

I worried that I would miss Jimmy, or regret killing him. But I shouldn't have. Jimmy lacked friction. He was so easy to ignore, it was hard to remember he'd been there at all.

FIVE FUNERALS

Ernest

Chapter 30: Stop. Don't. Come Back.

An Account of the Death of Ernest Bundy in March, 2015

Meatballs (1985)

He'd always been skinny. As a child, his uncles and aunts, every one of them the size of two or three people mashed together, remarked on his size every time they saw him. *What! Aren't you feeding him?* or *It isn't natural! He's not developing!*

His Aunt Helen would sneak him food. He would be playing video games in his room, and she'd walk in and silently place a sandwich on top of the television. Or she'd be helping his mother cook, and she'd bring him a plate of sausage. When she took him to school or Boy Scouts, she'd always stop and get him a few slices of pizza, a burger. Aunt Helen—all of them, all of the extended family of Bundys and Ciccerones who had united with his parents' marriage—fed him like it was a holy mission. He was always offered seconds, and thirds, and met with disbelief when he refused.

Still, he remained thin as a rail. He felt fine, and doctors assured his mother that he was healthy, but no matter how many extra servings of meatballs he got, he remained thin as a rail.

The mood at dinner always bothered him, though he couldn't sense why. His family was so large, so dense, so *everywhere* he felt crowded. When the plates hit the table, he felt even more crowded, like everyone was leaning in. He ate fast and always asked for seconds even when he didn't want any.

I Am the Walrus (1987)

When Ernie was small, before he went to Bishop Carlbus Prep and became a surly, cranky adolescent, every Friday night was Fast Food Night at the Bundy house, run on a regular schedule: Chinese, Pizza, Burgers, Tacos.

On Chinese Night, Ernie would take chopsticks and stick them in his mouth to form walrus tusks. He would then entertain his family by reciting famous speeches or poems.

On Pizza Night, Ernie was expected to make a long, humorous speech concerning the many ways that pizza counted as healthy food, beginning with the presence of vegetables in some form. He varied it every time, building an increasingly absurd argument that had his family in stitches.

On Burger Night, Ernie would take two onion rings from the box, hold them at his ears like earrings, and sing an appropriately ridiculous song.

On Taco Night, Ernie would place a hard-shell taco on his head like a Fez and delight his family by singing *Puttin' on The Ritz*.

Ernie's mother told him he was a born entertainer, and Ernie believed it. He loved being the center of his family's attention, and he enjoyed the short respite when they weren't urging him to eat.

Barfecue (1995)

Ernie could remember what he was eating before, during, or after every major life event. Birthdays and Little League championships, vacations, parties, graduations, weddings, every one of them was linked to hot dogs and linguine and porterhouses and ice cream and waffles and french fries. When he summoned specific memories, he could taste and smell the food again as if it was right there in front of him.

When he thought of Amy Keaton's Outing Party, he thought of barbecue potato chips. And then he got nauseous.

He always remembered that Amy had provided a ludicrously small amount of food for the party—a few bowls of pretzels, some store-bought vegetables and dip. He remembered everyone was starving, surviving off of bong hits and resentment. He remembered that Yorick, always a flushed, damp mess, located a cache of snacks in the locked pantry off the enormous, extremely beige kitchen, snapping the lock and tossing bags of chips and jars of salsa into the crowd like a rock star.

He remembered snagging the bag of barbecue chips out of the air and laughing, tearing it open and stuffing a handful of chips into his mouth, then just lifting it up and shouting I AM A GOD OF CHIPS as he poured the rest of the bag onto his face.

Everyone laughed. Olive Partridge bowed down to him and promised to tithe chips to him. And for the rest of the night people would hand him bags of barbecue chips and he would repeat the performance. I AM A GOD OF CHIPS. And after a few hours he kind of was: he smelled like chips, he could taste nothing but barbecue seasoning, he had greasy crumbs inside his shirt collar, in his hair.

Fit As a Fiddle and Ready for Love (1999)

After high school, Ernie moved to New York City and took

guitar lessons. He got a job at a call center guiding complaints back into the sales funnel via a 328-page guidebook that had been indexed according to every conceivable objection, profanity, argument, and personal threat. When followed scrupulously, the flowchart inevitably turned callers' dissatisfaction with a product or service into a desperate need for *another* product or service, and Ernie was surprised to discover that most callers hung up without getting a refund and actually out several hundred dollars.

He was neither good nor bad at the job. He continued to be employed, but he never hit the volume metrics to trigger a bonus payout, and so his income remained skeletal in a city like New York. He found a studio apartment on Monroe Street in The Bronx that was an hour away from work on the D train and made just a hair more than his rent each month. Something had to be sacrificed on the altar of his budget, and Ernie chose groceries.

He spent years living off crumbs. Instead of free drinks at the bars and coffee houses when he played open mics, he took home bags of peanuts and popcorn served at the bar or day-old baked goods from the coffee houses. At work, he stole people's lunches until one day he reached into a brown paper bag and a mousetrap snapped on his fingers. He found a note stuck to the trap that read HANDS OFF, MOTHERFUCKER.

He wrote songs that no one wanted to hear. He was frequently booed when he performed at tiny clubs and occasionally assaulted on street corners. He told himself that inspiring any sort of passion in people was proof that his art was worthwhile.

He shrank. Unable to afford new clothes, he cinched. He bore new holes in his belt. He stopped going home to visit his family after one visit ended with his cousins attempting to force him into the car for a trip to the emergency room, his mother wailing that he was fading away in front of her, that her little boy was a ghost.

He realized, one day, that the last twenty-seven songs he'd composed were about hunger.

Stay on The Scene (2006)

When he was offered a managerial position at the call bank, Ernie told himself it was a temporary accommodation. He had started to exhibit symptoms that the Internet informed him might be scurvy, and so he thought a few months of larger paychecks and actual health insurance would be useful.

His marginally better income allowed him to eat more regularly, but the stress of managing a churning group of malcontents burned it off him just as fast. He was amazed to discover that his years of service working the flowchart until his shoulder cramped from holding a phone against his ear was an anomaly, that most people stayed with the company less than six months. He began to suspect that his main qualification for promotion had been remaining in the same chair for five years.

He moved into a slightly larger studio in The Bronx which actually extended his time on the D train by fifteen minutes. He justified his recent decisions by aggressively trying to start a band. He put up and responded to advertisements, he met up with drummers and bassists and horn players and flautists, singers and slam poetry composers and keyboardists. He drank cheap coffee and stale beers and discussed music theory and the Scene, always with an implied capital letter.

Things always fell apart when the inevitable jam session was arranged. Ernie would listen politely as the flautist raged through some Jethro Tull or the drummer sweated through some Charlie Rich routine, but after approximately forty-three seconds of Polybius' epic *Excel Macrophage* the jam sessions typically ended, often wordlessly, sometimes with vitriol and insults.

Eventually, Ernie realized he was on his own. Blacklisted at most of the venues in the city for reasons that remained mysterious to him. Unable to get fellow musicians to sit through all 33 minutes of *Scab Soup*, an exercise he felt necessary to determine that their musical DNA was similar enough to work together.

He missed Hector.

He considered trying to contact him, because it now seemed like they'd written edgy, complex songs together effortlessly. But the thought of hearing Hector's voice reminded him of the Outing Party and filled him with terror.

Thinking of Hector, one day at work he played *Colonoscopies Me* on his computer while he reviewed time sheets. The volume was modest, but half an hour later he received a call from Human Resources informing him that there had been complaints. Employees were "disturbed" and "unsettled" and he had been terminated. She added that if he knew what was good for him, he would finish the time sheets before he left.

That night, he created a YouTube account.

Mukbangin' (2014)

He was staring down forty with a sense of helpless acceleration toward an unseen cliff. To cut expenses, Ernie took on a roommate who moved in, promptly stole a jar of peanut butter from the kitchen, and then refused to speak to him. He supported himself by working temp jobs, mostly in warehouses. On Monday, the temp agency would call at six in the morning and offer him a few days moving boxes, loading or unloading trucks, or other physical tasks for minimum wage minus the agency's cut.

He learned how to program drum beats on a used groovebox he'd acquired and began writing songs at breakneck speed—often two or three a day—for his one-man band, Cockamamy.

The song *Meatball Surgeries* turned out promisingly, and one night after a few hours drinking alone in his bedroom and plotting to defecate in his hated roommate's bed, he decided to make a music video for the song.

Walking briskly to the pizzeria on the first floor that served enormous, two-foot novelty slices of pizza, Ernie purchased two meatball subs, then returned to his apartment where he consumed them with noisy relish while recording himself and talking about the song's composition. He deliberately smeared tomato sauce all over himself as he ate, got onions and bread in his hair, and played up his inebriation. Then he fired up the backing track, grabbed his guitar without cleaning himself up and played along, screaming the vocals.

Ernie had uploaded a few videos before, and each one drew a few dozen views and some half-hearted comments. When he woke up the next afternoon, head aching and stomach flipping,

Meatball Surgeries had been viewed seven thousand times. Every time he checked the number had grown.

The comments were gold:

This man knows how to eat

tHis made me hungry for A-P-p-l-E-S

shreding That sub like a h8ungry Eddie Van Halen

his manifest joy at consumption brought joy to my heart

i could watch this man eat all day long.
guuiitar licks are solid, too.

Ernie understood, in a vague, academic way, that online videos could be monetized. When *Meatball Surgeries* hit 30,000 views, he formed a sudden interest in figuring out how, exactly, this was done.

His next video, for his song *Sushi Sunrise* (hastily retitled from *Heartafterburner*) followed the pattern: he got drunk, ate an immense amount of sushi in the sloppiest manner possible while rambling, and then played along to his own backing track. It was even more successful than the first, but metrics told a simple story: everyone stopped watching once he started to play guitar.

They wanted to watch him eat.

I'll Stop the World and Puke with You (2015)

When Ernie received his first five-digit payment from his streaming host, he moved into his own apartment without even telling the Dread Silent Roommate that he was leaving. He hired scriptwriters and a producer, upgraded his equipment, and began polling his growing list of followers for the foods they wanted to see him eat theatrically. He included music in the first few but then gave up and concentrated on entertaining ways of gorging himself.

He gained fourteen pounds in his first three months.

The money poured in. His subscriber list ballooned, and he established accounts on other platforms in order to take private orders for custom videos and offer extended content. He began making two or three videos a day. He was paid enormous sums to eat tacos, steaks, whole chickens, gallons of ramen, boxes of candy bars. He began buying oversize cutlery and dishware. He made a video where he filled a kiddie pool with pasta and sauce, using a man-sized loaf of bread he'd custom-ordered as a flotation device. He swam around in the lukewarm sauce and ate until the pool was empty. It was his most popular video to date, catching viral metrics and earning him what he thought of as stupid money.

He gained thirty-four pounds over the next six months. He bought a house and two BMWs. He hadn't spoken with anyone not associated with his channel in months. He had a whole new wardrobe custom made, then had to do it again six weeks later when nothing fit.

He attempted to eat a large bowl of ghost peppers and experienced such pain and discomfort that he began weeping and announcing that his life had been wasted; at one point, delirious and dehydrated, he begged Amy for forgiveness, giving rise to the viral hashtag #WhoIsAmy. The video sparked another surge in viewership, and Ernie began regularly crying and insulting himself during his videos, and asking Amy for forgiveness at least once each time, often with a wink at the audience.

He had a custom-made griddle built on the grounds of his new estate, capable of cooking pancakes or hamburgers the size of cars, which he would eat while weeping.

On a platform where wealthy donors could pay him tips and request special videos, several anonymous accounts appeared and began depositing large sums along with disturbingly specific instructions. Instead of huge volumes of food, the anonymous accounts asked Ernie to cook meals with defective recipes—replacing sugar with salt, quadrupling the vanilla extract, mixing in sawdust, or slashing baking time to produce a lukewarm, gelatinous bowl of potential salmonella. Ernie was careful to weep in each one.

By the end of his first two years making videos, Ernie had gained one hundred and sixteen pounds and was a multi-millionaire.

Peachy (2015)

When Ernie turned thirty-eight, he weighed over four hundred pounds and had a net worth of sixty-seven million dollars. Confined to his bed, he made his videos surrounded by an increasing number of medical devices. He stopped trying to clean himself or change the sheets after each shoot, and his viewing numbers soared.

People became concerned about his health. There were

lengthy posts on his channels, requests for interviews, demands that his hosting platforms step in and perform wellness checks. Each fresh wave of controversy around Ernie's ballooning figure and state of hygiene pushed his numbers higher.

Through it all, the anonymous accounts remained his highest revenue source, continuously donating large sums and submitting requests. It got to the point where any time Ernie failed to thank his unnamed benefactors at the end of his streams other fans would crowd into the chat demanding to know if The Unseen, as Ernie's fan base referred to the accounts—which had become something of an icon in the community despite being completely faceless and anonymous—were okay.

The final request submitted appealed to Ernie's fans: The Unseen wanted a video of Ernie eating peach pits.

"Not peaches," the post specified. "Peach *pits*. A lot of them."

Some of Ernie's followers complained that peach pits could be poisonous if consumed in large quantities, but they were shouted down. Ernie, others insisted, knew what he was doing. He was a famous and professional mukbang entertainer: he knew his limits. And so, the event was scheduled. As usual, Ernie ordered an enormous number of peaches and filmed sequences where he sat covered in them and ate the flesh from several dozen as messily as possible. But these were just the amuse bouche. His assistants dutifully filled a bucket with the pits from hundreds of peaches and Ernie went live, his face still crusted with peach juice and the remnants of a dozen prior meals. He began popping the pits into his mouth, announcing he was entering Hamster Mode, filling his cheeks with pits and ramming in more.

His metrics jumped. His audience was loving it.

When Ernie paused and began thrashing around in his bed—or as close to thrashing as his enormous size would allow—everyone initially thought it was part of the act. Ernie regularly feigned moments of insanity, shouting and throwing food, smearing it on himself, rolling his eyes and even drooling—his audience loved it.

As Ernie's exertions became increasingly panic-stricken, a growing wave of viewers began posting demands that the stream be ended and assistance summoned, but they were shouted down by the majority who believed it was all a bit, citing the lack of intervention by Ernie's staff as evidence.

Ernie's staff, in fact, were all underpaid interns whose main responsibilities included grocery shopping and video editing. They each had exactly zero first aid training, and they stood outside the shot with varying expressions of panic and terror.

Hundreds of thousands of people continued to watch the stream for approximately forty-five minutes after Ernie went still, staring up at his ceiling, froth leaking from the corners of his mouth. Finally, people ran into the shot, crowding around Ernie. Just before the live feed was cut, a heated argument could be heard concerning who was going to try to clear his windpipe.

Then, one by one, everyone logged off.

FIVE FUNERALS

Maud

Chapter 31: The Worst Trip I've Ever Been On

An Account of the Death of Maud Bluth in July, 1996

Now that I have some time to myself, time to just think and *exist*, god, you know? Now that it's just me for the first time in, Jesus, *forever*, I can look back and see where the mistakes were made, you know?

First and most importantly, I was the wrong kind of rich.

I mean, yes, sure, we have money. My family, I mean. And it's like, the moment you *admit* you have money, you're screwed, because that's all people who *don't* have money see. You just become this walking dollar sign. But to people who *really* have money—like, a *real* amount of money, like, you know, *generational wealth* and all that—we're just part of the other people. It's like, when you have a billion dollars people who have a million are the same as everyone else. We fly First Class, not private. No one takes you *seriously*.

But the worst of it is we were rich enough to be in the same room, you know? When the Taylors organized ski trips back in high school, I could go, and I had all the *stuff* and the cute outfits and I *knew how to ski*, and all that. But I still wasn't in it; I wasn't part of things. It's like all your friends are going to this great concert and you manage to score tickets but they're all in the pit right in front of the stage and you're in the back row in the upper deck. It always made me angry.

Mom and Dad didn't get it; they didn't understand. Because

they were poor. Not, literally—we had money, like I said—but mentally, because they both grew up poor. So they didn't understand money, not how me and Michael and Mandy do. For people like my parents it's, like, they *won* tickets to the concert, you know? So they're *there* and all, but they don't know how to *appreciate* it properly.

After the Outing Party, I was messed up, for a while. I mean, nothing was my *fault*, I didn't want anything bad to happen. I mean, I didn't *like* Amy, but I didn't want her *dead*, you know? But I got a little out of hand at the party. I was wild, back then. Angry. And Yorick convinced me to do mushrooms with him and I felt this *incredible*, *dark* energy, building and building until I had to destroy *something*. I'm not a violent person. I'm *not*. But I remember the pressure of it, like something immaterial boiling inside me, bubbles filling me up and stretching my skin, moving my limbs involuntarily. I stormed around Amy Keaton's house in a frenzy. I smashed bottles and slapped the braces out of Olive Partridge's face.

Mistakes, like I said.

After the party, it was like I had no friends. No one returned a call. It's hard to believe that *none* of those assholes had a party all summer long, but I heard nothing. It was like everyone went on vacation without me. Mike and Mandy didn't want me around, Mom and Dad never *left the house*—I mean, God, their idea of a fun night was sitting around the living room watching TV. And I didn't have the money to just do what I wanted. I had a car, a gorgeous RX-7, red—loved that car. But I had nowhere to go. There's *nothing* to do in Bergen City and if I wasn't invited somewhere, what was I supposed to do?

It was the worst, most boring summer of my life. And the worst of it was that Amy was everywhere. Big news. Everyone wanted to talk about it. And the investigation went on *forever*, despite what Mr. Sandford told us: that it would be fast, that we would all get on with our lives. That we were too *young* and too *full of promise* to let a terrible accident ruin us. That's what he said, but it just dragged on and on with the same questions over and over again and Mr. and Mrs. Keaton's bloated cry faces everywhere all the time.

I mean, we didn't *mean* to hurt anybody. It was an *accident*.

There's something meditative about treading water, don't you think? The repetition. It's *mesmerizing*. Lets you think. Maybe if we'd had a *real* pool, something bigger than a glorified bathtub, who knows. Maybe I would have had time to think back then, make better decisions. But that's the problem with being the wrong kind of rich: sure, you *have* a pool. But it's a *small* pool, not conducive to meditation.

The Taylors didn't invite me anywhere, and the Sandfords apparently didn't have any blowouts by that gnat-infested pond on their property, or if they did they didn't call *me*. It was like my entire life just vanished. Everyone pretending we'd never known each other. I needed new friends.

College was my chance. I was going from New Jersey to California, *infinitely* far away, and none of the drips from my class were going, so I could finally leave it all behind. I was going to find the right people—*my* kind of people, not boring like my parents, or different boring like my siblings. And not poor, Jesus, no. I mean, I'm not *judging* people, but being poor is so frustrating. You literally can't *do* anything.

The thing about people with real money is, they're everywhere. They look just like you and me, if you're not paying attention. Their clothes don't *look* special, they look like the usual stuff people wear. But they're *nicer*. If you look, there won't be tags. They're custom. It's just a pair of shorts and a T-shirt, but they're *tailored*, you know? Tailoring makes all the difference. You know, the tailoring.

And the Real Rich don't ever have any money. I know! It's *crazy*, but true. You're at a party with a billionaire, or, you know, the *son* of a billionaire, and you order pizza and they can't chip in. Rich people don't *need* money, which is really how you know you're not Real Rich.

But mainly you just *look* at them. No stress, right? I mean, not no stress; people are people and everyone's got stuff. Like, I have a recurring dream where I go down into Amy Keaton's basement and someone locks the door and I'm trapped and somehow Amy is there too and she starts eating me and then I wake up in a sweat. Real Rich people have *concerns*, right? But they also have *money*, in case I'm not being clear, and so they don't have to worry that they're going to end up living in their RX-7, which is a *super impractical* car to live in.

I found Harley by accident. *Honest*, I wasn't even looking. It wasn't, like, a *project* or something. He was sitting in the Student Center on move-in day, all by himself. He didn't stand out. He was wearing boat shoes, though, which caught my eye, and a really expensive watch. He had that relaxed look—you know, loose-limbed, just existing because he could afford to exist. His skin was dark and smooth, and his legs were muscular, athletic. Sports. Our eyes met as I walked in—I was looking for snacks—and he smiled a little before playing with the flimsy earphones connected to his little portable cassette player.

I don't know what *possessed* me, really, but I said, "You want anything?"

His eyes followed my arm to the general direction of the vending machines, and he shook his head. "Nah, I'm good."

Candy bar in hand, I sat down on the couch next to him. They were playing shit grunge on the PA. He smelled like soap, but it wasn't just *soap*, it was lavender-ish. He was probably the best-smelling boy I'd ever met. Though that isn't saying *much*.

"Why are you in here?" I asked. This was a tactic. It works! I swear it works. Maybe mostly for girls, but it seems kind of universal. You just ask a question. No easier way to start a convo.

He told me he'd flown in and had his bags shipped, but they got delayed in customs, so he had nothing to move into his room. I looked at his boat shoes, so white against his skin. They were sparkling. And *boat shoes*.

You swallow enough salt water, you get sick. But if you puke in the ocean and no one sees you, did you really puke at all?

I think I'm delirious. Sometimes I think Amy's here, head at the wrong angle, almost under water as she floats. Sometimes it's Olive, ruined mouth all scabbed over. Then it's just me and the sun sinking low and the waves and my tired arms.

If you look, I'm in the background. Of things. Of everything, you know? I'm always on the edge. I slip in, I just show up and stand in the back and if you're cool about it that's how you get in with people. They see you a few times, they think, Girl must have been invited. Girl must know somebody. Someone takes a photo; I'm in the back.

You can see me in Harley's pics—the infamous Polaroids he was always snapping, his thing. In his dorm room, red Solo cups in hand: there's me, by the closet, a head and a shoulder. At The Hut on fake IDs, everyone crowded in the booth, me leaning over from the back, my hair looking good. I mean, I don't think I actually had a *conversation* with Harley after that first day? Like, I don't think we ever *talked*? I just showed up. Like, when he organized the trip to Vegas in second semester, no one, like, *literally* invited me. I was just there when the plans got made, so I *assumed*. So in those pics, on the party bus he rented, or crowded around the sign, or hoisting huge plastic cocktail glasses, being silly, I'm on the edges, in the background. But *there*, you know?

That's the thing about the Real Rich, it's sloppy. Their staff: they do for everyone, they don't *ask* who you know or whatever. You don't have to show them your VIP pass or whatever. You're in the room; that's good enough. I mean, Harley could have kicked me out. He could have said, hey, who *are* you, anyway? Right? So maybe he wasn't sure who I was, but I was already in the room.

The boat seems really far away. I tried swimming after it for a while, but it was going a lot faster than you'd think. At least I'm far away from everyone else. I mean, *gross*.

Going home sucked, I can tell you that. Harley used to host brunch in his room—had it delivered. Just a local diner, nothing special, but *delivered*. And I was in the room, so Mimosas and scrambled eggs for *moi*, thankyouverymuch. Then it's winter break and I'm back in my *tiny* room in Morris Plains, New Jersey for a few weeks and it's like no time at all has gone by. Or I've *regressed*. Like I was still going to catch the *train* to Bergen City to hit Bishop Carlbus, stand behind Olive Partridge as she and Una Taylor giggled and made fun of everyone, the fake smile on my face straining every muscle.

I knew that Harley was in Malibu for the summer, hanging out with his uncle, who was a producer. It was just him, though, not some big thing. So, I was back in Morris Plains. Mom didn't talk to me. Still oh-so *shocked* about Amy and that shit show. Dad talked to me, but I wished he *wouldn't*. He thinks I'm damaged, and he kept trying to therapize me. It's so *sad*. And I hate being sad. It's why I hate being alone.

And they made me get a *job*, which made everything infinitely worse. No one from Bishop Carlbus was around—they either didn't come home for summer, or they just didn't answer my calls or chats. So, I'm at Arthur's in the stupid black skirt while Harley and whoever is getting a tan and probably hanging out with all these famous, beautiful people on the beach. And I smelled like steak all the time—*disgusting*. I started to worry I'd smell like a cow forever.

I decided, *never again*. I wasn't going to be stuck in my crappy room smelling like hamburgers with my Dad asking me if I was okay five hundred thousand times a day and my Mom acting like Amy's death was a personal affront of some sort, like the time me and Mike put all the bubble bath into the washing machine and the garage filled with bubbles. It took Mom *years* to stop talking about that, so I figured Amy would take forever. Or longer.

Then I got a call from Max, one of Harley's friends. He liked me—like *liked* me liked me. He was nice enough, but not my style, but he was nice to talk to, and he was a good excuse to always be in the room. And he tells me that Harley's putting together an end of summer blow out on his uncle's yacht in Majorca. And I'm standing there in my room in my beef-smelling skirt and listening to my parents fight and I know one thing: I'm going to be on that boat if it kills me, because this is no way to live.

The boat's really tiny now, and the sun's really low, and I'm freezing. And tired. I've stopped treading and I'm just floating on my back watching the sky turn purple. And I'll tell you this:

when you're floating in the ocean, all it takes is for you to think the word *shark* once, and then that's *all you can think of*.

Which is fine, because I don't like my other thoughts. I guess I never really had any friends. Or I wasn't really anyone's friend, I guess is a better way to put it. I mean, you collectively, *accidentally*, kill someone and you spend an entire summer being iced out by every single one of your co-conspirators—it makes you think. Makes you *reassess*, right? So, I hoofed it to the airport with all my tip cash and Dad's credit card with the intention of making a connection. Maybe Max, I remember thinking. He's cute, and if he isn't Real Rich, not really, he's in the room; so why not? Or anyone. Anyone at all, as long as they knew the difference between Vail and Aspen.

Dad canceled the card, but not before I scored a ticket to Palma. And everything went *so well*. Max met me at the airport, like a gentleman. The weather was *perfect*. There were a dozen of us, plus the crew, but Harley's That Guy, you know, who treated the crew like everyone else. *So nice*. Like, I could tell Harley hesitated when he saw me, like he wasn't sure who I was or didn't realize I'd be there, but he played it off. Smiled and hugged me.

We go out on the boat, the *yacht*, and it's *perfect*. It's so nice, and everyone is so cool, and relaxed, and I had that feeling I hadn't had in a long time, ever since the party. The Party. Like, I was part of things. Not on the edge, in the back, but right there.

Not everyone is cool. Two of the girls—the tall blonde everyone calls Sissy for some reason, and the tall brunette,

Cressida, who everyone calls Crissy—don't like me. I hear them talking about me and Max, making fun of my swimsuit. Of the fact that I didn't know which way *starboard* was, as if that's something real people actually know.

Harley suggested we all jump in and have a swim, and everyone cheered. People were cannonballing off the boat and there's nothing around us for miles but water and sun and it's just perfect. And Harley yells to the crew to join in, because he's a cool guy, and I am lucky to be with such cool people (minus Crissy and Sissy, of course) after my own Personal Nightmare of a year. And they do, the crew, they jump in in their uniforms, laughing, and then it's just me and Max and he's fiddling with something with his back to me, and everyone is shouting—like, the energy is *high*, and kind of reminds me of the old days with everyone back at BCP—and so I push Max in, flirty-like, let out a whoop! and dive in after him.

When I broke the surface, the water was warm and really, really nice, but the vibe was off. Everyone *glared* at me, and started talking all at once, with the waves and the splashing making it hard to understand—Max had been trying to lower the ladder, and now we couldn't get back on the boat.

"Why are you even *here*?" Crissy spluttered.

"Good taste in girls, as usual, Maxie," Sissy said.

I imagined myself drowning them one by one, the two absolute bitches. But then Max was looking at me and it wasn't a *friendly* look, and I could feel that old panic rising up.

So, there we all were, treading water, and God, they *blamed* me. They clumped up together, having a conference, and I drifted to the edge because no one would even look at me. I felt *terrible*. It was an *accident*, you know? And not my fault if the *crew* was going to ignore *protocol* and jump off the boat! And I said so, and Crissy just looked at me, the sun glaring off the water around her.

"Not your fault," she said, sounding angry. "Our fault for letting some gold-digging *whore* get her pincers into poor Max!"

"Why are you even *here*?" Sissy screeched. "If you don't know how the world works *stay the fuck home*!"

They tried a bunch of things, but it was no use. The boat was lighter without us and sat higher, and the current kept pulling us, so we had to keep swimming a little to stay close. Sissy tried climbing up on Harley's shoulders, but she kept tipping and sliding off. Someone else took off their trunks and tried to sling them over the bottom rung of the ladder—I thought he was going to pull it off, for a moment, but as he tried pulling himself up the shorts tore, and he splashed back down.

We were all getting tired. Sissy and Crissy took turns glowering at me and calling me names. The first couple of times, Max said something back, like *Hey now* or *That's enough*. But after a while he looked at me, breathing hard, and said maybe I should just hang back, put some distance between us. Then Harley, of all people, started to lose it, shouting about how he didn't want to die, about how tired he was, and then people started shouting at *him* to shut up and stop whining and how spoiled he was and what a baby he always was.

And I kept falling further behind and drifting further away and no one *noticed* or *cared*—not even Max—and I could feel their anger, and it was the same thing, again, as with the Outing Party. Everyone angry, everyone shouting, and after a while I just let them drift away, or maybe it was me drifting away and they were still there.

It wasn't *fair*. God! It was an *accident*!

FIVE FUNERALS

Yorick

Chapter 32: The Void is Ever Eager

An Account of the Death of Yorick Evans in May, 2000

The world is small, and Yorick was big. So big, so unspeakably large, that he tore his mother apart coming into the world, a fact his father reminded him about on a constant basis. From a large, loud baby he grew into a large, flush-faced boy who continuously struggled to join sports teams because no one believed he was his actual age. His father eventually resorted to having copies of Yorick's birth certificate in the glove compartment of his car, ready and able to prove his son's age whenever some asshole who took Little League a little too seriously objected that this boy was clearly fifteen or sixteen years old. By the time Yorick reported to Bishop Carlbus Prep at age 14, his mere presence was enough to spark rumors of a football program being established at the school.

Yorick hated being huge. He hated not fitting into any seats, hated the look of dismay people wore when he stepped on a bus or walked into a crowded movie theater. He hated sprawling, hated the jokes, how his clothes always fit slightly wrong, and the nicknames. What most depressed him about the nicknames was their predictability. Gigantor. Gulliver. Big Man. Hulk. Or the folks who considered themselves witty, who called him Tiny or Peewee.

At the same time, he had to admit there were advantages. His classmates treated him like an unexploded bomb, and teachers and adults often assumed he was older—he purchased his first six pack of beer when he was just twelve, with no one blinking an eye. The beer made him feel small, for a while. Light. And then heavier than ever.

What Yorick really hated, however, was the constant feeling of constraint. Every space was too small for him, every bed, every chair, every room. He spent his life wearing too-tight clothing and ducking under low ceilings, hunched over and uncomfortable. He developed a permanent hunch, he learned to hug himself at all times to prevent his monkey arms from an unpremeditated assault of people and possessions. This had the unintended consequence of making Yorick look *coiled*, as if preparing to detonate, which made people even more leery of him.

At night, in the Colorado King bed his father purchased for him, he liked to sleep skydiver style, on his stomach with his arms and legs splayed. In his dreams he was in space, all mass and no weight.

His career options seemed grim; he couldn't imagine physically fitting into an office cubicle, or finding suits that fit properly, and despite his size, his athletic ability simmered somewhere below *hapless*. But he liked math and sailed through algebra, geometry, and calculus with top grades. For some time during high school, he thought he might be an engineer; in the back of his mind he thought perhaps he'd join the Navy, become an astronaut.

His father was therefore surprised when, after graduation,

Yorick decided not to attend college at all. No amount of yelling could dissuade him. His father tried pointing out that he'd already been accepted; the housing, tuition, and meal plans had already been paid. He tried threatening to disown his son, to throw him out on the street. He tried arguing that going for one semester and then deciding if it wasn't right for him was a more sensible solution.

Yorick ignored all of these suggestions. He took a job in a bike shop and spent his days working and watching TV. He paid his father weekly rent and never responded to questions, provocations, or direct abuse. He would simply look his father in the eyes and listen, then nod and walk away. When his father finally kicked him out of the house in a rage, Yorick kept doing what he'd been doing, but redirected his rent to a studio apartment that was about half an hour away.

He tried burying himself in noise. In people. The louder and more crowded a space was, the happier he felt. He took the train into New York City and went to the clubs. CBGB. The Ritz. Webster Hall. Bands no one had ever heard of opening for bands that very few people had heard of. The mosh pit, the safest place in the world. Loud, fast, and Yorick would sail in wearing a knit cap and boots, and he could ricochet around, slamming into people in the pit with wild abandon. When he was knocked down, hands reached down and pulled him up. When he accidentally elbowed someone in the face, it was waved off. No matter how big he was, the pit was bigger. He would emerge, sweaty and shivering, into an empty city. Plenty of room, the buildings looming over him.

At an all-ages show in the summer, at a grungy little spot on West 21st Street, he was spinning, crashing into people, lost to it. He was never sure how it happened—he remembered slamming into a round, bald guy who was always at the shows. Round, bald guy never moshed, never *moved*, just stood there like a pinball bumper, shoving people back into it. He shoved Yorick and Yorick whooped, flailing his limbs and letting his momentum take over. Then he spun around, arms out, and felt the impact.

He sent the kid flying at the perfectly wrong moment. A gap in the crowd, and the kid—fourteen? fifteen?—went right into a column, slumping down, unconscious. Security swarmed, big guys in black T-shirts. The lights never came up, the band never stopped playing sixteenth notes. They dragged the kid off and the pit healed itself, closing in over the gap. Yorick stood there, suddenly immovable. It had been so effortless. He'd reached out and casually destroyed someone.

The kid was okay. A little loopy, he came to and begged everyone not to call his parents. His friends found him, bundled him out of the place with promises of medical attention, affectionate care.

Yorick felt big again. Bigger than ever.

He went on a diet. He stopped working out. He reduced his wardrobe to a few pairs of jeans and some T-shirts, a light jacket, his battered old Chuck Taylors. He stopped returning phone calls and letters, cut his hair extra short, and at night he saw himself looming over Amy Keaton at the Outing Party and felt intolerably huge, immense and unable to control his mass and weight. He saw himself crashing into the basement door over and over again, that fucking guitar lick in his ear, the cheers of his classmates. He saw himself, flushed and sweaty, a monster rampaging, and he wanted to shrink. He wanted to be nothing.

When his father died, Yorick wasn't surprised. The man had never taken care of himself, and every year he grew fatter and sicker, buying new clothes and drinking more, calling his son up in the middle of the night to alternatively offer verbal abuse concerning his lack of ambition and his epic levels of disappointment or to weep and tear at his virtual breast, informing Yorick that he was dying, would soon be dead, and then it would be too late for the two of them to have a rapprochement. Yorick, so skinny now that his ribs and tendons showed through his skin, listened wordlessly to these speeches, then quietly hung up the phone. When Yorick attended Amy Keaton's party in senior year of high school, he weighed two hundred and thirteen pounds. He now clocked in at one hundred and sixty. He intended to get smaller, so he would never accidentally hurt anyone ever again.

When Filip Evans finally caught the heart attack he'd been chasing, Yorick heard the news via a voicemail left by his Aunt

Nissa, who peppered the announcement with various judgments against Yorick as a son and human being, along with several threats focused on Yorick's attendance at the funeral. Yorick listened to the recording with the same grim silence he'd greeted his father's calls, then erased the message and turned on the TV.

He assumed that was the end of his connection to his family, but a few weeks later he received a letter from a law firm informing him that his father had named him his sole heir. There wasn't much beyond a drained IRA account and the house. Yorick considered selling the house, but in the end hired his own lawyer and took possession, paying off some minor tax debts to clear the title.

His Aunt Nissa left several angrier messages, which he dutifully listened to and then deleted.

The house was a preserved time capsule of his childhood. It was crowded with things: furniture, huge, monolithic antique pieces, each with an associated memory. Books, which his father had collected by the box full and never actually read, most of them piled around the house and covered in thick pelts of dust, placed there reverently by a man who thought there would always be some lengthy, amorphous retirement phase in which to read them. The shelves were populated with mementos of his childhood and remnants of his mother, the walls covered in photographs that tracked the family until he'd moved out.

Each room he stepped into felt smaller than the last. The living room carpet was the same rough green he remembered from his youth, the color of moss, a dense pile that burned knees and trapped dust; his breathing hitched and hesitated as he moved through it. The dining room was dominated by an enormous china cabinet, filled with ancient place settings he didn't think had ever been used. The kitchen had too much island, making it a challenge to move through the space. His old bedroom was full of the model ships he'd made as a kid, faded gray-green plastic laced with cloudy rock-like glue, guarded by moldy stuffed animals, game cartridges, his old bank—a terrifying clown that ate coins when you pressed a switch in the back, the sort of Monkey's Paw item you only gave to a child if you hated children and wished nightmares upon them—still heavy with coins.

Fifteen minutes after walking through the front door, he was struggling to breathe. He felt huge again.

Yorick considered selling the place, but as he moved restlessly through the house, smelling that familiar mix of garlic and stale beer, he realized that all the place needed was a renovation. He began studying the layout and the walls, trying to figure out which were load-bearing, which could be removed. He wanted to make the ceilings as high as possible, to have the floor plan as open as possible. He wanted the house to feel big again, like when he'd been a child. He wanted to feel unrestrained in it again. He felt inspired and excited for the first time in years. He moved in, ordered a dumpster, and began throwing away everything he could carry out the front door.

It took him some time to notice. The chaos and disorder, the house disassembled around him, hid it at first. And his sleepless nights as he pushed through, driven by a need to make room, to make space, left him fuzzy and half-awake.

It was little things. A roll of toilet paper. Some bottles of water. The sort of thing you could easily overlook—had there been five packets of tuna in the makeshift box he was using as a pantry, or only three? What happened to that extra roll of paper towels he *knew* he'd left in the bathroom? Or had he? He mopped his face with one shovel hand and tried to remember when he'd last shopped for sundries. Was he really noticing things going missing, or was he just forgetting? Was someone really coming into the house and robbing him blind, but instead of stealing his valuables, of which he had none, or his keepsakes, of which he also had none, they were stealing basic groceries and dry goods?

He became even more confused after a few more sleepless nights when he realized that, apparently, someone was then *coming back* and *replacing* the things that had been taken but putting them in odd places where they were difficult to find. Stumbling on a 12-pack of bottled water on the floor of the coat closet in the foyer early one morning, Yorick, bleary from hunger and lack of sleep, stared at it blurrily for a moment, wondering why someone would engage in this strange game of theft and restitution. And then he wondered if perhaps his largeness was turning terminal, his brain swelling in his head, his insides getting bigger while his bones and skin remained stubbornly, merely enormous.

The idea of a thief wasn't entirely crazy, he thought. He frequently left to go on supply runs or take trash to the dump, and the house wasn't exactly a fortress. He settled on the idea that some neighborhood indigent was doing some light thieving and then experiencing regret. Whatever the explanation, it was increasingly annoying. Yorick changed the locks on the doors and windows and turned his attention towards knocking down walls with a brand-new sledgehammer.

He lost track of more things. Sundry items simply vanished when he wasn't paying attention—things he'd thought lost reappeared in rooms he couldn't remember visiting. He bought wireless cameras and set them up in the kitchen and bathroom, where all of the crimes had occurred. For two days the recordings showed nothing, and then while sipping coffee and reviewing the overnight feed he almost choked, because on the grainy video the door to the upper cabinet next to the stove *moved.*

Yorick replayed the moment several times, squinting, leaning forward. His head felt fuzzy—shrinking was challenging work, and he was getting used to not eating much, or at all. He'd once been a man capable of eating entire pizzas by himself. Now, he was vaguely aware that he might have forgotten to eat the day before. His mind kept wandering, and he had to replay the moment—timestamped 3:09AM—over and over again.

Each time it was the same: the cabinet door appeared to move slightly, pushing outward, then settling back against the frame. Then the kitchen returned to the eerie stillness that had prevailed before, a static image slowly brightening with the rising sun. He sat and watched the whole recording, drifting in and out of alertness, but the door didn't move again.

Slowly, Yorick lifted his gaze to the cabinet. He sat there for some time, staring at it, his coffee growing cold, the video on his phone scrolling along. It was high on the wall—too high, the result of his father's imperfect understanding of how human beings used kitchens. It was tall, almost four feet. As long as he could remember it had not been used much because no one could comfortably reach it.

He stood and crept forward and opened it now, slowly, poised to duck or retreat if necessary. The cabinet appeared empty, as expected. He craned his neck and examined the interior, which was the same stained white pressed wood as the rest, remembered from a thousand grim, frantic breakfasts rushing out of the house to school, his father glowering at him.

He frowned, noticing a section of the cabinet, roughly two feet square, which caught the light differently. When he reached in to touch it, the area gave way—it was just contact paper, stuck over an opening, a patch of darkness. An example of his father's approach to home repair and maintenance, he thought—the man had always been fond of adhesive solutions to life's problems. Yorick contemplated it for a moment, estimating the contortions and grace level required to climb into the cabinet and then maneuver into the opening.

Something moved.

He blinked, trying to focus. It had been just a hint, a flash, but he was suddenly certain of it: something—some*one*—was in there. In the wall. He nodded to himself, climbed down, and went to retrieve his sledgehammer.

The first blow sent the hammer bouncing back towards him as if the cabinets were made of steel, a buzzing ache spiraling up his arms as he stumbled backwards, narrowly avoiding a broken nose. A few more tentative strikes confirmed that these were super cabinets, reinforced somehow, and Yorick thought this indicated they were capable of bearing the weight of a human being climbing in and out of them. He stood, sweating and panting, pondering the fact that someone had *built* this into the house. Someone had brought in *materials*. But the kitchen cabinets were the same ones he knew from childhood—the ones that had been there when his parents had purchased the place. They had been in the kitchen for forty, fifty years. Had this always been there? Had someone been *living in his kitchen walls* throughout his childhood?

He shook his head; he couldn't seem to get his thoughts organized. Feeling dizzy, Yorick took up the sledgehammer again and attacked the cabinets with fury. He was skeletal, but sinewy, and still oversize. On the fifth swing he was rewarded with a loud cracking noise, and after that things progressed quickly. After a few more minutes, the entire cabinet fell off the wall, smashing into the countertop and shattering it into several chunks, then rolling onto the floor, cracking the tile.

For a few seconds, the floor vibrated and a series of low groaning structural noises filled the air. Then it was just dust and the exposed wall, a different shade of yellow from the rest of the room, the hole an ominous black square.

Yorick dropped the sledgehammer and went to retrieve his flashlight and ladder. When he returned, flashlight clenched between his teeth and the heavy collapsing ladder in both arms, he stopped just inside the room. For a second—less than a second—he thought he'd seen a pale face peering at him from the rough square cut into the wall. He stood, heart pounding unsteadily, momentarily uncertain where he was or what he was doing.

Animation surged back into his face. "Oh no you fucking *don't!*" Yorick howled, the flashlight clattering to the floor. He dropped the ladder with a crash and seized on the sledgehammer again, adrenaline allowing him to swing it up over his head as if it weighed nothing. He smashed the hammer into the wall and with a loud snapping noise a jagged crack appeared, driving down towards the floor.

"Get out of there!" he shouted, spittle flying as he lifted the sledgehammer again. The floor was vibrating, and a low crackling hum filled the air. "Come on out or I will come in and *get you!*"

Suddenly, Yorick felt big again. He felt huge. In a dim corner of his mind, he recognized the purple energy that suffused him as the same feeling he'd had all those years before at the Outing Party. That sense of bigness and power.

The sledgehammer weighed nothing, and the room shrank as he raised it up again. He was a giant, and nothing could stand in his way.

He swung the sledgehammer. It smashed through the wall,

jerking Yorick forward. There was a rushing noise, like sand falling but tons of it, getting louder and louder. For a moment, Yorick struggled to extricate the hammer from the wall, pulling and grunting. Then there was an incredibly loud crashing noise, and then the second floor violently entered the first, knocking in Yorick's head seconds before compressing him into a thin sheet.

Hours later, the silence was broken by the scrape of movement. A tiny figure, long and furry with a lengthy tail, a shadow in the near-total darkness, emerged from the wall and dropped lightly on top of the rubble. For a moment, it looked around, whiskers quivering as it contemplated Yorick, pounded thin below. Then it picked its way gingerly toward the rest of the house.

Fanny

Chapter 33: To Serve Man

An Account of the Death of Fanny Heck in November, 2007

Transcript of eulogy for Frances Angel Heck by Frederick Hobart Heck

Thank you all for coming. Fanny—she hated that name, by the way, hated being called Fanny ‹laughter›—would have been pleased to see you all here. She would have worked the room, checking on everyone, making sure you were all comfortable ‹laughter› because—because that's who Fanny was. I have never known anyone more concerned with making the world a better place and taking care of people, even strangers, than my older sister.

Sorry, this is ‹clears throat› this is hard.

I want to say thank you again. I know some of you considered not coming. I know there has been some bad blood within the family—yes, Uncle Jim, I see you. I *hear* you. So, I wanted to say again that I—me and Mom and Dad, all of us—appreciate the turnout here. We have every intention of honoring Fanny's debts. It will—it's just—well, as you all know, I've been unemployable ever since "The Incident," so—but that's not what I came here to say. I just—thank you.

But it's important that you understand. That you understand *why* Fanny always asked for help. Aside from her own employment challenges, which were not my sister's fault. Fanny has never been "good at interviews." And her lack of past job experience of any kind or academic degrees or professional certifications didn't help, I'll allow. But it's not really fair that a note from a medical professional explaining her physical limitations—and Fanny had *several* such notes, from very reputable doctors—oh, fine, Uncle Jim, not *doctors* per se, but *respected professionals adjacent to the medical profession*, I know what the settlement stipulated—it's not fair that these notes didn't clear everything up. If a person is *physically incapable* of performing a task or being away from their bathroom for several hours every day, is it not the worst kind of discrimination not to hire that person?

But—look, I'm—I've lost—look, what I'm saying is, you'll all be paid back, and you should be proud to have been part of Fanny's efforts. Because my sister was truly one of the best people in the world. She needed money not for spas and massages—though those were medically necessary, as those letters attested—or the personal chef services because Fanny's digestive tract was one of the most sensitive in the world—you know, she once went to an allergist and they called in *all the other allergists* to look at her back because she reacted to just about *everything*—but because Fanny was dedicated to making this world a better place.

There was a time when I could not have imagined saying something like that. To be honest, I often think of my older sister as two different people. When we were in high school—I was a freshman at Bishop Carlbus Prep when she was a senior—she was—sorry, Mom and Dad—she was not a nice person. She was *mean*. I didn't like my sister when I was fourteen. I won't—I don't want to—I won't go into details. It was standard sibling stuff, I guess.

But something changed in her right before college. She would never talk about it, but something definitely happened to her. It changed her. She spent one semester at Wesleyan and then dropped out. I think our parents had matching heart attacks ‹laughter›.

I remember when she got home from school after that first year and she wouldn't come out of her room. She was such a different person. Her friend, Amy, had died right before graduation, just this horrible accident, and that hit her hard, I know. She and Amy had been close. But my sister was a fighter. You could see, even in those dark days, the fight she had in her—she kept trying to do good. Dad, you remember how you had to lock your credit card because Fanny kept donating to charities? That was my sister. When it came to doing good, she didn't let anything stop her.

When she told us she was going to go help build a house for poor people in Cambodia, no one believed her. But then she explained how it worked, and I swear, the sparkle in her eye when she talked about helping those poor people, it made *me* want to go build a house ‹laughter›. And I intend to do that, someday, in honor of Fanny. I want to keep doing the work that meant so much to her. Of course, ever since the consent decree I can't get a passport, but I'll find a way. Fanny always did. Which is why she died owing you all so much money.

After that, there was no stopping her. Over the next few years, she totally changed the way I looked at her. I asked her once why she was so determined to help everyone else in the world, and she said it was just what she had to do. Helping other people was something she felt driven to do. So, she went everywhere. She was in South America, Africa, the Balkans, Eastern Europe—there was literally no place she wouldn't go to help other people.

Fanny always said people help in different ways. Fanny went on these trips, and she faced down a lot of challenges. No one knows how *hard* these trips were for her. First, the airlines always fought her on the service animal thing. We all know Shade, her English Mastiff. Shade wasn't just a pet, he was a—Uncle *Jim*, I know, but you're *wrong*! She had the documents!—He was a *service animal*. Fanny got terrible anxiety on planes. Two Xanax and a little bottle of vodka barely helped. Shade kept her sane on those long flights, and yet the airlines—I mean, *all* of them—were so rude and unkind. Did you know Fanny was banned from *six* airlines when she died? *That's* how determined she was to help the impoverished people of the world.

People help in different ways—my sister was wise. Sure, Fanny couldn't carry cinder blocks, because her back was weak and doing so would leave her in excruciating pain for weeks. She couldn't use a hammer because of her carpal tunnel syndrome—we all saw her drop things because of her weak wrists—and she couldn't mix cement because she was sensitive to dust. That was *serious*. She could have *died*. But no Build Team ever had a better cheerleader than Fanny Heck. I have so many photos of my sister sitting under her giant umbrella on a build site, Shade at her feet, smiling under those trademark Caviar sunglasses.

She gave her fellow builders so much joy and support. *That* was Fanny's talent.

You could tally up Fanny's impressive statistics to show how much good she did. All those trips to exotic—I mean, impoverished places. Fiji. Bangkok. Anywhere there was need, Fanny would sign up. Selfless.

She paid in other ways, too. She got sick—a lot. You can't slave away in some of these places and not pick up every bug known to man. She was trapped in Malawi, once, for six weeks under quarantine. Six weeks! You can't blame her for that bill at the Protea—she was fighting for her life. And she had to have Shade's food flown in, because you all *know* that dog has digestive issues.

‹weak laughter›

You might—Uncle *Jim*, you can say whatever the fuck *later*, okay?—you might wonder how I *know* that Fanny was doing good. Well, I know it because the people she helped made that loud and clear. Because wherever Fanny went, she had fans. Locals, *natives*, who considered her to be a friend, a good person they wanted more of in their lives. There was Soth, who drove her an hour into the country to see his house, and who wrote to her regularly for years after the trip, asking for photos. There was K—Fanny couldn't remem—pronounce, I mean, his name, so she just called him K—who took her to dinner to show his appreciation, and gave her a lot of gifts, some quite valuable.

This meant the world to Fanny. It was important to her to show these people that she didn't think less of them just because their English was hilarious, or because their homes had dirt floors, or because they lacked education or what she considered basic hygiene. So, despite her sensitive stomach and the exhaustion that always plagued her on these service trips—she was frequently confined to her bed by medical advice—she would never dream of insulting these people by refusing something she was offered. And the food was terrible. I mean, you don't really understand how bad it was, sometimes. But Fanny would soldier through it with a smile and spend the next few days recovering, because that's who she was. She was fearless.

And that fearlessness killed her.

She went to Thailand to help people, and they repaid her by pushing her into a pond, a small lake. A pit filled with brackish water. She'd gone to the work site for the first time after being bedridden for three days, and she'd spent the morning cheering on her fellow volunteers, offering the light and joy that was Fanny's special gift. And she walked a little bit away from the site, into the country, and as she was walking past this gross puddle, someone raced past and shoved her in. Shoved her in!

She told us she couldn't identify the person who pushed her, but I got the sense, over the phone, on a terrible connection as we worked frantically to get her home, that she had seen them. She did know who had pushed her. She'd alluded to some problems with the other people on her build, some nasty people who were rude, but we don't know more than that. Fanny never said a bad word about anyone—the fact that she said even that much indicates to me that these people were very nasty indeed.

Unfortunately, I have a negative—and undeserved—reputation with law enforcement stemming from those warrants and that time I was detained at Charles de Gaulle, so, my efforts to contact local authorities by phone were fruitless.

But nothing could knock my sister down. Nothing could defeat her sense of purpose. She didn't feel well after the incident—she'd swallowed a lot of that water. But she got up the next morning and made it to the door of her room before the dizziness overtook her, forcing her back to bed to order room service. She did it again the next day, even though she felt worse, and didn't get further than the bathroom. The hotel, I have to say, was quite cruel. Something about a rejected credit card for sundries, and despite her obvious illness they refused to send anything up. They even apparently tried to evict her! While she was *literally dying*!

She developed a fever. She had a nosebleed, and told us she had something in her throat, and to their credit the build group sent her to the local clinic, where whatever kind of medicine man or whatever they had there examined her and told her she was probably suffering from sun stroke, gave her some aspirin, and sent her back.

And my incredible sister, who started to cough up blood, still got up the next day to try to go to the site to do her work. She told me she felt terrible—she had chills, her throat was so sore she couldn't swallow, she was still coughing up—but she told me ‹incoherent› ‹sniffling› I'm sorry.

I'll never forget that last conversation. She told me she deserved whatever she got. That she had to do whatever she could to be a better person. That's how dedicated Fanny was. Even as she was ‹incoherent›. Even as she was dying, she was thinking of others.

It was leeches. There were leeches in the water, eggs or larva or something, and she swallowed them when she was pushed into that pond. Something about cattle, cows. It doesn't matter. I'm told that even here doctors might have missed it, because it's not common and it's difficult to see in your ... in your throat. The leeches bled her to death. But to me, none of that matters. I hope the person that did this to her understands, somehow, what they took away from the world.

My sister was a great person. A truly great person. She gave her life trying to help others, and I'm gladdened to see so many people here today willing to set aside grudges and consider dropping out of the lawsuit—yes, Uncle Jim, I *am* looking at you—and let Fanny's legacy shine.

Thank you. Fanny would have been tickled to see you all here, and she would have wanted you to laugh, to smile, to celebrate her instead of mourning her. So, please, let's do that.

That's why I'm excited to announce the launch of the Fanny Foundation and invite you all to participate by becoming platinum-tier founding donors. We—Uncle Jim, of *course* you'll have the chance to review the paperwork, but now is not the time or place, is it? This will be our chance as a family to continue the spirit of Fanny's work—yes, Melanie, I'll be acting as Executive Director, which is a *great sacrifice* since, as you know, so much of my time is spent in litigation these days, but again, these details can wait—Uncle Jim, there's no need to—please stay in your—this is a place of worship, man!

‹incoherent shouting›

FIVE FUNERALS

Rhoda

Chapter 34: Miriam De Rasta's Last Stand

An account of the death of Rhoda Anderson in April, 2013

Glenn Anderson had been by all accounts a no-good, unreliable man who made everyone less happy by his presence. He left his wife and daughter when Rhoda was just five years old. Camille Anderson never missed him once in the remaining two decades of her life. Rhoda missed him desperately, all the time.

Rhoda's memories of her childhood were vague and hollow. Lots of empty space, many missing frames, subtitles that were just a series of question marks. She knew she did not think about sex once before the age of fourteen. Other girls on her block and in her classes began giggling about sex years before, but Rhoda was baffled. Boys were just other people. Girls were just other people. Rhoda had no strong feelings for either, but Rhoda was slowly discovering that she had no strong feelings for many—if not all—things.

At the age of fourteen Rhoda showed up at the Bishop Carlbus Prep campus wearing a pair of green overalls and a pink shirt, her dull brown hair pulled back in a simple ponytail, and the first person she met was Fanny Heck, who immediately asked if she had dressed in a watermelon costume on purpose. Fanny was simultaneously the meanest person Rhoda had ever met and the most interesting. Fanny had opinions. About everything. They were dark and aggressive opinions, smart in jagged ways. Fanny was a fourteen-year-old girl who had seen some things and judged them all to be vastly overrated.

For the second time in her life, Rhoda Anderson found herself thinking of another human being when they weren't standing right in front of her, making noise.

Rhoda remade herself in Fanny's image, even though she found many of the other girl's opinions to be opaque and difficult to comprehend. But she knew that when she was in doubt the correct answer involved being mean and cutting, something she practiced at home with her mother.

Camille Anderson had not flourished in the wake of her husband's vanishing. Whether Glenn was alive or dead, she couldn't say, and while this didn't particularly worry her, it did complicate her life to the point where she found herself exhausted more or less continuously. From the age of eight, Rhoda began engaging in a nightly ritual of turning off lights Camille had left on, closing cabinet doors that Camille had left open, and removing a burning cigarette from Camille's slack, unconscious fingers before going to bed. Camille found it increasingly difficult to remain awake and had winnowed the time spent conscious down to a bare minimum. The house grew quiet, and Camille did not tolerate noise at all.

Rhoda's contempt for her mother grew daily.

The entirety of Freshman Year was taken up with learning everything that Fanny Heck had to teach her. She learned the art of shitting on things. She learned the power of disinterest and disdain, more destructive than violence or bloodshed. She learned to apply makeup and to choose cute outfits, because even though she still had no interest in either gender she knew that Fanny regarded sex appeal as a key skill. She learned the power of secrets, and secret communication channels that rivaled the Cold War Superpowers in complexity and obfuscation. Fanny created a complex list of secret and super-secret nicknames for all 24 other kids in their class. The secret names were mean and not exactly secret. The super-secret names were meaner and as far as Rhoda knew only existed in her private communications with Fanny. Amy Keaton's secret nickname was *Roid*, as in roid-rage. Her *super-secret* nickname was *Pussy Face*.

Summer break between freshman and sophomore year at BCP was traumatic to Rhoda. Home was intolerable. Fanny was cool. Some of the other kids were cool. They had cool adventures and said cool things. Her mother was not cool. Her mother was depressingly square and hopelessly outdated, unable to understand even the simplest concepts. Rhoda felt like a caged rat in her room, in large part because Fanny had gone to visit her grandparents for the summer, and Rhoda found herself stuffed back into a life that no longer quite fit her.

One day, prowling the neighborhood in a desperate search for something to distract herself with, she ran into a boy from her class: Quentin Cunningham. They had never once spoken to each other, and Fanny's super-secret nickname for him was *Horse Boy*, because, she said, of his long, flat nose.

They walked around a little, awkward and nervous. Quentin told her a story about a dilapidated green house from when he was a kid where he and his friends had lost all their balls—baseballs and rubber balls, footballs, both foam and leather—as well as several kites. It was a story so pure and wide-eyed she felt, for the first time in months, the stirrings of regret for the Super-Secret Name he'd been given.

Years later, Rhoda could not recall how they fell in with each other. Boredom, certainly, but the details eluded her. Fanny's attitude towards Quentin should have made a friendship impossible, but Fanny was so far away, the radiation she was beaming was weak and the signal was easily lost. By the end of the summer, she and Quentin were spending most of their days together hanging out, watching TV. Rhoda liked that Quentin didn't treat her like a girl or a sexual object at all. He seemed content to just have her company. She ended her nights on the phone with him, whispering miseries, and then crept up to her mother's bedroom to pluck the burning cigarette from her fingers and head off to bed.

Back at Bishop Carlbus Prep, Rhoda began living a double life. Walking the halls next to Fanny, she dispensed sarcasm and sick burns. At home, on the phone, she cried and told Quentin how much she hated herself, her mother, her father. Then she would check on her mother, extinguish the cigarette, and go to sleep.

Quentin said with static all around his voice, "We're connected. Like, forever."

and Rhoda nodded, eyes heavy, swathed in her sweaty sheets, the smell of Camille's cigarettes everywhere, in her hair, in her skin—Pontifuss Maximuss' rising and falling belly as she breathed, purring.

and Quentin said, "No matter how much time or space comes between us, we'll always know exactly where we are. And someday when we need each other, we'll just know."

and Rhoda nodded.

Rhoda split into two. And for three years she existed as both people.

For Fanny, Amelia Dongle was just a lark, a way to keep her most scathing and terrible comments at arm's length so they didn't invite physical retributions. Amy's surface-level secret nickname was Roid for a reason, and Fanny did not wish to experience it.

But for Rhoda, Miriam de Rasta was a real person, a tight-fitting costume made of human skin that she slid into like a reverse snake every morning. She dressed the part, recited the lines Fanny had written for her, and stalked BCP's campus in a cloud of glitter.

Quentin was a risk. For both of them, but mainly for Rhoda due to her proximity to Fanny. At school, they were careful to limit their interactions. Rhoda knew how Fanny operated, knew that ignoring each other would be as much of a red flag as a lingering look. So, they had a calibrated friendship at school: nods, polite exchanges, the understanding that Rhoda would slag Quentin privately to Fanny.

At home, she peeled off Miriam's outer layer and became Rhoda again. She called Quentin and made plans. She lay in the dark and thought that all she had to do was survive until graduation, and then she would be free. She discussed moving to New York with Quentin. She would change her name, get a new phone number, forget Fanny Heck and Amy Keaton and the rest of them and do something, anything, everything.

And then Amy Keaton threw a party.

Quentin suggested they skip the party. He made persuasive arguments centered on the fact that they didn't much like Amy, or Fanny, or anyone else for that matter, the bunch of boring Normies. But Rhoda preferred an Irish Exit. She knew that Fanny would leave town to visit her grandparents over the summer as usual, and no one else would put much energy into staying in touch. She would be able to slip away and cut ties without any scenes. By the time Fanny returned, she would be gone, a mystery.

Rhoda considered Fanny Heck's determination to subvert Amy's Outing party to be a silly waste of energy, but had grown terrified of Fanny over the years, and so she went along. She felt shame as Miriam said mean things and egged Fanny on, but reminded herself that in just a few days she would graduate and Rhoda Anderson would vanish, along with the extremely bitchy Miriam de Rasta, never to be heard from again.

For years afterward, she wondered how things might have

been different if she'd listened to Quentin.

When Pontifuss Maximuss returned to the house every night, yowling for food and comfort, leaves in her fur and mud between her toes, Rhoda always stood in the doorway for a moment staring at her and wondering, why? Why do you come back to this terrible house? And then she would gather Ponts up in her arms and bury her face in the cat's fur and knew that if she ever lost the cat, she would have nothing left.

She sometimes sat in her room, the smell of Camille's cigarettes everywhere, and imagined she'd left with Quentin instead, that night, not even waiting for graduation. Just melting away. Quentin came to the house one last time. Stood at the bottom of the stairs looking up at her, the expression on his face the most painful thing she'd ever seen. She felt frozen. She wanted to say something—to shout something, to throw herself down the stairs and grab onto him like a life preserver. But she couldn't move. He left without saying a word, unable to even look at her. Rhoda understood. She couldn't bear the thought of seeing anyone, any of them. She just pictured them in that living room, cheering. Dancing. Ghouls.

Over time, though, Rhoda hoped Quentin would come home. Check in. Call her or write a letter. She took part-time jobs and drank beer in her room, ended most nights taking the cigarette from Camille's hands, studying the burning coal as she walked it to the toilet, thinking about Glenn Anderson and what he'd known, the future he'd glimpsed with apparent psychic powers. Rhoda once imagined her father being punished, in pain and regretting abandoning his family. Now she saw him smiling, secretly, a plump, well-fed billionaire, a man without worries because he'd had the good sense to walk away from his doomed family.

Quentin, too, had finally seen the truth. The years ticked by, and he never made contact.

Sometimes, when she looked in the mirror, she saw Miriam de Rasta. Grinning, pink lipstick and glossed lips, smoky eyes, hair curled and brittle, tits pushed up and belly button peeking out from a shirt that was precisely too short. Miriam was at fault, not her. Miriam and Amelia had egged Amy on, sown dissent, spread rumors. Not her.

Rhoda and her mother moved between four rooms in a strange asynchronicity that ensured they were never in the same room at the same time. The house filled with cigarette smoke, stinging Rhoda's eyes and afflicting her with a constant, burning cough. Pontifuss skulked, staying low where the air was fresher.

The phone calls began around this time. Random moments, unexpected. No one ever spoke. Sometimes she could hear static on the line. Sometimes breathing. After ten, twenty seconds, half a minute, the line would go dead. Always from the same, unfamiliar number.

She thought it must be Quentin, and she wished he'd speak. Say anything. Say that he'd seen her true self and been repulsed, that what happened to Amy had broken him, broken their friendship, broken everything. Anything. She began sleeping with the phone, startling awake when it buzzed in her sleep.

The calls continued for a few weeks, a presence she came to rely on. She would randomly dial the number. Each time, whoever was on the other end answered but said nothing. Every time, Rhoda felt paralyzed again. Frozen at the top of the stairs. She would sit and listen to the emptiness, and she wasn't able to speak.

When they abruptly stopped, Rhoda felt a searing pang of loss. She'd never been certain it was Quentin on the other end—there had been a menace to the calls, a strange subliminal anger to the breathing—but the loss burned like acid.

Rhoda stepped lightly down the stairs. The treads and floor were gritty under her stocking feet. The house hadn't been cleaned in months, years, ever. The house was dark, but her eyes had long ago adjusted, the lids receding into her head, her eyes glowing a soft mint green, every corner and dip in the house memorized long before.

She walked to the back door, whispering the cat's name. Pontifuss appeared, quizzical. When Rhoda opened the door, however, the cat did not hesitate: it chose adventure and vanished into the night.

She walked into the living room, pushing a wave of fast-food wrappers, paper plates, and magazines before her. She stood over Camille for a moment, the final nub of a cigarette burning between her fingers. Rhoda stared at the red coal for a moment. She reached for it, eyes on the kindling all around, the dry, brittle paper and assorted trash.

Then she pulled her hand back.

She left the burning coal where it was, held slackly between two numb fingers. She turned and crossed to the stairs. At the bottom, one hand loosely on the banister, she looked down at her feet and sighed, shoulders slumping. Then she started to climb up.

FIVE FUNERALS

Olive

Chapter 35: Awl Together Now

An Account of the Death of Olive Partridge in November, 2011

By the time Olive was thirty-four years old, no one had seen her face in sixteen years. No one called her Olive. When customers at Bierk's Books referred to her, it was almost always as The Girl with The Mask. The elastic bands dug cruelly into her head and neck, leaving deep red marks that never went away, but she always wore the heavy duty medical-grade masks in the hope that people would assume she had some terrible autoimmune disease.

When Olive ate meals, she would lift the bottom of the mask up and slip a fork or spoon beneath it.

When she brushed her ruined, crooked teeth, she closed her eyes.

She often thought of Maud Bluth. She often saw Maud's face from that night, so high her eyes were basically black holes absorbing all visible light. She saw Maud barreling towards her, sweaty hair in her face. What she always remembered was Maud's expression. It was an expression she'd never seen before, or since. An emotion she'd never experienced or seen anyone else experience.

The punch was random. An afterthought. She wasn't even

sure Maud knew who Olive was as she flashed past, lashing out one hand like a medicine ball. Olive wasn't even sure Maud remembered or realized what she'd done. She'd never see Maud again. Olive skipped graduation, receiving her diploma in the mail. She'd dropped the envelope on top of her admission materials for NYU and never opened either.

On the bus, Olive's phone *dinged* softly, and she pulled it from her pocket. A text from her mother. She went through the motions of blocking the new number and deleting the text unread. Every few months, Diana decided to try again.

As Olive settled herself back in her seat, something pricked the back of her neck. She looked up sharply. Across the aisle from her, a man was staring.

This wasn't unusual. Every few years her mask became normal thanks to some global pandemic, but it always faded, and people discarded theirs and left Olive as the only one left wearing one. Sometimes she was hassled about it, but most people just assumed she was a germaphobe and left it at that. Every now and then she met an Activist.

She stared back and waited for the inevitable diatribe.

He was perhaps a few years younger than her. Pale like milk, freckled in a way that implied anger, brown hair hanging in his face. He was smiling at her, but it wasn't a friendly smile.

"Take off your mask," he said. "Let me see your face."

The tone, also, wasn't friendly.

Olive looked away. At the next stop, she rushed off the bus at the last moment, slipping through the closing doors with a shouted apology. When she turned to look back, he was smiling at her through the window as the bus pulled away.

The weeks after the party were a blur. She remembered Mr. Drummond having them sign papers, telling them they all had to be careful. They could lose their scholarships, be fucked for life. She remembered being afraid to leave her room after being released from the hospital—her mouth full of metal, an appointment set with the oral surgeon, her parents giving her space for a few days, a week. The pain in her mouth became excruciating, lances of agony into her brain. When she finally had the courage to look, she almost fainted.

When she told her parents she wasn't having the surgery—she wouldn't have her mouth repaired—there was an explosion.

They ordered her into the car to drive her to the emergency room, but she refused. They called an ambulance, but she refused to leave her room. They called the police, and she sat, terrified, behind the locked door of her room and insisted that she was eighteen years old, that her parents were overreacting, that she did not need medical attention. The police had difficulty understanding her but were reluctant to intervene in what they termed a family matter. Olive packed her backpack and climbed out the window.

She ate the antibiotics she'd been given. Her mouth healed, to an extent. The crooked teeth solidified. The sores and cuts scabbed and closed up. It became a calcified monument to the Punch, a frozen moment of time.

But her mouth was never healthy. She battled constant infections. She lived on acetaminophen and ibuprofen, lying awake at night and imagining the stress on her kidneys and liver. She dreamed of Oxycodone, but worried that any connection to a hospital or emergency room would lead her parents to her. She would kill herself, she thought, before letting her mother see her like this.

Sometimes she fantasized about prying her teeth out, one by one, and replacing them with something else. Small, white stones. Or seashells. Or gold ingots. She dreamed of doing it herself. A pair of pliers. A bottle of vodka. Screams. Blood.

Eventually, she began wearing the masks. More people accepted it than she expected.

She changed phones on a regular basis, but after a few months her mother would slide into her texts again. It always began with cheerful care, her mother not wanting to spook her. But it always twisted into a desperate need to understand. Why had Olive run away? What had they done? What had happened?

She could hear her mother: *Of course, that terrible business at the party with the Keaton girl. That was a shock. But surely a terrible accident didn't cause Livvy to throw away the rest of her life!*

Olive imagined the usual explanations being discussed over glasses of red wine in that old painfully white kitchen. Drugs? Certainly. Bishop Carlbus Prep had a reputation as a party school, rumors of all kinds swirling about, the occasional parental panic when one of those rumors—cocaine at a sleepover, meth being smoked before midterms—surfaced high enough to catch their attention. A secret boyfriend, girlfriend? Why not? Pre-injury Olive had been a good-looking girl. Round face, good hair, clear skin. Only her teeth, poorly spaced and prone to cavities like they were made of chalk, ruined the look. The braces were supposed to correct them, elevate her to true hottie status. Her mother, petting her, brushing her hair, telling her how pretty she was, how lucky. How the boys would fall all over her in college.

Emotional problems? Mental breakdown? Pregnancy?

Olive was fairly certain her parents would never understand that the Punch had been a gift. She'd become a different person in that instant.

She got the job at Bierks' just a few weeks after leaving home. Ken Bierks was a befuddled old man who hired everyone who applied for a job. There were sometimes ten people working there at once, most with nothing to do. It paid just enough for her to rent a room from Mrs. Koshka, whose husband had died three years before, leaving her with a Social Security check that didn't leave her much margin for error. The room was small and windowless, which appealed to Olive.

Mrs. Koshka made no comment on the mask and asked no questions about a young girl paying cash to stay in a tiny room. She insisted on giving Olive a full tour of the house. Each room required several lengthy stories concerning her husband, relatives and other people Olive had never met and who Mrs. Koshka did not explain. The tour ended in Mr. Koshka's old woodshop in the converted garage, left exactly as it had been on the day he dropped dead of a stroke in church. The unfinished birdhouse he was building had been intended for their backyard, and remained on the bench, incomplete.

Olive came to love Mr. Koshka's workshop. She spent hours in it, just sitting, reverently avoiding upsetting anything. She would pick up the tools and weigh them in her hands—the mallet, the awl, the cold chisel—but she was careful to put them all back in the exact same spot, without even smudging the dust. She thought the room had good energy, that Mr. Koshka must have been a good person. She imagined him, sometimes, and saw a stolid, fleshy man who wore baggy clothes. A man who seldom spoke and who would seem unfriendly or even mean when you first met him, but who would silently bring you a cup of tea. A man who expressed himself with the things he made.

And those things were all over the house. Mrs. Koshka regarded Olive as a member of the household and invited her to go anywhere in the home she wanted, often inviting her to watch television with her at night. Mr. Koshka's handiwork was everywhere: picture frames, shelves, the napkin holder in the kitchen. Jewelry boxes and approximately one million carvings of cats in various poses. Olive loved being in the Koshka house, but she especially loved the old workshop.

Her shift at Bierks' was vaguely defined. She knew there would be at least four other people working in the tiny shop, so her presence wasn't mandatory, and Mr. Bierks did payroll on the honor system. People drifted in and out but knew they would be paid their pittance no matter how many hours they had actually worked.

No one wanted her to work in the children's section, which she was thankful for. She'd never liked kids, but after the injury they'd become little monsters that she avoided whenever possible. The adult section was sleepier, and she was able to spend her time thinking and reading.

She was thinking about Maud and the Outing Party when her phone *dinged* again, the specific tone signaling it was her mother, once again trying to make contact. She ignored it, thinking back on the party and tasting the faint echo of that sensation of spinning, of everything out of control. She remembered feeling increasingly nervous all night, the whole party like a scene out of a zombie movie, one of those early scenes when everything is still ostensibly normal, but everyone can sense things sliding into chaos. The Slide, that was what she remembered. Things going wrong. Things breaking, the power going out, Amy raging, and everyone being mean to her. Because she deserved it, maybe, but it still felt wrong.

And then Maud had punched her in the face and the pain had been incredible. Her eyes teared, but she was so shocked and in so much sudden, unexpected agony that her outward reaction was casual, muted. Then she went into what she now recognized as shock, feeling numb and distanced from everything. And then she got stoned, trying to ease the pain, trying to burn out the trembling fear, the flinch that kept going and going. And it worked. Until the next morning. Until they found Amy.

The bell on the front door jangled, and Olive glanced up. For a moment she was confused—the man standing just inside the store seemed familiar, but she wasn't sure how. A primitive buzz of anxiety bloomed in her chest.

Then he took a step forward and she realized it was the man from the bus. He smiled at her as he approached, but again the smile was mean, hard. He was wearing a black baseball cap, strands of limp, dark hair dripping out at his temples.

"Excuse me, miss," he said, maneuvering around the bestsellers table with angular grace. He was tall and skinny, his skin dry and mottled where she could see it.

She felt trapped, as if his stare was a tractor beam of some kind, holding her in place. A dread, familiar and choking, rose up inside her. This had happened before. Always men, always angry. Always.

The bell on the door jangled again.

"Excuse me, miss," he said again, the smile eerily unwavering. When he was right in front of her, he reached up. "*Take off your mask!*" he hissed, snatching the mask from her face. The elastic held out heroically, then snapped, drawing blood from her cheek as it did so.

She felt strangely calm, even though she'd just been assaulted. She looked up over his shoulder, and there was her mother. She was gray-haired and her face had a permanent sad sag to it, but it was her mother: tidy hair, colorful scarf.

Her mother's eyes widened. "Olive? *Oh my god, Olive!*"

Olive clamped a hand over her mouth and screamed through it. Then she turned and ran out the back.

Mrs. Koshka didn't look up from her crossword puzzle when Olive raced through the living room. In Mr. Koshka's workshop, she shut the door behind her and leaned against it. Tears dripped down her face. She'd imagined the moment when her mother would find her—she'd known it was inevitable, because she knew her mother, a woman who had once spent three weeks calling a customer service number in pursuit of a refund totaling four dollars. In her imagination she had remained in control. Calm and cool. She had refused to answer questions.

In her imagination, though, she'd been wearing her mask.

But seeing her, Olive felt the loss of time. She felt she'd punished herself enough. Sixteen years was enough. If she'd gone to prison, she imagined that would have been her sentence, and she would be emerging today, blinking in the sun, older and weathered by her time behind bars with true criminals—but with perfect, white teeth thanks to the surprisingly sophisticated healthcare in prison.

She began to shake. Reaching up, she tore off the replacement mask and felt the shock of air against her lips. She ran her tongue over the scarred wasteland of her mouth and couldn't bear to live with it one moment more. She convulsed with sudden despair, a low moan boiling up from within. Sixteen years, she thought.

Her eyes landed on the workbench where Mr. Koshka's tools sat. Pushing off from the door, she staggered over to them and picked up the awl. She would pry them out. Every jagged, broken tooth. Every solid, unharmed one. She would rip them out by the root and have them replaced with gemstones, with tiny sculptures, with knives.

Hands shaking with something like joy, she opened her mouth and pushed the tip of the awl into a gap between her front teeth. Her breathing was loud and ragged in her ears, but that day, the day she'd been living in for sixteen years, was finally ending.

Trying to steady herself, she closed her eyes and took a deep breath, preparing for the pain. It would be sudden and sharp, and her mouth would flood with salty blood. She pictured it. She'd dealt with pain. She was used to it. She pressed the palm of her hand against the bottom of the awl's smooth, timeworn handle, then retracted it a few inches, preparing for the jolting smack that would set her free.

When Mrs. Koshka found the body of Olive Partridge sometime later, she stared for a long moment, distressed; then she knelt down and gently slid the awl from Olive's head. She wiped the blood from it with the hem of her baggy floral dress, reached up, and set it precisely where it had been. Where it belonged.

Xerxes

Chapter 36: I'll Be Judge, I'll Be Jury

An Account of the Death of Xerxes Bartokomous in January, 2004

PEOPLE were always asking him if he would take some experimental treatment to get his hair back, but Xerc always told them he'd never *had* hair, so he didn't miss it. It was like asking him if he would do a surgery to get a third arm.

The strangest thing was, if he wore a hat most people didn't notice. They always knew something was off, though. They just couldn't quite place what it was, what was missing.

Eyebrows. Eyebrows were what was missing.

The House was out in the middle of nowhere, an ancient hulk of a place being crushed and digested by ivy and trees and other vegetation. He bought it for the back taxes, more than he'd thought, but then the state was always robbing you, always had its hand in your pocket. Old heads in town knew the story: it had been built by a successful farmer a century before, but hard times and tired soil had ruined him, so he'd packed up his family and left the house to rot. It had been empty for a long time, until a group of foreigners—no one remembered where they were actually from—set up a lab of some sort. When the feds raided it, they recovered all manner of medical waste and dangerous stuff.

This was ten years ago, and it had remained a mystery. Who would set up an unlicensed lab in the middle of nowhere?

Xerc told no one. It was his secret. Even before he started working on it, he would go there and sleep with the soft, rotting wood and the leftover equipment, rusted and ruined.

His father sat him down shortly after the family found out he'd used his inheritance to buy a rotting house in the middle of the forest. Xerc knew it was a serious talk when the old man poured him a shot of ouzo, always the sign of a respected guest in the house. They'd sat at the kitchen table for a long time while the old man stared at his liquor.

"Why?" he'd asked, genuinely baffled. "Why spend your future on this ... wreck?"

Xerc nodded. He didn't know what to say, so he said nothing. He'd tried to explain to his parents that the world was ending, that you had to be prepared. No one understood. So, it was up to him to prepare for them.

After New York, he'd started buying gold. And self-heating meals.

Once you started pulling threads, it all started to make terrible sense. The center could not hold. He knew what people were capable of—he'd stood there with Leo and Olive and Quentin and the rest, listening as Victor's dad explained it to them, how they moved on, how they protected themselves. The machinery of the state belching into life in order to protect them all, even though they didn't deserve it.

People exhausted him. Their pretending wore him down. Pretending they didn't notice his condition, pretending not to notice them not noticing. He often felt like he spent more energy willfully ignoring what other people were willfully ignoring, everyone acting like they were super tolerant, super caring, super cool. The idea of living out in the middle of nowhere, totally independent, became increasingly attractive. Amy Keaton's disaster of a party had planted the seed—he decided that morning that he would live apart from everyone. But then the world had gone to shit, and he knew he needed to move faster, be more prepared. He started studying self-defense. He got a gun license. And he started looking for a place off the grid.

The property wasn't hooked up to city sewer lines, had no running water, and no electricity. The city made it clear that it was not fit for occupancy, but he hiked out to the spot with camping gear and some basic tools. He determined he could drive something formidable to a trailhead about two miles from the house, then haul in whatever he needed by foot. He envisioned a sled.

Sweating and with an aching back, he stepped through the empty doorway, stamped snow off his boots, and set his pack on the soft, springy old floor. He looked around. The place still had the outlines of a home. He imagined everything in it being built by hand, crafted lovingly and installed with unstinting accuracy. But now everything metal was rusted, and every plank was warped. The glass was shattered, the paint peeled, the bricks spalled. He knew almost none of it was salvageable, but he hoped to find something—an ornament, a detail—that he could preserve, a link to the past.

He looked around and nodded. When society collapsed, he thought he could ride it out here.

A wave of movement made him jump. A band of a dozen mice, hairless and pink, surged through the room, their tiny claws scratching against the soft floor. He watched in horror. He knew that the cops had found a large population of the rodents when they raided the place. Hairless mice were often used in medical research and bred like a house on fire. But he'd assumed the creatures would have moved on to better pastures or been eradicated by predators. Xerxes didn't like mice, rats, or bugs, or anything else that crept along in the dark, and suddenly the old place seemed dirty and dangerous.

The image he remembered from Amy's party was the footprints. The basement was coated in red, rusty dust that shimmered down from the walls and ceiling, and the house was covered in ghostly red steps. Everyone had to go down to see, and then everyone was up and down the stairs during the general panic.

It was Leo who'd noticed the footprints. Before Victor called his father, before Mr. Drummond called the Chief of Police and Principal Murray and set the creaky machine that absolved them into motion. Xerc remembered the panic, thinking that people would think they'd all come down to stare, which they had, and used his foot to sweep them away until Kate shoved him, yelling. *When you sweep up footprints it fucking looks like someone swept up footprints!*

What he remembered is that everything was terrible, but it made sense: they'd done something bad, and they would be punished. And then Victor made a call to his father and his father made calls to the authorities and suddenly they were just kids who'd made some mistakes, and the world stopped making sense.

He set mouse traps, and every time he returned to the house, he had a crop of dead mice to clear out. The little bastards had been enjoying their independence, building a little Mice Nation out in the middle of nowhere, but the idea of mice scampering across his face as he slept—their smooth, gross, wrinkled bodies against his skin—made him unhappy.

It was getting cold, and the house was an icebox—Xerc's feet and hands were always numb—but the mice didn't seem to care. They thrived. No matter how many he killed, he found more. Whenever he moved something, a half dozen pink bodies would scamper away, squeaking. He began to wonder what, exactly, the illegal lab had been researching and what, exactly, had been done to the mice. His suspicions intensified when every exterminator he called hung up on him the moment he mentioned where he was.

He began stocking the place with supplies. He intended to fix it up, make it pleasant and livable, but he felt an increasing sense of urgency. If society collapsed, it would be sudden and violent. Pleasant and livable wouldn't help him much if he was starving and powerless.

He started with the gold and the weapons. He felt safer with the neat little bars off in the woods, security through obscurity. And he worried about his cache of guns and ammunition drawing attention before he could get set up.

While driving through the beginnings of a blizzard promised to be of the Century Storm sort, a box of gold bars in the car seat next to him, he was pulled over by a state police officer. The officer didn't seem to mind the snow and whipping wind and regarded his alopecia with suspicion. He responded to everything Xerc said with *Is that right?* as if unwilling to grant him any kind of shared commitment to a version of reality. This only worsened when Xerxes turned over his driver's license, as the officer clearly regarded Xerxes Bartokomous as a made-up name.

Xerc kept his eyes off the box, trying to remind himself what the local civil forfeiture laws were, and was mildly radicalized, wondering if perhaps the end of the world couldn't come soon enough. At least if someone tried to take his gold bars after the bombs fell, he could shoot them.

After the officer reluctantly let him go, he had to drive slowly because of the storm. Conditions had gotten worse as the temperature plunged, and he could barely see the road. When he got to the house, he added the box of gold to the pile he was forming in the center of a large room on the first floor. He'd recently secured several brand-new and never-loaded hunting rifles, two Glock G17s, and several boxes of ammunition, along with an enormous propane-powered generator capable of producing 15,000 watts.

He dropped the box, and the floor groaned and complained. There was a strange tearing sound that he felt more than heard, and then the floor gave way under him, and he plummeted into darkness.

He remembered playing Truth or Dare with Olive, Susan, Georgie, and Una. He remembered Olive got incredibly angry at him. He remembered he could feel her getting tight and quiet and annoyed even as they laughed at George doing his stupid little strip tease. He remembered dragging her into the off-limits formal living room, green painter's tape everywhere.

"Your eyes *follow* her," she'd hissed miserably, pushing him away. "You're, like, *obsessed* with her."

Her: Una. Tall, pretty, serious. Floaty. Xerc had always thought Una sort of floated.

"I don't," he said, feeling that embarrassing flush creeping up his neck. His skin betraying him, again, showing all of his emotions whether he wanted to or not. "I *don't*."

Olive shook her head. "You *do*. I see it."

She turned and ran off. He remembered thinking, *go after her*, but he didn't.

Later, he remembered thinking, *say something, don't go along with this*, but he didn't.

He woke up and for a moment he didn't know where he was. When he sat up, he cracked his head against something and fell back, cursing, the pain sinking down into his neck and shoulders and waking up the pain in his legs. It was dark and cold, and it smelled dank and mildewy.

The basement, he realized after a moment. He'd fallen into the basement. A root cellar, really, cold and slick, stone walls and muddy dirt floor, cobwebs and slithering things. There were no stairs; the ceiling was just four or five feet above him. He imagined in the distant past you would have lowered a ladder down to gain access, but it didn't look like anyone had been down there in a very long time.

Gold bars glinted dully all around him in the dim light. The generator had landed on its wheels and looked miraculously undamaged a few feet away. He supposed he was lucky it hadn't landed on his chest. As he sat there, feeling out the damage, he heard squeaking, high-pitched and insistent. Mice, he thought. In the darkness, hairless and pink.

He looked up, wincing. The hole in the floor was jagged and not as large as he'd expected. He could still make out the ghostly outline of his backpack, just a few inches from the edge. With a grunt, he got to his feet, his right knee almost buckling. He grabbed onto a joist for support and let the agony sweep past. With effort and some splinters in his hands, he was able to climb back up into the main part of the old house. He lay on the floor for a few moments, listening to the mice. When he tried to get to his feet, his knee refused to play along, sending a lance of agony up into his core.

He hadn't yet brought the medical supplies he'd accumulated. Searching his pockets turned up two Ibuprofens, which he swallowed without much expectation, and they delivered exactly zero relief from the deep ache in his knee, which erupted into white-hot pain whenever he moved.

In the dark, he made an ersatz nest for himself out of cardboard and a sheet of tarp, cursing himself for leaving his Go Bag in the car. Everything in the house was incredibly flammable, but he didn't even have matches. As he sat in the dark, listening to the wind howling outside, his knee pulsed painfully in time with his heartbeat, and he thought that preparing for disaster was harder than he'd expected.

A dull ache had settled into the center of his brain, and he shivered uncontrollably; nothing seemed to be keeping the wind out of the house. It just passed through the walls and turned the place into an enormous walk-in freezer.

For the first time in his life, Xerxes wished for hair. A real pelt. He imagined himself sweating under a pile of werewolf, Bigfoot-level fur.

Before Xerxes arrived at the Bishop Carlbus Prep campus as a freshman, he'd endured weeks of constant encouragement from his mother concerning his alopecia and appearance. The endless drone of optimism and reassurance had the opposite of its intended effect; after getting by with minimal awkwardness during his grammar school days, he began to approach his fancy prep school future with a sense of doom. His mother's anxiety, he reasoned, had to be based on something, some real experience or knowledge. BCP would be a hellscape.

When he was disgorged from his family's car, he remembered that the sun was bright and the skies clear—there was no hiding. He walked fearfully into the school with a comically bulky book bag strapped to his back, and was almost immediately intercepted by a chubby boy with lush, curly black hair and a nose shaped like a snail, dressed in a red tracksuit that shimmered in the bright sunlight.

"Jesus Christ," Leo Barone said. "You're, like, the baldest motherfucker."

This was conveyed in a tone that Xerc recognized as genuine wonder. Leo walked with him as if giving Xerc a personal tour of his strange, labyrinthine house, and began introducing him to everyone as The Baldest. The name was permanent by the end of the day. That night, lying in bed, Xerc realized that by pointing right at it and making it his nickname, Leo had normalized him immediately, effortlessly. He was The Baldest, and he was ride-or-die for Leo Barone from that moment forward.

Startling awake, he experienced a new kind of pain and found a mouse chewing on his earlobe.

He screamed, then screamed louder when his twitching response sent shockwaves of agony through his body. Shaking, he plucked the mouse from himself, a spray of his own warm blood hitting him in the face—and threw it, screeching, into the darkness.

He sat up in the gloom, hands numb. He was shivering, breathing hard, his heart pounding as his eyes slowly adjusted to the deep gloom of the place. All around him he could hear the mice dashing this way and that. Careful not to jostle his knee too much, he cast about his immediate area, seeking anything he might use as a weapon, but there was nothing within reach. A giddy laugh burst from deep within. He'd not only forgotten his Go Bag, but he'd also left all his weapons—the ones that hadn't fallen into the basement—out of reach.

The sound of tiny claws on the rough floor made him jump.

He could hear them—the mice. Dozens, moving freely around in the shadows. He tried to track them by sound, but didn't have a mental map of the space in his head.

The sounds stopped. The silence was worse. So much worse. He heard himself breathing, a whistle at the end of each breath, and he imagined them studying him with their black, blank eyes. Probing him for weaknesses.

The mice came in a wave. Dozens of them raced towards him. The sight of those wriggling pink bodies sprinting towards him was so terrifying he forgot his pain for a moment and tried to push himself up to escape. Screaming in sudden agony, he raised his arms and began violently sweeping them away.

After a moment, the mice retreated.

Survival was harder than he'd expected.

Leo was saying *we have to stick together.*

There was a murmur, everyone shifting their weight.

Kate was saying *all we have to do is nothing.*

Olive turned and looked at Xerc, her face swollen, her eyes red, her jaw miserably out of line. Her eyes latched onto his, asking him to tell her what to do.

Leo was saying *we have to stick together.*

Xerc remembered Leo on that first day. The Baldest. He nodded at Olive. Reassuring. *We have to stick together.*

She swallowed and nodded. And then she was incessantly nodding and wiping her eyes, like she was convincing herself.

Like she was telling herself if Xerc said so, then it would be okay.

The mice crept forward.

Xerc felt hot but was shivering. He was numb, but in agony.

The mice were hesitant, gauging his ability to strike. One stepped forward, creeping within a few inches and pausing, standing up on its hind legs, whiskers wiggling as it sniffed the frigid air. Behind it, several dozen more of the little pink mice advanced. Xerc thought it might be his fading coherence, but they looked ... organized. Like an army waiting for a signal.

He was finding it difficult to concentrate. His shivering had subsided, which he vaguely thought might be a bad sign. He was sleepy, despite the imminent danger. He let his eyes close for a moment and sank down into the tarp. It felt good. He wasn't even cold anymore.

He thought it was fitting: he'd left Amy to die, years ago. This was just a version of what was always going to happen. He felt the almost-gentle touch of the mice against his flesh, and he was glad he was alone. He knew they were nibbling at him, slicing his skin with their sharp teeth, consuming him, but it didn't hurt, and he found he didn't care.

As he sank into nothing, he wondered how long these mice had lived here, thriving in this abandoned house, their own little secret universe.

He wondered who else they'd eaten.

Susan

Chapter 37: Seize and Desist

An Account of the Death of Susan Petrie in January, 2015

The first time it happened, it took some time for her to realize *what*, exactly, had happened.

It was graduation day, six days after the Outing Party and she remembered just beginning to feel better. Not okay. Far from okay. But better. Able to take a shower and get dressed, able to smile, somehow, through the endless photos her parents insisted on taking. She remembered the phone in her room being almost dormant, with a single message on her machine that was just three seconds of silence. Susan had never imagined herself the most popular girl in the world, but normally her phone rang regularly, and there was always something going on. It was as if life had been put on pause.

It happened in the back of the car on the way to Bishop Carlbus Prep. She remembered sweating in her robes, holding her mortarboard in her hands, trying to forget about the enormous pimple that had erupted on her nose, no doubt from the stress. This pimple would be immortalized in every photo, video, and memory of the day, and Susan was disturbed that she wasn't entirely certain she didn't deserve it.

This sort of thinking had never afflicted her before. Susan had been born with a halo of soft, curly blonde hair and a tendency towards giggling, and this had been sufficient to convince everyone around her—and by extension, herself—that she was generally a good egg deserving of good things. No matter what she did. Pulled Stacey Hoga's hair until she cried in second grade? Her father took her for ice cream and mild admonishments. Dared Cousin Michael to urinate in the basement? Her mother brushed her hair extra that night, murmuring soft recriminations.

The car hit a bump in the road, and she lost time.

One moment she was resisting the urge to just pop her zit all over the back of her mother's headrest. The next, she was in Amy Keaton's kitchen doing Jello shots with George Heffernan and Xerc, feeling like she was floating an inch off the floor and unable to stop laughing. Ernie found a supply of chocolate syrup in the fridge and began squirting it everywhere, miming an ejaculation, and that sent her into a paroxysm of laughter. She had to kneel down and struggle to breathe, red dots in her eyes.

Then, Amy stormed into the kitchen. She looked rough. Her hair was pasted to her forehead by sweat. Her shirt was stained with at least three different substances. Her eyes were wide and bloodshot as they jumped around, taking in the mess.

"What. The. *Fuck*." she seethed.

Ernie made a sad trombone sound and dropped the bottle of syrup. "Annnd ... I've gone soft."

Susan laughed.

Then, she was back in the car, and they were parking. She blinked in confusion.

"Sweetie, you okay?" her father asked, studying her. "You kind of ... blanked out on us for a moment."

Susan managed a wan smile. "A lot on my mind," she murmured.

The second seizure hit her in her dorm room.

She'd been luxuriating in her bed before her roommate, the dreaded Doira, woke up and resumed what so far had been an existence defined by shouting and complaining.

And then Amy turned with a flurry of curses and stormed back out of the kitchen, and they all laughed. She held out a shot to Ernie, and he sketched a sloppy little bow and accepted it.

"Man, fuck that bitch," Georgie said as they toasted the tiny plastic cups.

Still floating, her head crackling with buzzy static and her fingers numb, she drifted into the living room. People were dancing. She studied Rhoda and Quentin as they jumped around to some kind of pop punk Hector had pumping from the speakers. They looked so *happy*, so in tune. They were flopping around like assholes, but laughing, eyes locked on each other. And Susan felt a familiar old acid rising inside her and she floated over to them and tried to match their smiles in intensity.

"Oh, just fuck already!" she shouted gleefully. "Quentin, you look like you're terrified you might accidentally touch her!"

There was a gentle ripple of laughter over the music. Quentin and Rhoda stopped dancing, and the acid level dropped with this expulsion of vitriol. Her eyes roamed over the rest of the room, and she saw opportunities, but the need to lash out, to destroy, to rip and tear, had faded.

She was in Plants and Hallucinogens, sitting next to

Murphy.

"—not even *close* to the blowoff class I was promised," he was saying. Then he paused. "You okay? You got all ... spacey. Haven't said a word in, like, five minutes."

She frowned, then blinked, a sense of panic filling her up and stretching her skin. "Wait," she said, leaning forward as a spasm of nausea cramped her stomach. "Wait, what ... what *day* is it?"

Murphy sighed, leaning back in his chair. "Thursday, kid. It's been Thursday for, like, weeks now. This fucking *class* ..." He scrubbed his stubbly face with his hands. "I'm going to have to actually study for this shit. And too late for add-drop."

Susan spent the rest of class sitting in rigid horror, heart pounding. She'd been lying in bed on Wednesday. She'd lost a day, 18 hours, some ridiculous amount of time. What had she been doing? Being back at Amy's party had seemed so *real*. It was already fading back to the smoky, half-glimpsed memories she was used to, but for a moment after ... waking up in class, she would have sworn she'd spent the last twenty minutes or so back at the Outing Party, being a complete bitch and enjoying it the way she once had.

She was in seat 33D, staring at the bare foot that had intruded into her airspace from seat 34D. It was enormous, and hairy, and the yellowed toenails were disturbingly talon-like. There were deep marks from a pair of socks that had been worn too long. She didn't need to smell the foot to smell the foot. One glance told her everything she needed to know.

People, she thought, were animals. She reviewed her options for tools. She had the small plastic fork that had been supplied with the heinous meal she'd refused to eat, several pens somewhere in her bag, and—her mind flashed to it with a surge of adrenaline—the broach pinned to her sweater, a gift from Murphy. She saw herself taking it off, bending the pin forward, stabbing it into the foot. She imagined the chaos, the blood. She began filling up with that old vinegar, searing her insides and threatening to burn her alive from the inside out. She reached for the broach.

She was spinning in the master bathroom, her stomach in knots, sweat all over her face. But there was electricity in her veins, a sweet buzz that kept her in motion. She could hear Polybius' third encore downstairs, shaking the floor, everybody cheering and booing simultaneously.

She opened the medicine cabinet and inspected the pill bottles. When she shut the cabinet door and faced herself, she was shocked: her blonde hair was pasted to her forehead, her skin was shiny, her cheeks red. She stared at herself for a moment, critically. Pretty, she thought, but not pretty enough. She wasn't Una, legs up to her ears and a face everyone dreamed of doing things to. But she was smart. *Smart bitch*, she thought.

She turned and opened the door. Standing there just outside was Yorick. He smiled, holding up a lighter. "Come on," he said. "We're burning shit on the patio."

She was on the subway.

She almost fell, the swaying momentum of the train sending

her stumbling into a wall of ill-humored people. She grabbed onto a silver-haired man's lapels, staring at him in sudden terror. She'd been ... on a plane ... she'd been ... at the party. And now she was here.

Silver Hair frowned down at her. "You all right, miss?"

She shook her head. "No," she said in a voice she barely recognized. She blinked rapidly several times.

Someone tugged at her ... suit? She was wearing a suit. "Miss?" a woman in a neat sweater and pencil skirt said, smiling kindly, "Take my seat. You just had a ... seizure, I think. Your eyes kind of ... rolled up, and you were shaking."

Susan managed a faint nod and smile. She sat down and glanced around again. She was *on a train*. She had been *on a plane*. Just ... she startled and inspected herself. Patting herself down, she found a phone in her pocket. She pulled it out and stared at the lock screen.

Three years.

She stared at the date again.

She probed the sense of distress that infused her. She felt wrong, somehow. Fat, she decided. She was suddenly at least ten pounds heavier, and she could feel the difference because of the sudden, shocking transition.

The kind woman leaned down, swaying easily with the motion of the train. "Feeling better, honey?"

She blinked through sudden tears. "*No*, you fucking asshole."

Three days later, she was nervously chewing a fingernail as her father leaned back in his chair. He looked concerned. "So, you've been having more of these fits," he said slowly.

She nodded. "I don't know what's happening. I ... lose time."

Her father was proficient in the art of weaponizing facial expressions. He had on many occasions elicited unwilling confessions from Susan simply by studying her with a raised eyebrow or a specific kind of grimace that Susan knew intimately but could never describe effectively. He raised an eyebrow, and she was flooded with panic.

"Losing time?" he asked.

She forced a smile. "That was a poor choice of words," she said, carefully considering what to say next.

She was by the pool, the fairy lights bouncing off the water. She had one of the pebbles from the planters set up around the perimeter of the outdoor area in her hand. As she stood there, a strange feeling of blankness filling her thoughts, Yorick threw one with surgical accuracy at an empty bottle of Jagermeister floating in the water. It shattered with a satisfying tinkle and several people cheered. She turned and found Fanny, Rhoda, and Victor standing behind her, applauding.

Her mouth was dry. Her head was buzzing. Her heart was pounding.

"Take the shot," Victor said, a slight slur thickening his words. "If you miss, you gotta take your top off."

Fanny and Rhoda both screeched out disapproval. Yorick just smirked. Susan blinked stupidly, then looked down at the pebble in her hand.

"Jesus is she *high*," Fanny said.

"Fuck off, losers," she said, but the words were rubbery in her mouth, like she'd been chewing them for hours. She turned and raised the pebble, squinted at the pool and went into a pitcher's windup. As she started to lean forward to throw the pebble, her feet slipped out from under her and she fell on her ass, teeth clicking, pain momentarily shooting up her back.

She burst into howls of laughter. A moment later Victor slid his arms under her shoulders.

"Come on, Funny Girl. You okay? Anything broken?"

From inside the house, the muffled music suddenly shifted.

"Oh! I love this song," Fanny shouted, clapping her hands. "Let's dance!"

Victor grinned at Susan and pantomimed brushing her off. Then he extended his arm. "Milady?"

She was inside some kind of metal tube, so small and tight she couldn't sit up. There was a loud humming all around her. She was freezing, and realized she was wearing a thin white gown and nothing else.

She began to scream and thrash. A metallic voice buzzed all around her.

"Susan, sweetheart, you're gonna have to be quiet and still like we talked about, okay? The scan is compromised if you move." There was a muffled voice in the background. "What? Oh f—Pull her out! Pull her out!"

The humming stopped. The platform she was lying on began to slide. When she was halfway out, she contorted herself and crawled free, slapping away the two men who tried to assist her.

She dashed to the far wall and pressed herself against it.

One of the men, broad-shouldered with dark skin and enormous glasses, held up his hands. "Susan, you had another seizure while in the scanner." He frowned. "Susan? Susan, do you know where you are?"

She shook her head. "What ... what year is it?"

She lay in bed and stared at the ceiling. Six years. She'd lost six more years.

"Tell me again."

She closed her eyes. Her father had aged. He was an old man, suddenly.

"You were on the subway," he said. "Look, Susie, we're ... we're all just worried. It's getting worse. Your Mom, me, Brooks—we're all just worried. And you telling me this stuff about losing time ... it doesn't make me less worried."

Her eyes popped open. Who the fuck was *Brooks*?

She found herself watching him again. As he drove the streetlights danced over his face, a face she still found unfamiliar.

He glanced over and smiled. *He thinks I'm adoring him*, she thought.

"One year," he said, smiling, reaching over and taking her hand as his eyes returned to the road. "One year without a ...

an incident! I'm glad we're celebrating."

She smiled. She'd learned to play along. She knew she'd come pretty close to being institutionalized, because she kept telling everyone about the Other Her. They weren't seizures, she was … sharing her body. With some other Susan, a mirrored sister. But then she'd had an epiphany: no one believed her. No one would ever believe her. So, she composed herself. She put on a smile. She pretended. And as the weeks went by and she settled into her role, she wondered if that's what she'd been doing, the other her, the one she couldn't remember who'd been living her life in the in-betweens.

Catching herself, she dutifully squeezed his hand. He wasn't a bad guy. She just wasn't sure if she liked him.

Turning her head, she looked at the buildings sliding past.

"Girl, your *eyes*!"

She dragged her gaze to Zillah. Moving any part of her body took effort and time. Zillah was worse off, her dark skin flushed, her eyes red.

"*Fucking bitch! Fucking liar!*"

Susan reversed course and laboriously dragged her eyes over to the basement door, where Amy was standing in apparent preparation for a demonstration of spontaneous combustion.

Susan started laughing. The giggles just bloomed out of her like bubbles, sharp and spiky. She couldn't be certain *what* was so funny. Was it Amy's ragey face? Was it the fact that she'd thrown a party that was making her so mad blood vessels were bursting in her face? Was it her clear and obvious mustache? Susan thought that these issues deserved a zine dedicated to them, and the thought of someone publishing a stapled, folded treatise seriously investigating whether or not Amy Keaton had a personal grooming problem—driving Amy, whose personal grooming was borderline obsessive, absolutely batshit—sent her into further hysterics.

"Motherfucker! I will not be *brutalized*!"

Susan felt like a balloon, tethered to the floor by some invisible string, drifting this way and that. There was commotion all around her, shouting, but she just laughed to herself, reveling in the way her heart raced *so fast*, and the air felt *so cold* on her sweaty skin.

And then Yorick was shouting above everyone else, and a door slammed, and the air filled with the rising wail of an epic, familiar guitar riff, and she felt her body start to sway as if floating on air currents, beyond her control but pleasant.

She was standing in the rain, shivering. It was dark, and for a second wisps of her high from the party lingered, buzzy warmth, maybe the last time she'd felt physically good. She stared around, but didn't recognize her surroundings. It was dark, and she was outside, and she was ... *fat*, sweet *lord* she was *enormous*. For a shocked moment her brain raced through explanations for having doubled in size—prescriptions, despair, marriage? She was freezing and numb, she itched everywhere, and her hair was long and soaked, hanging in limp, greasy strands like a curtain.

She looked at her hands. They had aged, plump but with thin, finely lined lines. Her nails had been chewed to scabby nubs. There was a tight sense of something under her flesh, too, a burning skein of throbbing need, like her bones were poking and dragging the inside of her skin.

Tears stung her eyes as she patted herself down, finding nothing—no wallet, phone, or anything else. It was just her, a pair of baggy old jeans, and a T-shirt. And the rain. And the darkness. She was standing in the middle of a road at a rail crossing, a highway overpass a few hundred feet away. She started for it, pausing only to look at her bare feet for a moment.

The overpass granted her a reprieve from the rain. It smelled like shit and urine and something else, something at the edge of her mind but opaque. She squatted down in the muddy dirt and cried, tears just pouring out of her eyes. She regretted every mean thing she'd ever said, every vicious cut, every hot bit of sarcasm. She knew, somehow, that it all ended when she relived the end of the Outing Party—something that had taken her entire forgotten, missed life to figure out. But now she understood.

Because Amy had cursed her. All of them.

She thought, *the only choice I have is to not go along. To not cooperate*. She stood up and walked steadily back out into the rain, towards the railroad tracks. She stepped out onto them and sat down on the gravel. If a train came, she was sure to be sliced to ribbons, obliterated. If not, she would probably get pneumonia and die. Either way, she thought, maybe she skipped the end. Maybe she got what other people got—a simple fade to black.

She closed her eyes. She felt the water raining down on her. She screamed and jumped up. "Assholes!" she shouted, flicking water at Titus and Leo, who ran off, laughing. She shook herself dry, noting the dry-mouthed hangover that was setting in like a sour weight, the way the sunlight streaming in through the windows made the Keaton place look almost nice. She was in the living room, which was her last memory from the night before. She looked down at the filthy carpet and was amazed she'd allowed herself to sleep on it.

Then the nausea hit, and she raced to the kitchen. When she arrived at the sink, she discovered she wasn't the first person to barf there. That made her throw up twice as hard, her eyes clenched shut.

"EVERYBODY!"

She slid down to the cold tile floor, breathing hard but feeling a little better.

"EVERY FUCKING BODY!"

She frowned. Was that Xerc? Far away, but it sounded like him.

"JESUS FUCKING CHRIST EVERYBODY! AMY IS FUCKING D—"

She was driving. The car fishtailed for a moment as she jumped, heart surging in her chest. Then instinct took over and she grabbed the wheel. The speedometer read 105. She'd only driven a few times before—the family minivan, with her mother white-knuckled in terror next to her.

At first, she thought the flashing lights were a remnant of her latest seizure, but a glance in her rear-view mirror showed several police cars behind her on the highway. Then she caught sight of her eyes, and the deep bags and wrinkles around them.

She looked ancient, and haunted. Like her hidden life had been a hard one. And she knew the next time she ... flashed back, whatever it was, she would be walking down those creaky stairs to see Amy, and she never wanted to see that again. Never wanted to go back to that party, the party that had never ended.

She looked back at the speedometer. Then back at the road, which was rising up to cross over a river. As she flashed by several cars, she pushed down on the gas. They would think she had another fit. They would think her eyes rolled up in her head and her body went stiff.

She jerked the wheel. She prayed she didn't wake up back in Amy's house.

ABOUT THE AUTHOR

Jeff Somers was first sighted in Jersey City, New Jersey after the destruction of a classified government installation in the early 1970s; the area in question is still too radioactive to go near. When asked about this, he will only say that he regrets nothing. He is the author of *Lifers*, the Avery Cates series from Orbit Books (avery-cates.com), *Chum* from Tyrus Books, and *The Ustari Cycle* from Pocket/Gallery, including We Are Not Good People.

Jeff's published over thirty short stories as well; his story "Sift, Almost Invisible, Through" appeared in the anthology *Crimes by Moonlight*, published by Berkley Hardcover and edited by Charlaine Harris, and his story "Ringing the Changes" was selected for *The Best American Mystery Stories* 2006. He survives on the nickels and quarters he regularly finds behind his ears, his guitar playing is a plague upon his household, and his lovely wife The Duchess is convinced he would wither and die if left to his own devices, but this is only half true.

Today, he makes beer money by writing amazing things for various people. Favorite whiskey: Glenmorangie 10 Year. Yes, it is acceptable to pay him in it.

Discover more about Jeff Somers and his work at **https://www.jeffreysomers.com/**.

SUPPORT

If you or someone you know is experiencing any of the following, here is a list of US-based resources. For resources outside the US, check with your local government.

Bullying

https://www.stopbullying.gov/

24/7 Crisis Text Line at 741741

Suicidal Ideation

24/7 Suicide and Crisis Lifeline dial/text 988

Substance Abuse + Mental Health Hotline

https://drughelpline.org/

844-289-0879

Domestic Violence

National Domestic Violence Hotline

https://www.thehotline.org/

Text 88788 or dial 1-800-799-7233

Eating Disorders

https://www.nationaleatingdisorders.org/

Winter in the City
A Collection of Dark Speculative Fiction
Edited by
R.B. Wood & Anna Koon

120 Murders
Meg Gardiner
Josh Malerman
Silvia Moreno-Garcia
Paul Tremblay
and more.
Edited by Nick Mamatas

A Collection of Dark Speculative Fiction
Spring in the City

The Black Fire Concerto
Mike Allen

Portraits of Decay
A Novel By
J.R. Blanes

Sinister Societies
Six Novellas of Secrets and Horrors
Michael Burke • Tom Deady
Errick Nunnally • Cindy O'Quinn
Sarah Read • Mercedes M. Yardley

RUADÁN
BOOKS